More THAN FRIENDS

More THAN FRIENDS

USA TODAY BESTSELLING AUTHOR
KAT SINGLETON

Entangled Publishing, LLC
644 Shrewsbury Commons Ave., STE 181
Shrewsbury, PA 17361
rights@entangledpublishing.com

Amara is an imprint of Entangled Publishing, LLC.

Visit our website at www.entangledpublishing.com.

Edited by Bird and Bear Editorial Services,
Sandra Dee of One Love Editing, and Salma R.
Cover design by Summer Grove
Edge design by LJ Anderson
Edge image by kritiyakorn Srikum/GettyImages
Title design by Jade M. Design
Interior design by Toni Kerr

ISBN 978-1-64937-994-8

Manufactured in the United States of America

First Edition March 2026

10 9 8 7 6 5 4 3 2

AMARA

ALSO BY KAT SINGLETON

Pembroke Hills

In Good Company
Bad for Business
More Than Friends

Black Tie Billionaires

Black Ties and White Lies
Pretty Rings and Broken Things
Bright Lights and Summer Nights

To my girls who love a single dad in slutty little glasses.
Jude Kensington is definitely for you.

More Than Friends is a sexy and swoon-y contemporary, standalone romance. However, there may be some elements that might not be suitable to all readers including an infuriating billionaire hero, child abandonment not by the main character, and explicit sex on the page…*lots* of pages. Readers who may be sensitive to these topics, please take note.

1

Charlotte

"Why do I never get good karma?" I whine, looking down at my lap, which is covered in the vanilla latte I bought ten minutes ago.

I steer my car to the side of the empty road and put it in park, trying to figure out what I'm going to do. I'm supposed to be at work in thirty minutes, and since I can't afford to rent in this part of the Hamptons, that's how long it'd take me to get back to my apartment and change.

If I were responsible, I'd have a spare uniform in my locker at Pembroke Hills Country Club, where I work. Most of the time, I do have a uniform in there. But my washing machine has been out of order recently, making it hard to keep up with laundry. I've been meaning to ask Jude, my best guy friend, if I can do laundry at his place, but I keep forgetting.

Jude!

Hope blooms in my chest at the thought of him. I pull my phone out of my cup holder and immediately call him. He only lives five minutes from Pembroke. Maybe I can stop by his house and get myself cleaned up before starting my shift.

"Good morning, Char," Jude drawls. I can't even see him, and I know he's wearing that typical grin of his that charms every woman he meets.

"I have an emergency," I tell him, switching the phone over to my car speakers so I can get back on the road. I head toward his house without even getting confirmation that he's home.

It's *Jude*. He'd do just about anything for me. I know that even if he isn't home, he's not going to have an issue with me using his place to get ready for work.

"Are you okay?" Jude asks, his voice void of its usual humor, concern taking its place instead.

"No," I complain, glancing down at my clothes again. This is only my second week as a cart girl for Pembroke's private golf course. The job is a coveted one—especially the weekend shift—and I'm about to jeopardize it because I was stupid and picked up my coffee by the lid.

"Tell me what happened," he rushes to get out. There's movement on the other side of the phone. "Where are you? I'm on my way."

I try not to smile. I don't know if I've ever heard Jude so concerned. He's not a concerned kind of guy. He lives life as if nothing can go wrong. "Are you home?"

"Yes, but where are you? Are you okay?"

"I'm fine, I just have an entire iced latte in my lap and have to be at work in thirty minutes. Can I swing by your place and wash up? I don't have an extra uniform, and I can't show up looking like this."

Jude lets out a long sigh before I hear a low, familiar chuckle. "Fuck, Char," he begins. "You had me worried something was wrong."

I frown as I make my way to his house. I've been to his place countless times. I could get there with my eyes closed. I just hope I have enough time to get myself pulled together before my shift starts. "Something *is* wrong, Jude. I splurged on a very expensive coffee this morning because, for once in my life, I wasn't running late, and I wanted to treat myself, and of course, I didn't even get two sips of it before my lap got to taste it instead."

Jude snickers. "Oh, I'd love a taste of that, then."

I roll my eyes. If it were any other man, I might be flattered by the obvious flirting, but because it's Jude, I'm not putting much weight into the comment. If you looked up "playboy" in the dictionary, you'd find a picture of Jude Kensington. He flirts with everyone. I'm no exception right now.

"Jude," I scold, turning on my blinker and waiting to turn onto the street that leads to his house. There are more people on the road this morning than I was expecting. We still have a month before the summer busy season begins. I smile at how close it is to my favorite time of the year. I love the Hamptons in the summer, and it's even better because it means all of my closest friends will be here for three months.

I can't wait.

"You didn't really tell me I could come over, but you should know I'm two minutes from your house. Time to put your pants on."

He laughs. "You know you don't ever need an invite, Char. You're welcome anytime. And what if I want to keep my pants off? Think of all the fun we could have."

My body heats at his words. I wish I could say that his flirting doesn't have an effect on me, but it does. It has since I met him, but I do what I always do—I ignore it.

"You better have pants on when I get there."

He lets out a dramatic sigh. "*Fine.*"

"Be there in a minute," I respond before pressing the button on my steering wheel to hang up.

It doesn't take me long to make it to his house. I type in the code to open the gates at the end of his driveway and pull my car around. I've been to Jude's house numerous times since we struck up a friendship last summer, but every time I see the Hamptons home he spends a lot of his time at, I can't help but marvel at it.

I fell in love with the Hamptons when I was eighteen, flipping through a magazine in a hair salon in Arizona, when a feature on some reality TV star's Hamptons home caught my attention. At first, it was the photographer's laid-back, inviting style, not overly styled or posed, that drew my eye—I'd always loved photography, and the cozy beach oasis captured in those photos stirred a reaction in me that would ultimately become a fixation. Once the idea was in my head, I couldn't think of anywhere else I'd rather be. I told myself that if I ever got the opportunity to move out there, I would.

So, at twenty-four, I packed up and moved from Arizona to the Hamptons. Before moving, I applied to work at Pembroke on a whim, not expecting to get the position. So many people apply to work at one of the most expensive country clubs money can buy, I didn't think I actually had a shot. When I was offered the position, I had to accept. It was my sign to commit to moving. While my degree was in business and my lifelong dream was to open up a photography business in the Hamptons one day, I couldn't say no to the waitress job. Pembroke is a country club for the richest of the rich, and they pay their employees well. Even though it wasn't a job I thought I'd have after graduating, it was a way for me to move to the Hamptons and make enough money to be able to live there. Working at

Pembroke has allowed me to save money to hopefully open up my dream photography business one day, while also living in the place I fell in love with years ago.

Little did I know that moving to the Hamptons and accepting a job at Pembroke would lead me to becoming best friends with one of Pembroke's most prominent members.

I park in front of the house. From the front, it looks like the cottage-inspired homes that line the roads of Southampton, modest even. You wouldn't know there's an extra addition to the house and that inside it's *massive.* Jude takes pride in the renovations he's done. He's here more than his friends, opting to escape here even in the off-season. He turned the home into something beautiful, and I can't help but appreciate the view every time I visit.

I'm staring at the gray shingles of the house when the front door opens and Jude steps outside.

The moment my eyes meet his, my lips turn into a smile as I push my car door open. I can't help it. Jude has one of those smiles that makes you immediately want to smile back—and he's *always* smiling.

"Char!" he exclaims, his long legs eating up the distance between us quickly. His eyes rake over me before going wide. He lets out a whistle. "Wow, you really did spill coffee all over yourself."

I roll my eyes before stepping out of my car. "I told you it was an emergency." I look back at the coffee that's all over my seat but decide to clean that up later. Right now, I need to get my clothes clean before doing anything else.

Jude opens his mouth to respond, but my view of him is cut off as I strip out of the polo golf tank that is my uniform and head inside.

2

Jude

A strangled noise leaves my throat as I follow closely behind a half-naked Charlotte.

"I didn't realize we were stripping," I remark, following her to the laundry room on the main floor.

Charlotte tosses a dirty look over her shoulder. "How else am I supposed to get my clothes clean?"

Her response wipes the smirk from my face. She's got a point.

She walks into the laundry room with me close behind her. "Please tell me you have stain remover," she mutters, beginning to open up cabinets. I take her coffee-stained shirt from her hands and let her resume looking as I take it over to the sink on the other side of the room.

"Yeah, I should." I lay the shirt flat on the counter next to the sink. Luckily, the classic Pembroke green hides the coffee well. With some water and stain remover, she should be able to go to work with nobody knowing of the spill.

"Have you ever even been inside these cabinets?" she asks, a teasing tone to her voice. I turn around to find her walking closer to me with a bottle of stain remover in her hand. She sets it down next to me before bending over and pushing her skirt down her thighs.

There's a split second where it's hard to breathe as I try not to focus on the fact that she's standing next to me in nothing but her bra and underwear.

Is that a thong?

I force myself not to look. "I do know how to do my own laundry, thank you very much," I rasp. My pulse spikes, but I close my eyes in an attempt to gather myself and play it cool. It doesn't matter that Charlotte is standing next to me in tiny scraps of fabric. It's a normal Friday morning, where I'm just helping out a friend to clean up a mess.

"I didn't know if that was taught at boarding school or if you just had people do it for you."

I step to the side as she comes up closer to the counter next to me. She wets the fabric of her clothes before laying them flat once again and starts to spray them with the solution. I watch her as she works, making sure I keep my eyes safely pinned on her face.

Charlotte has been one of my best friends for almost a year now. No matter how much I've flirted with her, she's always made it clear that she has no interest in being anything other than friends. I've respected it. At first, her disinterest was a bruise to my ego. But the more she denied me, the more I wanted to get to know her. The more I got to know her, the more I liked her being my friend. She's incredibly cool. Not many women call me on my shit, but it's one of her favorite things to do.

"Did you manage to *drink* any of—" My words fall short as I make the mistake of looking at her, completely forgetting for a moment that she's almost naked. Another weird noise comes from deep in my throat at the sight of her in nothing but her bra and panties.

I know I shouldn't, but I can't look away from the way her breasts pool over the cups of her lace bra. The bra is a nude color, and her thong is a bright pink. My lips part, and suddenly, all I can think about is how dry my mouth is and how desperately I need a drink of water.

Charlotte sticks her hand in my face, her fingers snapping. "Eyes up here, lover boy." She laughs at the same moment I feel blood rush to my cheeks.

I meet her eyes immediately. I expect to find her upset, but instead, she looks at me with a lifted blonde eyebrow.

"Sorry, I..." My words trail off because I don't know what to say. It feels like I can't take a full breath. I just really wasn't expecting to see my best friend in nothing but her bra and thong, and I definitely didn't expect the sight to steal the air from my lungs. This is Charlotte. *My best friend.*

"You were checking me out?" She pulls her gaze from mine and works on getting the large stain out of her skirt. She really has to scrub at the fabric. There's more coffee on the skirt than there was on her shirt.

"I wasn't checking you out." My words come out hurried and jumbled. I wasn't checking her out. I *can't* be checking her out.

I stare at the side of her face, making sure my eyes don't drift lower again.

"Sure you weren't." She laughs and shakes her head, her focus staying on the skirt and treating the stain. "It's nothing you haven't seen before. I've worn bikinis that showed more skin than this."

She has a point. The thing about the bikinis, though, is that I was expecting to see her in those. I prepared myself not to look at things I shouldn't be looking at. I can flirt with her all I want because it's fun, and I don't know how *not* to flirt, but I'm well aware of the line she's drawn for us, and I never want to cross it. Her friendship means too much to me to do that.

Needing a change of subject, I rip my gaze from her face and look at the clothes she's busy treating. "I can't believe you don't have an extra uniform." I give her a smirk. I actually *can* believe it. Charlotte spilling coffee all over herself and not having an extra outfit to change into is just like her.

"Lesson learned," she mutters, scrubbing at her skirt to remove the coffee.

Wanting to help, I grab her shirt and repeat the same motion as her. Luckily, the coffee comes out pretty easily.

"If only all your fangirls at the club could see you scrubbing coffee out of my shirt for me. Jude Kensington doing laundry? They'd fall in love with you."

I meet her gaze with a cocky smirk. "They're already in love with me. Plus, I only do laundry for the special women in my life."

Charlotte rolls her eyes. "Your charm doesn't work on me, Jude. Stop wasting your lines on me." She snatches the shirt from me and grabs the skirt before walking over to the dryer and throwing them inside.

I make sure I keep my eyes safely on her face when she turns around and meets my gaze. I swear there's a hint of pink to her cheeks that wasn't there a moment ago, but I could be wrong.

"Nothing with you is ever a waste." My grin gets even wider before I wink at her.

Her entire face breaks out into a smile. I'm pretty sure she crosses her arms over her chest before leaning up against the dryer, but I can't be sure because my gaze is safely locked on hers. "Another line wasted on me."

"Not wasted," I immediately respond, lifting an eyebrow and daring her to argue with me. She doesn't. It's silent in the laundry room for a few beats before I decide to break it. "Were you able to drink any of your coffee before spilling it all over yourself?"

Her bottom lip juts out in a pout. She lets out a low groan. "I wasn't lying. I really only got, like, maybe two sips. All I wanted was a Friday treat before starting my busy day, but the universe had other plans for me."

"You didn't trade shifts with anyone, right? You're working all day?" I have her new schedule memorized, but I know the cart girls sometimes switch things around.

Charlotte nods. The motion causes a piece of her curled blonde hair to fall into her face. My fingers twitch at my side as I fight the urge to tuck it behind her ear. I know I shouldn't. That'd cross a line I shouldn't cross, but it doesn't stop me from wanting to. Luckily, she beats me to it and tucks the stray strand herself. "Yep. Hoping it's a good day, lots of good tippers. Devin keeps reminding me how low my rent is and how much more he could make if he rented out my place to someone else for the summer, so I want to give him extra this month."

"Are you trying to bribe your landlord?"

Charlotte purses her lips. "Maybe. Don't judge me. We can't all afford houses like this." She waves her arms above her head.

"I'd never judge you, Char," I rush to say. My body feels tight at her insinuation that I ever would. "Let me know if you need me to talk to your landlord."

Charlotte shakes her head before clicking her tongue. "Nope. I don't need you to swoop in and save the day. Plus, I don't know if your charm would even work on him anyway. I'll just hope I make extra money that I can give Devin, and I won't have to worry about finding a new place to live this close to the busy season. I'm nervous he's going to find renters at the last minute, and I'm going to be out of a place to live. Maybe paying him more will prevent him from doing that."

I nod. My jaw clenches as I force myself to keep my mouth shut. She's been going back and forth with her landlord for weeks about her rent and being able to stay there. I know the unknown is stressing her out, and I want to help her with it, but I also don't want to overstep. If she believes that the landlord thing isn't a problem and that paying him more will keep things how they are, then I'm going to stay out of it. That doesn't mean I don't like that she won't let me help her, but I know her well enough to know she's too stubborn to ask for help.

Neither one of us says anything else, and eventually, the dryer lets out a loud chiming noise. It slows down before the clothes stop tumbling.

Charlotte turns around, and I peel my gaze from hers.

"How much time do I have left to get to the club?" she asks.

I look at my watch. "About ten to fifteen, depending on how fast you get dressed," I tell her. Just then, I remember the coffee that was spilled all over her seat. I turn around. "I'll meet you outside."

"Oh, so now you leave the moment I put my clothes on?" Charlotte calls out, her tone teasing.

"I've got something I need to do!" I yell over my shoulder. I stop in the kitchen and grab a roll of paper towels and some all-purpose cleaner before walking back outside.

Opening the door to her car, I find coffee all over her seat and even some in the cup holders and space between the seats. I get busy wiping her car clean, making sure to check all the nooks and crannies.

She really meant it when she said she didn't get to drink any of her coffee. It's everywhere.

"I feel like I should take a photo of this." Charlotte's voice comes from behind me.

I look over my shoulder, finding her dressed and smiling a few feet away from me.

"And why is that?" I ask, turning around to continue wiping down her seat to make sure it's fully dry before she gets in.

"Because never in my life did I think I'd see you on your knees, cleaning out a car."

I smile, even though she can't see it. Technically, I'm only on one knee, and I needed to get lower to make sure I didn't miss any of the mess.

With a sigh, I rise to my full height and turn around to face her. "Your car should be clean and ready for you."

"My hero," Charlotte practically sings. She dramatically bats her eyelashes, completely poking fun at the situation.

I roll my eyes before grabbing onto her door. "Get in and go before you're late."

Charlotte's blue eyes gleam with mischief as she follows my directions. Before she sits down, she leans around her car door and plants a kiss on my cheek.

"Thanks for being my savior," she mutters before sliding into the driver's seat.

I smile because I can't deny how much I love being the one she called when she needed help. "You can call me anytime,

Char. Now, go before you're late."

"I'm going," she responds, pretending to be annoyed.

I make sure she's safely tucked into her car before I close the door for her and watch her pull away.

As soon as she pulls out, I slip my phone out of my pocket and shoot off a text to a friend I'm supposed to be meeting at the club.

Jude

Going to be late to our tee time. I've got to run an errand real fast.

3

Charlotte

"I've got a delivery for you," Mia, one of my fellow bev cart girls, tells me as I pull up to the pro shop at Pembroke. I've only been at work for a little over an hour, and things have been slammed. I'm having to stock up on more blue Gatorade because, apparently, that's the preferred flavor this morning.

"A delivery for me?" I ask, sliding out of the cart and walking up to her. She stands in the open garage at the back of the pro shop with a knowing smile. I don't know what she knows or what the delivery is, but she's acting suspicious.

Mia nods. "It came from a very cute *deliverer* too."

I narrow my eyes at her as I follow her into the garage. She opens the door to the walk-in cooler, and I follow behind her because I do need to grab those Gatorades.

Mia pulls a coffee off one of the shelves and holds it out for me. "Jude Kensington dropped it off for you. He was adamant that it was kept cold."

I stare at the coffee cup. It's from the same coffee shop I stopped at earlier.

"Jude brought this?" I ask, a little shocked.

Mia nods, rubbing her lips together in an attempt to hide her smile. It doesn't work very well. "Do you know he's in love with you?"

I let out a loud snort before grabbing the coffee from her. She's crazy to think he'd ever be in love with anyone, let alone be in love with *me*. "Jude's in love with himself. He's not capable of falling in love with anyone." I take a sip of the coffee, shocked to find it's my exact order. We've gone to this shop numerous times together, but I didn't realize he was paying that kind of attention.

"He isn't bringing any of the other bev cart girls a coffee," Mia points out.

"None of the other girls are his friend," I respond, turning and walking out of the cooler. I walk to my cart and take a long drink of the coffee before placing the cup in one of the cup holders.

Mia, a coworker who I'm quickly developing a friendship with, waits for me in the same spot. She watches me carefully as if she still has something else she wants to say.

I grab the carton of blue Gatorades. "It's nothing, Mia," I call over my shoulder. "Jude's my best friend and brought me a coffee because I spilled mine this morning, and he knows that. He isn't bringing anyone else coffee because he's probably already slept with all the bev cart girls."

I scrunch my nose at the idea. I truly have no idea who he has and hasn't slept with at the club. I don't want to know. It's frowned upon for anyone who works at Pembroke to get involved with the members, but people still do it. Jude openly flirts with everyone in front of me, but as far as who actually goes home with him, I have no idea. I'm happy not knowing.

"Well, I want to know how to find myself a mega-hot, rich,

thoughtful *best friend*," Mia remarks.

I start to fill my cooler with the bottles. "I'm not sure I'd call him thoughtful. Plus, it's not like I was looking for a new friend. Jude and I just got thrown together when his best friend and my best friend started dating. Then he was annoying and decided to never leave me alone."

Jude's best friend, Cal, is now engaged to my best friend, Lucy. Jude and I first met last year when Lucy became Cal's private chef. They had a little bit of history—she dated his brother—and she quickly went from being his employee to being his girlfriend to being his fiancée. Cal and Jude are always together, and Lucy and I try to spend as much time as we can together too, so Jude and I becoming friends was inevitable. Cal and Lucy spent the off-season back in the city like everyone else, but Jude spent a lot of his time here. Since I live in the Hamptons full-time, we found ourselves spending a lot of time together. It was easy to want to spend time with him, even when no one else was around. I never thought about how lonely the off-season could be, but I've never once felt lonely because I've had him here.

Speaking of Jude, I walk around the bev cart and pull my phone from the compartment on the passenger side. I pull up our text thread and fire off a text.

Charlotte

A special coffee delivery for me? You shouldn't have.

I go to put my phone away again, but it vibrates in my hand before I can.

Jude

I didn't want you to have to conquer the day without any caffeine. I pity the poor members who had to deal with an uncaffeinated Charlotte this morning.

I can't help but smile.

Charlotte

I'm a professional. I was very nice this morning. I've even made some generous tips already.

Jude

Good. Everyone should be tipping you well. If they don't, let me know.

I roll my eyes at his comment. He's always trying to get me to tell him who is and isn't a good tipper. He did the same thing when I was a waitress at Pembroke Grill. I've kept my lips sealed on who tips terribly or who doesn't tip at all. Luckily, Jude is a good judge of character when it comes to who he spends his time with. All of his friends and colleagues tip extremely well.

Jude

I'm waiting for my thank you.

Jude

"Thank you for the coffee, Jude. You're the best, Jude. You're my hot, swoony hero, Jude." ;)

Charlotte

Thank you for the coffee, Jude.

I consider sending him the middle-finger emoji but decide to leave it out. I really do appreciate him going out of his way to bring me the coffee this morning. If I remember right, he had a tee time early this morning that running out and grabbing coffee might've made him late for.

Jude

One of these days you'll call me hot and swoony and it'll make me the happiest man on Earth.

I shake my head at his text.

Charlotte

I'm not here to stroke your ego. You're not hot and swoony. You're more of a bridge troll.

Jude

A bridge troll?!

Jude

That's cruel.

Jude

Going to ignore the second part of your text and focus on the stroking part.

I grimace. He's absolutely ridiculous. I toss my phone back into the compartment and finish stocking my cart. Since I'm already here, I walk back into the garage and grab a bucket of ice. The weather is beautiful this morning, cool enough that I might even ask one of the guys at the pro shop to lend me one of the fancy Pembroke Hill jackets they have. I keep meaning to get myself one, but I know if I sweet-talk one of them, they'll lend me theirs.

"How's it been this morning?" Mia asks before sliding into her cart.

"It's been good. I didn't expect so many people to be here for the weekend already, but it's been steady. What about you?"

Pembroke Hills has two eighteen-hole courses. On a day like today, when it's steady, two cart girls work the bev carts. We each take one of the eighteen holes. As long as the players don't have a preference, they alternate which course they send the group to, so that way things don't get congested. As a private club, we try to do everything possible to make sure all members have the ultimate experience every time they step onto the course.

Mia adjusts her ponytail before putting her cart in drive. "It's been good. There are more people out than I was expecting. Good tippers too," she yells over her shoulder with a wave.

I wave back at her, smiling as I watch her drive away. Hopefully, the good tipping continues throughout the morning. The pay at Pembroke is better than at any other country club around. I make good base pay at Pembroke, but it's expensive to live in the Hamptons. I'm trying to give more to Devin so he lets me stay in my apartment for the summer instead of renting it out to tourists who can pay more. I need as many tips as I can to compete with the typical renters Devin's used to having for the busy season.

I slide back into my cart and take a sip of my coffee, my eyes fluttering shut in euphoria. It tastes amazing, and I didn't realize how much I needed the caffeine. It hits my soul, giving me the pick-me-up I need to continue the rest of my shift. My morning started out rough, but it has turned around with Jude coming to the rescue. On top of that, it really was thoughtful of him to drop off the coffee. I make the mental note to tell him how much I appreciate it, but for now, I plaster on a smile and pull up to the group of men waving me down.

4

Jude

"Hey, Tyson," I mutter from the driver's seat of the golf cart. We're on our tenth hole for the day, and I'm really enjoying his company. He isn't someone I've spent a lot of time with in the past, but all of my friends are finding girlfriends and getting married and becoming too busy for me, so I'm clinging to whatever single friends I can find.

"Yes?" he asks, looking at me over his shoulder. I know I've interrupted him setting up his shot, but I've spotted Charlotte two holes away from us, and I know she'll be here soon.

"Can I ask you to do me a favor?" I question, reaching into my back pocket and pulling out a hundred-dollar bill.

Tyson raises his eyebrows as he looks at the cash in my hand. "Whatever it is, I don't need the cash, Kensington. I'd like to remind you how well Bishop-Moore hotels is doing right now."

I laugh and roll my eyes at him. Tyson runs the Bishop-Moore hotel empire alongside his sister, Winnie, and her husband, Archer. They've only been at the helm of the company for a couple of years, and their increase in revenue is more than impressive. We've recently started a partnership where some of our luxury brands are featured in their hotels, and it's really helped both our companies financially. "I know you don't need the money, but in about a minute, a cart girl is going to pull up and ask for our drinks, and I want you to tip her this."

Tyson narrows his eyes but closes the distance between us and snatches the bill from my grasp. "And why can't *you* just tip her?" he asks incredulously.

"Because she won't take it from me."

"Does Jude Kensington have a girlfriend?" he asks, his lips lifting in a half smirk. "I know I prefer to stay clear of the social scene in our circle, but even I know the gossip when it comes to you."

My cheeks feel hot as I watch Charlotte get closer to us. "She's a girl who's a friend. Don't forget to tip," I whisper before plastering on a smile. "Char!" I yell before sliding out of the golf cart.

Her mouth turns up in a radiant smile. Why does she have to be so damn beautiful? I aim a look in Tyson's direction, hoping *he* doesn't notice just how stunning she is. "I was wondering if I'd run into you today. Do you two want a drink?"

"Always," I answer, coming to a stop next to her bev cart.

She grabs the club's iPad and stands up, a smile staying on her face the entire time. "What do you want? Beer? Or are you switching to liquor?"

My eyes rake over her body, and I'm just about to answer her when my mouth snaps shut. I cock my head to the side. "Since when do you have a pro shop jacket?"

Charlotte looks down at her jacket. On the left side, right over her chest, is the Pembroke Hills logo, and it doesn't take long for my eyes to focus on the name stitched underneath.

"And since when is your name *Teddy*?" I ask, my gaze bouncing between Charlotte's eyes and the name stitched over her chest.

She looks down before lifting a shoulder in a shrug. "I was cold, and Teddy let me have his jacket. I still need to order myself one. What do you want to drink?"

I tell myself that it doesn't matter that she's wearing Teddy's jacket. It's just a jacket, but something hot runs through my veins at the knowledge she's wearing something of his. I stare at his name stitched across her chest for a few more seconds before shaking my head and turning my focus to her face. She smiles at me with a lifted brow, clearly waiting for me to answer her.

"I'll take a beer. What about you, Tyson?"

I look over at him, finding him taking a step closer to us. "A beer's perfect. And they're on me." He hands the cash over to Charlotte.

She gives him a warm smile. "Perfect. I'll grab your beers and your change."

Tyson's eyes skirt over to me for a moment before his gaze snaps back to Charlotte. "Keep the change."

Charlotte's eyes go wide as she focuses on removing the bottle caps from the beers. She regains composure as she finishes, meeting both our eyes with a bright smile. "Thank you for the tip, Mr. Bishop."

Tyson tosses a knowing look in my direction before returning her smile. "Of course."

"How's your coffee tasting?" I ask, changing the subject and catching her attention. I need her to stop looking at Tyson and look at me. My chest still burns at the sight of her wearing Teddy's jacket, and now that she's smiling at Tyson, I think

I might be feeling jealous, and I have no idea why. This is Charlotte.

Luckily for me, she looks away from Tyson, and with her attention on me, I'm finally able to take a deep breath and get rid of the tightness in my chest. "The coffee's been delicious. I'm trying not to drink it too fast. Thank you again, *troll*." She bites her lip after saying the nickname, clearly amused with herself for continuing to use the name she called me when we were texting earlier.

I place my hand on my chest and pretend to be offended by the nickname. "You're hurting my feelings, Char. I'm not a troll."

"How are you both doing today?" she asks as she hands me my beer.

I try not to frown when she focuses on Tyson again.

"Jude's kicking my ass today." Tyson laughs as he takes the other beer from Charlotte.

I smirk and try to push away the sudden jealousy I'm feeling when it comes to Charlotte. I lift my shoulder in a shrug. "I'm having a good day."

Charlotte aims a beaming smile in my direction, and I try to ignore the way my pulse spikes because of it. "Good for you." She wipes her hands against the fabric of her skirt before clapping her hands together. "Well, I'm going to get on with it. There's a lot more of you out today than I was expecting."

"There's definitely a lot more people here at Pembroke for it not being the busy season yet."

"Everyone's in on your secret of how great it is during the off-season," Charlotte quips.

She slides onto the bev cart seat and gives Tyson and me a wave before leaving.

I'm watching her drive away when Tyson's deep laugh breaks me from my thoughts.

"What are you laughing at?" I ask, putting my focus on him.

He tucks his free hand into his pocket while using the other to bring the bottle to his lips. "Nothing, Kensington. It was nice of you to be so insistent on tipping your *friend*."

I narrow my eyes. "She's told me how cheap people can be here. I knew she wouldn't take anything from me, but I just wanted to make sure she made good money."

"Mm-hmm." Tyson takes one more sip of his beer before setting it in the golf cart's cup holder.

I roll my eyes and plaster on a smile. "So, are you going to take your shot, or are you going to keep grilling me about being nice to my friend?"

Tyson ignores me and returns to the green to line up his shot.

We don't see Charlotte again for the rest of the day, and he doesn't bring her up again. It's the first time I've spent so much time with Tyson, but I like the guy. He comes off quiet and reserved, but he's cooler than I thought. And he doesn't want to talk business the entire time or make everything a pissing contest. I'm glad he's choosing to spend more time at Pembroke Hills. With Cal busy being madly in love with Lucy, and Ryker attached at the hip to Camille, it's nice to have someone who has a fairly open schedule. Usually, I spend a lot of time with Charlotte, but with this new job, she's busy working every weekend.

I keep quiet as Tyson lines up his shot. For some reason, I can't stop thinking about Charlotte in that damn jacket. It shouldn't bother me that she was wearing Teddy's jacket, but it did. Add in the way she was smiling at Tyson, and I'm wondering what's up with me today. I don't ever get jealous, but that's exactly what I felt when watching the two of them together.

I scrape my hand over my mouth and wipe all thoughts of Charlotte from my mind. I was up late working, and then seeing her first thing this morning might just be messing with my head.

5

Charlotte

I have a personal vendetta against whoever came up with the saying “when it rains, it pours.” No one should’ve ever spoken that mindset into existence. My day started rough with my coffee spilling all over me, some rude members at the club, and now it’s ending even worse.

“There’s really nothing I can do?” I ask, trying to keep my voice steady as I meet my landlord’s eyes.

Devin grimaces for a moment, clearly uncomfortable with the conversation we’re having. “I’m sorry, Charlotte. You know how it goes. I found last-minute renters who can pay full price to rent the apartment for the summer. With it being so close to the busy season, I thought maybe you could keep your discounted rate for the summer, but this is too good an offer to pass up.”

I nod, trying to keep my lip from trembling as I look at the ceiling for a moment. I don’t want to make Devin feel any worse than he already does. He’s got a wife and a two-year-old at home to take care of. It isn’t fair of me to ask him to turn down a lot of money just so I don’t have to find a new place to live for the summer. He needs to take the long-term rental tenants that can pay the full price; I just don't know what I'm going to do.

"I understand," I whisper, panic about what I'm going to do next settling deep in my gut. I should've known today would end badly when it started with me spilling my coffee all over myself first thing.

"I'll give you a couple of days to get your things. If you want, you can put some of it in the attic. As soon as this rental is over and it's off-season again, the place is yours again if you want it."

There's a lump in my throat, making it impossible to respond to him. I'm stressed about finding a place I can afford to live last minute, and I'm also feeling guilty for making Devin feel bad. Those two things combined make my throat thick with emotion, making it hard to say anything.

"I'm really sorry again, Charlotte. I wish it didn't have to be..."

I tune him out and close my eyes for a moment, mustering up the courage to put on a brave face. I knew this was a possibility for the summer. I was just really hoping luck would be in my favor and Devin wouldn't find any renters.

"It's okay," I manage to get out. I'm impressed by the steadiness of my voice. "Thank you for giving me time to pack and for allowing me to use your storage. I'll probably take you up on that."

"I'm also happy to help you move to your new place. I could ask around if any of my friends have rentals that are open..." His words drop off, and he looks at his feet.

He's being kind, but it doesn't take a rocket scientist to know that finding another rental this close to the busy season in the Hamptons will be impossible. I hate asking others for help, but I might have to ask to stay at one of my friends' places. Lucy and Cal aren't here yet, but I know if I were to ask, they'd let me stay with them. But this is their first summer here as a real couple. They're engaged and busy planning their wedding for the end of this summer. The last thing I want to do is feel like a bother.

"I'll be able to handle my things," I speak up, forgetting for a moment that Devin had said something. "Thank you again for letting me stay here as long as possible. I'll be out by Wednesday."

Devin nods before scratching the back of his neck. If I weren't so sad about having to find a new place to stay, him being so uncomfortable might make me feel the same, but I'm too deep in stress to reciprocate. Now, all I want is for him to leave so I can have my cry and breakdown in peace.

Unfortunately, Devin is a man and has no idea how to read the room. He stands there, shifting on the balls of his feet, not taking the hint that he can go now.

I sigh before having the nerve to meet his eyes. Hopefully, I don't look as sad as I feel. I'm seconds away from losing it, and I just need him to leave, because the last thing I want to do is to let him see me get upset. "Have a good rest of your night," I say, hoping this makes him take the hint. "Tell Erica I said hi."

Devin nods. "I will. Let me know when you're all moved out and if you need anything."

He turns around to leave, and the moment he walks out the front door, the tears I've been desperately trying to hold in fall down my cheeks.

I knew there was a chance he'd find renters willing to pay more than I can, but I was hopeful it wouldn't happen, and I could stay for the discounted price just like I was able to last summer. The apartment isn't in the same part that most tourists like to spend the season. It's farther away from the typical spots, and because of that, I got away with renting the apartment last year. I thought I could be lucky two summers in a row, but I was wrong.

I need to find somewhere to live, and I'll have to figure it out fast.

My mind is spinning with where to even start when my phone vibrates in my pocket. I pull it out, finding my mom calling me.

I let out a long sigh. She's got that kind of intuition that if I don't pull myself together fast, she'll know I was crying, and then she'll ask a million questions I'm not ready to answer. I could ignore the call, but she'll just call again or send one of my sisters to do it for her, since it's been a few days since we last spoke.

I have to answer and find a way to convince her that everything's fine.

I swipe to answer and hold the phone up to my ear. "Hey, Mom."

"Charlotte!" my mom exclaims, shock in her voice that I'm on the phone when she's the one who called in the first place. There's a slight rustling before she speaks up again. "See, Hailey, I told you she would answer."

My sister laughs in the background. "I said I hoped she didn't answer and that she was out having fun instead."

"Your sister worked all day. She's probably having a nice, relaxing night before having to work again tomorrow," Mom points out.

Hailey snorts. "Live and have fun before you have kids, Lottie. Soon enough, you'll be spending your evenings covered in baby food and running from one sporting event to the next."

I can't help but laugh at my sister and Mom. Hailey and I are closest in age, but she's still over a decade older than me. Her life—all of my siblings' lives—is very different than mine. There's an ache in my heart that I'm not there with them, but even though I miss my family like crazy, I'm still happy to be out in the Hamptons.

But it is nice to hear their voice, even if my sister and Mom called only to bicker on the phone with each other, with me listening in.

"How was your day, Lottie?" Mom asks, using the same nickname my entire family uses for me. "Are you liking the new job?" There's concern in her voice, but it isn't any more than usual. She's a mom who loves to be involved in all of our lives, despite every single one of her five kids being grown adults who don't need her to meddle the way that she used to. Because I'm the youngest—and the one with their life the least together—my life is the one she likes to meddle in the most. My two sisters also like to join in on the fun, the three of them constantly asking if my life in the Hamptons is what I want it to be or if I'm ready to come home yet. If I told them I lost my place to live for the summer, they'd pretend to be sad but would probably be thrilled and tell me it's a sign to return home instead.

"My day was great," I lie. "I'm really loving the new job. It pays great. I'm excited to see what I can save up this summer when it really gets busy at Pembroke."

My mom huffs, and the sound makes me smile. I know all she wants is for me to be happy, but she couldn't be more obvious that she wishes my happiness brought me home instead of to the Hamptons. "Is everyone nice to you there?" she finally asks.

"Yes, Mom, everyone's nice."

"How's that hot friend of yours? Have you dated him yet?" Hailey asks.

"Hailey Marie!" my mom scolds. "And his name is Jude. You should remember that by now. Charlotte's always talking about him."

I frown. I'm not *always* talking about him. He just happens to be the person I spend the most time with because all of my other friends have very busy lives, and his is a little slower. Or he makes it slower. I still don't know how he's able to help run a company and have the free time that he does, but I don't ask questions. I'm just happy I'm able to spend time with him.

There's incoherent whispering on the other line, followed by the sound of my sister laughing. "What?" Hailey asks innocently. "I've been married for what feels like an eternity. Let me live vicariously through my young and hot little sister. And you've said it yourself that you don't understand why Charlotte hasn't gone for Jude and how handsome he is."

I roll my eyes. If Jude could hear the current conversation, he'd have a field day. I make the mental note that he can never meet Hailey. She's the more vocal of my two sisters. Carly is the oldest and is good at keeping her thoughts to herself. Hailey, on the other hand, is a lot more like me—we like everyone to know our opinions.

"Jude—my friend who I will never date because he's a *friend*—is great. I spilled coffee all over myself on the way to work this morning, and he brought by a new one for me."

I can almost hear my mom melt on the other line. Maybe I shouldn't have told her about the nice thing Jude did. Now she might join in with Hailey and ask questions about him every time we talk. "What a man," Mom swoons. I scoff. Dad makes her coffee every single morning and brings it to her in bed.

"What a shame you won't date him. At least take him for a ride and be friends with benefits or *something*. Let me live through you, Lottie! Have *fun*."

She can't see it, but I can't help but roll my eyes at my sister. "You're way too worried about what I'm doing. I'm having plenty of fun without having to make things weird with my best friend, thank you very much."

Hailey groans. "Are you at least getting laid by someone else?"

There's a loud thumping noise. "*Ow*!" Hailey yells. "Mom, did you just hit me?"

"You can't ask your sister if she's getting laid."

"I always ask my sister if she's getting laid. I want to know the details. My sex life is planned and once a month on the calendar. Let me ask questions about all the fun my hot, single, younger sister is having."

Mom lets out an audible gasp.

My nose scrunches. "I don't need to know that, Hailey." I dodge her question about my sex life because my sister is still having more sex than I am, but she doesn't need to know that.

To be honest, I can't even remember the last time I had any kind of action that wasn't from one of my toys. I've been too busy with work and spending my free time with Jude to meet someone and get involved with them.

"How's Lucy doing? Or Camille? I can't believe she's now the publicist for Scarlett Astor. I *loved* her new movie. The one where everyone thinks she's dating that cute co-star."

I smile at my mom's change of subject. Our phone calls often consist of me giving the rundown on my friends' lives so she won't ask me about my own. One perk of moving out to the Hamptons last summer is the people I've met and become close with. Mom loves to hear all of the gossip when it comes to the members at Pembroke Hills, and I love giving it to her. Any conversation about someone else prevents her from prying into my life. Plus, I like to remind her that if I moved back to Arizona and left the Hamptons, I wouldn't have as much gossip.

"They're great. Lucy's busy preparing for the wedding at the end of the summer, and Camille is keeping busy with her new firm and wedding planning of her own."

"Lucy emailed me over some recipes last week. I got them before she posted them online," Mom says smugly. I can picture her smiling and lifting her chin, proud that she's getting something before the rest of the world.

I smile because with how busy Lucy is, it was thoughtful of her to make time to send things over to my mom and make her feel special. "I love that for you, Mom."

"I want the recipes," Hailey chimes in.

"You can find them on her page or website when she posts them."

Hailey gasps, and I can't help but laugh. As much as I love it here in the Hamptons and don't want to leave, moments like this remind me how much I miss my family and wish I were there with them.

"How's your friend with the cute little girl?"

I smile, thinking of Margo. "Margo's great, and Celeste is cute as ever. I'm so excited for them to be here for the summer. I'll be talking Margo into letting me have a girls' night with Celeste."

"Don't let your nieces hear that," Hailey pipes up. "They've been asking when you're coming home to visit."

"Hopefully soon," I respond, giving the generic answer

I always give. I know I need to get back there; it's just hard scheduling it. But I miss them all like crazy, so once I figure out where I'm living for the summer and I get more into a routine with the bev cart job, I'll find a time to get back to Arizona for a few days.

"You better. Lottie, I love you, but I've got to get going. I just wanted to prove Mom right and show that you were out having fun, but instead, you've let me down by being lame. Get out there and have fun, wild sex. Love you!"

"Don't listen to your sister," Mom immediately speaks up. I can imagine her aiming a stern look in Hailey's direction. I'm sure they're sitting in the kitchen of my childhood home, Mom sitting in her chair as Hailey circles the space, trying to round up her children. All of my siblings live within fifteen minutes of home. They're at the house constantly, and it's hard not to feel a little left out of the family dynamic with how much time they spend together. I don't let it get to me too much. I chose to come out here. Missing out on the everyday family antics is something I signed up for.

"I promise I'm in for the night," I assure my mom. The words make me sad. The last thing I want to be is alone tonight after the news I just got, but I also don't know what to do. I look across my kitchen at an old bottle of wine that sits on my counter. I haven't opened it because I don't think it's one that I like, but maybe I'll still pop it open tonight to help drown my sorrows about not having a place to live come next week.

"I love you, Lottie," Mom says, breaking me from my thoughts. "We'll talk again soon. Don't forget it isn't me who has to call you. The phone works both ways."

I nod. I probably should be better about being the one to call her. "I love you too, Mom. Tell everyone I love them."

"Good night, honey."

"Night." I hang up the phone, a sudden lump forming in my throat.

I think I'm just more emotional than normal because of the day that I had, but right now, I wish nothing more than to be closer to my family. I wish I could drive to my childhood home and get a hug from my mom. But I can't. I chose to move away, and I don't regret the choice. I want to be here. I just miss them. I know if I told my mom about losing the apartment, she might be able to give me advice about what to do, but I can't tell her. I don't want her to think I'm not able to handle things by myself out here.

Plus, all my other siblings have their lives so perfectly planned out. They've got it all together. Good jobs. Families. Houses. Kids. And then there's me—the daughter who moved across the country and doesn't use her degree or have any kind of serious relationship. While I'm happy with where I'm at in life—despite the current hiccup of finding where to live—I can't help but wonder sometimes if my parents think I'm a failure compared to my siblings.

It's always been hard being so much younger than them. Because of the age difference, they've always been ten steps ahead of me in life. I used to blame my age on it and hoped my parents realized that too. But now at twenty-four, it's hard not to wonder if my parents wish I were doing more with my life than what I am.

I shake my head.

I can't think like that.

I know my parents—my entire family—is proud of me. I left the only life I've ever known to come out here and chase a dream. And while actually getting to the part where I could open a photography business out here seems still so far away, I've found a good job that allows me to save money. I've found my own family of friends out here. And I'll figure out my living situation too.

I'm doing it all on my own, and I'm proud of myself for it.

But that doesn't mean that the thought of finding a new place to live doesn't stress me out.

I stare at the bottle. Opening it up and polishing off a bottle of wine alone doesn't seem like the worst idea.

But talking to my family, hearing them together, makes being alone the last thing I want to be right now.

If only I knew what Jude was doing.

Before I can talk myself out of it, I'm grabbing the bottle of wine from my counter and walking back out to my car.

I get so lost in thought, trying to brainstorm places I could look for somewhere to live, that one moment, I'm at my apartment, and the next, I've made it to Jude's.

Showing up at Jude's unannounced at night probably isn't my best idea, but I just really didn't want to be alone, and it seemed like a good idea to spend time with him. He's always there for me when I need him, and tonight's a night I just need my friend. He's smart and levelheaded—most of the time—maybe he can help give me some insight on my next steps. At the very least, he can make me not feel pathetic by drinking with me instead of making me drown out my sorrows alone.

I don't know if he's even home, but it doesn't stop me from pulling into his driveway to find out. The gates are open, making me pause for a moment, wondering if maybe he has company. Typically, I have to type in his code to pull in, but not tonight. I'm wondering if it's open because somebody's already there.

I slowly pull up the driveway, telling myself that I'll turn around and pretend I was never here if he has someone inside. I don't want to bother him if he's on a date or busy, but if he's alone, I'm hoping he won't mind me inviting myself over.

I let out a small sigh of relief when I don't see any cars besides his in the driveway. The lights in the house look like they're on, and that's all the invitation I need to park my car and grab the bottle of wine from my passenger seat.

I'm walking to his doorstep when my steps falter for a moment.

I'm suddenly feeling self-conscious. I didn't give myself the time to think about showing up at his house without telling him first.

Maybe I should rethink this. Jude and I hang out all the time—I spend more time with him than I spend with anyone else—and he often shows up at my house unannounced, but I don't typically show up at his house without texting him first. It's mostly because I never know when he's in meetings and working or not, but now I'm second-guessing if he'll be annoyed by me showing up without any kind of warning.

Just because there isn't anyone parked in the driveway doesn't necessarily mean he's alone. After golfing with Tyson, he hung out at Pembroke. I've seen him flirt with many members and guests throughout our friendship but have never actually seen him take any of them home. That isn't to say he doesn't do that though. He's Jude Kensington. Of course he brings women home. I just somehow have never witnessed it. I wouldn't be shocked if he found someone at the club to bring home and spend time with.

I stop at the doorway, my eyes dancing along his front lawn, which is bathed in the brilliant orange of the setting sun.

"This might be a bad idea," I whisper to myself. Maybe I

shouldn't come here unannounced. Maybe I can give him a call instead. The panic of finding a new place to live for the summer made me have a momentary lapse in judgment. I wanted someone logical like Jude to tell me it'll be okay and I'll figure it out, but now that I'm here, I'm wondering if I should've given him a warning before coming to him for comfort.

"Back home alone we go," I mutter under my breath. I'm taking a step back toward my car when Jude's front door swings open.

6

Jude

"Char?" I ask, propping my shoulder against my open doorway as I meet Charlotte's wide-eyed gaze.

"Jude," she exclaims, my name coming out shocked. She blinks a few times, as if she can't believe that she's running into me in my own driveway.

"What are you doing here?" I ask, my lips forming a smile. "Wasn't expecting to find you talking to yourself on my doorstep."

Charlotte's head rears back as her lips form the smallest frown. "I don't talk to myself."

My smile gets even wider. "Char, you're always talking to yourself. What are you doing here?"

I was sitting in my home office, going through some emails that my assistant had flagged, when a notification on my phone caught my attention. I opened up my security app and was surprised to see Charlotte standing at my front door through the phone screen.

Charlotte gives me a sad smile before lifting up a bottle of wine. Now that she's in the light, I'm able to see that her eyes are red. *Has she been crying?* My chest feels weirdly tight at that thought. I can't stand the thought of her crying.

I hate the unsure look on her face as she looks at me. It makes my chest hurt to see her upset and unsure. "I brought wine, but if we're being honest, it's cheap wine, and you'll probably hate it. Maybe we can trade it out with one of your nice ones from your wine room."

I'm quiet for a moment as I try to figure out if there's sadness in her tone. She doesn't necessarily sound upset, but there also isn't the typical bubbliness to her personality either. Something's off, and I want to know what.

"Any reason we're drinking?" I ask, holding my hand out to take the bottle from her. She can have any wine from my collection that she wants. I just want to know what's bothering her enough to lead her to my doorstep tonight.

Charlotte takes a step closer to me, and I know I should move out of the doorway to give her more room, but the look in her eyes when she meets my gaze makes my entire body freeze. She bites her lip, and she doesn't have to say a word for me to know that something's happened. I've gotten to know her so well and have spent so much time watching her that I can tell just by the way she works her bottom lip between her teeth and stares at her feet that something's bothering her.

"Devin got renters for the summer." Her voice breaks slightly at the end, showing the crack in the composure she's trying to keep.

"Fuck, Char," I mutter with a sigh. Without putting any thought into it, I wrap my arms around her and pull her in for a hug.

Her body is stiff against mine for a moment. We've never hugged like this. I've put my arm around her neck more times than I could ever count. We've done plenty of the quick, one-armed hugs in the last year, but we've never done this. This is more of an embrace, but I don't want to overthink it. It seems like she needs a hug, and I want to be the one to give it to her. She's obviously here for a reason, and while I don't know how to fix her problem yet, I can hold her for a moment to hopefully bring some sort of comfort.

It takes a few moments, but her body relaxes against mine as she accepts that it's okay for me to hold her like this. The hug is strictly platonic. Even though we don't have the kind of friendship where we hug like this often, it feels nice to have her body pressed against mine. There is comfort in it. I've never seen sadness in her eyes until tonight, and it's something I never want to see again. I want to find a way to strike all sense of sadness from her demeanor until she's back to being the bubbly Charlotte I'm used to.

I keep a tight grip on the neck of the wine bottle but use my free hand to softly pat between her shoulders. "So he won't let you stay there for the summer, even though you're paying rent?"

I've only met Devin a handful of times, but I thought I liked him. He seemed to have a soft spot for Charlotte. He was kind to her. But knowing he's the reason she looks so defeated makes me second-guess whether I should like the guy or not.

Charlotte slides out of my grasp and takes a step back. I miss the feeling of her body against mine the moment she's gone, and I try not to put much thought into why. Charlotte lets out a long, sad sigh. "I was paying rent, but the off-season rate. Now that the summer season is about to begin and he found renters able to pay full price, he had to do what's best for him and his family and accept their rental request. They could pay more than what I was giving him, and I can't blame him for that. I knew there was a chance this would happen."

I cock my head in the direction of the house. "Let's get inside, and we can talk more."

Charlotte nods and steps inside. She looks over her shoulder, giving me what I know is a fake smile. "Don't forget, we're drinking your wine, not mine."

I look down at the bottle of wine she brought. It's a little dusty, making me wonder how long she's had it. "Want me to pick out a bottle, or do you want to?"

I follow closely behind her as she makes her way to my kitchen. She slides into one of the counter stools and aims her gaze at me. "You're the wine snob. Pick something good."

Her comment makes me smile. It's not my fault I enjoy a good wine. I normally opt for red, but I know Charlotte prefers white, so I walk over to the wine fridge on the other side of the island. I keep white wine chilled there, just in case she ever wants a glass when we spend time together at my house, but I don't need to tell her that. "I have a bottle I bet you'll like, and it's already chilling." I lean down, open the fridge, and pull one out. "How's this look?"

Char pretends to inspect the bottle from where she sits, but at the last minute, she smiles—a real one—and lifts her shoulder in a shrug. "I'm deferring to you. If you think I'll like it, let's get that baby opened already. I need a drink."

I nod. I'll do anything she wants right now if it means she won't be so sad. "Want me to talk to Devin?" I ask her, setting the bottle on the counter. I watch her closely as I reach into the drawer next to me and pull out a wine opener.

Charlotte shakes her head. "I don't think there's anything you can say that'll change his mind. He's already signed a rental agreement with the new renters, and my rental agreement has a clause that if he finds tenants willing to pay full price, then I'm out of a place to live. You can't flirt your way out of this one for me, Jude. Plus—" She lets out the smallest giggle as she leans back. "—I don't think your charm would even work on Devin anyway."

My mouth falls open as I pretend to be hurt by her comment that I wouldn't be able to sweet-talk him. "Don't count my charm out yet. I'm known to be very persuasive."

I'm busy grabbing two wineglasses, but I don't miss the way Charlotte rolls her eyes. "Your charm won't work for this one. I'm just fucked and have nowhere to live for the summer."

"You're not fucked. We'll find you somewhere to live for the summer."

"You have to remember that I can only afford so much. Any place still open is probably *way* out of my budget."

"Like I said, we'll find you somewhere to live. I don't want you to stress about this."

Charlotte looks up for a moment, and it breaks my heart to see her like this. She's trying to put on a brave face and not show me she's upset, but in between her fake smiles and jokes, it's obvious how stressed she is about this.

My eyes scan my kitchen for a moment before focusing on Char once again. "Why don't you just live with me for the summer?"

7

Charlotte

I blink a few times, wondering if I heard Jude correctly. Surely I didn't hear him right.

"What?" I ask, taking the glass of wine he offers me. I take a large drink of it, wanting to feel a buzz as quickly as possible to deal with the ending of my day.

"This house is huge, plenty of guest rooms... Just stay with me for the summer."

I crinkle my nose before taking another drink. I watch Jude closely as he ambles around the counter and takes the seat next to mine.

"Jude, I'm not staying in your bachelor pad with you for the summer."

He stares at me over the top of his wineglass. He lifts an eyebrow before taking a drink, making me wonder what he's thinking.

His eyes pull from mine as he looks around the large kitchen. "I wasn't aware the house I spent months and months renovating gave off bachelor pad vibes."

I follow his gaze as I take another drink of my wine. I've

already drunk half the glass, making me a little sad because the wine he chose is delicious. I'm sure it cost more than I ever want to know, and I'm meant to savor it and sip it slowly, but tonight is not a night for taking my time with a glass of wine. I'm looking to down a bottle to forget that I have nowhere to live for the summer.

I keep the glass of wine pressed to my lips to buy myself time. The truth is, his house looks nothing like a bachelor pad. It's beautiful. The cream-colored cabinets and the original hardwood floors give the house character. He kept the history of the old Hamptons house and made it his own. It has the charm of the house I saw in the magazine that made me want to move to the Hamptons in the first place.

I let out a long sigh when my eyes find his still staring at me. "Your house doesn't look like a bachelor pad, but I'm still not staying here for the summer. Maybe I'll ask Lucy."

"You don't have to ask Lucy. I've already offered. I can assure you I'm way more fun than Lucy and Cal." He sets his wineglass on the counter and keeps his gaze pinned on me. There's a whisper of a smirk on his lips as he waits for me to respond.

I bite my lip for a moment, following his lead and setting my own wineglass down. I already feel a slight buzz from the wine, making my cheeks feel a little flushed.

His fun is the exact reason I don't want to stay here for the summer. The last thing I want is to watch him have a revolving door of women through his house. We're basically a year into our friendship, and I've managed not to have any awkward encounters with any of the women who fall at his feet, and I want to keep it that way.

"Jude, we're not meant to live together," I offer, giving him the first excuse that pops into my head.

Two wrinkles form between his eyebrows, accompanied by a slight frown. "What's that supposed to mean? Two friends can't live together? I'm just trying to help, Char."

There's a slight twinge in my chest at his words. The look on his face tells me all I need to know. He's just trying to do the right thing and offer me a place to stay for the summer. He's a good friend. I just don't think it's a good idea to live with him for the summer. Things might get weird, and I don't want that to happen.

"I know you're trying to help, and I appreciate it, but I'll figure it out. I always do."

His lips press into a thin line. It's obvious he wants to say something else, but he keeps whatever he was thinking to himself. Instead, he picks up his glass of wine and takes a large gulp. Now we're both over halfway through our first glass.

The silence between us gets to me. I sit forward and prop my elbows against the counter. "No more talking about me being homeless for the summer. For tonight, I want to forget about the problem."

Jude's sandy-brown eyebrows rise to his hairline. The serious look on his face that was there when I denied his offer is gone, and the constant look of humor he typically wears is back. "How can I help you forget?"

There's a deepness to his voice that I feel throughout my entire body. It makes my spine straighten and my toes curl against my rubber flip-flops.

My throat feels suddenly dry, and all I can do is swallow to try and wet my mouth enough to speak. I open my mouth to say something, but I still can't form a coherent thought. Since I can't get words out, I opt to take another drink of wine instead.

I take one gulp and then another until the glass is empty.

Jude chuckles. "So drinking is how we're forgetting tonight. Got it." He reaches across the counter and knocks his half-full glass of wine with my empty one. "Cheers, Char." His eyes stay pinned on me as he tips the glass up and chugs the rest of his wine.

• • •

"You're cheating!" I yell, pointing my finger at a grinning Jude.

He gives me a casual shrug before looking at the cards in his hands. "Or maybe I'm just better at this game than you are."

I shake my head. "No one's better at Go Fish than me. I've played it countless times with my nieces and nephews." The words come out perfectly clear in my mind, but the multiple glasses of wine running through my bloodstream make me wonder if my words maybe came out a little jumbled.

"Maybe I'm a Go Fish connoisseur," he jokes, his brown eyes pinned on me. The light from the candle on the table between us reflects in his eyes.

I scoff. "Not a chance. Have you even played before tonight?"

He lets out a bark of a laugh before covering his mouth with his cards in an attempt to hide his smile. "I don't think I've played since I was a kid," he admits, his shoulders shaking with the hint of another laugh.

I try to fight my own smile, but it doesn't work. I know Go Fish might not be the most refined card game we could've chosen, but all the other games Jude wanted to play seemed so complicated. I'm too tipsy to learn the rules of a new card game, so we settled on this one.

"Well, I still think you're cheating," I declare before taking a sip of my wine. Together, we're on our third bottle of wine. I know I'll have a terrible headache tomorrow at work, but I don't care. I'm having too much fun to stop. Despite the shitty news I got hours ago, Jude's been able to turn the night around for me. He'd done what he sought out to do—made me forget—and it feels like there's still so much of the night left.

Jude stares at me for a moment. He doesn't say anything for what feels like the longest time, and it makes me nervous. Jude is a talker, just like me. He says exactly what comes to his mind the moment he thinks it, but something about tonight has been different. I know he isn't saying everything he's thinking, and for some reason, it's unnerving me. He's looking at me longer than normal and keeping his thoughts to himself. This is unfamiliar territory when it comes to him, and I don't know how to feel about it.

Finally, he clears his throat and speaks up. "Weird that you think I'm cheating just because I'm winning."

"Do you have a seven?" I repeat, looking at my hand of cards.

"Go fish," Jude immediately answers. He keeps his gaze pinned on me, and I can't help but squirm under his intense stare.

The way he looks at me gives me butterflies, and that's never happened before. I groan and close my eyes for a moment as I try to ignore my body's reaction to him. I open my eyes to find him still staring at me with an intensity he hasn't shown before. "Jude, you *have* to have a seven."

"I don't have a seven. Go fish."

I stare at him for a moment, trying to do the math in my head. I'm tipsy, but I've been paying enough attention. He has to have a seven.

I know it's dramatic, but I let out the loudest sigh as I draw from the deck of cards between us. I swear he's cheating, but unless I crawl across the coffee table and force him to show me his cards, I just have to trust that he doesn't have the card I could have sworn he has.

I try not to show any sort of reaction to picking up a two. Two turns ago, he was looking for this card. As long as he doesn't ask for it again, I'll have a chance to catch up to him.

"Do you have a two?" he asks. He smirks before I can even react to his question.

I toss my cards down. "You're cheating!"

He laughs before his eyes go wide. I follow his gaze, finding my glass of wine spilling all over the table—and on me.

"Shit," Jude mutters, standing up and running to his kitchen.

I look down, finding my shirt covered in wine. "I'm so sorry," I rush to get out, feeling terrible. Leave it to me to invite myself over to his house and then spill his expensive wine all over his vintage restored coffee table that I'm sure cost way more than I could ever imagine.

He crouches in front of where I'm kneeling, that smirk he's always wearing still on his lips despite my mishap. "No need to be sorry." He quickly unravels sheets of paper towels from the roll. I try to help him by peeling off a few sheets and soaking up the wine from the table.

"What do you mean?" I ask, trying to stifle a giggle at the situation. "I spilled your nice wine on your nice table. I'm sorry, Jude."

He moves his attention from the spill on the table and onto me.

"Fuck, I didn't realize it was on you too." He quickly rips another paper towel off the roll and starts dabbing at my shirt.

"It's not that bad," I say, trying to keep my voice composed as it hits me how close Jude is.

His face hovers in front of mine as his eyes stay trained on the wet spot across my shirt. I blame the multiple glasses of wine for the reason why my entire body heats. It isn't because he's standing close. It isn't because I can feel the heat of his hand through the fabric of my shirt.

It isn't because I just realized that Jude Kensington's lips are inches away from mine. The heat blooming across my cheeks isn't because the only thought running through my head right now is how easy it'd be to kiss my best friend…and how badly I think I want to.

8

Jude

I shouldn't have drunk so much. After Char and I polished off the second bottle of wine, it seemed like the right idea to open up a third. But now I'm feeling things I shouldn't be feeling and thinking things I shouldn't be thinking, and it's all because of this stupid wine.

Or maybe it isn't the wine at all. Maybe it's her.

I'm too close to Char.

I'm not close enough.

She's got wine all over her shirt, and I'm just trying to help her dry off, but my head is spinning, and I can't think straight.

My entire body stills. Her stomach rises and falls underneath my touch.

"What's with you spilling your drinks on yourself today?" I ask, my voice coming out far more hoarse than I was expecting.

Charlotte lets out a small breath of a laugh. "Apparently, I'm a mess."

I smile and try to pretend that pressing my lips to hers isn't every thought going through my mind. I've never hidden my attraction to Charlotte. She's witty, incredibly smart, an amazing friend, and stunningly beautiful. It'd be impossible not to be attracted to her, but I've learned to bury that attraction. Sure, I'll make comments here and there because I love to make her blush. Sometimes making her blush is the only way I can tell if I have some sort of effect on her. I love having proof that she isn't completely immune to me, but never did I think we'd end up here, with my hand pressed against her stomach, feeling the proof of her reaction to our proximity with her sharp inhales and exhales.

"Char," I whisper, my gaze flicking to her lips. I don't think I've ever been this close to her. If I have, it didn't feel like it does now. The air around us is thick with tension. I feel like I can't even bring air into my lungs because of it.

Her lips part, and her tongue peeks out the smallest amount. She wets her lips, and I swear my heart races so fast that it feels like it could beat right out of my chest. I blame the alcohol, even though it has nothing to do with the buzz I have from the wine. It's because I'm drunk off Charlotte.

It's dark in my living room; the only light we have is from the dim lights of the kitchen and the candle on the coffee table. Her eyes are normally a stunning bright blue that reminds me of the sky on a summer day here in the Hamptons, but because of the lack of light in the room tonight, they appear darker.

"Jude." My name comes out strained, and it might be the drinks playing tricks on me, but I swear she looks at my lips.

Does she want me to kiss her?

God, I really want to kiss her.

I know I shouldn't.

She's been upfront from the very beginning that nothing will ever happen between us.

But she's also never looked at me like she was starving for my kiss.

"I…" My words fall off because I don't know what to even say. Do I ask to kiss her? Do I tell her I want to kiss her? Or do I back away and let the moment pass and not risk messing up our friendship?

I've known Charlotte for almost a year at this point. We've had drinks together plenty of times and been alone more times than I could ever count. Never once has there been tension between us like there is right now. I don't know if it's the alcohol, the candlelight, or something else entirely, but all I know is for the first time in our friendship, I'm considering crossing the line that's been drawn.

The resolve I'm desperately holding on to threatens to snap. Instead of resting my hand against the wet spot on her shirt, I let the paper towel drop and fist the fabric instead. My fingers latch onto the material tightly, and I toe the line by pulling on her shirt slightly, bringing her body closer to mine.

She doesn't protest. In fact, she takes me by surprise by bracing herself with her hands on my thighs.

And then she looks at my lips again at the same moment a small noise of surprise—that sounded a lot like a *moan*—falls from her lips.

My resolve snaps. I lean in and press my mouth against hers. It's so soft that our lips barely touch, but it's enough to send shock waves through my entire body. Everything fades away with the press of her lips against mine.

I know I shouldn't kiss my best friend, but I can't think of anything else. I'm not thinking of the consequences. I'm not thinking about what happens after we kiss. All I'm thinking about is the desperate sound she let out and the hungry way she was staring at my lips.

I'm about to open my mouth and coax my tongue into hers

when she tears her mouth from mine.

"Jude." My name comes from her lips like a plea; I just don't know what she's begging for. I hope it's for more of what we just started, but her wide-eyed stare tells me that it's probably the opposite. "We shouldn't..." Her words trail off as she brings her fingertips to her mouth and presses them against her bottom lip. She sits back, and I take the hint to let go of her shirt.

I miss the warmth of her mouth, of feeling her rapid breathing under my touch. I want to close the distance between us and kiss her again, except this time, I want to deepen it. I want to figure out what she tastes like and discover what sounds she'll make with my mouth against hers. I want so much more from her, but the way she stares back at me tells me all I need to know. I want more, and I can tell just by the look in her eyes that *more* is the last thing she wants.

I swallow, my fingers twitching at my side to reach out and touch her again.

Fuck, what have I done?

I close my eyes, trying to push the memory of her lips against mine to the very back of my mind. It was a terrible idea to want to kiss her. I know that, but it doesn't change how, for a few perfect moments, the only thing I needed was to feel the press of her lips against mine.

When I open my eyes, I make sure to plaster on a smile. It feels incredibly forced, but I hope she doesn't recognize it as that. I pick up the discarded wet paper towels before standing up. I whistle, trying to come off as if I'm completely unfazed by what just happened. My mind races with things I can say that can ease the tension as I try to find a way to pretend we didn't just kiss.

"We were about to make things totally awkward between us, weren't we?" I laugh, trying to play it cool. I hope she doesn't see right through my lie. It didn't feel awkward at all. It felt right, and the realization is jarring. I try to push all thoughts of that away, knowing just by the look on her face and the way she keeps looking down at her lap instead of at me that no matter how right it felt for me, it didn't feel right to her. Me calling it awkward when it was anything but is just an attempt to make her feel better about what just happened.

Char looks up at me. She chews on her lip for a moment before plastering on her own fake smile. "Yeah," she mutters. I can't help but look away from her blue eyes for a moment to notice the way she twists her hands in her lap before making eye contact again. "It's just the wine," she offers, her words coming out so quiet I almost don't catch them.

I nod. "Of course it was the wine. You and me kissing?" I force out a laugh. "That would be *so* weird."

There's no denying that the wine has gone to my head, but it hasn't clouded my judgment in the slightest. Now that I'm being honest with myself, I still would've wanted to kiss Charlotte completely sober, but I'm not going to tell her that.

I can't.

I clear my throat in an attempt to get myself under control. Standing up, I grab the dirty paper towels and walk to the kitchen to throw them away. "If you want to follow me to my closet, you can pick out a new shirt to wear," I offer.

Charlotte nods before her eyes skirt over the coffee table. "I feel like I should help you finish cleaning up."

I don't tell her that I need to get away from the living room for a moment. All I can think about when I stare at the coffee table is the fact that we almost kissed in front of it. If we leave the room, maybe I'll stop replaying the feeling of her lips against mine over and over in my head.

"The coffee table is fine. The only thing still covered in wine is you. Let's go find you a new shirt."

I walk to my room and hope that she follows. My head feels fuzzy, and I know it isn't because of the wine. It's Charlotte. Kissing her—no matter how brief it was—has unlocked something inside me. It's like the floodgates have been opened, and now I can't think about anything other than her.

I don't have to look over my shoulder to know she follows me into my room. I take a deep breath as I turn on my closet light in an attempt to clear my mind of her.

When I turn around, it doesn't work. All I can think about when my eyes meet hers is how much I still want to kiss her.

"Do you want a T-shirt or sweatshirt?"

The long pieces of her blonde hair cover her face as she looks to the ground. "A T-shirt is fine."

I nod and turn around to sort through my T-shirts, trying to decide which one to give her.

Which one have I worn recently? I want to give her one that smells the most like me, although I won't tell her that. It won't smell like my cologne, but it'll smell like my detergent, and for some reason, I'm crazy about her wearing anything that smells like me.

I pull a Pembroke one I know is freshly clean from a hanger and turn around to face her again.

"How's this?"

Charlotte looks at the shirt. "Good."

I nod and take a step closer to her. Now that we're standing so close, I'm wishing I had turned more lights on in my closet. I only turned on the ambient lighting, and it makes things feel far more intimate than they should.

Or maybe the way she stares at me makes it feel intimate.

Her chest rises and falls in quick succession, mirroring my own rapid breathing.

Neither one of us moves or says a thing. We stand in the middle of my closet, staring at one another, and there's never been a moment when I've ever wanted to read someone's mind more.

I'm dying to know what she's thinking.

Is she recalling our kiss? Is she wishing it'd happen again? I know I am.

My eyes rake over her face. I've always known she's beautiful. I accepted my attraction to her the moment we met. But I didn't pursue her the way I typically would because she made it clear early on that nothing would ever happen between us. I made sure to bury the attraction because I didn't want to mess anything up. She was off-limits, and because of that, I've never taken the time to appreciate just how stunning she is until now.

She's *still* off-limits. Her stopping the kiss proves that. But at this very moment, there's no use in burying my attraction. It runs rampant through my veins. There's no burying it.

I trace the curve of her cheekbones with my gaze. Even in the dim lighting, I can see the flush to her cheeks. I can't help but wonder if I could turn them from the soft shade of pink to a scarlet just from kissing her…from touching her.

I swallow and close my eyes for a moment.

I feel dizzy, and I'm not even touching. All I'm doing is looking at her and I feel lightheaded.

I close my eyes for a moment as the truth settles deep in my chest. I can try and blame the drinks all I want, but it's no use.

I'm not drunk off the wine. I'm drunk off Charlotte.

I open my eyes to find her still watching me carefully. I needed out of the living room desperately to try to wipe the memory of our kiss from my mind, but it turns out maybe I just need to be away from her to forget it.

The only problem is I don't want to be away from her. I want to wrap my arms around her waist and pull her body flush to mine and finish what we started in the living room.

"Arms up," I hoarsely demand.

Charlotte looks up at me in confusion but does as she's told. She lifts her arms over her head slowly. Or maybe it just feels slow because my head is fuzzy because of her as I pay close attention to her every move.

"Good girl," I whisper with a smirk. My attempt to lighten the tension between us doesn't work. I thought she'd roll her eyes or scold me for the saying, but instead, her breath hitches, and her eyes go wide as she stares expectantly up at me.

I know she's fully capable of taking off her own shirt. It'd honestly probably be smarter for me to leave her alone in the closet to get changed, but I can't get my feet to move. They stay planted as I reach for the hem of her shirt.

With every move I make, I watch her closely. If she gives any indication that she feels uncomfortable with what's happening, I'll stop. I'll leave the room and do my best to pretend that none of this ever happened.

But she doesn't say anything. As I begin to inch the fabric up her body to remove the wine-stained shirt, she stays perfectly still with her arms raised above her head.

"Why are you looking at me like that?" Charlotte asks, breaking the silence.

I pause, the fabric of her shirt still fisted in my hands and lifted enough to show off her stomach but not quite high enough to get a glimpse of her bra. "How am I looking at you?"

Her eyes flick to my mouth, and I swear she's testing every bit of restraint I have. "Like I'm not just your friend." Her words are said so quietly I wouldn't have been able to hear them if it weren't for how close we're standing.

Because of the proximity, I'm sure she hears my sharp intake of breath at her words. I hadn't expected her to call me out like that. My mind races with how I can even respond. Should I be honest with her? Or do I do the right thing for our friendship and tell her it's just the drinks so we can wake up tomorrow and pretend none of this happened? I swallow. My mouth suddenly feels incredibly dry. "I don't know how else to look at you right now," I confess.

She doesn't respond, and it's just another moment I so desperately wish I could get into her mind to find out what she's thinking. Is she feeling the same tension I am? She stares up at me with her wide, beautiful, big blue eyes, and I can't help but wonder if the way she looks at me is a way she looks at a friend or if there's more to it.

I ache for there to be more to it, but I'm not brave enough to ask.

My heart slams against my chest as I continue what I started. I pull the fabric up, revealing more of Charlotte's perfect skin inch by inch. I fight every urge to look down and appreciate her, but I know that wouldn't be appropriate. Instead, I keep my gaze on hers as I lift the fabric up until it's over her head and off her body completely.

She stands in front of me in nothing but her skirt uniform and a bra. From the corner of my vision, I can tell it's the same bra she had on this morning. It takes everything in me for my gaze not to move from hers as I toss her wine-stained shirt to the side and grab mine. I'm quick at getting the shirt onto her body to stifle the temptation to look at her bare skin.

"Is that better?"

Charlotte nods. "Yes. Thank you." The smile she gives me slices right to my heart.

Fuck. I want her. Desperately.

I scrub my hand over my face and rip my gaze from hers because I need a moment of relief. "Sweet." My gaze focuses on the bathroom as I try to think what to say now. I want to get as far away from her as I can, while at the same time, I'm still fighting the urge to pull her body into mine.

"Want to watch a movie or something?" Char asks.

The question takes me by surprise. I can't help but look at her again. "A movie?"

She nods as she gives me a tentative smile. "Yeah. A movie. We love to watch movies, and I figured I'm too buzzed to go to sleep yet, and…"

Her words trail off, and I give her a few moments to continue her thought. When she doesn't, I choose to fill the silence instead. "Is watching a movie your way of ending the card game so you don't officially lose?"

Charlotte's eyes go wide, and I try to ignore the way her soft giggle feels like a punch to the gut. "Oh, if we kept playing, I would've made a comeback. But the wine's getting to my head too much to play a game. I want a movie instead."

My jaw tenses as I fight the urge to tell her that it isn't the wine getting to my head…it's her. I know I should probably say no to the movie and go to bed instead so I can maybe sleep off these funny feelings she's giving me.

But I can't.

If she wants to watch a movie together, I'm going to watch a movie with her. No matter how much it might torture me to do so.

I hold my hand out in point to the exit for my closet. "Then let's go watch a movie."

9

Charlotte

I wake up with a pounding headache and my back pressed against something solid and warm. I blink a few times, trying to wake myself up enough to figure out where I am.

Last night is a little blurry. I remember playing cards, but I don't remember what happened after. I look down, finding a tan arm sprawled across my middle.

My eyes go wide, and my entire body stills as I realize where I am and, more importantly, who I'm with.

I slowly turn my head to look over my shoulder, my eyes immediately landing on a peacefully sleeping, *shirtless* Jude. In his deep sleep, his long eyelashes rest against his sharp cheekbones. His hand rests against my stomach, and even though my shirt provides a fabric barrier between his skin and mine, I swear I feel the heat of his hand through the shirt.

Speaking of shirts. I glance down, realizing that the shirt I'm wearing is not the one I showed up in last night. It's looser and far softer. It's Jude's.

"Oh, fuck," I whisper, immediately glancing over at Jude the moment the words accidentally slip from my mouth.

Luckily, he stays fast asleep, giving me time to figure out what the hell happened last night.

Did we have sex? I gently lift the blanket that's tucked around me, letting out a sigh of relief when I find out I'm at least still wearing my underwear.

I squeeze my eyes shut, trying to remember what happened last night.

I showed up at his house, we had a glass of wine. One drink turned into finishing off three bottles of wine. Or was it more? The throbbing pain between my eyes tells me that we might've had more.

Although it's a little foggy, I remember playing cards with Jude. I remember spilling the wine, and I swear I remember a moment with him that almost felt like…more. I swear I remember our lips brushing against each other's for a moment. I swear I remember him looking at me in a way he's never looked at me before.

But I had a lot of wine. I don't know if my mind's playing tricks on me.

Everything after us playing cards is a blur. I don't know everything that happened.

I squeeze my eyes even tighter, as if that will force the memories of the rest of the night to appear.

What happened after we stopped playing the game?

I remember standing in Jude's closet. Maybe that's when I changed out of my shirt and ended up in his. But something gnaws at my memory. Something more. We were both in his closet, but I swear I remember an intense look in his eyes as he helped me out of my shirt and into his.

I open my eyes, knowing I have to be imagining things.

I look over my shoulder again, trying to remember what led

us to cuddling on the couch. I close my eyes again, but for the life of me, I can't remember.

I sigh, beginning to slowly slide off the couch. I need to find my phone and figure out what time it is. I have to work this morning, and it's going to take me longer to get ready, thanks to this hangover.

I'm also going to have to go back to my place and get a clean uniform.

My home.

Reality hits me as I remember what even led me to show up at Jude's house in the first place.

I need to find a new place to live.

I stifle a groan, wishing I hadn't had the bright idea to forget the fact that I have nowhere to live this summer. If I hadn't drunk so much, I wouldn't have ended up cuddling with my guy best friend all night. I wouldn't have woken up and immediately started panicking that we kissed last night.

My foot softly hits the ground as I try to inch myself off the couch even more. I don't know if it'd be better to lift his arm off me or if I should continue slowly rolling away, allowing his arm to gently fall against the plush cushion of his couch.

I opt for the latter option, taking my time slowly rolling my body away from his until my other foot hits the ground and I'm no longer on the couch. I pause for a moment, watching him closely to make sure he stays asleep.

From what I can remember, he drank just as much as I did, maybe even more. All I can hope is that he'll wake up with fuzzy memories like I did too. We'll be able to pretend nothing happened, and things will never be awkward.

I rise to my feet, keeping my gaze locked on him. Even after I rolled away from him, he hasn't moved. His sandy-brown hair falls over his forehead, and his lips part slightly in his sleep. The sunlight from the living room window drifts in through an opening in the curtains, causing sunbeams to dance across his skin.

Once I'm sure that he isn't waking up, I turn my attention to the living room. I need to get my clothes—or at the very least, some sort of pants—and then I need to rush home and get to work. The orange glow of the sunlight gives me hope that I have plenty of time to make it home, get myself together, and still arrive on time for my shift at the club today.

I spot my phone on the ground near the coffee table. I crouch down and grab it, relieved to find that I still have over an hour until I have to be at Pembroke.

My eyes scan the room as I try to decide if I should try and clean up or not. There's a bottle of wine still on the table and our empty glasses right next to it. There are even empty plates from what was apparently a late-night snack that I don't remember.

Jude makes a sound behind me, and my head immediately whips in his direction. My stomach drops at the thought of facing him before I even get a grip on what did—or didn't—happen last night. I know I'll have to see him again, and I'm sure things will be totally fine and not awkward at all, but I at least need to get rid of this hangover and attempt to regain my hazy memories from last night.

With his eyes still closed, Jude adjusts his body slightly on the couch but doesn't wake up. I feel guilty for leaving the living room the way it is, but I start to tiptoe toward Jude's room to find my pants.

My heart races the entire time I collect my things. I'm hoping that if I'm able to sneak out of here while he sleeps peacefully, by the time I see him again later today, or whenever, we can just pretend that we didn't drink too much last night.

I tiptoe toward his front door, keeping a close eye on his sleeping form as I make my way outside.

I'm able to get out of the house and to my car without waking him up. The moment I get in my car, I finally let out a deep breath of relief.

I back out of his driveway and hope that I can find a way to get rid of this massive hangover before starting my shift. The entire drive home, I try to force myself to remember if anything else happened between us last night, but I keep coming up empty. I don't think we crossed any lines. I can't remember exactly though.

Things won't be awkward at all the next time I see him.

Everything is fine.

So why, when I let my mind wander, do I almost wish that something *did* happen?

I'm not immune to Jude's good looks and charm. I am attracted to him, but I'm smart enough to know that a man like him doesn't settle down. He'd be a great one-night stand, and if he weren't one of my best friends, I'd absolutely go for that. But he is my friend, and I do care for him in a way that makes me not want to lose him. I can't let the fact that he's good-looking and has the charm of any good playboy cloud my judgment. I can't cross a line with him that can't be uncrossed. Because of that, I can't hope that something more did happen between us. I can't want more from him. He's staying in the friend zone because I don't have many friends out here in the Hamptons with Lucy gone as much as she is. Because of that, Jude and I have grown close, and now…I don't know what I'd do if I lost him.

We're staying friends. *Just* friends. We'll never be more than friends.

The problem is, even as I rush to pull myself together for work, I can't stop picturing the desperate way he looked at me last night. I know I was pretty tipsy, and I can't trust my memories, but I swear he looked at me in a way that no one's ever looked at me before. It was in a way that screamed he didn't want to *just* kiss me, and I don't know what to do about the hazy recollection.

I'm still thinking about it as I park my car at Pembroke Hills. I know I have to be making it up. Jude wouldn't look at me that way, and I need to stop fantasizing about him doing it. Nothing happened or almost happened last night.

He's going to show up at the club later and act like his usual self. He'll say something to annoy me, and we'll be back to normal. I'll be annoyed at myself for spending all morning worrying about it, and we'll move on.

Nothing's going to change at all.

At least, that's what I keep telling myself as I work my shift at Pembroke.

10

Jude

The sound of my doorbell ringing pulls me from a deep sleep. I groan, adjusting my position on the couch. I wrap my arms tighter around Charlotte, wanting just a few more minutes with her in my arms instead of answering whoever is at the door.

Except I quickly realize it isn't Char's body that I'm cuddling anymore—it's a throw pillow.

My doorbell rings again, and the sound of it has me leaping off the couch. The gates must've been left open overnight, and the front door auto-locks. It could be Charlotte at the door. I've told her the code to the keypad, but I'm sure she's forgotten it.

I smile and run to the front door, more excited at the thought of seeing her than I should be. I know we drank a lot last night, and at first, she turned me down after kissing her, but the mood still shifted after that.

Once we both got ready for bed, we put on a movie, and it hadn't even started before she was lifting my arm from my side and tucking her body next to mine. I don't remember when exactly we fell asleep watching the movie, but I know nothing will ever beat the feeling of falling asleep with her in my arms.

The night was perfect. So perfect that part of me wants to do something I never expected to do—I think I want to ask Charlotte on a date. It was on the tip of my tongue last night to ask her, but I never did because it wasn't something you ask when you're not sober.

But now, we'll both be sober—both probably fighting a hangover—and I can ask her on a date. The tension between us last night can't all be in my head.

My cheeks spread in a wide smile—despite the dull ache at the back of my head—as I yank the door all the way open before even looking through the peephole to see who it is.

My eyes land on the woman in front of me, and my smile falters.

Because it isn't Charlotte standing at my door.

It's someone from my past, a face I wasn't really expecting to see again, and someone I certainly wasn't expecting to see carrying a baby.

"Hi, Jude," she says, her voice void of any emotion.

"Karina?" I ask, my fingers holding tightly on to the door. I hadn't thought of anyone but Charlotte being at the door, so I hadn't bothered putting on a shirt. It feels weird to be standing here in nothing but a pair of athletic shorts while Karina stands in front of me dressed up for an event. I try not to feel too weird about standing in front of her without a shirt on. After all, this woman has seen me naked. Although at this point, it must've been a little over a year since then.

She gives me a tight smile before taking a deep breath. Her eyes move to the baby, who is sleeping peacefully in a car seat.

"I don't know how else to say this," Karina begins, her voice stiff. She watches the baby, still without any hint of emotion on her face. I watch her closely, wondering what's even happening.

Am I still dreaming?

Maybe this is a dream. It has to be.

There's no reason Karina Walters would be standing on my doorstep with a sleeping baby. She was a model I met at some party last spring. It was weeks before I was set to return to the Hamptons, and we shared a great night together. But she didn't seem like the type to ever reach back out, making seeing her on my doorstep even more odd. Especially with a baby. Karina never struck me as someone who spent time with babies in her spare time.

"How else to say what?" I ask, unable to wait for her to offer the answer herself.

Karina meets my gaze, and there's something about the way she looks at me that tells me exactly what her next words are going to be.

"This is your daughter," Karina explains, lifting the car seat slightly. "She's four months old, and she's yours."

My grip gets even tighter on the door. It's the only thing holding me up at this point as my eyes bounce between Karina and the baby she claims is mine.

"What?" I croak, my vision going blurry with the way my head spins with questions.

"This is your daughter," Karina repeats, setting the car seat on the ground. With the movement, I notice she's also holding a large duffel bag. She sets it down on the ground next to the baby.

"My daughter?" My mind flashes to our night together. I know I used protection. I always use protection. Plus, I never heard from her again. There's no way that the baby in front of me is mine. She wouldn't have waited a year later to tell me about it.

"Yes, *your* daughter." She has the nerve to sigh as if there's something wrong with me clarifying what she said.

"I don't understand," I mumble, my head spinning as I try to figure out if this is really happening or not.

"We had sex a year ago, I got pregnant, I didn't want to keep the baby, but my family convinced me to, and now I'm just… I never wanted a baby, Jude. I didn't want to be a mom. I *don't* want to be a mom. I want to be a model. I want to be the best model. And I can't do that while taking care of her."

My jaw flexes as my brain tries to play catch-up with what she's just said. Not only is she telling me that this baby is apparently mine, but it also sounds like she wants nothing to do with the infant.

"Karina," I begin, letting out my own sigh. I take a deep breath, trying to force myself to think clearly about what's happening. "You can't just drop a baby off on my doorstep and say she's mine."

"I didn't have sex with anyone else, Jude," she explains, her tone annoyed. "I was too busy with work, and no one interested me until you. And the weekend after we hooked up, I went on a four-week safari, where I spent half the time throwing up and in denial that my period was late. She can't be anyone's but yours."

I shake my head as I look down at the sleeping baby. She's cute, with her round cheeks and her blonde hair, but I can't look at her and have any idea if she's mine or not. She looks like a baby. All babies look like babies to me because I don't have any experience with them.

"You still can't leave her with me. We'll do testing, and if she's mine, I promise I'll help. I'll be there for her and for you, but you can't just drop her off and leave her. She might be mine, but she's yours too." By the end of my words, my voice is barely above a whisper. My words come out strained and choppy, because for some reason, I believe her that this baby is mine. There's something about the way she looks at me that makes me believe she's telling the truth. But still, I'll need to confirm that. We'll need to do testing and plan schedules and…

"I don't want her, Jude. As harsh as that sounds, it's my truth. Everyone told me once I had her that I'd want to keep her, but I don't want to keep her. I can't. She deserves more. And I couldn't decide what to do with her next before telling you that she's yours if you want her."

I swallow through the emotion that clogs my throat. I think everyone should have the choice if they want to be a mother or not. But she's talking about this baby as if she were some inanimate object. She isn't talking about her like she's a real baby, and something that feels a lot like anger blooms in my chest because of that.

"We have to talk about this," I manage to get out through the countless different emotions completely taking over.

Karina shakes her head. "I don't want to talk about this. I've had months to make this decision, and my mind has never changed. I'm trying to do the right thing by giving you the chance to take her if you want her."

The baby makes a cooing sound in her sleep and catches my attention. I stare at her, wondering how things have even come to this.

I have a daughter?

I stare at her and feel it deep in my bones that she's mine. It's a weird feeling, one I've obviously never felt before. It's like everything just clicks, and some weird sort of sixth sense tells me that Karina is telling the truth. I have a daughter. She's *mine.*

I tear my eyes from her and look at Karina. "So that's it? You're going to drop her off and pretend that you're not her mom? So...what? You just forget about her forever?"

It's the first time that Karina actually looks sad. She glances over at the sleeping baby once before meeting my gaze.

"I'm not her mom," Karina offers, her tone dry and void of any emotion. "Not in the ways that matter. I won't ever be, and I don't want to be." She emphasizes the last part, leaving no room for interpretation on how she feels. "I've already spoken with a lawyer, but before I can fully sign my rights over to you, you're going to have to do a paternity test. But it'll come back that she's yours, and I will do whatever I need to in court to make her fully yours."

I close my eyes to try and escape the ringing in my ears. It almost feels like I'm having an out-of-body experience. I know I'm standing on my doorstep in front of a woman I slept with once and that I'm not dreaming, but it feels like none of this is real.

When I open my eyes, the ringing subsides, and an eerie kind of peace settles over me. I have no idea what's happening, but I know that I can't abandon this baby.

"You're sure about this?" I ask, keeping my eyes trained on her.

It's not that I've never pictured myself as a dad. I always figured if I ever met the right girl that I'd settle down and maybe have kids, but I never could've pictured it happening this way. I thought I had more time. I thought I'd have someone on the journey with me. I never thought I'd venture into fatherhood completely alone.

Karina's shoulders sag with what might even be relief. "Yes, I'm sure. I've been sure since the moment I figured out I was pregnant, but I held off on the decision because the people around me told me I'd change my mind."

"And you haven't? You won't?" My voice breaks a little at the end because the last thing I want to do is confirm this baby is mine, form a bond with her, make her mine, and have Karina come back and decide she wants to take her back from me.

Karina shakes her head. She doesn't show any emotion as she opens her mouth to speak. "I won't change my mind. She's yours, Jude. Just yours."

An unfamiliar feeling runs through my body when I look down at the sleeping baby. I don't know the first thing about taking care of an infant, but I'll learn…for her. "I don't even know what to say to you," I confess. This still doesn't seem real. It seems like some plot out of a movie.

"Her name is Ava," Karina tells me. I don't look at her. I can't, not as I'm still trying to process how she can just hand over her daughter like this. "There was this nurse in the hospital who said she looked like an Ava. I went along with it because I hadn't really ever thought of giving her a name until then."

Her honesty feels like a punch to the gut. I don't understand how she never even thought about giving her a name. My eyes travel over the sleeping baby's face—*Ava's* face. "Ava," I whisper, getting used to the way it falls from my lips. I like it.

Karina lets out a long sigh, making me look back in her direction again. "There are diapers in this bag. Extra clothes. The formula she's been drinking, along with bottles. You're going to need to buy more, but I wanted to make sure you had enough for now."

All she does is stare at me, and all I can do at the moment is stare right back. I can't wrap my head around what's happening. I can't pretend to even begin to understand how she could've hidden a pregnancy—a *baby*—from me and then decided to tell me by dropping the baby off and leaving forever.

I don't know how much time passes as we just stand there staring at one another. My entire life has changed in a span of a few minutes. All I know is I apparently have a daughter, and she needs me.

I clear my throat, wondering how life can change so abruptly, and meet the eyes of the mother of my child. "My lawyers will be in touch with yours."

She nods and takes a step back. It's only now that I notice the idling car in my driveway. A man sits in the driver's seat, his eyes pinned on the phone in his hands. I look back at Karina and wonder if I'll ever see her again.

"My lawyer's card is in the bag as well. Take care of her, okay? And please, Jude, don't tell anyone who her mother is. I went to great lengths to hide the pregnancy…to hide the birth and the baby. No one can know about this."

I feel dizzy as I watch her walk away. My fingertips press into the doorframe so hard that I'm sure there's got to be marks on my skin. I grew up with a mother who loved me and dreamed of being a mother. All she ever wanted to be was a mom. It took a lot of years—and some science—for my parents to have me. I was surrounded by my mother's love every single day, but I know not every woman dreams of being a mother. I respect Karina's right to choose; I just can't wrap my head around how she cared for Ava for four months only to decide to abandon her.

Just as Karina walks away, the baby at my feet begins to grunt.

I look down, finding her eyes open and staring right at me.

The air leaves my lungs the moment my eyes connect with

hers. I crouch down, my hand shaking as I reach to touch the baby—*my* baby. Her eyes meet mine, and it's like my world comes into focus. I have no idea what I'm going to do with her—I know nothing about kids and have no business raising a baby—but as I look into her dark blue eyes, I know that I'm all she has now.

"Hi, Ava," I whisper. My throat feels tight, and my eyes sting with the threat of tears. The reality of the situation is kicking in, and I have no idea what to do.

I don't even know how to unbuckle her from the car seat she's in.

She lets out a little coo before kicking her legs. Her eyes stay on me as I try to figure out how the hell to unfasten the buckle between her chubby little legs.

I finally get the button pushed down enough for the two clips to pop out. After that, I figure out how to get the buckle undone, and she's free. My heart hammers against my chest at the thought of picking her up. I've never held a baby. I guess I held Beck and Margo's daughter, but she wasn't this little by the time I had the courage to hold her.

Ava's tiny. And she stares at me, wide-eyed and curious, having no idea that her mother just left her and now I'm all she's got.

"I'm your dad," I tell her, letting my fingers drift underneath her.

She seems so fragile. I haven't even picked her up yet, and I'm terrified I'm doing something wrong.

All she does is let out a little squeal. I think it's an excited squeal. Or maybe she's mad. I don't know babies and their sounds enough to know the difference, but I do know she doesn't look upset as I pull her out of the car seat and into my arms.

I cradle her head, not even knowing if it needs to be supported or not. I don't know what I'm doing as I pull her into my chest. I'm probably already fucking this up, and she hasn't even been in my care for five minutes.

Ava lets out another squeal, and I hope the sound is a happy one. I don't want to already be messing this up.

The sound makes me smile as I bring my forehead to hers while cradling her gently. "Ava, I have no idea what I'm doing here, and I'm probably going to mess things up, but we're going to figure this out. Okay, baby girl?"

I lean in and press my lips to her little forehead because it feels like the right thing to do.

"We're going to figure this out," I repeat, realizing the words are said more for my benefit than for hers.

11

Charlotte

"There's my favorite bev cart girl!" Tony Baldwin cheers as I pull my cart up to him and the three men he's golfing with.

I give them all a smile. "Need anything?" I ask, hoping they all say yes. It's been a busy day here on the course, and I've welcomed it. At first, it sucked because I was still fighting a hangover, but there's nothing that a little vitamin D and a yellow Gatorade won't fix. Thirty minutes after my shift started, I forgot all about the hangover and have been raking in the tips. The only problem is, I'm almost done with my shift, and I haven't heard from Jude once.

"We'd all love a Fireball shot," Tony answers, walking up to the golf cart.

I nod and slide out of my seat. Tony was a regular when I worked at Pembroke Grill, and I know he's a good tipper. Plus, he's friendly without being creepy. "Anything else besides the shots?" I ask, opening the cabinet to pull out four shots.

"We'll need four Transfusions as well." I grimace, wondering if I still have enough grape juice to make the cocktail. Everybody on the course today has ordered one, and I'm trying to remember if I finished it off a couple of stops ago or not.

"I'll have to check if I have enough juice for that," I tell him, trying not to immediately jump and run to my phone the moment I hear it vibrate against the dash of my cart. I've been waiting for Jude to text me with some funny comment about the night before to break the ice.

"Popular day for Transfusions?" one of Tony's companions asks as I hand out the shots. I know I should remember his name, but it's slipped my mind.

I nod before stepping to the side to open the cooler and see if I have enough juice for their drinks. Luckily, I only have one more hole to drive by before I reach the pro shop, and then my shift is over.

I shift the ice around and look through the bottles in my cooler until I finally find one last grape juice bottle. I pull it out with a smile and look at Tony. "It looks like today's your lucky day."

He laughs. "Send that energy to my golfing as well. I can't putt worth a damn today."

I give him a sympathetic smile as I grab a bottle of vodka and a can of ginger ale. "Your day's just starting though. You have time to get better." I nod toward the shot he still holds in his hands. "Maybe that'll make you putt better."

He laughs before holding it up and waiting for his friends to do the same. They all clink their glasses together and sling the shots back as I finish making their drinks. I rip off the bottom of the straw wrappers and place them all in the lids before handing out each drink.

"Will this be charged to your member account?" I ask

Tony, pulling out my work iPad.

Tony nods before setting his drink down on the counter of the bev cart and reaching into his back pocket. He pulls out a hundred-dollar bill and hands it over. "And this is for you, my *favorite* bev cart girl."

I give him a warm smile, thankful for his generous tip. "I'm totally going to tell Mia you said that."

Tony's mouth falls open. "You wouldn't dare. She's also my favorite."

It's my turn to feign that I'm upset. I've learned this job is a delicate balance of playful friendliness and banter. You want to skirt the edge of flirting without actually flirting. "Don't go breaking my heart, Tony." I lift the twenty before putting it in the fanny pack around my waist. "And thank you for the tip."

He swats at the air. "You deserve it. Just don't tell Mia what I said." He winks before grabbing his drink and stepping away.

I finish putting the transaction through before I make sure all my cabinets are closed and nothing's loose. "You guys have a great rest of your day." I walk around the cart and slide into my seat, anxious to pull my phone from the dashboard and check to see if it was Jude who texted me.

"Bye, Charlotte!" Tony calls as he follows his friends out to the green.

The moment I drive away, I check the text.

Lucy

I'm counting down the days until I see you again. It's been too long!

I try not to be disappointed at seeing Lucy's name instead

of Jude's. The great thing about being busy today is that I haven't had much time to overthink what happened last night and why I haven't heard from Jude. The bad thing is my shift is coming to an end, and all of the thoughts I've pushed away while trying to focus on work are starting to creep in now that I'm not distracted.

I let out a long sigh before beginning to type out a response to Lucy. Just as I'm about to send it, my phone dies.

"Ugh." My head falls backward as I toss the phone in the seat next to me. Of course it dies while I'm waiting for a text or call from Jude. I'd been too tipsy last night to charge it, and now it'll be a while before I'm home and able to.

I groan as I pull up to the pro shop. Now that I'm done for the day, I could go home and take the nap I've been dreaming about all day. Or I could walk around the club. It's possible I've just missed Jude today and he decided to hang out inside instead of golfing. If his hangover is anything like mine was, maybe that's what makes the most sense. Maybe he's hanging out at Pembroke Grill or even meeting with friends in the Gentlemen's Lounge.

I nod, coming to the decision that I'll do a lap around Pembroke to look for him. A walk might be good to help clear my mind anyway.

I try not to let myself get disappointed by the fact that every place I look, I still don't see Jude. I check rooms, hoping that the next one I stop in, I'll see him. I expect to hear his infectious laugh or see his sandy-brown hair, but he's nowhere to be found.

When I get into my car, an unease settles over me. I check my glove box and center console to see if I happened to have left a spare charger in here to charge my phone and see if Jude's texted me now, but I come up short.

I pull my lip between my teeth as I try to reassure myself that nothing with Jude has changed. He's probably still nursing his hangover and hasn't had time to call or text. It's just that it isn't like Jude to leave me alone. His favorite thing to do is blow up my phone with funny videos and play-by-plays of his day, but just because he didn't today doesn't mean anything's wrong or that anything has changed. It just means he might be feeling the wine from last night more than what he's used to.

I tell myself that over and over again, but I must not believe it because instead of going home, I head back to Jude's instead.

12

Jude

"How do I even make this?" I mutter, looking at the can of formula in my hands. I've read the directions ten times at this point, and I still don't know if I understand what to do.

How warm should the water be? Do I microwave it or just use warm water from the sink? Is the water from the sink even okay for her to drink? I think it should be—I think I have a filtration system, but now my brain can't seem to figure out if I'm even qualified to make my daughter—I still can't believe I have one— a bottle of milk.

I glance at where Ava is lying on the floor and quickly realize I have nothing to contain her in. All Karina gave me were diapers, clothes, the car seat, bottles, and formula. I need so much, but before I can even begin to stock up on baby essentials, I need to feed my daughter. For now, I laid out my nicest, softest blanket on the ground and tossed a bunch of throw pillows on top of it to lie her on. She stays on there for the most part, but it seems like she's close to rolling because she keeps kicking her legs up and attempting to turn over.

She hasn't acted like she's hungry at all, but I don't know how often babies eat. She was dropped off about an hour ago, and I don't know how long ago Karina fed her. It feels like she should be hungry soon. Now, if only I could figure out how to make a damn bottle.

I sigh, slipping my phone out of my pocket and calling Charlotte for what my call log says is the fifteenth time in the last hour. I know she worked today, but if I remember her schedule correctly, she should have been off about an hour ago. Every time I call, her phone goes straight to voicemail. Either she's blocked me, or her phone is dead. I really hope it's the latter, but there's a small part of me that wonders if the events from last night got to her more than I was expecting.

I close my eyes for a moment, my grip tightening on the formula can. I got so swept up in Karina dropping a baby off at my doorstep that I haven't even had time to think about what happened with Charlotte last night.

We almost kissed.

Technically, we *did* kiss. Our lips brushed against one another's for the briefest, most perfect moment.

With my eyes closed, I vividly remember everything about that moment. Her smell, her taste, the sound of her labored breathing as she angled her body closer to mine in anticipation. I squeeze my eyes shut even tighter, doing everything I can to not remember it all.

I wanted more, and by the way she looked at me all night, it felt like she wanted more too. I didn't try again. She made it clear she didn't want to kiss me, and I respected that. But the way she looked at me the rest of the night had to have meant something. We fell asleep with her cheek pressed to my chest and my arms effortlessly wrapped around her body like they were meant to hold her.

But then I woke up without her in my arms and shortly after found out that I'm a father to a sweet baby girl. I don't have time to analyze what did—or didn't—happen with Charlotte last night.

Right now, I just need my friend to answer her phone. She's told me all about her siblings and taking care of their kids. I know she has experience with babies, and I could really use her guidance right now. I'm not ready to call anyone else I know who could help me. I don't even know how to begin to explain Ava to anyone else. But I do know I want to tell Charlotte. I want her here.

I'm mentally kicking myself that I might've jeopardized our friendship last night by kissing her when I hear the front door open.

I jump, not expecting anyone to walk in. I hadn't even thought about locking the door after bringing Ava in because I was too focused on how I'm supposed to take care of a baby.

I have so much to figure out and so much to do, and I don't even know where to start. There's no protocol for finding out you have a four-month-old daughter. And not only do I have a daughter, but her mother has left me as the sole caretaker.

My eyes meet Charlotte's, and for the first time since I found out about being a father, I'm able to let out a small breath of relief.

Charlotte's here, and it isn't fair of me to ask this of her, but I need her help.

"Hi," Charlotte says, her tone unsure. She steps into the house and closes the door behind her before taking a step toward me.

"Hi," I respond, giving her a small smile. I've been calling her for an hour now, needing to tell her about what's happened, but now that she's here, I don't even know how to tell her how much my life has changed since she left this morning.

I take a moment just to look at her before she notices the formula canister in my hand or the baby on the floor on the other side of the island from where she stands. She's still dressed in her Pembroke Hills uniform, and she's pulled her hair out of her face using a clip. Her cheeks are a little pink from the sun, and her blue eyes watch me carefully as she walks toward me.

"I hadn't heard from you today and…" Her words trail off as she rounds the corner of the island and her eyes land on Ava.

"Um…" It's quiet for a moment as she just stares at Ava. "Jude, why is there a baby in your kitchen?"

13

Charlotte

I don't know where to look. A million different questions run through my mind as my eyes dart between Jude and the baby lying on the ground, who looks almost identical to him.

Jude whistles before tucking his hands into his pockets. He pulls his gaze away from me to stare adoringly at the baby for a moment before meeting my stare once again. "So," he begins, taking a deep breath. "I don't really know how else to say this. It's been a crazy morning, and I still haven't really even processed what's happening, but it turns out that I have a daughter."

I blink.

And then I blink again.

"I have a daughter."

The comment runs through my mind on a loop as I try to make sense of what he's just said. I don't think I heard him correctly. There's no way I heard him correctly. And yet, I know I did because the baby on the ground, kicking her feet and cooing, looks exactly like him.

"A…a daughter?" I manage to get out.

I focus on Jude, trying to push all the questions running

through my mind away and instead wait for him to explain before I try to fill in the blanks myself.

He nods as his shoulders rise and fall with a deep breath. "This morning, I woke up to someone knocking on the door. When I realized you weren't…" He stops and clears his throat for a moment before running a hand over his mouth. He doesn't finish at first, but I realize I know exactly what he was going to say.

When he woke up and found out I wasn't here anymore. I blush, wondering what he remembers from last night.

"When I realized you weren't here, I thought the person at the door was you," he continues. "And then I was shocked to find out it wasn't you. It was…" He pauses, and I wait for him to continue, hanging on every word of his story so I can try to make sense of the fact that he apparently has a child.

His eyes scan my face carefully. His features are tight, his lips pulled together in a straight line as if he's unsure if he should tell me the next words or not. "It was someone I had a one-night stand with over a year ago. It was right before I met you, actually. She informed me today that the baby is mine and that she didn't want the baby—*Ava*—at all."

I can't hide the gasp that leaves my lips. I bring my fingers to my mouth, wondering if my gasp was as loud as I think it was. Jude's daughter lets out a little squeal, drawing my attention to her.

Sadness washes over me as his words sink in. She has a mom who doesn't want her. As someone who has the best mom in the world and who's always dreamed about eventually becoming a mother, it's hard to process that Ava's mother doesn't want to be involved in her life. I swallow, trying to make sense of his words. Surely I misunderstood him. "I don't understand," I confess. "What do you mean she didn't want Ava at all?"

"I mean, she told me she didn't want to go through with the pregnancy at first but had Ava anyway, hoping that it would change her mind. But she realized that she didn't want to be a mother and thought it'd be better if I took her."

"She's her *mom*. How did she just decide now that she doesn't want her daughter?" I shake my head, looking over at the squealing baby on the ground. She continues to keep herself entertained by kicking her feet.

"Except she did decide that," Jude offers, taking a step closer to me. It's only now that I notice he's holding what looks like a can of formula in his hand. "She said she'd sign over all parental rights to me."

"Holy shit," I mutter, not knowing what else to say. This is too much to process at once. I can't even imagine what Jude is feeling right now.

Jude chuckles before pointing a finger at me. "Don't cuss around my daughter." He wears a lopsided smile, his words more teasing than they are serious.

My mouth falls open. "Your daughter. God, Jude, you have a *daughter*."

Jude nods, his eyes moving to Ava's moments before mine do. "I know I'll have to do a paternity test, and there will be a million hoops to jump through to really make sure no one can take her from me once it's confirmed, but is it weird that I already know she's mine?"

"She looks just like you." I walk over to Ava and crouch down in front of her. She smiles the moment she sees me, showing off the same deep dimples that her father has.

"You think?" Jude asks, closing the distance until he stands at my side.

I look up at him from the ground. "I do. Except she's way cuter."

He laughs and doesn't even pretend to be hurt by my comment. We settle into a quiet moment as we both focus on Ava. She's still happy as can be as she finds her toes and attempts to put them in her mouth. I try not to smile at the area Jude's created for her. She rests on top of a pile of throw pillows, her little body wedged comfortably between them so she can't get into any trouble.

"What am I going to do with a baby?" Jude asks from my side. His voice breaks a little, and it's the first time I see a crack in his demeanor. I know him well enough to know he's trying to hold it together, but it's a lot to take in. Jude's as carefree as they come, but even he has limits, and it's clear that a baby getting spontaneously dropped off at his doorstep might be his.

I get so lost in worrying about him that I forget to even respond to his question. He lets out a sad laugh, breaking me from my thoughts. "I can't even make her a bottle of milk without second-guessing myself. I'm not cut out to be a dad. And I definitely don't know how to do this alone."

"Hey." I place my fingers against his cheek, pulling his attention to me. When his eyes find mine, I smile. "You're not alone. You have me. And lucky for you, I'm great with babies."

I take the formula canister from his hand before standing to my full height. I was a big *oops!* for my parents, so all of my four siblings are quite a bit older than I am. The oldest, Carly, had her first baby when I was only twelve, so I grew up taking care of her kids. I love kids, and I'd do anything to help Jude.

"We're going to start out giving her six ounces and go from there. She might not drink it all, she might want more, but we're going to start with that. Your water is filtered, right?" I ask, setting the formula on the counter and looking in his direction.

Jude just stares at me for a moment before nodding. "Yes, it's filtered."

I give him what I hope is a confident and reassuring smile before turning on the sink. I let it run for a moment before sticking my fingers under the stream of water to test the temperature. "We'll probably want to get a formula dispenser or at least a bottle warmer, but for now, I'm just going to test it on the inside of my wrist to make sure it isn't too hot for her to drink."

Jude still doesn't say anything. All he does is stare at me with an unreadable expression. Eventually, the uneasiness of the quiet between us gets the best of me. Once I get the bottle filled with six ounces of water, I set it on the counter and aim my gaze at a silent Jude once again.

"Tell me what you're thinking." My words come out soft and unsure. I stare at him, waiting for him to answer me. I can't even begin to imagine everything that's going through his head right now, so I don't push him to talk before he's ready. I just wait patiently, my gaze staying trained on him the entire time.

Eventually, he looks from Ava to me. He swallows slowly before opening his mouth to speak. "You said we'll probably want to get a formula dispenser."

I frown a little, wondering why his words come out hoarse. "We don't have to if you don't want to. It's just that I though—"

Before I can get the rest of my words out, Jude is closing the distance between us and stopping right in front of me. He lifts his hand as if he wants to touch me before letting it fall in front of him.

"You said...*we*," he says, his words coming out so quiet it's almost as if he's in disbelief. "You said we, and it's the first time I didn't feel completely alone in this."

14

Jude

Charlotte blinks a few times before her eyes scan my face. "Of course I said *we*," she whispers. Her hands twist in front of her as if she's trying to find a way to keep them busy. "You're not in this alone. Not unless you want to be. If you want to handle this alone, just let me—"

I cut her off by pulling her body against mine. My arms wrap around her as I pull her in for a hug. I didn't realize just how badly I needed a hug from her until this moment.

Her arms hang at her sides for a beat before she tentatively lifts them and wraps them around my middle. I let out a relieved sigh as I tuck her head under my chin.

I don't know how long we stand there. It could be seconds, it could be minutes. Neither one of us moves for the longest time. Ava stays content the entire time, too entertained by trying to get her feet into her mouth to care that the bottle is taking a while.

"I don't want to handle this alone," I tell Char, keeping my arms tight around her, even though I know I should probably let go. "I don't know if I even know *how* to handle it," I admit, hating how weak and hoarse my voice sounds with the admission.

The reality is, I don't know how to take care of a baby. I don't know the first thing about kids. It's new and foreign, but my biggest fear in the world now is letting down the baby girl who is depending on me to figure it out. Ava deserves a dad who gives her everything, and in giving her everything, I have to admit to myself—and Charlotte—that I don't think I can do this by myself. Not in the beginning, at least.

"I'm here," Charlotte tells me, pulling me from my thoughts. Thoughts of all the different ways I can fail my daughter.

"I know it's a lot to ask of you, and you have every right to tell me no, but I think I really need your help, Char." I pull away, even though every part of me wants to keep her in my arms. My hands drop to my sides, and I stuff them into my pockets before I give in to the temptation of pulling her body against mine once again.

She gives me a smile before looking over at Ava. My gaze follows hers, the two of us lost in our own thoughts for a few moments.

"I'm here, Jude. I'm not going anywhere." I feel her timidly place her hand against my chest. The simple touch pulls my gaze from Ava as I focus on Charlotte once again. She smiles, as if my attention is exactly what she wants, before she opens her mouth to speak again. "You're stuck with me. We're going to figure this out. And the first thing we're going to do is feed Ava and then run to the store and grab all the things she needs. How does that sound?"

I nod, having to swallow past the lump in my throat. I'm not normally an emotional person. My default setting is to be silly and casual. I'm not used to being run by my emotions, but now

I'm being overrun with so many of them at once that I don't even know how to handle them.

All I know is I want to be the best dad possible to Ava, and I know the first step in doing that is to accept Charlotte's help in that.

"Char," I say, watching her closely as she takes the lid off the can of formula. I narrow my eyebrows when she sticks her hand in the container, but I figure out what she's doing the moment she pulls a little scoop from inside. "This isn't your responsibility to take on. I know you've got a lot going on in your life, and the last thing I need to do is add to your plate by asking you to help me figure out how to be a father."

"The milk is the perfect temperature." She completely ignores what I'm saying by wrapping her fingers around my wrist and lifting my arm between us. She taps the top of the bottle against the inside of my wrist. "Feel that? Not too hot, but not cold either. She should take this." She hands the bottle to me and gives me an encouraging smile. "Time to feed her."

I don't know why I suddenly feel so anxious, but my heart hammers against my chest at the idea of feeding my daughter.

Charlotte bumps her hip against mine. "I'm right here with you. You can feed her. You've got this, Jude."

I stare at her for a moment, wondering how I got so lucky to have a friend like her. I haven't even wrapped my head around having a daughter myself, yet somehow, she seems to have full confidence in me. She doesn't ask questions I can't even begin to answer. All she does is step up and help me in my time of need, and I wish my mind wasn't spinning so I could properly thank her for it.

Charlotte takes the bottle from my hand and nods toward the living room. "How about I hold the bottle, and you grab

Ava, and we'll go to the couch together to feed her?" She keeps her voice soft and reassuring, knowing what I need from her without me having to say anything.

I nod and swallow the lump in my throat. My pulse spikes the closer I get to Ava. This won't be the first time I hold her, but with Charlotte's eyes on me, I suddenly get self-conscious about how I hold my daughter. I have no idea if I'm doing it right, and it's something Charlotte's done countless times.

Is she going to judge me?

Will I hold Ava the right way?

Is there an angle I'm supposed to hold the bottle at?

Will Charlotte think I'm not qualified to raise a baby?

Ava lets out a little squeal the moment I crouch down in front of her. "Hi, baby girl," I whisper, unable to fight the smile on my lips when I carefully place one of my hands behind her head and the other at her back. Ava excitedly kicks her legs as I lift her off the pillows. She's squirmy, making me even more anxious to lift her from the ground.

I carefully pull her to my chest, closing my eyes for a moment as I stand to my full height with her. I don't have to look at Charlotte to know she's watching me carefully, and it makes me nervous. I know she knows I'm brand-new to this, but I still don't want her to believe I'm not cut out for being a father.

Except...am I cut out for this?

I try to push the thought from my mind as I slowly walk to the couch where Charlotte sits. When I'm finally brave enough to meet her gaze, all I see in her eyes is encouragement. Her lips curve up into the hint of a smile, her stare never wavering from mine as I take a seat on the couch next to her.

"She's so cute I can't handle it," Charlotte mutters, easing some of the tension I feel.

I carefully adjust my position next to her before returning her smile with my own smirk. "She gets that from me." I wink and savor the way Charlotte rolls her eyes at me. The last day has been one unexpected thing after another with her, and seeing her react to me the way she always has is oddly comforting.

Everything has changed, and yet nothing has changed at all. The realization causes the knot of anxiety in my chest to loosen.

Maybe I can do this…as long as I have Charlotte.

"You'll learn this early on," Charlotte begins, gently tickling Ava's belly, "but your daddy isn't humble in the slightest. He's full of himself, and we love him anyway."

We love him anyway. I don't know what it is about those words, but they make me smile.

"Is it really being full of myself if it's just the truth?"

I get another eye roll from her, and I love it. There's no awkwardness between us, even though we haven't talked about what happened—or *almost* happened—last night. She isn't acting like she regrets anything from last night, but isn't acting like anything has changed either. Instead, she's focused on helping me with Ava.

"So you'll want to cradle her in the crook of your arm," Charlotte instructs. Her fingers brush against my skin as she helps adjust Ava's position in my arms. It feels like she's lying too far back, but I trust Charlotte knows what she's doing.

Charlotte's breath tickles my cheek as she makes sure Ava's head is supported well. I meet her gaze, unable to calm my racing heart. With her this close, all I can think about is last night.

About how it felt to press my lips against hers.

About how she looked at me in a way she's never looked at me before.

I blink, trying to push the thoughts aside, because the last thing I need to be doing is thinking about kissing her when she's trying to help me learn how to be a good father to another woman's baby.

"Now you'll just give her the milk. About halfway through, we'll pay attention to whether she's uncomfortable or not. If she seems like something's bothering her, we'll burp her in the middle of the feed. She might not need it until the end though. We'll just have to see."

I nod as Charlotte hands over the bottle. I shouldn't be so nervous to feed Ava, but I am. I don't want to mess it up.

"You're not going to mess it up," Charlotte says, making me wonder if she can somehow read my mind or if I said the words out loud. I look away from Ava for a moment and meet Charlotte's reassuring stare. She smiles, and it's just what I need. "You've got this," she adds on, her smile only growing.

I swallow before looking at Ava. I tentatively bring the bottle to her lips. Her dark blue eyes stay focused on me as I place the tip of the bottle in her mouth. Before wrapping her lips around the top, her face lights up, and I swear she gives me a smile.

I smile back, wondering if what she gave me was actually a smile or if I'm just seeing things. Either way, the moment she begins to drink the milk, I let out a breath of relief.

I'm feeding my daughter.

She isn't crying or complaining.

She's eating.

And I swear she smiled at me.

With Charlotte's help, it's the first time since the moment Ava got dropped off on my doorstep that I feel like maybe I really can do this.

15

Charlotte

"Something tells me we're going to be here awhile," Jude mutters as we walk into the store. He sets Ava's car seat into a shopping cart as I grab a second one. We're definitely going to need the extra space.

"Babies need a lot," I tell him, setting my notebook onto the handle of the cart so I can go over my list. I spent the entire car ride creating it, wanting to make sure I didn't miss anything that Jude would need. I started researching baby things as he fed Ava. It was obvious he was nervous to give her the bottle at first, but he did great. His confidence started to build as he changed her diaper and got her dressed for our shopping adventure.

Figuring out how to install her car seat into the back of his luxury SUV was a different story. I don't think I'd ever heard Jude let out so many curse words. He even watched videos about how to install the specific brand of car seat she has, but it was still a struggle.

"Where should we begin?" he asks, flipping up the visor of the infant seat to check on a sleeping Ava. He made me sit in the back seat with her on the way to the store, too nervous about how quiet she was while sleeping and wanting someone to have eyes on her.

It's kind of adorable, but I keep that thought to myself.

It was only this morning that he found out he is a dad, and he's already doing so well at it. It's clear that Ava already has him wrapped around her little finger, and I feel some sort of pride at being the one to walk with Jude on this new adventure.

I look at my notes as we both begin to push our carts. He falls in line slightly behind me, letting me steer the way.

"I have things separated into needs and wants. First, I say we make it through the needs list. Some of these things we could also order online in the event that Ava wakes up and decides that maybe shopping isn't for her."

"What's at the top of the needs list?" he asks. A tiny line forms at the center of his forehead, and I can't help but love the sight of it. I've never seen a serious Jude. Normally, he wears a smirk at all times. But jumping into the role of being a dad has brought out this new side of him that I can't wait to see more of.

"First and foremost, we need to find a crib. Or at least a Pack 'n Play."

He frowns, making the line across his forehead even more noticeable. "A pack and what?"

I laugh, realizing that if you aren't around kids a lot, you'd probably think it's a pretty weird name. "A Pack 'n Play. It's like a portable crib. We're probably going to have to start with that—or a bassinet—and wait for a crib to come in." I stop and turn my body to face him, a question popping into my head. "Have you thought about which room the nursery will be? I should've asked you that at the house so that I'd know the size of the room and what furniture we'll need to order."

Jude's shoulders sag slightly. "Is it horrible of me to admit I hadn't even thought about what room she'll be in?"

I shake my head and softly place my hand on his arm. He doesn't shy away from my touch, so I keep it there, hoping it makes him believe in what I'm about to say. "You've had a lot thrown at you today. It's okay if you don't have everything figured out yet. Today, we'll just get a portable crib of some sort and then focus on ordering nursery furniture another day when we know which room will be hers."

Jude nods, and I fight the urge to give him a hug. His stress is obvious by the way his fingers are almost white in clutching the handle of the shopping cart. "I really don't know how I'd be doing any of this without you," he admits, his eyes scanning my face.

I blush under the intensity of his gaze. I look at my feet for a moment, hoping he doesn't notice the pink that's spreading across my cheeks. "You'd have figured it out," I respond before pushing the cart forward. I can't help but remember another time when he looked at me with an intensity like he just was. It was last night, seconds before our lips touched for the first—and *last*—time. Jude's got so many things going on in his life now, it feels wrong to even think about kissing him.

What he needs right now is a friend. And friends don't think about kissing their friends. No matter how charming they are or how much they make you melt with just the intensity of their gaze.

"I'm glad I don't have to," Jude says from behind me.

I turn around and look at him. "What?" I was so lost in my thoughts I forgot what we were even talking about.

"I'm glad I don't have to figure it out without you." He gives me a smile—an unforced one—and God, it does things to my heart it shouldn't be doing.

I quickly turn back around and focus on my notebook. Jude needs me to be his friend right now, so that's what I'm going to be.

"Let's go find a Pack 'n Play." I change the subject and walk the long pathway to the back of the store. I have no idea where the baby aisle is, but I'd rather spend my time looking for it than looking into Jude's big brown eyes, which are suddenly making me feel things I shouldn't be feeling.

• • •

"Do we like the pink one or the purple one?" Jude asks, holding up two onesies on either side of his face. We've been shopping for over an hour, and Ava is still sleeping peacefully as we make our way through the list of things to buy. It's only my first day with her, but Ava seems far more chill than my siblings' babies. So far, she's easy and calm, which might be just what Jude needs as he gets used to being a father.

I smile, something about the sight of Jude holding the two frilly onesies pulling at my heartstrings. "I like both. Can't go wrong with either one."

He looks between the two and then nods. "You're right. My girl needs both." He tosses the clothes into the cart with a wide grin.

I look at the ground for a moment, trying to compose myself after the adorable way he called Ava his girl. Something about it dangerously made my heart squeeze in my chest.

"What size are they?" I ask. We just made it through getting essentials in other aisles, and now we're tackling clothes.

Jude's eyes go wide as he looks at the onesies, shifting from one foot to the other. "Well…" he begins, pulling at the tag. "This one says three months."

I close the distance between us and grab the hangers from his hands. I check the tags before giving him a smile. "These are both three months, which means three months old is typically the limit for wear. Three months means zero to three months old, six months means three to six months old, and so forth. Before we left, I checked the clothes Ava was sent with, and they are all six months. That seems to fit her, so we should probably get some more in that size and some nine-month options as well."

Jude stares at me for a moment, and I hate the vulnerable look in his eyes. He seems disappointed that he didn't know this information himself, and I hate that I'm the reason his face fell. "I didn't even think about the sizing," he admits, pulling his gaze from mine in an attempt to hide the sadness in his eyes.

"It's confusing. Plus, different brands fit differently. Those three-month ones you picked could fit her perfectly."

He narrows his eyes at me. "Are you just saying that to make me feel better?"

I bite back a smile. "Of course not. Baby clothes sizing is tricky."

He stares at me for a moment before turning to a rack of infant sleepers. He fiddles through the hangers before throwing different variations of them in the cart—all six- and nine-month sizes.

Before we continue, he places a hand on my shoulder, his normal grin making an appearance on his face again. "I really don't know what I'd do without you, Char. Thank you."

And before I can respond, he turns his attention to Ava and checks on her once again before pushing the cart forward, completely unaware that he's made my stomach do a weird flip-flop thing that I hope to never feel again when it comes to him.

16

Jude

"What do you think of this one?" Charlotte asks in an excited tone, holding Ava in front of a stuffed animal that's as big as Ava is.

My daughter lets out an excited squeal as she flaps her arms in front of her, trying to grab the pink teddy bear.

Charlotte's eyes meet mine as a beaming smile overtakes her face. "I think Daddy should get you the pink bear, shouldn't he?"

Despite how unexpected and stressful my day has been, I feel like a smile hasn't left my face this entire shopping trip. I might have said it countless times to Charlotte today, but I really don't know what I'd do without her. I'm so clueless when it comes to kids, but because of her, I feel like I can handle this. She's been incredibly patient with me, taking time out of her day to help me get all the necessities for Ava and never laughing at me when I show just how completely clueless I am when it comes to raising a baby.

I prop my shoulder against the shelf, focusing on Charlotte as she shows Ava the different stuffed animal options.

According to Char, we should have enough to get started, so now we're in the toy aisle, finding out what Ava is interested in.

My lips twitch with the blooming of a smile, watching Charlotte with my daughter. She holds her against her chest with Ava facing out so she can really look at all the toys. Ava seems to be having the time of her life looking at the different options, and the sight of her so happy with Char does something to my chest.

I'm lucky enough to have made many close friendships in my life. I have numerous people I know who love me and support me in anything. Eventually, I'll tell everyone about Ava and allow them to be there for me, but right now, I'm still figuring things out. I feel the need to have my footing better before telling everyone else about Ava. For the moment, it feels right for only Charlotte to know. The way she's shown up for me today makes me realize just how lucky I am to have *her.* I still haven't processed the fact that I have a daughter and that I missed four months of her life. Instead of bombarding me with questions or making me feel guilty about having a daughter I didn't know about, she's stepped in without hesitation. I don't know what I did to deserve a friend like her, but as I watch her playfully use the bear to pepper kisses along Ava's cheeks, I make a promise to myself that I won't do anything to mess up this friendship.

I can't.

I need her.

And something tells me that Ava is going to need her too.

Whatever feelings I have for Charlotte, no matter what I wanted to happen last night, and no matter how attracted I am to her, I push it all aside. With Ava now in my life, I'm in no position to ask for more from Charlotte. I've never been known to be good at commitment or taking things seriously, but all of that has changed. And for my daughter's sake—and my own—I have to keep things platonic with Charlotte and not let it go any further.

I can't lose her.

Ava can't lose her.

It hasn't even been a day, and she's already made all of this easier. I don't even want to think about what all of this would be like without her. I can't imagine it.

"I think he needs to get you the pink bear *and* the puppy," Charlotte says in a higher pitch than normal as she talks to Ava. Her words break me from my thoughts before my eyes connect with hers.

She smiles, completely unaware that I was lost in thoughts about her.

"He's got lots of money," Charlotte continues. "If you play your cards right, he'll buy you anything you want."

I smile before stepping closer to them and tapping Ava's tiny button nose. "Anything for my baby girl."

Charlotte bites her lip before her mouth spreads into a wide smile. "She's going to be so spoiled, isn't she?"

I lean closer and place a kiss to Ava's cheek. I didn't think about how leaning in to Ava would also bring me closer to Charlotte. My lips linger against my daughter's cheek for a moment before I step back. "Of course she's going to be spoiled. I've got to make up for her somehow being stuck with a dad like me."

Charlotte's lips turn into the smallest frown as her blue eyes scan my face. "She's not *stuck* with you. She's lucky to have you."

I lift a shoulder before grabbing the teddy bear and the

stuffed dog and tossing them into the cart. It's our third cart; the other two sit at the front of the store, ready to be rung up whenever we're done. I'm hoping I have everything I'll need for Ava. I don't want to mess this up, and buying as much as possible makes me feel slightly prepared to take on my new role as a dad. Truth be told, I don't know if Ava is lucky to have me or not. I hope one day she'll think so. I'm going to do my best to make that a reality for her.

Charlotte takes a step closer to me, and my heart soars when Ava reaches her arms out, making it seem like she wants to be handed over to me. I outstretch my arms and take my daughter, everything in the world feeling right the moment she's in my hold again. I expect Charlotte to take a step back after handing her over, but she doesn't. She stands close to me, her eyes pinned on me in the middle of the toy aisle. Ava squirms in my arms, but I can't look away from Charlotte's earnest blue stare.

"Ava *is* lucky to have you." She keeps her voice strong, and something about it makes me believe that she might actually mean what she's saying.

"Ava hasn't known me a day. I still have plenty of time to fuck this up."

"You're trying. That's all that matters. She's lucky to have you, Jude. I believe it. I know she'll believe it. And I hope someday soon, you'll believe that too."

I look at the ground because I can't stare into her eyes for another second. Not without showing emotions I don't want her to see. It's been such a whirlwind of a day that I haven't even been able to really process what all of this means and what all is going to change. It also means that I haven't had time to let the doubt creep in too much, although I know it's only a matter of time until it does. I don't know when—or if—I'll ever feel confident about raising Ava, but Charlotte has a point...I'm trying my best.

And my best is all I can do.

I look at my daughter before running a hand over her small head. She watches me closely, looking completely content and not at all scared about the fact that she's been placed in my care.

I hear the sound of some more items being placed in the cart, but I don't break the moment with Ava. I can't. My baby girl stares up at me like I'm the only thing that matters in this world, and I have to swallow a lump of emotion as a realization hits me.

I'm truly all she has, and I'm going to make damn sure that's enough for her.

When I look up, I find Charlotte watching us with her hands clasped next to her cheek and a warm smile on her lips. "Ready to check out?" she asks, keeping her voice soft.

I nod. I don't even remember everything we've thrown into the cart since we got here, and I know I don't know how to use half the things Charlotte insisted we needed, but I feel better now that we've gone shopping. It feels good to have more than just the duffel bag full of clothes she was dropped off with.

"Let's go buy all your new things, baby girl," I tell Ava, leaning in to press my lips to her temple and following Charlotte and the cart to the checkout counter.

17

Charlotte

"Motherfucker," Jude curses before running his hand through the longer strands of his hair at the top of his head.

"Maybe we should read the instructions?" I offer, trying to fight a smile. Ava is fast asleep in my arms, completely tuckered out from all the shopping, which is a good thing because her dad isn't being quiet at all about his feelings toward putting together the Pack 'n Play.

Jude glares at me before attempting to shift one of the pieces. "I shouldn't need directions. It's basically four walls, and that's it. It shouldn't be this hard to put together a little baby cage."

My lips twitch as a laugh threatens to escape, but I fight it off by burying my face behind Ava's little head. We got back from the store two hours ago, and once we sorted through everything and fed Ava again, we figured the first thing we should put together is the portable crib so Ava has somewhere to sleep that isn't in our arms. Jude's been trying to figure out how to set it up for almost an hour now, and no matter how many times I offer to look at the directions, he shoots my idea down every time.

"A little baby cage," I mutter. I tilt my head to the side. "It really is basically a baby cage."

The laugh finally escapes me. I try to keep it quiet so I don't wake up Ava, but it does completely rattle out of me. Jude's eyes meet mine, and for a moment, I think he's going to be upset, but instead, his face breaks out in a grin. He tosses his head back and lets out a laugh. It's loud, and it's the first time I've really heard him laugh today.

I love the sound of it.

Our laughter fills the room for a few moments before it dies down. Ava peacefully sleeps through it all. I don't know if she's always this good of a sleeper or if today is just a fluke, but she's been a champ throughout the chaos of the day.

"It really doesn't feel like I should need directions to put this together," Jude finally says, putting his hands on his hips as he stares down at the pile of pieces. "It shouldn't be this complicated."

"It's okay to accept that you need to read the directions to figure it out."

Jude aims a glare in my direction, and I think it's the first time I've ever seen him give a dirty look. I try not to smile all over again. "*Char.*" My name comes out of his mouth like a warning. "You're really hurting my pride right now."

"No, *you're* hurting your pride by taking double—maybe even triple—the amount of time to put this together just because you refuse to open a tiny paper booklet and read it."

Jude furrows his eyebrows as his lips press into a thin line.

I smile at his reaction. "And you know I'm right, and that's why you have nothing to say to it." I raise an eyebrow as I reach for the instructions manual. I hold it between us playfully, letting it hang in my grasp as I wait to see if he'll take the bait or not.

Jude lets out a frustrated sigh before snatching the booklet from my hand. "Fine," he grumbles before opening the booklet and holding it in front of his face. "But I'm only reading this so you can finally put Ava down and get home and be done with us for the day."

I frown, hating the idea of leaving the two of them alone tonight. I don't want to overstay my welcome. I'm sure Jude wants alone time with his daughter, but I can't shake how wrong it feels to leave them. Here with Jude and Ava, I've been able to forget all about my problems. I haven't thought once about how I still have no place to live. I haven't stressed about packing up all my things or wondered what I'm going to do next.

It's been nice.

Luckily, Jude is so focused on finally reading the directions that he doesn't even notice that I've gone quiet.

I'd been so swept up in helping him get everything he needed for Ava that I hadn't even thought about leaving and going back to my place. Of course he wants that with his daughter; it just seems even more lonely to go back to my rental tonight. Especially with the added stress of knowing I need to find somewhere else to live for the summer.

"I did it!" Jude excitedly says, breaking me from my thoughts. I jump a little before blinking rapidly, my gaze focusing on a grinning Jude. I was spaced out long enough for him to fully assemble the Pack 'n Play.

I smile despite the sadness I feel at having to leave soon. "Proud of you. Now think of how much time you could've saved if you had just started with the instructions from the beginning."

He attempts to give me a dirty look again, but the smile on his face is too wide to make it work.

"Are you going to remind me of this forever?" he teases before picking up the portable crib and setting it down in the corner of his room closest to his bed.

"Of course I am." I point to the laundry basket on his bed. "Those sheets are clean. Once they're on the mattress, I'll carefully put her down and hope she stays asleep."

Jude walks over to the bed and grabs the pink sheets with little butterflies all over them. "Is there a chance she won't stay asleep?"

I laugh at his question, my gaze immediately going to a sleeping Ava to make sure the noise didn't wake her up. "I think every baby is different, but most of my nieces and nephews would wake up the moment you tried to put them down. Babies love to contact sleep."

He stares at me wide-eyed for a moment, as if he hadn't even thought about what happens if Ava doesn't sleep. So far, she's been a great sleeper, but she's also always been asleep in our arms or in her car seat while moving. I have no idea how she feels about sleeping completely independently, but we're about to find out.

"Put the sheets on so we can find out." I point to the bed as if that'll make him move any faster.

He does as he's told, quickly getting the sheets on the mattress—with only a few cuss words this time. Once her bed is ready, I stand up, careful not to jostle Ava too much.

Jude watches me closely as I close the distance to her bed. I don't think either of us breathes as I bend over the edge and softly place her in it. The moment she's fully down, I place my hand against her chest to try and not make the loss of being held so sudden for her.

We're both silent as we stare at Ava, waiting to see if she

wakes up or not. I suck in a breath when she turns her head and the Binky in her mouth looks like it might fall out. Luckily, Ava sucks it right back in.

I look at Jude, wondering if I should risk removing my hand and backing up or if I should stay another minute or two.

He cocks his head over his shoulder in the direction of the door.

I nod in understanding before slowly removing my hand from her chest. My heart hammers against my chest in anticipation.

I keep my eyes pinned on her as I slowly back away. As I make it to the door, Jude gradually turns up the volume of the sound machine until white noise fills the room.

We both stop in the doorway. Ava stays asleep the entire time. I give Jude a look of relief as he quietly pulls the door shut.

The moment it's closed, he reaches into his pocket and brings out the baby monitor we set up earlier.

Neither of us talks as we stand in front of the shut door, both of us staring anxiously at the monitor screen as it turns on.

I don't know whose sigh of relief is louder—mine or Jude's—but we both let out a deep exhale when we find Ava still fast asleep.

Jude gives me a crooked smile, and it makes my entire body warm. "Should we each have a small celebratory glass of wine to celebrate putting her to bed for the first time?"

I should probably leave. I know I should. Especially with knowing how the last time we had wine ended. But something about the way he's smiling at me right now has me wanting to stay, and I find myself answering him before I can talk myself out of it.

"Yes."

18

Jude

"I don't know how I'm going to get any sleep tonight," I tell Charlotte as we both stand at my kitchen island. I work on pouring us both a glass of wine, even though a drink is the last thing I want right now. It was just the only thing I could think of to get her to stay a little longer.

I don't want her to leave. I don't want to be left alone with Ava tonight, but I don't have the right to ask Charlotte to stay. Ava isn't her responsibility; she's mine. And Charlotte's already helped so much. I can't ask more of her.

I just don't want her to go. And not because I don't feel like I can do this alone. It hasn't even been a day, but she's helped me feel confident about taking care of Ava. I think I can do it on my own. I just don't want to. Her presence has been calming, and I'm not looking forward to the absence of that feeling.

"It seems like you might be lucky and Ava's a good sleeper. Maybe you will get some sleep," Charlotte offers, taking the glass of wine from me. She doesn't take a drink, just holds the glass to her lips. I'd been so lost in thought about how I don't want Charlotte to go home that I forgot I even said anything about Ava's sleeping.

"Maybe." I pour my glass of wine but don't take a drink either. "But even if she sleeps all night, I don't know if I'll be able to. What if something happens to her while I'm asleep?"

Charlotte smiles, and I try to ignore how the sight of the beautiful upturn of her mouth immediately calms me. "She'll be okay." She keeps her voice soft and encouraging. "But I understand the worry. It's cute, seeing you being a concerned dad."

I raise my eyebrows. "Did you just call me cute?"

She rolls her eyes and shakes her head. "You know you're cute."

"That doesn't mean I don't like hearing you say it." The words come out before I can think better of them.

I wince, knowing I shouldn't have said that, but not regretting it either. I don't know if I can regret anything when it comes to Charlotte. Because of Ava, things are far more complicated than they were last night, but that doesn't mean I feel any differently today than I did then. It just means I can't act on the attraction I have for her.

"I should go," Charlotte interrupts my thoughts. She places her glass on the counter; I don't think she took a single sip.

My jaw flexes as I try to keep myself from asking her not to go. I pull my gaze from hers, looking at the monitor for a moment to give myself time to think of a way to convince her to stay.

Ava still hasn't moved. She sleeps peacefully, completely unaware that she's no longer on Charlotte's chest and is instead in her own bed. The events from today run through my mind. It still hasn't quite hit me that I'm a dad and I'm now the only person responsible for Ava. I know there are countless things

I'll need to do to make sure Ava can't ever be taken from me, but right now, the only thing I can think of is asking Charlotte to be here with me, not only for my sake but for Ava's too.

"Let me know if you need anything tonight," Charlotte says, breaking me from my thoughts again. "I'll keep my phone close in case you call."

I swallow, pinning my gaze on her. I know I have no right, but asking her to stay is on the tip of my tongue. Everything with Ava is uncharted territory. I don't know what the rules are, but I know I really need my friend right now. All I want to do is ask her to stay with us; I'm just terrified of how she'll respond. She's got her own problems. It's unfair of me to ask this of her when she's still dealing with the fact that she just got kicked out of her place for the summer. She hasn't mentioned it once, and with everything that's happened today, I completely forgot why she even showed up on my doorstep last night in the first place.

"Stay with me this summer," I blurt, the proposal I made to her last night falling from my lips before I can think better of it.

Charlotte's blue eyes get wide. She shakes her head, acting like the question is ridiculous. "Jude, I told you this last night. I'm not staying with you for the summer. I'll ask Lucy and Cal. I just haven't gotten the chance yet."

"I need you," I confess. I run a hand through my hair as my eyes scan her face. She looks back at me with an unreadable expression. I sigh, knowing I shouldn't be doing this but continuing anyway. "I don't know a thing about taking care of a baby. I'm learning, but if today taught me anything, it's that I need some guidance. And I figured…since you need a place to stay, maybe we can work something out to help each other."

My heart slams against my chest as she thinks through

my words. She chews on her lip for a moment, still giving no indication about what's running through her head. I haven't thought through the details yet, but I don't think my idea is terrible. I have plenty of space in this house for her. It's nicer and closer to work for her than the place she was renting anyway. It might actually work.

"You won't have to pay a thing," I hurriedly say, using her silence to my advantage. "You'll be closer to Pembroke, and you can have whatever room you want. I promise not to bother you or make you watch Ava—that's not why I'm asking," I add, realizing she might think I'm asking her to move in to take care of Ava, which isn't the case. I just want to know she's here, and I try not to think too deeply about what that means or everything that could go wrong by wanting that. "I'll find a nanny for when I need to work or figure something out." I give her a grin as my mind goes in countless different directions with everything I still need to get sorted out. "To be honest, I haven't had the chance to think about what I'll do when I have to work or childcare or anything, really, but I'll figure it out."

"You don't need me here interrupting your time with Ava."

"That's the thing, Char. I *want* you here with us. Not because I expect you to do anything. I fully understand she isn't your responsibility. I just…I don't know, it feels like perfect timing that this stuff with Ava happened right when you need a place to stay."

Charlotte stares at me. I wish I could get into her mind and figure out what she's thinking. Now that I've asked, I'm desperate for her to say yes. It seems like the most logical solution for her to stay here instead of anywhere else.

"You have so much going on right now. All of this with Ava is so new. I promise I can find somewhere else to live. You don't have to take me in."

I pinch the bridge of my nose as I think about how to convey to her that I want her here without making it seem like I expect her to help with Ava. I can do everything with Ava on my own, but knowing she's here just in case is enough to help put my mind at ease.

"I'm not asking you because I feel like I have to. I want you here. I think it makes sense." I give her what I hope is a convincing smile. After what happened last night, it might not be the best idea to ask her to live here, but I can't find the will to care about that right now. I've put up my own mental boundaries when it comes to her. I plan on sticking to those boundaries. I know I need to keep her as a friend and not let my attraction get in the way. I believe I can do that. I just want her here with us for the summer. Nothing more.

I run my fingers through my hair and take a step closer to her. There's still a safe distance between us, but I want to make sure she can see me clearly with my next words. "Just say yes, Char."

19

Charlotte

Jude's eyes scan my face. He's so close that I can see the muscle ticking in his jaw. He seems to be forcing himself to keep his mouth shut, something that isn't like Jude at all.

I sigh, wondering why I want to tell him yes. I was already feeling guilty about asking Lucy for a place to stay for the summer. Staying with Jude would make it so I don't have to ask the favor from Lucy at all. I could leave her to enjoy the summer with Cal alone as they get ready to tie the knot.

But it's Jude.

I can't live with Jude.

He needs a friend right now, and more than anything, I want to be a friend he can lean on. Because of that, I don't know if moving in with him is a good idea. Not when we've already blurred the lines after last night.

"I want to say yes," I begin, pausing for a moment as I try to choose my words carefully. "I want to be there for you and for Ava, but I don't know if it's a good idea for me to move in for the summer."

Jude's face falls just a fraction. "Why?"

I pull my bottom lip between my teeth. If he wasn't going to bring up last night, I wasn't going to either. But I didn't expect him to ask me to stay with him and mean it. His puppy-dog eyes and lopsided grin make me want to fold though. Maybe if I do bring attention to what happened between us last night, it'll speak some reason into his mind.

"I think we kissed last night."

We *did* kiss, however brief it actually was. I know things are different now that he has Ava, but that doesn't erase what happened between us.

Jude's smile doesn't falter. If anything, it gets wider, which makes my head spin with questions. "My memory is a little fuzzy, but I know we *did* kiss."

A choking sound leaves my throat. "Okay, so…" I pause, wondering how to even respond to his remark. "We drank a lot and kissed and almost made things way more complicated than they need to be. We're friends and need to stay friends. I don't know if living together is a good idea."

Jude nods. I expect the smile to leave his face, but it doesn't. "You're thinking you won't be able to keep your hands off me." He winks, and I can't help but roll my eyes at him.

I'm sure he's got to be exhausted and overwhelmed after the day he's had, yet somehow, he's still giving me a casual grin as if it was all totally normal. "Jude," I scold.

"What?"

"Are you even sure you're going to stay in the Hamptons? What if you decided you wanted to go back to Manhattan to be near your family?"

A crease forms between his eyebrows. "I haven't told them yet. Ava got dropped off, and you showed up shortly after. But I don't know if I want to take her back to Manhattan right away. I'd rather figure things out here, where it's more quiet and peaceful." He taps his knuckles against the counter as his eyes scan my face. "I'd rather figure it out here...where you are." The words are said quietly, and he swallows immediately after, making me wonder if he didn't mean to say them at all. Before I can respond, he's running his hand through his hair and opening his mouth to speak again. "Plus, my family can be a lot. I need to get my feet under me first before I take Ava to them. I don't plan on keeping Ava from them for long. I just want to have some footing before I tell them about her."

I nod as I process everything he's saying. I haven't ever met his family. I was out of town last year when they all came to visit, but he talks about them a lot. They seem to be really involved in his life. It's a shock to find out I knew about Ava before they did, but it makes sense. We've fit so much into today that it's easy to forget that it was only this morning that Ava's mother dropped her off with Jude.

"I still don't think I should live here." I chew on my lip, hoping he doesn't keep pushing. I'm running out of reasons to tell him no. I need a place, and he has more than enough room. I'm just terrified of what being around his charm day and night will be like.

Jude looks at the monitor for a moment when Ava lets out a little noise. We both freeze, waiting to see if the transfer wasn't as successful as we originally thought. She wiggles a little but ultimately stays fast asleep.

"I see no reason for you to live anywhere else," Jude responds. I pull my gaze from the baby monitor and already find his eyes on mine.

"I've already given you a reason."

"Look, Charlotte, I'm not going to lie to you. Last night,

I did want to kiss you. I even woke up this morning thinking maybe things would be different for us. Maybe we could figure it out. But after Ava, I'm not in a place to start anything. I've got to figure out how to be a good dad before anything else. I promise I don't have any ulterior motives for asking you to stay. I'll allow you to keep me in the friend zone. Scout's honor." He kisses his fingertips before holding three of them in the air.

"I don't think the kissing part was necessary."

He shows off his dimples with his cocky grin. "It added a little flair."

I tuck a piece of stray hair behind my ear and roll my eyes. "If I say yes, you have to promise that you won't use your charm on me. We're *both* locked in the friend zone. We don't ever talk about the kiss again, and absolutely *no* flirting."

Jude lifts an eyebrow. "Flirting is part of my personality, and I can't help it that I'm always naturally charming. I can't promise you those two things, but I can promise to stay just friends. Nothing more. I swear it." He does the ridiculous thing with his fingers again, and I can't help but laugh.

"It really isn't your job to take me in and give me a place to live."

Something flashes in Jude's eyes for a moment before he recovers quickly. "I know it isn't my job, Char. I think I've been very clear that I want you to be here with me and Ava. I wouldn't have offered if I didn't want you here."

I hold out my hand and smile. "Then you have a deal. You're stuck with me as a roommate for the summer."

I swear his dimples get even deeper as his entire face lights up. "*Yeah*? You'll move in?"

I shrug before giving him a nod, unable to come up with any other excuses to say no. Not wanting to make things awkward between us was the main reason I was refusing to begin with. Besides, with how early people book things in the Hamptons, I know it'll be almost impossible for me to find somewhere to live on my own. And if I'm going to stay with a friend, I might as well stay with Jude over anyone else. I spend the most time with him anyway. Lucy and Cal are sickeningly in love, and they spend all their time together. Even Camille and Ryker are with each other every spare second they have when they're not both running their own companies. Margo's busy being a mom and an artist, and even Emma and Winnie are so busy that I'd feel bad asking to stay at their places. Jude is kind of my only option. And if we're both agreeing to being just friends and forgetting about last night, then there's no reason for me to say no.

My gaze travels to the monitor. I focus on a sleeping Ava. Her little lips are parted slightly, and I already miss snuggling up to her chubby cheeks. I love the idea of living here and seeing her more. I know Jude won't ask for the help, but I know he could use it when it comes to Ava. Especially if he doesn't want to get his family involved yet.

"So, when are you going to move in then, *roomie*?" Jude asks, breaking me from my thoughts.

"I'm off tomorrow. Is that too soon to bring my things over?"

He immediately shakes his head. "That's perfect. Let me know if you need any help. I can bring Ava with me, and we can help you get packed up."

I give him a smile. "I don't have a lot. I think I can handle it. You focus on spending the day with Ava, and I'll handle packing my things and coming over. Are you sure it's okay for me to stay here? I can pay ren—"

"I'm not taking your money," Jude hurriedly gets out. His tone makes it seem like he might even be insulted that I offered. "I asked you to stay here. Yes, I'm sure. Save your hard-earned money, and stop overthinking this."

I narrow my eyes on him. "I'm not overthinking anything. It's logical for me to ask if you're sure about me staying with you for the summer, especially after how much your life has changed today."

"Then it should also be logical for me to admit how much you helped me today. You ease my mind about things with Ava just by being here. I want you here for the summer, Char. What part of that is hard for you to understand?"

My mouth snaps shut. There's a vulnerability to his voice that I'm not used to. I don't know if I like hearing it or not. It makes my stomach flip and my heart race, neither of which is good when just minutes ago, I was promising to keep him firmly in the friend zone.

"Okay," I whisper, unable to say anything else. It looks like I'll be staying with Jude for the summer. This might end up being the worst idea or the best, but right now, all I can think about is how excited I am to spend more time with him and Ava.

"Then it's settled. You'll be back tomorrow with your things, and we'll be roomies for the summer."

"Please never say the word 'roomies' again."

"I know you're excited to be my roomie, *roomie*." He winks, and all I can do is roll my eyes.

I step away from the counter and make my way to his front door. It's been a long day, and my exhaustion is starting to catch up with me. I'm ready to get out of my work uniform, treat myself to a bath, and put off packing up my things until tomorrow morning.

"I'll see you tomorrow, then." I don't look at him over my shoulder as I slip my shoes on by his front door. I know he's probably excited to get rid of me and have some alone time of his own before Ava wakes up. "I'll leave my phone on ringer for the night. Don't hesitate to reach out if you need something with Ava." I finish putting on the other shoe and look up, finding Jude closer than I expected him to be.

His face looks tight as he watches me carefully. The muscles along his jaw pulse as he quietly watches me.

"Enjoy your quiet time tonight, and again, don't hesitate to call if you need anything. You're a great dad already. You've got this."

Jude nods. His arms lift before they drop at his sides. He stays silent, which is so out of character for him.

It's quiet in the foyer as I wait for him to say something. All he does is keep his mouth closed so tight I wonder if it hurts.

I give him a shy smile before opening the door. "Good night, Jude."

"Night, Char," he finally responds as I step to the door.

I risk a glance over my shoulder and find him watching me with wide eyes. He almost looks scared, but I know that can't be right. Jude Kensington doesn't get scared. He barely even gets unsure. I give him one more smile before getting out of his way for the evening and walking to my car.

The entire drive back to my rental, I can't get the mental picture of him out of my mind. The more I think about it, the more I'm sure he was scared. Was it the right thing to leave him alone tonight? I thought he'd want to be alone on his first night with Ava, but maybe it was the opposite.

I fight the urge to text him, offering to come back once I've gathered my things. If he wanted help, he would've asked. I need to leave him alone.

But still, even as I get home and slip into a hot bath, I can't forget the fear I swear I saw in his eyes.

20

Jude

"It's okay, baby girl," I whisper, bouncing back and forth as I try to settle my daughter.

It doesn't work.

Nothing's working.

Every time I feel like I get her to sleep, she's up twenty minutes later, crying all over again.

Ava lets out a loud cry before burying her face against my shoulder. I know she has to be exhausted. *I'm* exhausted. I just can't figure out how to get her to stay asleep.

I continue to rock back and forth at a pace so fast that I'm wondering if it's maybe too much for her. Charlotte had mentioned I might want a rocking chair in Ava's nursery when we have time to get that set up. I've already come to the decision that as soon as Ava gets to sleep and we reach an acceptable hour of the morning, I'll be calling around to find a rocking chair that can be delivered today. It's a necessity. Although the constant rocking back and forth and pacing the room with Ava in my arms has made my legs burn the same way any workout with my trainer would.

Ava cries again before spitting out the Binky I just got her to finally take.

"What am I doing wrong?" I grumble.

All Ava does is cry again, clearly unable to understand or answer my question.

The night started out great. Well, kind of.

I wanted to ask Charlotte to stay the night tonight. I know Ava is *my* daughter and that she's my responsibility, but I'm still learning what it takes to raise a baby, and Char's just so good with her. Truthfully, I was nervous to be alone. The moment my front door closed, I considered running after her and confessing my anxiety about this first night.

But I let her leave. I already had a victory by getting her to agree to stay here for the summer. I didn't want to ask too much of her and scare her away. For a couple of hours, Ava stayed fast asleep. I watched her closely on the monitor, watching her little chest rise and fall on the tiny screen to make sure she was still breathing. Eventually, I climbed into bed and continued to watch her sleep on the monitor before exhaustion from the day took over, and I drifted off to sleep myself.

I couldn't have been asleep long before Ava finally woke up.

She's barely slept since.

It's our first night together, and now that I'm alone, I can't even get her to stay asleep on her own. Charlotte made it look so easy. Ava's persistent crying and squirming show it isn't, in fact, easy at all.

I'm terrible at this.

I continue to shush her, wondering if it'd be frowned upon if I turned up the volume on the white noise machine in the room. Maybe that'll help make her sleepy and stay asleep?

Fuck if I know.

I look down at my daughter, and my chest constricts because of how tired she looks.

"Just go to sleep," I plead softly, wishing she'd listen. Instead, it has the opposite effect. Her bottom lip juts out and trembles before she lets out a loud wail.

"Maybe you're still hungry?" I ask, wishing she could actually answer me. All of this would be so much easier if she could just tell me what's bothering her.

I try my best to bounce up and down in the same rhythm that Charlotte showed me earlier. It does nothing to calm Ava. If anything, she lets out an even louder wail.

"Okay, we'll try the bottle again."

I walk over to my nightstand and grab the bottle from the edge. I continue to rock Ava back and forth, even as I take a seat on my bed and get comfortable. I hold her at the angle Charlotte told me to and press the tip of the bottle to Ava's lips.

Instead of drinking it, she blows a loud raspberry before thrashing her head back and forth.

"Okay, *not* hungry," I mutter, setting the bottle down before letting my head fall back against the headboard. I rifle through all the different tricks Charlotte told me about. I've tried everything possible to soothe Ava, and it just won't work.

Maybe I'm just not cut out for this.

I shake my head, pushing the thought from my mind. I can't think like that. I'm all Ava has. I *have* to be cut out for this. I have no choice. It's just our first night together, and I'm still figuring all of this out. I can't keep doubting myself. That doesn't help anyone.

"Why won't you sleep, baby girl?" I whisper, looking down at my daughter. I trace my thumb over her eyebrows. The movement makes her eyelids flutter shut.

I sit up a little straighter, wondering if I found a trick. “You like that?” I ask, cradling her small head in both my hands. I bring my knees up, getting her in a comfortable position before I run the pads of my thumbs over her eyebrows once again. Excitement blooms in my chest at the hope that maybe I’ve found something that’ll help.

A sleepy smile forms on my daughter’s lips as her eyelids drift closed once again.

This time, they stay shut.

Did I figure it out?

I hold my breath as I repeat the motion. I sway a little, hoping the combination of movements is what’s needed to finally get my daughter to sleep.

Pride blooms in my chest as I watch her closely, her eyes not opening again. Her long eyelashes kiss the apples of her round cheeks as her chest rises and falls in long, sleepy breaths.

She looks so adorable in this moment that I fight the urge to lean in and press kisses all over her face. No matter how strong the temptation is, I’ll do anything to keep her asleep right now, and that means fighting the urge to kiss her perfectly chubby cheeks.

She’s beautiful.

And she’s mine.

I still haven’t had time to fully wrap my head around the fact that I have a daughter. There’s a sharp pain in my chest when I think about the four months of her life I’ve missed. Maybe if I’d known her from birth, I’d be much better at this. But I can’t let myself dwell on that too much.

I missed four months with her, but that won’t happen again. I’m going to find a way to be the parent she deserves. I’ll make up for our lost time together and be a father she can be proud of when she gets older.

I don't know how long I watch her sleep. I know I need to put her in her own bed and fall asleep myself, but now that she isn't crying and she's dreaming peacefully, all I want to do is watch her.

I've always wanted to be a dad, but I thought it'd be in the more traditional way. I didn't think I'd be figuring it out on my own, and I definitely never imagined raising a daughter on my own. A pit forms in my stomach that one day I'll have to be honest with Ava about her mom not wanting to be a mother. I already dread it, but all I can do is make sure that I do everything to give Ava a happy, fulfilling childhood. I grew up incredibly lucky, having two loving parents who gave me the world. Mom and Dad were the perfect role models of what parents should be. I had a happy childhood, and I so desperately want to give that to Ava, even if she won't have the traditional family dynamic that I did.

I swallow past a lump in my throat as guilt washes over me while I stare at my daughter.

I know I need to tell my parents about Ava.

It's not that I'm hiding her. I just know the moment they find out about her, they'll be on the next flight out. They'll start meddling and asking questions, and I don't have the answers yet. I'm not ashamed of Ava, but I'm also not looking forward to explaining to my parents, who have been married for over forty years, that not only did I have a child from a one-night stand but that I also missed the first four months of that child's life. I wish I had found out about Ava at the same time as her mother, but I can't change that.

I'll tell my parents. I want them to be involved in Ava's

life. They were made to be grandparents and have used every opportunity to remind me of that, but first, I want to gain my footing as a dad. I want them to see that I can handle this on my own. That I'm a good father. I just need a little more time.

My eyelids begin to feel heavy. I let them close for a moment, knowing I need to muster up the courage to put Ava back in her bed so I can catch what sleep I can.

I just need one minute like this.

I'll move her in one minute.

Just as I find myself drifting off, Ava begins to squirm before letting out a cry so loud that I jump with her still in my arms. My movement makes her scream. Her entire face scrunches together and turns a bright red.

I sigh before sliding out of bed and beginning to rock her again.

So much for sleep. This is going to be a long night.

21

Charlotte

I roll from one side to the other before letting out a loud sigh. I can't sleep.

I'm completely exhausted from working and spending the evening helping Jude, and yet I can't stay asleep.

Every time I drift off, I wake up thinking about Jude and Ava. I want to know how the first night is going. It feels like I should be there helping him. I grab my phone from the pillow next to me and look at the screen. My ringer is on, so I already know Jude hasn't called, but I check just in case.

Is it weird for me to call him?

What if he's sleeping and I wake him up?

I roll to my back and stare at the ceiling. I know I shouldn't worry about Jude. He's probably asleep and has been handling the night with Ava just fine.

But what if he is having a rough night?

Babies are temperamental. Even though Ava was fast asleep when I left, it doesn't mean she's still asleep. Because it's three in the morning, I fight the urge to call Jude to check in.

What if I just text him?

I grab my phone before I can change my mind.

Charlotte

How's everything going?

I stare at my phone. It's so late—or early, depending on how you look at it—and I know he probably isn't going to see this text for a few more hours. I still feel better for sending it though. At least if things aren't going great, he knows I'm up and thinking about them.

I'm about to place my phone back on my pillow and force myself to fall back asleep when Jude's face pops up on my screen. It's a silly picture he took of himself last year when we were out golfing. Every time I see it, I smile. Except now, my stomach drops at the sight of his name on my caller ID.

"Is everything okay?" I ask the moment I swipe to answer.

"Char." My name comes out raspy. Before he can say anything else, the loud sound of a cry makes me jump.

Before I realize what I'm even doing, I'm out of bed and shuffling around in the dark to find some clothes. "What's wrong?"

"Nothing. Everything. I don't know." Jude groans. "I've tried everything. Feeding her. Rocking her. Changing her. Feeding her again. Ava just won't stop crying. She'll fall asleep for a few minutes and then wake up crying again."

"I'm on my way," I get out, grabbing a pair of jean shorts from the one box I started packing before crawling into bed.

"You don't have to come over," Jude hurriedly gets out. "It's just that you texted, and since you were awake, I figured I could call and ask what I'm doing wrong."

My chest hurts at the vulnerability in his voice. "You aren't doing anything wrong. She's just a baby. Sometimes babies just cry. I'll be there soon."

"You really don't have to come, Char. I can handle it. Get some sleep. I only called to see if you had any tricks I didn't know about."

"I know you can handle it, but I'm awake, and I've already decided I'm coming over. I'll be there as soon as I can. Try walking around the house with her. Maybe a change of scenery from your room will help."

Jude sighs, but he doesn't argue anymore. I hang up the phone before he can try again to convince me that he doesn't need help. I button my jeans shorts and grab a jacket and zip it up. I'll need to come back later today to pack, but that can wait. Right now, I want to get to Jude's and help him with Ava. He sounds exhausted, and I don't want to waste any time getting over there.

• • •

Before I can knock on the front door, Jude's pulling it open with red-rimmed eyes and disheveled hair. "You're here," he remarks, his voice low and full of exhaustion.

I smile before turning my attention to Ava. She's in his arms, looking just as tired as he does. She cries before her head falls against his shoulder.

"Oh, sweet girl." I carefully take her from Jude and cradle her to my chest. She lets out a small little whimper as I hold her close.

"I don't know how she's still awake right now," Jude mutters. I look at him, and it's only now that I realize he's wearing a pair of glasses.

I've never seen him wear glasses.

It gets worse.

I swallow as I can't help but let my gaze travel over him.

He's shirtless.

In a pair of gray sweatpants.

It must be because I'm also short on sleep, but my head feels fuzzy at the sight. I rip my gaze from him and focus on Ava.

How can he look so good on so little sleep?

How did I not know he wore glasses?

I rock back and forth, watching carefully as Ava's eyelids flutter open and shut.

"She hates me." Jude's deep voice breaks me from my thoughts of what seeing him shirtless in a pair of glasses is doing to me.

I look at him and make sure I keep my gaze locked on his instead of looking at his abs, which are on full display. "She doesn't hate you."

He lifts an eyebrow and cocks his head in my direction. I look down to find Ava fast asleep. Her little lips are parted, and drool has already started to pool.

I roll my eyes, understanding the point he's trying to make but not agreeing with it. "She's probably just so overtired that she finally couldn't fight it anymore."

"Mm-hmm." He walks into his kitchen, and I try not to focus on the way the muscles of his back ripple with his movements.

I walk slowly with Ava and make sure I bounce with each movement. If it's been a struggle to keep her asleep, I want to make sure I don't do anything to mess up the fact that she's finally sleeping.

"I've got terrible news for you," Jude drawls. My eyes move

to him, finding him leaning against his kitchen island. He props his elbows against the surface, his head falling forward in exhaustion.

"What's the terrible news?"

Despite the lack of sleep, he manages a smile as he looks back up at me. "Clearly, you're her favorite, which means you can never leave us. Not until I figure out how to calm her down on my own, at least."

I shake my head. "I'm not her favorite. She's just a baby and is in a new place with new people. In no time, I'm going to have to pry her away from you to get snuggles in because she'll be so obsessed with you and not want to go to anyone else."

He lets out a defeated groan. "I hope you're right, Char. I don't want to fail her. I want to be her comfort person, and it's killing me that I couldn't get her to stop crying tonight."

I hate to see him look so sad and defeated. It's not something I'm used to with Jude.

"It has nothing to do with you. I promise. Why don't you go get some sleep, and I'll watch her?"

His eyes scan my face. It takes everything in me to keep my gaze locked with his when he pushes himself off the counter and straightens his spine. "I didn't call you to make you watch her for me. I can handle it."

"I'm not offering because I don't think you can handle it. I know you can, but you're going to have to learn to accept help, Jude. You've had a long night, and I'm already here and wide-awake. Go get some sleep."

Ava stirs in my arms. He focuses on her for a moment, keeping whatever he's thinking to himself. Her eyes open, but her exhaustion eventually wins out, and after a few rocks back and forth, she falls asleep once again.

"I just don't want you to think I'm using you. I only called for advice. Not free childcare."

I roll my eyes at him. If I weren't holding his daughter, I would push him in the direction of his room myself. But since I'm trying desperately to keep her asleep by rocking from one foot to the other, I keep my hands to myself instead. "I'm about to stay in your house for the summer. I fully plan on helping with Ava when I can because I *want* to. Now, stop arguing and get to sleep."

Jude lets out a deep, throaty laugh, and it does funny things to my body. "You're kind of cute when you're bossy."

"Jude," I warn. He can't flirt with me when he's shirtless, wearing glasses, and in a pair of gray sweatpants. That's basically illegal and definitely against the rules.

He puts his hands up in surrender but begins to back up to his room. "If she becomes too much to handle, please wake me up."

I nod. I'm not going to wake him up unless there's an emergency, but he doesn't need to know that. "Okay. Now, go get in bed."

His eyebrows raise to his hairline. "Trying to get me into bed, Char?"

I scoff. Even when exhausted, he finds a way to still be a flirt. "*Jude*." His name is said as a warning. It reminds me of the way my mom used to say my name when I was about to get in trouble for something.

He takes the hint because he smiles and changes the subject. "Thanks, Char. I know I probably sound like a broken record, but I don't know what I'd do without you. Wake me up in an hour or two, and I'll take back over."

I nod, thankful that he doesn't say anything else. He turns

around and walks to his room, disappearing from sight.

The moment he's out of view, I let out a deep breath.

I softly run a hand over the top of Ava's head. "Who knew your daddy looked so good in glasses? This is a *very* dangerous discovery."

22

Jude

The sound of my phone vibrating wakes me up from a deep sleep.

I groan, pulling a pillow over my face in an effort to ignore it.

I'm trying to force myself back asleep when my phone vibrates again.

Ava.

I bolt up in bed and grab my phone, swiping to answer without even checking to see who is calling me.

"What's wrong?" I ask, throwing my legs over the side of the bed. I figured if something bad were to happen with Ava, Charlotte would just come in the room and wake me up, but maybe it's *so* bad that she can't even make it in here.

"I think I should be asking *you* that," a familiar voice says from the other line. I frown before reaching to my bedside table and sliding on my glasses. I pull my phone away from my ear and check the caller ID.

It isn't Charlotte calling me. It's Matt, my assistant.

"What?" I ask, letting out a deep breath. Nothing's wrong with Ava.

"I've been texting you all morning with questions about the acquisition of Bowden Jewelers. Your dad wants a report on his desk by Monday morning, and as far as I can tell, it's Sunday, and you still haven't finalized the report. Are you still planning to?"

Fuck.

I scrub a hand over my face. After everything with Ava yesterday, I'd completely forgotten about the Bowden deal. As director of acquisitions at the Kensington Corporation, a company founded by my grandfather, I'm in charge of every acquisition we take on. The family business started out as a luxury handbag brand that's turned into much more. I'm lucky enough to have been given a seat on the board. My dad took over being the chairman and CEO of Kensington Corporation from his dad, and one day, the position will be mine, but I want to earn it the same way my father did.

Dropping the ball on what will be one of our most profitable acquisitions in the last decade isn't the way to do that.

"Jude?" Matt prods, his voice full of confusion. I'm lucky enough to have a team of people underneath me who do their job well. It allows me to not work as much as I did in the beginning and have more flexibility with my life. But this Bowden Jewelers acquisition was all my idea. Dad didn't know if they were worth the expensive price tag, but I talked him into it. I can't drop the ball now by not giving him the report he needs.

"Sorry, I'm here," I tell Matt, my brain spinning with all the things I need to do before tomorrow morning.

"Should I have Emerson write up the report?" Matt asks.

I like that he minds his own business. He doesn't ask why the report isn't already done or chastises me. As my assistant, he handles a lot for me. He keeps me organized. I just don't normally drop the ball in this way. It's not a bad idea to ask Emerson, one of the higher-ups in acquisitions, to take over the job for me.

I shake my head. "No, I can write it. Will you and Emerson just work together on pulling all the numbers and organizing it for me? Whatever information you can collect to give me the best chance at quickly writing the report would be great."

Matt's been my assistant for ten years. After I graduated from college and started at Kensington, my dad quickly let me interview personal assistants. He said his assistant was the best hire of his career and to choose wisely. It took me six months to find the perfect fit, but I'm so happy I went with Matt.

"Need anything else from me?" he asks. Even though it's out of character for me to forget things, especially something as important as this Bowden deal, Matt doesn't ask me what's going on. Eventually, I'll tell him about Ava. Maybe he can give me advice as a dad of three girls himself. But for right now, I focus on work.

We talk for a few more minutes before hanging up the call. The moment it ends, I let out a long groan. The time on my phone tells me that Charlotte allowed me to sleep for almost six hours. I can't believe I was able to sleep that long without waking up, but I also can't believe that I got so distracted by things with Ava that I forgot all about this Bowden deal. I'm exhausted, and my head is all over the place. Maybe sleeping like the dead for six hours isn't so odd after all.

I move my glasses out of the way for a moment to rub my eyes with the heels of my hands. Despite getting six straight hours of sleep, I still feel exhausted. I could easily go back to sleep, but between work and Ava, that isn't going to happen. I slide my glasses back on and take a deep breath.

I'm going to need an industrial-sized cup of coffee today.

I know I should probably look at my appearance in the mirror before opening my bedroom door and stepping out to the hallway, but I don't. I miss Ava, and I want to check in on things. I don't know if I should be nervous or relieved that Charlotte let me sleep that long.

"C'mon, sweet girl," I hear from what I think is the living room. I haven't made my way down the hallway yet to find out. "Give me that smile," Charlotte continues in a high-pitched baby voice that makes me smile before even seeing her.

I stop in the opening of the hallway before leaning a shoulder against the wall. Charlotte hasn't spotted me yet, and I want it that way. For a moment, I soak in the sight of her with Ava.

She's moved the coffee table to the side and laid out some sort of play blanket we purchased at the store. She holds a camera up as she continues to talk to Ava in a baby voice.

I fold my arms across my chest and take in the moment.

It feels like someone's reached inside my chest and squeezed. I can barely breathe because of the intensity of it.

An overwhelming amount of gratitude washes over me that I'm lucky enough to bear witness to this moment.

"Let me see that smile, Ava girl," she coos, reaching down and tickling Ava's belly. "So close!" she excitedly mutters to herself. She beams while continuing to hold the camera to her face, and I already know that I wear a matching smile.

If you'd told me a year ago that Charlotte would become one of the most important people in my life, I wouldn't have believed you. It was about a year ago that I met Charlotte because my best friend, Cal, hired a private chef who happened to be Charlotte's best friend. He's now engaged to that chef, Lucy, and the closeness of those two meant Charlotte and I became close as a result.

We developed a fast friendship. My usual charm didn't have any kind of effect on her. She didn't fawn over me the way other women did. She told me from the very beginning that nothing would ever happen between us. I wasn't used to the honesty, and it drew me to her even more. When summer ended last year and everyone left the Hamptons, I found myself coming back here more and more in the off-season just because Charlotte was here.

I don't know what it is about her, but I'm drawn to her. I've always found myself wanting to spend as much time with her as I can. And now with this new season of my life, I can't imagine figuring it out with anyone by my side but her. I'm lucky to have her. And walking out this morning to catch this moment between her and Ava is just another reminder of that.

"Oh." Charlotte lets out a sound of surprise, which pulls me out of my thoughts. I blink and focus on her, finding her staring at me, still wearing a smile. "Good morning."

I push myself off the wall and head toward her and Ava. "You didn't have to let me sleep that long." I give her a smile, hoping it conveys my gratitude.

Charlotte shrugs. "You needed to sleep, and we were having fun. Weren't we, Ava?" She looks down at Ava and tickles her belly.

Ava excitedly kicks her legs. I think I'm still too far away for Ava to see me, but I'm able to take in the pink outfit Charlotte's changed her into. It's one of the ones I picked out at the store, but what really catches my attention is the giant bow on her head.

"Oh my God." I laugh, closing the distance to my daughter. I bend over and grab her from the blanket and lift her up. "That bow is as big as your head, baby girl."

Ava gives me the biggest smile, and I swear all the exhaustion leaves my body, and my world makes sense for the first time in I don't know how long.

"Ah!" Charlotte yells from my side. A clicking noise fills the living room as she must begin to take pictures as I stare at my daughter with a matching grin on my face.

"Did you just smile at me?" I ask, even though she can't answer me.

It feels like my heart swells in my chest as Ava shows off her deep dimples. She lets out an excited squawking noise as she continues to smile at me, almost as if she's excited to see me.

"I've been trying to get her to smile like that for thirty minutes," Charlotte says from my side. The camera continues to make clicking noise after clicking noise as she captures another moment where my daughter completely steals my heart.

23

Charlotte

It should be illegal to witness Jude with bed head fresh after waking up. His hair sticks up in different directions, and it makes me wonder if it'd look the same if my fingers had been pulling at the longer strands at the top all night.

And the hair isn't the most illegal thing about him right now.

It's the damn *glasses* again.

The same gray sweatpants.

No shirt.

A raspy morning voice.

All of it combined makes my cheeks heat and my mind go to places it shouldn't be going.

I know I shouldn't be capturing it on film to go back and look at later, but it also seems like a crime not to picture him like this. I tell myself I'm only continuing to take pictures to capture the wide smile on Ava's face and the way Jude's entire face lights up looking at his daughter. I want him to have these memories with Ava forever.

It's not because I'll go back later and look at the photos of

Jude shirtless, in gray sweatpants, wearing glasses, holding a baby. I totally won't go back and admire the view.

"You saw her smile at me, right?" he asks. His voice is so giddy that it pulls on my heartstrings.

I nod, putting the camera down and stepping closer to them. I tickle the bottom of Ava's foot. "You wouldn't smile at me, no matter what silly face I made, but you smiled right away when you saw your daddy again."

Ava continues to smile before leaning forward and resting her head against Jude's chest.

Jude's eyes meet mine. "I think my heart just actually melted. She's going to get everything she ever wants."

I laugh, biting my tongue and fighting the urge to respond that my heart also just melted. It's a puddle at my feet at the sight of Ava smiling big at her dad before resting her head against his chest like he's her favorite person in the world. "I see nothing wrong with that." I lean in to run my fingers over Ava's chubby little cheek. "Kids are spoiled all the time and turn out just fine. Don't they, Ava girl?"

It isn't the same smile she gives Jude, but one corner of her lip twitches just the way Jude's does sometimes, and I take that as her smiling at me. It kind of counts.

"Did you sleep well?" I lift my camera to my face and wait for it to focus on Ava and Jude before snapping a few more photos. I can't help it. I know he missed four months of Ava's life, and I imagine that's hard on him. I want him to have countless albums full of her baby pictures to look back on one day, and today seemed like the perfect day to start. Plus, the way she snuggles against his bare chest is too cute not to take a picture of. Luckily, one of my cameras was in my car. I was able to grab it when the idea popped into my head that I could take pictures of Ava for him.

Jude rests his cheek against the top of Ava's head but keeps his eyes locked on me. "I slept great. Thank you for letting me sleep. You didn't have to let me go that long. I feel bad you had to watch Ava all night."

"Stop telling me I don't have to do anything. I know I didn't have to. I wanted to. Ava and I had lots of fun, didn't we?" I press my fingertip to her nose before making a funny face. It doesn't get me a full smile, but the corner of her mouth turns up again.

"Well, thank you. I needed it."

"Good. I'm happy to help."

Jude pulls his gaze from mine and leans his head back to look at Ava. "I'm happy you're not screaming at the sight of me this morning, sweet girl. I thought you hated me after you wouldn't stop crying last night."

I set my camera down on the coffee table and begin to pick up some of the toys I got out when playing with Ava. I stole the decorative basket off one of the built-in shelves in the far corner of Jude's living room. If he notices that I used his decor to hold baby toys, he says nothing.

"She was just overtired. It took me a while to finally calm her down enough to sleep, but I did get a three-hour stretch out of her."

"Or maybe I'm just bad at figuring out what my daughter wants." Jude plops down on the couch with Ava still in his arms.

I roll my eyes. "You can't take it personally when a baby doesn't sleep. It happens all the time."

"I don't know if I'd ever felt so defeated." Even the tone of his voice changes with his admission. It's obvious that he's being hard on himself about last night. I don't know how to get through to him that it isn't personal. Ava's going through a hard transition right now, and she's just a baby. There will be times when it's probably easy to calm her and figure out what she needs, and there will also be times when it will be more difficult. That's just how it works.

I sit down on the couch next to him. My leg brushes against his as I pull my knees to my chest and turn to face him. "Jude," I begin, trying to keep my voice soft, "stop beating yourself up. You did your best, and that's all you can do. Look at the way she's looking at you right now. She doesn't hate you. She's just a baby, and babies are temperamental sometimes."

He nods and stares at his daughter. It's not like Jude to let his vulnerability show, but it's written all over his face. There's a crease between his eyebrows I'm not used to seeing, and instead of his lips turning up in his normal smirk, they slightly turn down.

This version of Jude makes my heart hurt. His world has changed so much in such a short amount of time. I wish he'd give himself more grace on getting it figured out.

I know Jude well enough to know there isn't much more I can say. All I can do is change the subject and hope that eventually he believes what I'm telling him. "While Ava was sleeping, I got all of her laundry done. It's folded in baskets in the laundry room. I wasn't sure how soon you wanted to get a nursery put together and how soon she'd have a dresser, so I figured keeping them in the baskets was the safest option for now."

"You should've slept while she slept," he responds, his brown eyes scanning my face.

"Since her bed was in your room, she just slept on her mat on the floor. I wanted to be able to have eyes on her at all times, so I just tried going through our purchases from yesterday."

Jude closes his eyes for a moment and shakes his head. "I just don't deserve you, Char. You've got to be exhausted."

I give him a smile when he opens his eyes and our gazes connect. "I helped myself to a coffee from your fancy machine."

"This house is now yours. You can help yourself to anything."

There's something about the intense way he looks at me right now that sends shivers down my spine. I know he means the house is only mine for the summer, but it doesn't stop my body from having a reaction to it. My heart races, and I have to rip my gaze from his and change the subject before I start getting any crazy ideas just from the way he's looking at me.

"What's your plan for the day?" I push myself off the couch and walk to the kitchen. I left some bottles drying on the rack that I can put away to give myself some space from Jude.

Maybe it's my own lack of sleep and the sight of him shirtless and wearing glasses that's giving me funny feelings I'm not used to getting around him.

That's got to be it.

Jude turns around so he can look at me from his spot on the couch. He lifts Ava above his head, making her let out a happy squeal as he quickly lowers her closer to him. "Just spend time with my girl and hopefully squeeze in some work when she sleeps. Do you need any help getting packed or getting your things here?"

I shake my head. I want him to get as much time with Ava as he can. I hadn't even thought about how he was going to factor in work with Ava. I know he doesn't have a strict schedule for work, but I do know it keeps him fairly busy. I want to ask him how he plans on juggling both, but I don't want to overwhelm him. Instead, I focus on answering his question. "No, I'm good. If everything's good here, I'm going to run home now and pack, and then I'll be back."

Jude lifts Ava in the air again before repeating the same motion by dropping his arms. The smile she gives him is massive when he does it again. "Everything's good. I know you stepped in last night with Ava, but I didn't ask you to stay here for the summer because I wanted you to watch Ava for me. Hopefully, last night was a fluke. You're free to come and go as much as you need. Ava isn't your responsibility."

I want to tell him that I don't mind helping. I *want* to be here and help. But he's so insistent on wanting to be able to do it on his own that I don't argue. I pull open a cabinet I made some room in and place the clean bottles inside. I chew on my bottom lip, a little nervous to ask the question at the forefront of my mind. "Are you sure you're okay with me moving in? I was going to let Devin know I'm leaving and it'll be ready for the new renters, but I don't want to tell him that until I'm sure I have somewhere to stay for the next few months." My words come out hurried while I stare at the bottles in the cabinet because I'm nervous that he might have changed his mind

When he doesn't answer right away, I turn around to look at him.

He cradles Ava to his chest before standing up. He rounds the couch and walks toward me with furrowed eyebrows. He looks almost confused that I even asked the question at all. "Of course I'm sure. I want you here. Now, go get your stuff, and I'll make sure your room is ready for you when you get back."

I stare at him for a few moments, searching for any clues that he doesn't mean what he's saying. From what I can tell, he's genuine about not minding me crashing here for the summer.

I work my bottom lip between my teeth for a few moments before nodding. “Okay, I’ll go get my stuff, and I’ll be back.”

“Our first official day as roomies.” He winks, and I have to leave the kitchen before he can see the way my cheeks heat from the gesture.

24

Jude

My daughter gives me the biggest smile as I stare down at her with my mouth hanging open. "I think you're going to need a bath." I'm scared to even pick her up as she makes sounds I've never heard come from a tiny baby.

She happily kicks her legs up and down, completely unbothered that she just shit her pants…and I'm pretty sure it's going to be everywhere.

I've changed plenty of her diapers, but this is the first poop.

And based on what I just heard, it seems like it might be a big one.

"We're going straight to the bath, baby girl." I carefully lift her from her playmat. There's nothing on the playmat or on her back, but I'm still nervous to get to the bathroom and find out if Ava had a blowout or not.

I turn the bathtub on and set Ava down on the plush bathroom rug and unzip her pjs. We've had a great day together, just the two of us. Charlotte left to finish packing up her apartment hours ago. I didn't think she'd be gone so long, and I've fought the urge to text her and check in, but I also don't want her to get annoyed with me, so I refrained. I've kept myself busy playing with Ava and bonding with her.

After our rough night together, I needed today with her. We've had the best time. Every time she's fussed, I've been able to figure out what she needs almost right away, and it's been the confidence boost I didn't even know I needed.

While she slept, I was even able to get some work done and get in touch with a highly recommended family lawyer. I don't want to wait long at all on getting things sorted out about Ava being mine and only mine. My lawyer got me connected with a way to discreetly take a paternity test, and I should have it confirmed soon that Ava is biologically mine.

I carefully pull Ava's feet out of the pjs, bracing myself for what I'm about to see.

"Holy shit," I mutter, bringing my T-shirt over my nose to cover the smell.

I laugh. Literally, holy *shit*.

I realize as I pull Ava's arms out of the sleeves that I don't have wipes in the bathroom. I leave her on the rug and run into my room. Once I have the wipes, I work on quickly getting the diaper off her and wiping her down before putting her in the baby bath inside my large claw-foot tub.

She kicks her legs in the water before letting out a happy squeal.

I can't help but smile as I kneel next to the tub. "Do you like the water?" I grab the basket of bath supplies from next to the tub and pull out a whale-shaped rinse cup. Ava continues to happily kick her legs and splash while I fill the cup with water.

Her smile gets even wider and her dimples deeper as I slowly pour the water from the cup over her little body.

"You really like the water." My mom always said I was a

water baby and it was where I was happiest. I love that it seems Ava might be the same way.

"Hello?" Charlotte's voice comes from somewhere in the house.

"In the bathroom," I yell back, a sense of relief overtaking me that she's back.

Char taking longer to pack up her things than I expected had me second-guessing if she wanted to still stay here for the summer. I don't want to think too deeply about how disappointed I'd be if she did change her mind.

"Are you clothed?" Charlotte's voice is closer this time. I stare at the open door, waiting to see her walk into the bathroom.

I can't help but smirk at her question. "Why don't you come in and find out?" I tease.

Even though I still can't see her, I can perfectly picture her rolling her eyes at my comment.

She steps into view with her hands on her hips. "I haven't even fully moved in, and you're already flirting with me?"

I place a hand on my chest and give her a smirk. "Who said I'm flirting?"

"*Come and find out.*" She repeats what I said in a husky tone that's supposed to make fun of me but instead only makes my smirk grow. "That was absolutely flirting." She drops to her knees next to me and smiles when she looks at Ava in the tub.

"Maybe *you* flirted first by asking me if I had clothes on or not. Would you have preferred I was naked?"

Charlotte's lips part, and her cheeks turn crimson at my words. "I don't want to picture you naked," she hurriedly gets out.

I lift an eyebrow. "Everyone wants to picture me naked. It's a sight to see."

Charlotte snorts. It's an adorable snort, even if it's at the expense of my ego. Her blue eyes focus on me. "Not everyone. Not me."

It's at the tip of my tongue to remind her of the other night. She wasn't looking at me like she didn't want to see me naked then. She was looking at me like she wanted to rip my clothes off. I could remind her of that, but I know I shouldn't. I can't start anything with Charlotte because I need to focus on Ava. That doesn't mean I can't do a little bit of harmless flirting though. It's too hard not to. I love watching her cheeks get red.

"How did packing go?" I change the subject as I focus on Ava once again. She's still happily splashing in the water as the tub slowly fills around her. I continue to let the warm water run, keeping a close eye on it to make sure it doesn't fill too much with the baby bath inside.

"I'm all packed up," she answers from my side. "I was even able to pass the keys off to Devin, so you're officially stuck with me for the summer, unfortunately."

I pull my gaze from Ava to look at Charlotte for a moment. I bite my tongue, resisting the urge to tell her that it isn't unfortunate at all that she's here for the summer. She's here with me and Ava, which is exactly where I want her. "Poor me," I tease, ripping my gaze from hers before I get lost staring into her beautiful blue eyes.

I fill the bath cup with water and carefully pour it over Ava's head. She smiles, not bothered by the water on her face at all.

"How did your day go?" Charlotte asks. She places her hands on the corner of the tub and rests her chin on top of her forearm. I glance over at her again; the new position she's in puts her closer to me than I was expecting. She watches Ava with a smile, and I try to ignore how much more at peace I feel with her back here.

"Turns out maybe she doesn't hate me," I respond, turning my attention back to my daughter. I turn the water off for a moment and let her splash in it for a little bit. "We had a good day. We were having a lot of fun until she decided she was going to shit her pants, making noises I didn't know could come from something so tiny."

Charlotte giggles from my side.

Fuck, I love her laugh. It makes me smile and creates a tightness in my chest I can't describe.

"Yeah, I've definitely heard some intense sounds come from my nieces and nephews. But congratulations on handling your first blowout. Up all night *and* a massive blowout…you've been initiated on having an infant."

"Turns out Ava loves the water though. We haven't been in here long, but she seems to love the bath."

As if she understands me, Ava kicks at the water and lets out a happy squeal when some of the water hits her in the face.

Charlotte reaches into the bath and runs her fingers over Ava's cheek. "Are you a water baby?"

"I think she is."

"We'll have to get her in the pool one of these days. I bet she'd love that."

I nod. "Yeah, I thought about doing that today with her, but I was nervous. What do I do about the sun? Can babies wear sunscreen? Is it even warm enough outside yet for her to be in the pool?"

It's quiet for a moment. I expect Charlotte to answer my questions, or at least comment, but she doesn't say anything. I try to wait patiently for her response, pouring water over Ava to keep her warm, but the silence eventually gets the best of me. I look over at Charlotte and find her staring at me with a soft smile gracing her perfect pink lips.

My eyes narrow. "What?"

Her lips twitch for a moment. She pulls her bottom lip between her teeth in an attempt to fight her smile, but it doesn't work. Her entire face lights up, and she beams at me. "Nothing," she responds.

My mouth falls open. "No, you can't say *nothing*. I asked you questions, and you didn't answer any of them. And why are you smiling?"

Her nose crinkles when her smile grows even wider, and fuck, why is she so adorable? I've always been attracted to Charlotte. There's no denying she's absolutely gorgeous. With her long blonde hair, bright blue eyes, and heart-shaped face, she makes every man do a double-take at the club. But it's different now. I see her, and it's not that I'm just attracted to her. There's a pull I feel to her that I've never felt before. I'm starting to notice everything about her—the crinkle to her nose when she smiles, the way she blushes a perfect shade of red, or when she bites her lip when she's nervous. None of these are things I've noticed before.

"Char," I prod, speaking up to get out of my head and stop obsessing over the fact that I'm starting to get a little too attracted to my best friend. "Why are you smiling and not answering my questions?"

She shakes her head and bites her lip again, and *fuck*...why do I want to be the one biting her lip instead? Would she like that? I desperately want to find out.

"It's just kind of cute when you're worrying about Ava. I obviously have never seen this side of you. I like it."

I swallow, ripping my gaze from hers. My ears feel hot, and I think it's her turn to make *me* blush. No one ever makes me blush, but something about her compliment makes my entire face feel hot. "Did you hear that, baby girl?" I ask Ava, pulling out the bottle of soap from the basket next to me. "Charlotte just called me cute again. Do you think she likes me?"

Charlotte scoffs from my side before softly pushing my shoulder with her wet hand. "I give you one compliment, and it goes to your head. That'll be the last time you get one from me."

I give her a cocky smile over my shoulder. "No it won't."

Charlotte rolls her eyes before leaning forward and turning the water back on. "Stop flirting and finish cleaning Ava. I want to give her snuggles."

I do as I'm told, loving how right it feels to do something so simple as giving my daughter a bath with Charlotte.

I'm really going to love having her here with us this summer.

I just hope I don't love having her here a little too much.

25

Charlotte

"Why does she sleep so good during the day and not at night?" Jude asks. He bounces on his feet in the living room, going from one foot to the other as he tries to calm Ava down.

"Because she's a baby," I answer from the kitchen. I work on warming up her bottle, hoping maybe that's the reason she's refusing to eat anything and, therefore, refusing to sleep.

Jude paces the living room. He swings his body from left to right so hard I'm shocked the motion isn't enough to get Ava to go to sleep.

She lets out a loud cry and refuses to let Jude place her head against his chest.

"The milk's almost done," I tell him, testing it on my wrist. It's warmer than it was the last time I tried offering her a bottle, but still a good temperature that isn't too hot for her.

Before closing the distance to Jude and Ava, I check the time and find that it's just after midnight. We spent the rest of the day getting my boxes into the house, and I unpacked while Ava slept and Jude got some work in. We ordered in for dinner, and as far as my first night staying here goes, it was going well until Ava woke up at nine and decided she didn't want to go back to sleep at all.

"You can go to bed," Jude tells me for what feels like the hundredth time.

"I didn't know I needed permission to go to bed," I tease, trying to keep the mood light despite Ava's crying. I'm exhausted and should probably sleep, but I want to keep spending time with him. I'll sleep eventually.

Jude cradles her in the crook of his elbow and gets her in the position to take a bottle when I hand it to him. "I don't work again until Thursday this week, so I don't mind staying up with you while we figure this out."

He doesn't respond. We both seem to hold our breath as Jude offers Ava the bottle. If she'll drink it, I feel like we'll have a better chance at trying to get her to sleep. She had her last bottle three hours ago, so there's a chance she's hungry, and now that the milk is warmer than normal, maybe this will do the trick.

Jude and I share a hopeful look when she starts to drink the milk. She drinks maybe an ounce of it before turning her head and letting out another cry.

I step closer and rub my thumb along her forehead. "Your little eyebrows are so red, sweet girl. Go to sleep. I promise you'll feel better."

It calms her for a minute until she gets back to being upset all over again.

I frown, wondering what else we can try. I think about all the different things we used to do when my nieces and nephews were little…then get an idea.

"Let's drive around," I offer, a smile growing on my lips

because I think this might actually work.

Jude frowns. He wears his black glasses that do things to me that they absolutely shouldn't. Apparently, he only typically wears his glasses at night before bed. I need him to go back to wearing his contacts more often so the glasses stop having an effect on me. Paired with his T-shirt and thigh-hugging joggers, I've been struggling not to ogle my friend on our first night living together. I try not to think about how good he looks, even with the stress of not being able to get his daughter to sleep. It's honestly unfair.

Jude's eyes are full of questions as he scans my face. "Let's go for a drive with a screaming baby?"

I can't help but smile. I get why the idea might sound crazy to someone who hasn't had a ton of prior experience with infants. "Sometimes babies love to sleep in the car. There's something about it that calms them. I feel like we've tried everything else. Maybe just driving around will do the trick."

He stares at me for a moment before looking back at Ava. She isn't crying right now, but she isn't falling asleep either. She's just staring at her dad with a look that says she might break out in tears at any moment.

Jude sighs before leaning forward and pressing a soft kiss to the top of Ava's head. "How does a car ride sound?"

She doesn't cry. She stays quiet. Her eyelids are heavy as she looks up at Jude.

I lift an eyebrow and give Jude a smile. "That sounds like a yes to me."

Jude laughs. He runs his free hand through his hair before lifting his shoulders in a shrug. "It's obvious I don't have any fresh ideas on how to get her to sleep, and you're the baby whisperer. I'll take her for a drive."

I try not to let my disappointment show at the way he says *I'll* instead of *we'll*. Maybe he doesn't want me to go? I rub my lips together as I think of what to say in response. I don't have anything better to do, and I want to go. It feels like we're in this battle together. I don't want to stay here while he drives around.

"I can go too," I offer, keeping a smile on my face.

"Char," he begins. I hold my breath as I wait for him to continue, bracing myself for him to tell me that he doesn't want my help. "It's your first night here, and I already feel bad about how much you've helped tonight when it isn't your responsibility. I can take her for a drive so you can actually get some rest. You had her early this morning while I got to sleep."

"It was my idea. I'm going for the drive too. And one of these days, you'll learn that I'm not going to do anything I don't want to do. I was the baby of my family, remember? I'm used to getting my way, and I also got away with anything because everyone was too busy to pay attention to me. If I didn't want to go for the drive or help with Ava, then I wouldn't. But I *want* to. So stop trying to tell me what to do, and let's get on the road before she starts screaming again.

Jude's lips twitch as he stares at me with wide eyes. He quirks an eyebrow.

I fold my arms across my chest. "What?"

"I like it when you're bossy."

"I like it when you listen to me."

I swear his eyes light up. "Guess I'll start listening to you more, then."

"Good boy." I laugh as I back away from him and begin to pack a travel bag for Ava. I know we won't be going anywhere, but I want to have a spare diaper and some clothes just in case the car ride doesn't go the way I think it will.

It takes a few minutes to get everything packed up. I realize this is the first time Jude's leaving the house with Ava since we went shopping, and it's kind of adorable how many things he thinks we need to take with us just to drive around long enough to get Ava to sleep.

I'm busy buckling her into her car seat and shushing her through her cries when he runs in from the kitchen.

"Should we bring the bottle warmer?"

I look over my shoulder and find him holding it up with an unsure look on his face.

He's totally serious.

I have to rub my lips together to hide the smile that threatens to overtake my mouth. I don't want to make fun of him, but if I weren't here, I really think he would've packed everything we bought yesterday just to drive around mindlessly for a while.

"I think we'll be good without the bottle warmer. I already put her milk in a thermos of warm water in the car just in case we need it."

He nods before looking down at Ava. She's stopped crying now that Jude's here, but the little whines she makes tell me we're close to another meltdown, and we should get her into the car and drive as soon as possible.

"Your idea is better," he admits. He steps forward and picks up her infant seat carrier. I sling the bag I packed over my shoulder and follow him out to his parked SUV.

I try not to focus on the way he holds the carrier. Why is it kind of hot? He's got this hot dad walk that I can't look away from. It's no secret that women always flock to him. He's like a magnet everywhere he goes. He's got charm and is too ridiculously good-looking for his own good. It's hard to resist him. But now that he's a dad, I think it's going to drive women even more crazy.

And I come to a terrible realization as I watch Jude load Ava into the car.

Jude without a baby was incredibly attractive. He was hard to resist *then*.

But Jude with a baby? That's a lethal combination that even I'm struggling to be immune to.

26

Charlotte

"I'm waiting for you to tell me *I told you so* or something close to that." Jude briefly looks over at me before focusing his attention back on the road.

I stare at his profile for a minute, trying to figure out what he's talking about. "What?" I keep my voice quiet in an attempt not to disturb Ava.

He hooks a thumb over his shoulder as a corner of his lip rises in a smirk. "Ava's fast asleep. You were right about a drive doing the trick."

I look at the screen on Jude's dash. There's a camera on Ava's seat that allows us to watch her from the front seat. At the store, I just wanted to get a mirror for the back, but when Jude saw the camera, he insisted we go this route instead. I'll admit that it's nice not to have to look over my shoulder to check on her. "Something about the movement of the car does it every time," I note, smiling as I stare at the image of Ava on the screen. Her little cheeks puff out in the most adorable way as she peacefully sleeps.

"How long should I drive for?" Jude asks as he comes to a

stop at a red light.

I shrug before looking over at him, finding him already staring at me. "I'm in no rush to get home yet. Maybe we drive around long enough to let her get into a deep sleep. We'll have a better shot at successfully transferring her to her bed when we get back to the house."

Jude doesn't answer. All he does is glance at the light before looking back at me. The quiet makes me nervous. Maybe he doesn't want to spend the extra time together. He did try to get me to stay home in the first place.

"Or we can just go back to the house if you don't want to keep driving. She's asleep, and I bet if we—"

"I want to keep driving." His words come out confident and leave no room for argument.

My mouth snaps shut at his directness. He keeps his voice low, so the words are raspy, making goosebumps pop up on my skin, even though I'm not cold.

"Okay," I manage to get out, wondering if being alone with him in the car was the best idea.

It seemed innocent at the time I offered it. I really did just want to help. Driving worked all the time with my nieces and nephews. But there's something about being in the dark car, with him with only the moonlight and the occasional streetlamp to illuminate the space, that makes this feel far more intimate than I imagined. I've spent so much time alone with Jude, and I didn't use to think twice about it.

But now that we've kissed and now that I'm getting to know him on a deeper level, it's different. I'm not able to keep him at arm's length. Before, he was my charming friend whom I enjoyed spending time with. I was attracted to him, but I knew better. Because I knew better, I was able to keep up walls with him. Now, those walls seem paper-thin. Watching him step so effortlessly into the role of being a dad has opened up something inside me that's getting harder to fight.

I've always been attracted to Jude Kensington. It's just that I knew better than to act on it. I didn't want things to get messy because I knew he was never the commitment type. Now, I wonder if I had it all wrong. It seems like maybe he could be the commitment type if he just met the right girl, and I can't help but catch myself wondering if that girl could be me.

"What are we going to talk about, then?" He steps on the gas and leans back in his seat, and I'm suddenly aware of just how big he is. Even in the roomy SUV, his elbow bumps against mine as he rests it against the center console between us. I don't know exactly how tall he is…it's got to be over six feet. I've always *known* he was tall, but it feels more pronounced right now with his broad shoulders and how far his seat is pushed back to account for his long legs. His elbow used to bump against mine in the car, and I'd joke about him staying on his side. Now, when his skin grazes mine, I don't mind it. I don't want to tease him about touching me because I don't want him to stop.

"Char?"

I jump at hearing the nickname he uses for me. I hadn't realized I was spaced out until he tore me from my thoughts of him. "Um," I begin, tucking my hair behind my ear as I try to think about what he was saying before I got lost in thought. "You pick," I finally get out.

"Tell me your secrets."

My head whips in his direction. "My secrets?"

Jude smiles, and why does his smile now make my chest tighten? He's given me that same smirk countless times in the year we've been friends. I used to easily pretend it had no effect on me. Now I'm fumbling for words when he aims that smile in my direction.

"Yeah. We need to pass the time, and spilling secrets seems like the perfect way to do it."

I shake my head. "I'm not giving you my secrets." I don't even know what secrets I have kept from him. Up until recently, I had no problem telling him everything that came to my mind. He's my friend. Now, the only secret that I can think of is that it's getting harder and harder to keep him in the friend zone.

But then again, nothing about our friendship has been typical lately.

He turns onto another street and slows down slightly as we drive through a neighborhood. "I'm scared of clowns," he admits, taking me completely by surprise.

"You're scared of clowns?" I repeat the question slowly as I process exactly what he said.

He nods before briefly glancing over at me. "Yep. *Big*-time."

"That doesn't count as a secret. Isn't everyone afraid of clowns?"

His eyes go wide, and his mouth falls open. "I'm confessing one of my biggest fears to you—one that I used to get made fun of by my friends at school for—and you're telling me that it isn't even a secret? Way to wound me, Char."

I can't help but laugh and shake my head. "I'm just saying I thought it was common knowledge that everyone was scared of clowns. They're creepy."

"I don't just find them creepy. It goes deeper than that. If I see one, I'm running in the opposite direction. When I was in school, the guys on my floor all decorated my room with clown posters. I walked in from spending the weekend with my parents to find creepy clowns plastered all over my room. I didn't talk to any of them for weeks."

"Even Cal?"

"I didn't talk to Cal for almost two weeks. I was so pissed off at him. He had to have been the one to tell everyone."

"What if Ava loves clowns? She might want one for one of her birthday parties down the road."

Jude hits the brakes. I rock forward, my hand finding the dash in front of me to steady myself. He looks at me with a horrified expression. "Why would you ever put that into the universe? I'll give Ava anything she wants in this world, but she isn't having clowns at a party. That's my only limit."

I know I shouldn't, but I laugh. I haven't ever seen Jude like this. He keeps the SUV at a stop in the middle of the road. Luckily, we're in a neighborhood with no other cars around as he stares at me with wide eyes and his mouth hanging open.

"I'm sorry," I start, trying to cover my laugh, but it doesn't work. The fact that I know I shouldn't be laughing only makes me laugh more. "I just can't get the mental picture out of my head of you running for your life at a child's birthday party just because a clown showed up."

He pushes on the gas, softly accelerating as we continue to drive through the neighborhood. I briefly glance at the monitor to find that Ava is still fast asleep despite her dad abruptly stopping the car moments ago.

"It's a secret for a reason, Char. I'm terrified of clowns, and if you ever tell anyone else, our friendship is over."

"Would you forgive me if I hung clown pictures all over your house this summer?"

"I think I'd forgive you for anything," he instinctively

responds. The car slows down, and his eyes find mine again.

My lips part, and my pulse spikes. His answer wasn't what I was expecting at all, and suddenly, my mouth feels too dry, and my head feels too fuzzy to even respond. There was something about the huskiness to his voice that made his words feel more raw.

I think I'd forgive you for anything.

What did he mean by that? The words felt like an admission, but of what? Am I thinking too much into it? Maybe that's just what friends do…forgive each other for anything. That's got to be what he meant.

Jude stares at me for a few more moments before ripping his gaze from me and focusing back on the road. We pick up speed once again. Even in the dimly lit car, I can see the way his jaw flexes. I wonder if he keeps his jaw tight like that because he regrets what he said or if he's fighting the urge to say more.

Before I can think too much about it, he wipes away the thick tension between us by smirking once again and looking over at me. "But I'd rather you not witness me lose my shit at the sight of a clown, so please don't put clown posters all over the house. I've got to keep up appearances." He winks, pretending everything is normal again, and I wonder if I was reading too much into the way he so easily said he'd forgive me for anything.

"No need to impress me." I try to keep my voice light and like I'm not replaying his words over and over again as I attempt to dissect what they could mean.

Jude smiles so wide that it shows off his deep dimples. "I always want to impress you, Char." He lets the words linger between us for a few moments before speaking up again. "Now it's your turn to share a secret."

"No, I need a different secret. Give me something more intense." I don't know why I push him to tell me more. Admitting he was scared of clowns should be enough, but it isn't. I want more. "Tell me something no one else knows." My words come out barely above a whisper, and I try to tell myself they don't come out desperate, but I know they do. I just want to feel like I matter to him…that he trusts me enough to tell me something he's never said to anyone else before.

"Something no one else knows?" He sits back in his seat and lets out a low whistle.

"Yes. I want to know a real secret."

He briefly looks over at me before focusing on the road once again. His jaw flexes as he keeps quiet. I want to know where his mind goes, but I don't say anything as I hope that he actually answers my question.

Finally, he sighs before opening his mouth. "I told you clowns were my biggest fear because it didn't feel too vulnerable to do so, but the truth is, my biggest fear is that I'm going fuck up being a dad somehow. I'm terrified of letting Ava down. She just has me, and it'd kill me for her to grow up and wish that she'd had more."

I swallow, because although I've suspected he's scared of how he's doing as a father, him admitting that to me still comes as a surprise. "Ava is *so* lucky to have you," I assure him. I try to put as much conviction as I can into my words.

He looks at me, and there's so much vulnerability in his eyes that it slices right through to my heart. This is the side of Jude I never expected. The one who allows me to see what's really underneath the surface and not just what he wants you to see. "Is she? I'm not sure I agree."

"Why?"

"Because I'm a thirty-six-year-old who has never been with someone long enough to even begin to discuss children with. It's not that I didn't want to be a dad; I always thought I eventually would become one. But I haven't taken anything seriously enough to really think about it. I'm not prepared to be a dad. I don't know how to explain it. It's just that everything in life has always been easy for me until Ava came into my life. Now, it's just so hard to imagine doing this alone and not fucking it all up."

I stare at him as he stares at the road ahead. It's at the tip of my tongue to remind him he doesn't have to do any of this alone. I'm here for him as long as he'll let me be, but for some reason, I can't say the words out loud. It doesn't feel right to say right now because I know he means that he doesn't have Ava's mother to help raise her. Ava doesn't have her mom, and that scares him, and me reminding him that I'm here for him—and her—doesn't change that.

"You're not going to fuck it up. I don't know if anyone's ever really prepared to become a parent. It's just something you do. You show up for her every single day and give it your best. That's all you can really do. But I mean it when I say she's lucky to have you, Jude."

He shakes his head as if he doesn't agree, and it breaks my heart.

"And it's normal to be scared. You're scared because you care."

He opens his mouth like he wants to say something else, but he snaps it shut. A few more seconds pass by before he runs a hand along his jawline. His shoulders relax with a long sigh before he opens his mouth to talk once again. "Your turn for a secret. And since you got two out of me, you also have to tell me something you haven't told anyone else before."

I stare at him, and it feels like I'm seeing him for the first time.

He isn't the Jude Kensington I met a year ago. He looks like him. He even acts like him. But the Jude from last year…I was able to see right through that Jude. The charm didn't work on me. Not really. But now there's more to the Jude sitting next to me. Underneath the charm and confidence, there's a man with fears and feelings. I've known him for a year. I've been close with him. But I haven't seen the side of him that he's been showing me since he found out about Ava. I like this raw and real version of Jude. The one where he isn't afraid to let me see him be vulnerable.

I swallow, realizing that I might like this version of him *too* much.

I might be catching feelings for my best friend, which is the worst thing that could possibly happen because he's made it more than clear that the only thing he needs from me right now is to be there as a friend for him.

So why am I sitting next to him, wondering what it'd be like if we were something *more* than friends?

27

Jude

Charlotte is quiet. She's rarely quiet. I don't know if her silence should worry me, and I don't think I like it.

Maybe I shouldn't have told her how scared I am of fucking things up as a dad. I hadn't planned on saying that. The words slipped out before I could think better of them. But it doesn't matter if they were intentional or not, they were still the truth.

She wanted me to tell her something I haven't ever said to anyone else, and my fear of being a terrible dad is the most real and raw thing I could tell her. I wish I could say I regret saying them, but I don't. For some reason, it feels right to admit that to her. Everything with Charlotte feels right—too right.

No matter how hard I'm trying to fight it, Charlotte means a lot to me. She means more to me than I think I even realize. And if she continues to be there the way that she has been for me and Ava when she doesn't have to be, the harder it'll be to keep walls up that prevent me from caring about her more than I should. The lines are bound to get blurry, and I already know it's going to be hard to look at her and just see a friend when I inevitably care for her more than I ever have any other woman who was just my friend.

It feels impossible to stay quiet as I wait for her to give me a secret. I feel almost naked beside her after what I just admitted. She wanted something I've been afraid to say out loud, and she got it. Now, I'm desperate for her to be just as vulnerable with me. I don't mind opening up to her, but I want her to feel like she can open up to me as well.

I clear my throat and risk a glance over at her for a moment before looking back at the road. "You must really be thinking about that secret." I can't help but break the silence. It feels too quiet between us. I need to fill it with something, even though I desperately wish I could get into her head and find out what's running through her mind as she sits there staring at me, not saying a word.

Why am I so desperate for her to open up to me?

I can't explain why, but I just want to know things that she might not tell anyone else. I want that closeness to her, no matter how dangerous that might be, especially since we've agreed to keep things between us strictly platonic.

"Lately, I've been wondering if my parents are disappointed in me," she admits.

My grip on the steering wheel tightens as my head spins in her direction. "What?"

I don't know what I was expecting her to say, but it certainly wasn't that.

She gives me a sad smile as she pushes a stray piece of blonde hair from her face. "Sorry, was that not what you were wanting?" There's a hesitant tone to her voice that makes me sad.

I swallow and shake my head. "No," I rasp. "That isn't it at all. I just don't understand how you could ever think that."

She's incredible. How could anyone ever be disappointed in her?

She pulls her gaze from mine and stares ahead. I follow her lead, but I can't help but wish I weren't in charge of driving the car right now so I didn't have to look away. I want to guess every thought running through her head just by studying the different movements of her face. Instead, I'm left staring ahead as I wait for her to explain what she means.

There's a soft *thud* as her head falls back against the headrest. "After college, I didn't know what I wanted to do with my life. I graduated with a degree in business because I wanted to run my own photography business, but it was hard to make any money from it. I worked as a waitress back home before coming out here to the Hamptons to work at Pembroke. My biggest dream was to come out here and open up a photography business. Pembroke wasn't quite that, but it was a way for me to make money. It felt like enough at the time. Like something they could be proud of me for. Now, I can't help but wonder if I've let them down by not wanting…more from my life."

I keep my mouth shut as I try to think of a nice way to tell her there's no way in hell that could actually matter to her parents. And if it did, then I'd like to have a serious conversation with them. They should be happy as long as she's happy.

I'm so lost in thought, being confused how she could actually think anyone could ever be disappointed by her, that I don't even realize I've stayed quiet until she speaks up again.

"It's just that my siblings all have these careers and families. And then there's me. Working at a country club and completely content doing that for now. I don't have any big plans. I know I love photography and would love to open up a business doing that one day, but I'm realistic enough to know it'd take a lot to actually pay the bills with it. What if they're disappointed that I'm just a cart girl?"

I can't help but scoff. "You're a cart girl at one of the best country clubs in the country. People apply for years to work at Pembroke and never even get an interview. The fact that you not only got an interview but also got the job is incredible. Plus, you got a promotion after only working at the club for a year. Everyone wants to be a cart girl because of the tips. Having Pembroke on your resume can get you a job at any other place you want. You're doing amazing, and I know your parents are proud of you."

When I glance over at her, I find her smiling. The tilt of her lips soothes something inside me. Maybe that beautiful curve of her lips means my words got through to her. "You haven't even met my parents. What if they have ridiculously high standards?"

"For one, I'd love to meet your parents." Now that I've said the words out loud, I realize just how much I'd love to be lucky enough that she wants to introduce me to her family. "And two, the way you talk about them tells me there's no way they're disappointed in you."

Charlotte is so quiet that I have to look over at her in an attempt to find out why she hasn't responded. I find her eyes already on me, a wide smile still on her face.

"What?" I ask.

"Have you been paying attention when I talk about my parents?"

I look back at the road as my eyebrows draw in. "Of course I have. I listen to everything you say."

"Prove it." The sassy tone to her voice tells me she doesn't believe me at all.

I sigh as I turn my SUV into a different Southampton neighborhood. "Your dad's name is Kyle, and your mom's name is Ruth, but you've told me one of your favorite things is that your dad has always called her Ruthie, and you think it's romantic. Your parents met right out of high school. You're the baby of five siblings. There's an age gap between you and the rest because I remember you saying that you were a bit of an *oops*. You have two sisters and two brothers, and all of them have kids that you helped watch while growing up. Your family's lived in Arizona your entire life, and they all still live there, and—"

"Okay, so it turns out you do listen," Charlotte interrupts, surprise laced in her tone.

I glance to my right and give her a cocky grin. "I told you I did. Why do you sound so shocked by that?"

"I don't know. You've got so many important things to remember."

I frown. "Yeah, and I remember what you tell me because you're important to me too."

Charlotte groans, and the sound has me looking over at her.

"What?" I ask, finding her with her head in her hands.

"Nothing," she rushes to get out. "It's just weird. I know you. We've been friends—*good* friends—for basically a year at this point. But it's like I'm still finding out things about you that take me by surprise. It's weird, that's all."

I tap my fingers against the steering wheel as I think about her words. "Is that a good thing or a bad thing?"

My question comes out more hesitant than I intended it to. I just can't tell if she likes what she's finding out about me or not. I think about her words again, realizing she has a point. We've spent so much time together in the last year. I can easily call her one of my best friends. But I do feel like I'm seeing new layers to her in the last couple of days since Ava came into the picture.

"I think it's both," Charlotte quietly admits.

My eyes find her for a moment, but instead of her blue gaze meeting mine, she stares at the monitor on the dash instead. I focus back on the road as my entire body feels tight with nerves at her answer.

"Both?" I ask hoarsely.

I want to look at her without having to worry about the road. I cut the wheel to the right and pull over in front of a random house before putting the car in park.

"What are you doing?" Charlotte asks.

I turn my body in my seat and really look at her for the first time this car ride. She has my full attention, and I'm ready to catalog every detail of her answer to my question.

"Waiting for you to tell me why it's both a good and bad thing that you're still finding out new things about me." I smile as I try to ignore the way my heart pounds. I don't know why I'm pushing this. Maybe I don't want to know her answer. It could crush me, or it could make me want things I absolutely shouldn't be wanting with how complicated things already are as I try to navigate being a dad.

Charlotte swallows, her gaze dropping to my lips for a fraction of a second before meeting mine again. There's a hungry look in her eyes that I've only seen once before—when we kissed in my living room. It disarms me because I'm not used to her looking at me like this. She never stares at my lips like she's hungry for them. She looks at me like she's begging to be kissed, and it's not something I'm used to, but it's something I desperately want.

I close my eyes and try to forget how she's looking at me. I try to wipe the sight of her looking at my lips from my mind. It's only been a couple of days since we agreed to keep things platonic. I thought I'd be so distracted by Ava that it'd be easy to look at Charlotte and not want her.

It turns out not wanting Charlotte might be impossible.

My life is as complicated as ever, and there are a million reasons why I need to not cross any lines with Charlotte. I need her in my life, and historically, I don't know how to do romantic relationships. With time, I would probably mess things up and lose her. I can't lose her. But I can't not want her either.

I open my eyes to find Charlotte staring right at me. Her chest rises and falls in short succession. The SUV feels far smaller than it actually is with how thick the tension is between us.

"Why is it both a good and bad thing, Char?" I ask again, not caring at this point how hoarse my voice is.

She opens her mouth to speak, but before any words come out, Ava lets out a loud wail from the back seat.

I swear Charlotte's shoulders relax at the sound of Ava crying.

We both look at the monitor to find Ava with her eyes wide open and her mouth poised to let out another cry.

"Looks like you should start driving again," Charlotte says.

All I do is nod before putting the car back in drive. Ava waking up to interrupt that moment is just another reminder that I shouldn't be wanting the things I'm wanting when it comes to Charlotte.

Maybe it's best that I don't know her answer to my question. At least, I keep reminding myself of that for the rest of the drive. Ava falls asleep instantly, but neither Charlotte nor I say another word. The silence between us only leads my head to wander to places it shouldn't.

It's wandering to the sight of her staring at my lips. At the groan she let out. I'm left spending the entire car ride wondering if I'm doing the right thing by trying to keep things platonic between us. It doesn't feel like the right thing. Not when all I want to do is smash my lips against hers and finish what we started a few nights ago.

28

Charlotte

I walk into the house after a long shift as a cart girl and find Jude lying on the ground in the living room as Ava rests on his chest. It's so adorable, and I wish I hadn't left my camera in my room this morning, because I want to capture the moment. My camera is quickly filling up with photos of Jude and Ava, and I love it and wish this were another one I could capture on film.

It's been two weeks since I moved in with Jude and Ava.

Two weeks of me always taking photos of them.

Two weeks of spending every spare second with them.

Two weeks of lingering stares from Jude.

Two weeks of him making me coffee every morning.

Of me going to bed thinking about him.

Of us taking care of Ava. Of it feeling like we're a family when I know we're not.

Two weeks of torture because as much as I love living with Jude and being there for him as he navigates this new life with Ava, it's also brutal to live with him.

I used to be able to pretend I was immune to him. His flirting didn't work. I didn't notice if he looked at me too long.

Now, I'm all too aware if he's looking at me when he doesn't need to be. If his skin brushes against mine, it's all I can think about for days after.

I thought I'd be able to push all nonplatonic thoughts of him to the back of my mind and focus on being friends, but it's getting hard. I think I'm catching feelings for Jude. Feelings that won't go away, no matter how hard I try.

"People at the club are wondering where you are," I tell Jude, setting my bag on the kitchen counter and immediately making my way to him and Ava.

"Doubt it," Jude notes, giving me a smile as I sit down next to the two of them. The moment Ava sees me, she smiles, and it completely melts my heart. She's only started doing that recently. She smiles at Jude way more, but I'll still take what I can get.

I narrow my eyes on him as I get comfortable on the floor. "You're typically at the club every day, and you haven't been there in over two weeks. People are absolutely asking about you. I had to tell them you were in the city because I'm not a good liar, and I didn't know what else to say." I hadn't realized how much people associated me with Jude until he didn't show up at Pembroke for two weeks, and suddenly, everyone was asking me about his whereabouts.

"Telling them I'm in Manhattan is perfect," Jude responds. He presses his lips to Ava's forehead before lifting her off his chest and handing her to me. "Want some baby snuggles?"

I laugh and gladly take Ava from him. I love my job at the club, but after working three days in a row, I'm excited for my days off again so I can spend more time with her. I'm lucky to have the weekend shift. It's when we get the best tips, and now that it's warming up, it's getting busier and busier. "I do need baby snuggles, but I feel like we should maybe talk about what your plan is regarding Ava. You can't hide here forever."

Jude sighs. He folds his hands behind his head and lies back, his gaze staying pinned on me. "It's not that I'm *hiding*. I'm just figuring out how to tell everyone about Ava. I want to do it the right way."

I nod because I understand he's in a tough position. He knows everyone at the club. They'll immediately notice it when he shows up with a baby all of a sudden. But I also don't want him to feel like he has to stay locked away all summer because of her. I play with Ava for a moment before I look back at Jude. "You show up, you tell everyone she's your daughter, and you leave it at that."

He laughs, and I hate how the deep, throaty sound makes my entire body warm. It's been over two weeks since I moved in with him, and I wish I could say that it's been easy keeping him in the friend zone, but that would be a lie. When we're not working, we spend every second together, and things just don't feel the same as they used to. He used to laugh without me feeling it through my entire body. My heart didn't race just at the sight of his smile. He used to just be *Jude*, my charming best friend. Now, he's someone totally different. Someone I have feelings for that I can't even begin to understand.

"I don't know if your plan will work or not. I think people will have lots of questions. I know my mom and dad did," he adds on at the last minute.

A week ago, Jude finally told his parents about Ava after getting the paternity test back. It was obvious that Ava was his child, but I can't help but wonder if part of the reason he waited to tell his parents was to confirm she was his biologically. I wasn't with him when he got the results, but I know he was stressed beforehand. He already loves her so much, and he was afraid of losing her if they came back negative.

I look over Ava's head to narrow my eyes at Jude. "You said your parents took the news great."

He smiles as if he wasn't expecting me to call him out like that. "They did," he responds slowly, the cocky tilt of his lips doing funny things to my stomach. "They're thrilled to have a grandchild and upset that they're out of the country with commitments and can't make it here for a few weeks to meet her. Even with all of their excitement, they had a ton of questions. I answered what I could, but I don't want to have to answer the questions of people who aren't family. I want to keep Ava as private as I can."

All I do is nod as I try to think how to respond. To be honest, I have questions for Jude as well when it comes to Ava, the biggest one being who her mother is. Does he still talk to her? Does she really want no involvement? I want to know, but I also don't want to be rude. If he wanted to tell me, he would. "You show up and introduce her as your daughter, tell everyone she's perfect, and then say you won't be answering any more questions about it. You're Jude Kensington. People listen to you. And even if they do ask questions, it doesn't mean you have to answer them."

He stares at me for a bit before his gaze flicks to Ava, then focuses back on me again. "Why do you have to be right?"

I can't help but smile. "Telling me I'm right? You might as well be talking dirty to me."

Jude's eyebrows rise to his hairline, and I freeze because I realize I definitely shouldn't have said that.

Ava squirms in my lap as she plays with a piece of my hair, but I can't focus on her. I can't focus on anything but Jude. His lips spread into a smile I can only describe as lethal. He lets his gaze slip to my lips for just a moment before his brown eyes meet mine. "Give me a chance, Char, and I can talk far dirtier than that."

My entire face gets hot. Even my chest feels flushed as my lips part, and I fail to even come up with a response.

We're toeing a dangerous line. I know it. He's got to know it too. But that knowledge doesn't stop my body from shivering, even though I'm not even remotely cold.

Before I can say anything else, a knock at the front door captures our attention.

Jude rips his gaze from mine, his smirk disappearing as he stands up and makes his way to the door.

"Were you expecting anyone?" I ask, my voice coming out breathier than I intended it to.

Jude shakes his head as he stops in front of the door. "Not that I know of." He looks through the window and then looks over at me with wide eyes. "Oh shit," he whispers.

My grip on Ava tightens. "What? Who is it?"

Jude presses his back to the door as his eyes scan the room. "It's Lucy and Cal."

It's my turn for my eyes to go wide. "What? She told me they weren't coming until next week."

"Well, they're here," Jude mutters. He leans to the left and glimpses through the window next to the door again.

"You know we can see you, right?" Cal yells from the other side. "Stop ignoring me and open the door."

I frown. "Have you been ignoring him?"

Jude shrugs. "I just didn't know how to tell my best friend over the phone that I'm a dad." His words come out quiet but rushed.

"Jude!" Cal yells from the other side of the door. "You're being weird. Open the door."

I know it isn't the time, but I can't help but laugh at the sight of a wide-eyed Jude. He stares at me as if I'm supposed to help in this situation, but I don't know what he expects me to do. Cal's already seen him, and he's incredibly stubborn. He won't be leaving until Jude opens the door.

"Everything okay in there?" Lucy asks, my best friend's voice softer and gentler than her fiancé's.

"I think you're going to have to open the door and tell them about Ava," I whisper. I give him an encouraging smile. "Think of it as practice for telling everyone else at the club."

Jude groans before turning around, grabbing the handle, and opening the door.

29

Jude

My heart slams against my chest as I open the door and meet my best friend's gaze. I plaster on a smile, hoping I don't look as guilty as I feel about avoiding him for so long.

Cal and Lucy stand on my front doorstep with curious looks on their faces.

"Why have you been ignoring my calls?" Cal immediately asks.

Lucy gives me her typical warm smile. "What he means is that he was bothered that you weren't answering him, and I was anxious to see Charlotte anyway, so we came a week early." She lifts a finger and pokes me in the chest. "Don't tell her we're here yet though. I want it to be a surprise."

I give a tight smile as I fight the urge to step out of the doorway and show them that it might be a little too late on the surprise front. "Well..." I laugh before looking back at Cal. I outstretch my arms and give him a cocky grin. "You missed me so much, you came a week early? I'm flattered."

I step in to give Cal a hug, but he pushes me away with a laugh. "You normally never leave me alone. I wanted to make sure something didn't happen."

Oh, something happened…

"I made you some food," Lucy announces, holding up a canvas bag that looks filled to the brim with different items. "Let me put the food in the fridge for you." She steps inside before I can stop her, and multiple things happen at once.

Lucy's shoes squeak against the hardwood as she abruptly stops in the middle of the foyer, her eyes pinned on Charlotte and the baby.

Cal follows her in and immediately looks from Charlotte to me.

I step inside and let the door close behind me.

"Surprise?" Charlotte smiles and adjusts Ava in her lap as she nervously looks around at the three of us in the foyer.

"Char, what are you doing here with a baby?" Lucy asks, her voice soft and full of confusion. She blinks a few times, as if she's trying to figure out if what she's seeing is real or not.

"Jude, why is there a baby in your house?" Cal adds on, his gaze still stuck on me.

I take a deep breath and plaster on my own fake smile. I'm incredibly excited to see Lucy and Cal. It's been entirely too long. I just thought I'd have time to really think about how I'd tell them about Ava.

"So…" I begin, letting out a low whistle as I try to think about where to even begin.

"Charlotte, is that *your* baby?" Lucy asks in disbelief. "It can't be…oh my God, did you have sex with Jude and have a baby?"

Charlotte blanches as her eyes go totally wide. "No, Jude and I didn't have sex," she hurries to get out. "And Ava isn't mine," she adds on, this time a little quieter. "You've seen me enough in the last year to know I haven't had a baby."

I tuck my hands into my pockets and close the distance until I'm standing next to Charlotte. Without me having to ask, she lifts Ava up to me, and I take her and cradle my daughter to my chest. "She's mine. It was a bit of a surprise, but she's perfect, and I'm excited for the two of you to meet her."

Lucy's eyes soften as she basically shoves the tote full of food against Cal's chest and heads in my direction.

"Jude Kensington, you're a *dad*?" She doesn't bother to hide the shock in her voice. She closes the distance and immediately reaches out to hold Ava's little hand. "Well, you're absolutely adorable and look just like your dad."

Cal lets out a grunt from where he places the bag on the kitchen counter. "Lucy, don't call Jude adorable."

I smile because as nervous as I was to tell two of my friends about Ava, it's going surprisingly well. At least so far. Things could still change.

Lucy looks over her shoulder at Cal. "I'm not calling Jude adorable. I'm calling baby Ava adorable. She just so happens to look just like her dad." Lucy pauses as her gaze rakes over Cal. "You're cute when you're jealous though."

Cal pulls his attention from his fiancée to look at me. "So this isn't a joke? You have a baby?"

I look down at Ava, who still rests in my arms, although I don't know how much longer I'll be allowed to hold her. By the way Lucy's looking at my daughter, she's moments away from snatching her from my grasp. "I'd never joke about something like this. I'm a dad. I don't know if I'm a good one or not, and it's still so new, but that doesn't change the fact that I have a baby."

Charlotte scoffs before she stands up and steps next to Lucy and me. "Don't talk like that. You're a great father. Ava's lucky to have you."

I give Charlotte a smile. It isn't the first time she's said that to me, but for some reason, it means even more to hear her say it in front of our friends.

Lucy keeps a grip on Ava's hand as she looks between Charlotte and me. Her eyes are wide as she continues to scan us. "So, not to keep asking questions, but if you and Jude haven't had sex—which I wouldn't judge, by the way. It'd be about time, actually—then why are you here right now?" Lucy's gaze stays pinned on Charlotte.

Char looks over at me as if she doesn't quite know how to answer the question. All I can do is smile, completely interested in what exactly she's going to say.

"Jude and I aren't going to have sex. He's my friend. He's a new dad. And I'm here because I live here now."

Lucy's mouth pops open as she looks between Charlotte and me. I risk a glance over at Cal and find him to be as shocked as Lucy, which is really saying something because Cal is usually great at keeping a poker face. "Since when can dads not have sex?" Lucy asks, and I can't help it, but I snort because the question takes me by surprise coming from her. Lucy's not normally the blunt one in their friendship; that's typically Charlotte's job.

"I'm not saying he *can't* have sex," Char hurriedly gets out. I try not to notice how her cheeks turn an adorable shade of red. "It's just that he and *I* aren't having sex. And I meant he's a dad and busy right now, and..." Her words fall off as she looks to me for help. All I do is stare at her with raised eyebrows as I keep my mouth shut. I'm looking forward to how she plans to fill in the blank myself.

She lets out an annoyed sigh when she realizes I'm not going to rescue her from Lucy's questions. "And I can't tell you a single detail about his sex life because it has nothing to do with me."

To be fair, my sex life is nonexistent. It has been for a while. Sure, I like to flirt, but I can't actually remember the last time I was intimate with someone. It's been months and months at least, but I don't find it necessary to point that out at the moment. Luckily, Charlotte continues to talk and leaves the topic of my sex life behind.

"And I'm living with Jude because I lost the place I was renting, and he offered me a place to stay for the summer." She grabs Ava's other hand and places a kiss to the top of it. "Which works out perfectly because I get to help out with my best girl and get all the baby snuggles."

"To be clear, I'm not forcing her to help me with Ava in exchange for a place to stay. She could stay here either way. It's just nice to have someone else here in case I fuck something up."

Charlotte rolls her eyes as she gives me a warm smile. "How many times do I have to tell you that you're a great dad until you believe me?"

Before I can respond, Lucy holds out her hands. "Can I hold her?"

I nod and pass Ava to her. Something in my chest tightens when I see Cal take a step closer to Lucy and the two of them begin to interact with Ava. It's so good to see two people I care about immediately accept Ava into the fold.

"Don't get any ideas." Cal laughs as Ava reaches for his nose. He playfully blows a raspberry, and I've never seen my best friend like this. He looks at his fiancée with raised eyebrows. "We need to make it to the wedding before we start trying for a baby."

Lucy gives him a guilty smile. "Oh, but Jude and Charlotte have a baby. Now *we* need a baby."

Charlotte sucks in a deep breath as her eyes immediately find mine. She gives me an apologetic smile, but I don't know why she feels the need to. I don't mind Lucy's words at all. The truth is, it does feel like Ava is both of ours. It feels like we're raising a baby together, and that realization doesn't bother me in the slightest. I can't imagine it any other way. I don't want to.

30

Charlotte

"Spill," Lucy demands, her eyes pinned on me as she bounces Ava on her leg. Cal and Jude have just walked away to grab a drink in the kitchen, and she's wasted no time demanding news from me.

I sit back on the couch. "What do you want me to spill?"

Lucy raises her eyebrows. "How about *everything*? You're living with Jude…he has a baby you're helping him raise…you two are basically playing house. Are you dating?" She asks the question so loud that I wish I could melt into the couch from embarrassment because there's no way Jude didn't hear it.

My eyes go wide as my head whips in the direction of the guys. Cal and Jude are on the other side of the kitchen, doing their own catching up, and luckily, they seem to be so deep in conversation that neither one of them heard Lucy's question.

When I look back at her, I can't help but narrow my eyes. "You're one of the quietest people I know, and yet, when you ask me if I'm dating Jude, you ask it so loud?"

Lucy shrugs. "I didn't ask it loud. Look at them…neither of them heard me."

I look over my shoulder again to find Jude and Cal still locked in conversation.

Jude has a wide smile on his face, and I try not to focus on how it makes me feel to see him happy like that. He didn't say it out loud, but I'm sure it was bothering him to ignore Cal. I'm sure he's feeling much better now that his best friend knows about Ava and that he doesn't have to hide anything anymore.

"Charlotte, did you fall in love and not tell me?" Lucy accuses, her tone full of shock and still *way too loud*.

I let out a choking sound, and apparently, Ava finds the noise hilarious because she gives me the biggest smile. "What the hell, Lucy?" I whisper, repeatedly aiming glances over at Jude to make sure he can't hear the intrusive—and completely false—questions my best friend is asking. "What's up with you today? You're never this nosy."

"To be fair, I've never seen you look at someone with actual heart eyes. This is new for me, and the only reason I can think of for you to be looking at Jude like that is if you're in love with him."

I scoff and shake my head. "Of course I'm not in love with Jude. We're just friends."

Lucy raises her eyebrows. "The way he keeps looking over here at you makes it seem like you might be *more* than friends."

I groan as I scrub my hands over my face. Lucy never interrogates me like this. She minds her own business. Maybe all the time she's been spending in Manhattan has made her more bold. "We're not more than friends. We're just…close. But close friends. You know we've spent a lot of time together in the off-season. Everyone else was so busy, and Jude's fun and a good time, and we hung out a lot and grew close, but that's all there is to it."

Lucy tickles Ava's stomach before giving me a look that tells me she doesn't believe me in the slightest. "Mm-hmm. And you living with him? Helping raise his baby? There's nothing more to that?"

I shake my head. "Besides you, he's my closest friend. I'd do anything for him, including helping him figure things out with Ava. Plus, how could I not help when he's giving me a free place to live? I love helping out with Ava."

Lucy's back to her normal self and keeps quiet. I stare at her, waiting for my best friend to respond, but it seems like now she's deciding to keep her thoughts to herself. I wait some more, hoping the quiet between us will prompt her to say whatever she's thinking. As I do, I let my gaze travel over her. It's been a couple of months since I've seen her in person. We text daily and do the occasional call, but it's been a long time since she and Cal have made it out here. She's been so busy planning a wedding and putting together her first cookbook, so she hasn't had time to come for a visit. I've missed her and am so excited she's here and will be spending most of her time in the Hamptons this summer.

Finally, her shoulders rise and fall with a deep breath. "Can I just say one thing about this, and then I'll mind my own business?"

I can't help but smile. "So *now* you want to mind your business? There's the Lucy I know."

Lucy gives a quick eye roll. "Listen, I remember you asking a million questions when you found out about Cal and me. I'm just doing my job as a best friend by ask—"

"Yeah, but you and Cal were a thing. Jude and I aren't."

Lucy gives a slow nod, but the way she looks at me through slightly narrowed eyelids tells me she might not fully believe me. "Well, I'm going to say what I want to say anyway."

All I do is nod, and my stomach twists in anticipation. I can tell just by the anxious way she looks at me that I might not like whatever's about to leave her mouth. "I love Jude. He's one of my favorite people on the planet. He's always been an incredible friend to Cal, and he has a big heart..."

"I can tell there's a *but* coming," I mutter, anxiously tucking a piece of hair behind my ear as I wait for her to continue.

"I just worry about you, Lucy. We all know Jude. He's fun and carefree and the biggest flirt there is. He has this way of sucking you in, but he's not the settling-down type."

All I can do is swallow, because a few weeks ago, I would've said the same thing about him. He's never pretended to be anyone but who he is. But something's changed. I think he's only shown everyone who he wants them to see. Underneath the flirting and the charm and the ridiculous jokes is a man who can be vulnerable and does want to be taken seriously; he just doesn't show it.

"We're friends," I manage to get out before she can say anything else. "I don't care if he's the settling-down type or not. That doesn't matter to me."

Lucy cocks her head to the side as her eyes scan my face. "Just be careful, okay? You're living with him, helping him raise his baby, and you guys have always had this flirting thing going on... I just don't want you to get so lost in playing house that you lose your heart to him."

I blink a few times as I stare at her, dumbfounded. I could tell by her demeanor she was going to say something I might not like, but I wasn't expecting this. My head spins at her words. She hasn't even been here twenty minutes, and somehow, she can see right through my lies. I plaster on a smile and lean forward to tickle the bottom of Ava's feet. "You have nothing to worry about, Lucy. Jude and I are just friends who are living together for the summer. There's nothing more to it."

"You promise?"

I hate lying to my best friend. I feel guilty even before the words leave my mouth, but no matter if my feelings toward Jude have changed, I'm not going to act on them. I know he's got a lot on his plate, and I'm not going to add to it by asking him to try and start a relationship with me. I know better. Plus, I have no idea what would happen between us if we did ever try being more than friends. I know I don't want to jeopardize the friendship we already have, so no matter what feelings I might be developing, nothing can come from them. I give Lucy what I hope is a convincing smile.

"I promise. Now, tell me about what's new with you."

31

Jude

"Well, that went well," Charlotte notes as we close the door behind Lucy and Cal. They spent two hours with us before leaving so we could put Ava down for bed for the evening.

I lean against the wall next to the front door and let out a relieved sigh. "Yeah, that went great. Better than I could've expected, honestly."

Charlotte smiles. "And what were you expecting?"

"For Cal to grill me with questions or for him to be pissed that I waited as long as I did to tell him."

"Did you guys have a good talk?"

For the better part of an hour, Lucy and Char sat on the couch catching up and playing with Ava while Cal and I stood in the kitchen. I hadn't realized that much time had passed until Lucy finally came into the kitchen, saying she was hungry and that we should eat the food she brought. It felt normal to have them here, even now with Ava in the picture. Lucy and Cal were both great with Ava. I honestly couldn't have asked for it to go any better, which is a huge relief.

"Our talk went really well. I'm excited they'll be here all summer."

Charlotte adjusts the position in which she holds Ava before walking to the kitchen. "I am too. It'll be a fun summer with everyone. You'll get to meet lots of new people, won't you, Ava girl?" She leans in and playfully kisses Ava on the cheek.

"Now that Cal and Lucy have met her, I think I'm more comfortable with taking her to Pembroke and letting everyone else meet her as well."

Charlotte pauses, grabbing a bottle from the drying rack. "Yeah?"

I nod. "Now that my parents and two of my closest friends know about her, I don't feel as nervous about letting everyone else know too."

I'm not sure what exactly I was expecting from Cal and Lucy, but the way they just accepted the news without asking many questions wasn't it. I don't know if I'm just naturally more curious than anyone else, or if they could just tell I wasn't ready to divulge more, but I know if the roles were reversed and Cal suddenly had a baby, I'd have a million questions.

There was something about watching Lucy, Cal, and Charlotte play with Ava that made me feel like everything was going to be okay and that I might actually be able to handle all of this. Today was only the first day that Lucy and Cal met my daughter, but there was something about the effortless way we all interacted that proved that maybe I'm the one overthinking this, and I need to just live my life.

"That's good," Char responds. She keeps her voice gentle as she begins to make a bottle one-handed. I already offered to take Ava from her or make the bottle myself, but she refused it. She said Cal and Lucy stole all the time with Ava while they were here, and she wanted to get her "Ava fix" before her bedtime. "You shouldn't be locked away at home all summer because you have a baby. You don't deserve that, and neither does she. No one is entitled to information you don't want to give them. If they ask you personal questions, politely tell them to fuck off."

I laugh as I grab the edge of the kitchen island and lean forward. "Did you just cuss around my daughter?"

Char's eyes go wide. She gives me an apologetic smile as she sets the bottle in the bottle warmer. "Maybe. Luckily, she isn't old enough to repeat anything yet. I promise I will not be dropping the f-bomb around her at that point."

There's a tightening in my chest at the mention of her still being in our lives years from now. It's not that I expected Charlotte not to be around by then—she's been so deeply ingrained in my life over the past year that I really can't imagine life without her—but she's also never really talked about her long-term plans. I know she wants to open a photography business here, but I don't know how serious she is about it. With how close she is with her family, I can't help but wonder if the appeal of the Hamptons will wear off for her and she'll want to return to Arizona. I hate the thought of her moving so far away, and I can't pretend it isn't scary to think about the possibility of her not always being a part of our lives.

"Maybe we'll start a swear jar when she gets older. She'd make a fortune off the two of us."

Char throws her head back and laughs. "Yes, she will."

I smile as my body relaxes slightly at her agreeing with me. If she thinks Ava will make a fortune off both of us, then maybe it means she doesn't have any intentions of leaving us. I hope that's true. Even when I think about the future and what things will look like for my daughter and me years from now, I can't help but picture Charlotte still in our lives too.

Ava wriggles in Charlotte's arms as she lets out a small whine. I tilt my head toward my daughter. "Want me to take her?"

Charlotte shakes her head. "No, I've got her. I might go sit on the couch and get her comfy if you want to bring the bottle over once it's warm."

"Of course."

Charlotte lifts Ava up and brings her closer to her face. "Your bottle's almost done, I promise." In an attempt to keep her from fussing, she leans in and blows a raspberry against Ava's neck. Instead of crying, Ava lets out an excited squeal.

Charlotte's eyes immediately find mine. "Was that a laugh?"

I can't help but smile at her excitement. Charlotte said that Ava is now around the age where babies can start laughing, so the two of us have been trying hard to be the first person to get her to do it. "It was close," I respond.

Charlotte leans in and blows another raspberry against Ava's neck. Ava's tiny body scrunches together as she lets out another squeal.

"Ugh, so close," Char mutters as she pulls away from Ava's neck with a smile. "I'm going to get the first laugh out of you, Ava girl."

I shake my head and close the distance so I'm standing right next to them. I lean in and place a kiss against my daughter's cheek. "I don't think so. You've got to laugh for me first, baby girl." I repeat the same thing Charlotte just did and blow a raspberry against Ava's neck.

She lets out the same excited noise, but I don't stop. I blow another one against the ticklish spot between her neck and shoulder in hopes of finally getting a real laugh out of her.

Ava reacts the same way she has been, holding out on giving us a laugh despite my best attempts.

"You're cheating," Charlotte mutters. She turns slightly, pulling Ava away from me in an attempt to prevent me from being able to try to make Ava laugh.

My eyes go wide as I shake my head. "Oh, no you don't."

"I'm going to get you," Charlotte says in a baby voice before leaning in and blowing another raspberry against Ava's neck. She glances at me while she does it, clearly amused with herself.

I grab Charlotte by the hips so she can't move as I lean in and press my mouth against Ava's neck. We're both blowing raspberries against her skin. She lets out one excited squeal after another before letting out the most adorable little laugh.

Both Charlotte and I continue to blow the raspberries against her skin until she lets out another laugh, this time an intense belly laugh that is the cutest sound in the world.

I freeze.

Charlotte freezes.

Our eyes connect as both of our faces break out into deep smiles.

"She did it!" Charlotte gets out, her words coming out rushed from her excitement. The joy is all over her face, and it makes my body heat and my chest feel tight again.

"That was a laugh, right?" I ask. My heart completely soars because I swear I just heard my daughter laugh for the first time.

Charlotte nods, and I can't help but think how absolutely beautiful she is in this moment. Her eyes are bright and crinkle at the sides, thanks to her wide smile, and I'm so happy that I get to share this special moment with her. There's nobody else

I'd rather share it with.

"Yes. That was definitely a laugh." Charlotte huffs out a quiet laugh herself, her gaze focused on me.

I don't know how long we stand there and stare at one another. We both wear the biggest smiles, and my hands are still on the small of her waist. Our shoulders rise and fall in quick succession, her inhales happening at the same time as my exhales.

Time seems to stand still, and not for the first time, all I can think about is kissing Charlotte. I don't know if I'm relieved that Ava is between us or not. If she weren't in the middle, I don't know if I'd be able to resist leaning in and pressing my lips to Charlotte's.

It's harder and harder to fight my attraction to her, especially after a moment like this. A moment where I'm so grateful to be going through this season of life with her. My feelings for her grow deeper by the day, and it's getting harder to not want more.

I don't want to ruin the friendship Charlotte and I share. It's important to me. One of the most important relationships I've ever had. But I also can't imagine just being her friend for the rest of my life. Not when the smile she gives me lights up my entire world. Not when it seems like all I can think about these days is her.

"It was me who made her laugh," Charlotte points out, tearing me from my thoughts. She pulls her bottom lip between her teeth as she looks up at me through her eyelashes. If only she knew what she was doing by looking at me like that. How could I not develop feelings for her?

I shake my head. "Not a chance. She wasn't laughing until I joined in. It was all me."

"Sure it was."

I lift a brow at her sassy tone. "*Sure it was*?" My grip on her waist gets tighter as I mock the way she talks to me. I squeeze her sides, my heart soaring at the loud laugh she lets out.

"Jude! I'm holding your daughter. Don't tickle me."

I lean in, causing my nose to brush against Charlotte's cheek as I continue to squeeze her sides. "Hold on tight, Char."

Charlotte's laughter is so loud that I can't help but laugh along with her. She squirms to avoid me, but it's no use. She can't get away from me.

I don't know if it's my laugh or Charlotte's laugh, or maybe it's a combination of the two, but Ava lets out another deep belly laugh.

The three of us fall into a fit of laughter in the middle of my kitchen, and it's one of those moments I never want to forget.

Me.

Ava.

Charlotte.

Just the three of us.

The perfect moment with my perfect girls.

32

Charlotte

Jude needs to get out of the house.

It's been over three weeks since Ava came into his life, and while it's been incredible to get so much one-on-one time with the two of them, he's got to leave the house eventually. Lucy and Cal have come over a few times in the last week, which has made it so he sees someone other than me, and as happy as I am that he's seeing friends, I still think he needs to get out more. Every time I'm at Pembroke, it feels like all I do is dodge questions about Jude and where he's been. Even the always-quiet Tyson Bishop has started asking about Jude's whereabouts.

Today was another day of making up lies about where Jude has been while working my cart shift at Pembroke. Now that the busy season in the Hamptons has officially begun, we've been slammed at work. It's nice because I'm making more money off tips than I could ever dream of, but after working my three-day shift every week, I'm exhausted. It's Sunday evening after another long weekend of work and I'm so excited for a low-key night in with Jude and Ava.

But Jude's about to find out that his *nights in* are done for.

This Friday, Pembroke is throwing its annual party to kick off the season, and if I have anything to say about it, Jude will be attending with Ava.

I'm walking into the house, thinking about how I can convince Jude to finally go to Pembroke, when I notice how quiet it is. Jude normally spends most of his time with Ava in the living room if she's awake. A glance at my phone in my hand to check the time tells me that Ava should be awake right now. We've been doing our best to get her on a schedule so she sleeps better at night. I've read way more about wake windows than I ever thought I would, and where it's been great during the day to have her sleep on a strict schedule, we're still waiting for that to translate into nighttime sleep. We've only been on the new schedule for a week, so it's still a work in progress. Some nights, she's slept great; other nights, Jude and I have spent a few hours driving around the Hamptons while she slept peacefully in the back. I haven't said this out loud, but I haven't minded the late-night rides.

It lets me spend more time with Jude. There's something about driving around with him in the dark of night that makes it feel like it's okay to let down my walls with him. We're able to tell each other secrets and get to know one another on a personal level without physically crossing any lines we shouldn't. He has to keep his focus on driving, and a center console and a seat belt prevent me from doing anything crazy…like leaning in and kissing him.

I walk through the quiet house, wondering where Jude and Ava could be. There are still toys strewn across Ava's playmat in the living room, and a glimpse into Jude's room tells me they aren't in there either.

I frown as I continue to search for them. If his car weren't sitting in the driveway, I'd wonder if maybe he did finally decide to go out with Ava during the day. But since it was still parked in the same spot it always is when I got home from work, I know that he's got to be here somewhere. I almost give up looking and call him when I sneak a peek into Jude's office.

I don't come in here often. If Jude has to work, he typically shuts the door and doesn't have time to chat. It's at the very end of the hallway and isn't a room I ever visit. If I could find him anywhere else, I wouldn't even think about trying his office, but I take a glimpse into the room, stopping in my tracks at what I see.

Before I can think better of it, a smile spreads across my cheeks. I cross my arms over my chest and take in the view.

Jude sits at his desk, his glasses askew on his face due to how his cheek is pressed against his office chair, and he's fast asleep. It's funny that I never even knew he wore glasses until recently—he always wore contacts—but the lack of sleep and leaving the house has him wearing glasses most of the time. I both love it and hate it. I love it because he looks phenomenal in glasses. I hate it because he looks *phenomenal* in glasses. I already start my mornings with a pep talk on why I can't fall for my best friend. Him walking around in a slutty pair of glasses doesn't help with that.

My eyes move from his sharp cheekbones and angled jaw down to his chest. Ava lies against it, also fast asleep, her little butt in the air.

I have to pull my eyes away from him for a moment because I can't handle the sight of him sleeping so peacefully with his daughter on his chest. It makes my heart flutter and my body warm with how incredibly adorable it is. My ovaries basically scream at the sight.

His laptop sits open in front of him, but it's since gone to sleep, showing a screensaver instead. He makes my heart soar all over again, and he doesn't even know it, because his screensaver is a picture of the three of us.

It's a selfie I took that he insisted I send to him. We were all lying on the couch one day when I couldn't help but snap a photo. When he asked me to send it to him, I never imagined he'd make it into his computer's screensaver.

This is another thing I both love and hate. I think it's incredibly sweet that of all the photos he has, especially all the ones I've sent him that are just Ava, or just him and Ava, he chose one that included me. I can't help but love that. But I'm so conflicted, because all I can think about is what Lucy said when she first learned of Ava. It does feel like I'm playing house with Jude. I wouldn't change it for the world. I want to be here with him and Ava, but with every day that passes, it does feel like we're becoming this little family, which is incredibly dangerous for my heart.

I let my gaze travel over Jude's face as he sleeps peacefully at his desk. I soak in the opportunity to really get a good look at him when he can't catch me. From the very first day I met Jude, I thought he was one of the most attractive men I'd ever seen. The problem was…he was hot, but it was clear from the very beginning that he was a womanizer. I knew how men like him worked because I'd dealt with them before. They charm you, make you feel like you're the most interesting and special woman in the world, and the moment you finally give in and sleep with them, they're gone.

I didn't want to do that with Jude. I knew Cal and Lucy were inevitable, and if I wanted to still see my best friend even after she got a serious boyfriend, I needed to get along with her boyfriend's best friend.

So I wrote Jude off from the very beginning. He was a member at Pembroke anyway, and I could use that as an excuse to keep him at arm's length. I told him I didn't date members, which wasn't technically a lie. I hadn't ever dated a member before. But if he wasn't Cal's best friend, I might've been foolish enough to think I'd be the girl to change him from playboy to committed in no time.

The more time we spent together, the more I genuinely started to like him. It was hard not to. He quickly became a good friend of mine. I liked spending time with him. And once everyone left last summer and he was still here, it felt right to keep seeing him. We flirted because it was fun, but it was clear we both knew we wouldn't be more than friends.

And then…we kissed, and everything changed. I don't know if it was the kiss, or Ava showing up, or a combination of both things, but all the reasons I used to think it was better for Jude and me to just be friends no longer make sense.

Yes, he's a playboy. He's charming and appears not to take anything seriously, but that's just what he wants you to see. I think he's never settled down because he doesn't want to get hurt. When he cares about something, he cares *deeply*. That has become obvious with his desire to be the best possible father to Ava. Now that I've seen this side of him, I think Jude would be an incredible partner if he wanted to be. And sometimes, by the way he stares at me when he thinks I'm not looking, it makes me wonder if things were different, uncomplicated, that maybe he'd want to try with me.

I close my eyes for a minute, needing a break from looking at his perfect features.

A harsh realization sets in as I realize it's too late.

I want things I shouldn't want when it comes to Jude Kensington.

I want it *all* with him.

I want to be his friend. His best friend. The kind of best friend that you fall in love with because things between you are too perfect.

I want to try for a future and to make things serious and to give the two of us a real shot.

But I can't want those things. Not when I can't ask him to try with me. His focus needs to be on Ava, and I understand that. I don't want to make things more complicated. Plus, I know it hasn't been long, but I love Ava as if she were my own blood. It's impossible not to. I don't want to try something with Jude, and something bad happens between us, and then I never see Ava again.

That would destroy me.

I open my eyes and let out a long sigh before looking at my feet for a moment. I know that it's for the best that I continue to not act on my feelings for Jude. He doesn't need *complicated* right now. It's just getting harder and harder not to take things further.

When I look back at Jude, I find his eyes slowly opening. The moment our gazes connect, he gives me a lazy smile, and I have to stifle a groan at the sight of it. It's perfect. He's too handsome for his own good, and I can't handle it. Not when he smiles at me the way he is right now. Not when he makes me feel like no other woman matters to him.

I think not falling for my best friend is going to be impossible.

33
Jude

I blink a few times, wondering if it's actually Charlotte standing in my office doorway or not. I don't know if she's really there or if it's just a dream. She stares at her feet, her shoulder resting against the doorframe as she seems to be deep in thought.

I use the opportunity to just look at her. I'm still in that in-between state of being asleep and waking up, and I'm not confident she's actually there. It'd make sense if I were just imagining things. If I'm not thinking about Ava, I'm thinking about Charlotte. It's impossible not to constantly think about her. Her never leaving my mind has bled into me dreaming about her as well.

Maybe this is just another dream. No matter if it's real or fake, I allow myself to really look at her for a few seconds without being caught.

She wears her Pembroke uniform…the *dreaded* uniform. The one that taunts me every morning when she goes into work and every evening when she gets back. The hem of it always dances along her upper thigh, making me think about what it'd be like to push the fabric up her skin to reveal more of her to me. I hate the thought of her wearing it all day at work, but I keep my jealousy to myself. She doesn't need to know the envy that boils deep in my gut when I think about her wearing that short skirt all day on the course, around the other members. I don't want her to wear a skirt for anyone but me, and the daydreams I've had about her wearing nothing but that pleated skirt for me are happening far too often.

Charlotte pulls her gaze from her feet, and the moment our stares collide, I can't help but smile. I don't know how to explain it, but life just always feels a little better when Charlotte looks at me. Maybe it's because it feels like she sees a version of me others don't, or maybe it's because no matter how hard I try to fight it, I'm developing feelings for her. Either way, I let the feeling in for a moment instead of trying to stifle it the way I always do.

She rubs her lips together before a slow smile spreads across her mouth.

Those lips.

The ones I'm desperate to kiss again.

I want her to smile at me just like she is right now, but instead of seeing it, I want to feel it against my own lips.

I want so many things when it comes to her.

"Did I wake you up?" she asks, keeping her voice quiet.

I shake my head. The movement makes my glasses shift on my face, reminding me that I was even wearing them at all. "No, you didn't. You just get home?"

Charlotte nods and takes a step into my office. "Yeah. It was so quiet, and I couldn't find you. Didn't expect to find you fast asleep at your desk with Ava in tow."

A small rumble of a laugh leaves my chest as I look down at Ava. Charlotte's been working hard at getting Ava on a sleep schedule, and she's supposed to sleep in her crib, but she wasn't having it today. "I promise I tried putting her in her bed. She kept screaming instead of sleeping, and I needed to get some work done, so I let her sleep on me instead."

Charlotte tilts her head to the side. "Which led to you sleeping too?"

I shrug. "I was trying to at least catch up on my emails, but apparently, my lack of sleep caught up to me, and the emails finished the job."

"Speaking of you working, I had an idea while at work today, and I want you to listen to it before you tell me no." She steps farther into my office before leaning against the edge of my desk.

I smile, unable to resist messing with her. "No."

Charlotte's mouth falls open. "I told you to listen before you told me no." She keeps her voice barely above a whisper, but even so, I can tell that she isn't amused by me immediately saying no.

My smile grows. "If you're telling me to listen before saying no, then I already know I'm not going to like whatever you're about to say."

She purses her lips and narrows her eyes. "Jude, you're going to listen to the one thing—no, actually, *two* things—I have to say before saying no." With every word she says, she leans in closer as she continues to scold me.

God, I love messing with her. I resist the urge to point out the truth: with her this close to me, I think I'd agree to anything. "I'll listen, but I bet the answer is still going to be no," I finally get out. I try to ignore the way in which my heart races at our close proximity. Yet again, I'm thankful for my infant daughter being between us so I don't do anything I shouldn't.

Charlotte pouts for a minute before leaning back slightly. She tosses her hair over her shoulder. "So, I've been thinking…"

I adjust my position in my office chair, my hands resting against Ava's back as I make sure she stays snug against my chest with the movement. "I'm nervous," I admit with a laugh.

"I know you said you were going to look into a nanny for Ava, but you haven't, and what you're doing now isn't working. You need to be able to work without worrying about Ava as well."

I frown because I wasn't expecting her to lecture me on this. I meant it when I said I'd look for a nanny; I've just been putting it off. I've only been in Ava's life for almost a month. It feels wrong to hand her off to some stranger while I work. I don't know how people find childcare, but I'm just not ready to leave her with anyone but me or Charlotte.

"*Char.*" Her name comes out more as a warning than I was expecting it to. I quietly clear my throat in an attempt to make my next words softer. "I promise I'm handling it. I can watch her and get my work done too. I don't need a nanny."

Charlotte nods in understanding. Her gaze rakes over my face for a moment before she opens her mouth to speak. "I understand you're not ready to hire a nanny yet, and to be honest, I can't imagine just leaving Ava girl with someone random anyway, but you still help run an entire company, Jude. You need help."

"I don't need help. I've got it." I try to lace as much conviction as I can into my words, hoping that gets her to believe me.

"You do need help. Most weeks, I only work Friday, Saturday, and Sunday. Let me watch Ava at least a few weekdays while you work."

"No."

She lets out an adorable little huff. "What did I say about saying no?"

"I listened to your idea and then said no. I'm not making you watch my daughter for me so I can work on your days off. You work long days all weekend and deserve your days off."

"I spend them with you and Ava anyway."

I grind my teeth together as I think of how to respond. She has a point. She typically spends her days off with us, but I've tried telling her not to. I don't want her to feel like she's responsible for Ava. It isn't her job to watch her. "You're not using your days off to watch Ava."

"Yes, I am."

"No, you aren't."

"Are we going to keep arguing about this, or will you just listen to me?"

I open my mouth to respond, but she lifts her hands to stop me.

"No. I don't want to hear that Ava isn't my responsibility and that you didn't have me move in with you so I could watch Ava. I want to watch Ava, and you're not going to stop me."

My jaw flexes, and I try to think of another reason to tell her no. I just don't want to feel like a burden to her or for her to feel like she has to fix things for me. "Char, you deserve days off."

"Let me worry about that. I'm perfectly fine spending my days off with Ava. We'll have girls' day while you work, because what you're doing now isn't sustainable, Jude. Accept the help, and just say thank you."

I don't know why I do it. It happens so fast that I can't even think better of it. One moment, my hand is pressed against Ava's back, and the next, it's reaching out and taking

Charlotte's hand in mine. "Thank you." The words come out a bit hoarse. "I'm not taking all your days off, but maybe this week, we'll start with you watching her for two days and then go from there."

"Okay," she responds, her voice barely above a whisper. Her gaze darts to where my hand still sits on top of hers. I hadn't even realized my thumb was brushing over her skin until I follow her gaze and find our hands still entwined.

"But you have to promise if it feels like too much, or if Ava starts to feel like she's a burden, that you'll tell me." My words come out hurried because it's one thing to worry in my head about Ava ever feeling like a burden for Charlotte, but it's another thing to say it out loud. I just don't want Charlotte to feel like things with Ava and me are too much to handle.

I don't want to give her any reason to leave. And that includes asking too much of her, especially when it comes to my daughter.

Charlotte's head rears back slightly. "Ava could never feel like a burden to me." Her words come out a little louder than they have been, but it doesn't wake Ava. She stays fast asleep on my chest, completely unaware of her surroundings.

"You say that now, but what happens when you're tired and you just want a day off, but instead, you're having to watch a baby who isn't yours?"

She winces but recovers quickly. Her smile is soft as she looks from our joined hands to me. "I know myself well enough to know that I won't feel that way. I wouldn't be offering to help if I thought I couldn't handle it or if I didn't want to. I know Ava isn't mine, but I still care about her—and you—so please let me help."

It's silent as the two of us stare at one another. I'd give

anything to get in her head to find out what she's thinking. She hasn't pulled her hand from mine, and I'm dying to know if feeling my skin against hers is driving her as wild as it's driving me. It feels like a million different things go through my head. I want to tell her that I'm getting far too used to her being in our lives. I want her here forever, and I've never wanted someone the way I want her, and that's terrifying.

She woke up one day and decided she was going to move to the Hamptons. She left her entire family and everything she's ever known to come out here. I respect the hell out of her for it. She had a dream of moving to the Hamptons and chased it, no matter who she had to leave behind and miss to achieve it. But now, with my feelings growing deeper for her with every day that passes by, I can't help but be scared about what happens if she wakes up one day and decides to leave. Nothing ties her here to the Hamptons…to us. What if she decides she'd rather do photography somewhere else? She could leave at any moment, and there's nothing I can do about it. Because of that, it's scary to lean on her, especially with how deep the feelings I'm developing for her are.

"You're not arguing, which I can only assume means you're going to let me help you."

My cheeks twitch with the hint of a blooming smile. "It's as if you know me so well."

This makes Charlotte smile—a real one. Her fingers move underneath mine, but she still doesn't make an effort to move, so neither do I. I soak in the connection of our skin for as long as I can, even if it is just a hand hold.

"Well, perfect. While you're staying silent, it's time for you to hear the second thing I have to say. The same rules as before apply. No talking or saying no until I finish."

My grip on her hand tightens as I keep my gaze locked on her. "Lay it on me."

The way she bites her lip and pauses before speaking up tells me that I might like this idea even less.

34

Charlotte

Jude's hand on top of mine feels nice. I know I should probably pull my hand out from underneath his, but I don't want to. I like feeling his skin against mine. Plus, I know that with what I'm about to say, he might be the one to break the connection anyway.

I pull my bottom lip between my teeth as I watch him carefully. We've briefly talked about him leaving the house and taking Ava to Pembroke, but it's been days since then. I'd let it go for a bit, but now I'm ready to push it and really convince him that he needs to get out of the house.

"The second thing is, it's time for you to go to Pembroke… with Ava."

The only reaction he gives my words is the twitch of his fingers against mine. He keeps his face the same, his eyes wide and staring at me, while there's the slightest hint of a smirk on his lips. "Why do you say that?" he finally asks.

"Because you can't hide away in this house forever. Ava deserves to get out, and so do you."

"I'm just fine here with you and Ava and the occasional visit now from Cal and Lucy." He looks down at Ava for a moment. Despite the two of us no longer talking in hushed tones, she still stays fast asleep and completely unbothered. "And Ava's seemed happy as can be recently."

I frown, wanting him to know that I don't love the answer he just gave me. "Jude, you love Pembroke. Before Ava, you spent every day there. It's time for you to get back to the club. You're going tomorrow."

He pulls his hand from above mine, and I miss the warmth of it the moment it's gone. I try not to let him see the disappointment on my face about no longer feeling his skin against mine.

"I didn't realize you were the boss of me." There's humor in his tone, and that smirk still hasn't left his lips. If anything, the corner of his mouth has lifted a little higher.

"I *am* the boss of you when you become unreasonable. You're a little social butterfly who has been cooped up far too long. It's time for you to spread your wings and go back to Pembroke. I've scheduled you a tee time with Tyson tomorrow morning while I watch Ava."

He leans back a little as his eyebrows rise to his hairline. "Babies aren't allowed on the course."

I can't help but smile because he hasn't said no. "Well, I figured you could go alone and tell the people most important to you about Ava before bringing her there. Tyson's been asking about you, and so I arranged for the two of you to golf together tomorrow. I think Cal's going to try to join, but he and Lucy have some wedding planning meetings first."

"What if I don't want to golf with Tyson tomorrow? If you're watching Ava, shouldn't I be working during that time?"

I roll my eyes and swat at the air. "You'll golf in the morning, work in the afternoon. You need to get out, even for just a few hours. Tell who you want to tell about Ava, because by Friday, when Pembroke has their big welcome party, you're going to be there, and Ava's going with you."

"I'll go on Friday under one condition."

I straighten my spine and smile because this is easier than I thought it'd be. "What is it?"

"You go to the party with us."

My lips part, and I hope he can't see the blush creeping up my chest and into my cheeks at his one condition. "Oh, you don't have to bring me with you."

"I know. But I want to bring you. If I'm going to Pembroke on Friday, I'm going with my girls. *Both* my girls."

There's a loud whooshing sound in my ears, and I swear I can hear my own heartbeat.

My girls.

Both *my girls.*

I know he doesn't mean anything by it. He probably doesn't even realize what he's said, but that doesn't matter. I realize what he said, and it's something I can never unhear.

His girl.

I rub my lips together because if I don't, I might not be able to fight the giddy smile threatening to overtake my mouth.

I know I shouldn't want to be his girl, and I know that I'm reading way too much into what he just said, but none of that matters right now. I'm both elated and devastated to be called his because there's nothing I want more than for our circumstances to be different so that could be possible.

Jude gently adjusts Ava on his chest before leaning forward. "Char." My name comes out soft and gentle, and I swear there's affection in his tone, but I don't know if that's just my own wishful thinking or the truth.

"Mm-hmm?" I still can't really form words. All I can manage is a small hum as I try to internally calm myself down at being referred to as *his girl*.

What is wrong with me?

Jude Kensington is getting to my head.

"Will you go to the welcome party with us on Friday, or are we all three ditching it to stay home instead?"

"You're going," I manage to get out. My words come out barely above a whisper.

"I'm not going if you're not going."

He smirks and lifts an eyebrow, a silent dare for me to argue.

I can't.

I look at my lap for a moment as I think about what to say. I want to go to the welcome party with him. I've never been. Unless you're working the event, which I never did when I worked at Pembroke Grill, and won't be as a cart girl, then Pembroke employees aren't invited. Members on the course the last couple of weeks have been gushing about how fun it is. I've secretly wanted to go, but I was too nervous to ask Jude to take me.

When I look up, I find him still looking at me, waiting for an answer.

I sigh before finally failing at hiding my smile any longer. "Fine. We're going."

His smile gets wide, and he shows off his dimples, which drive me more mad with each day that passes by. "Good. It's a *date*."

A choking sound comes from the back of my throat. It's so loud that it wakes Ava up. She stretches against Jude's chest, her lips pressing together in a thin line as she lifts her head.

"Jude!" I scold. I try to keep my voice down to a whisper, but I don't know if it matters. Ava's eyes pop open, and she immediately smiles.

"What?" he asks innocently. He leans in and presses a soft kiss to his daughter's head while he waits for me to respond.

"You're flirting, and that's breaking the rules."

"Char, I don't know if we're really playing by the rules anymore."

My mouth snaps shut, and my pulse skyrockets. He has a point, but I didn't think he'd say it out loud. I rip my gaze from his to look at Ava. She blinks repeatedly, the cutest little smile on her face as she shows off the same dimples she got from her dad.

"Friday is a *friend* date." I try to really emphasize the word *friend*, even though it feels weird leaving my mouth. Jude is my friend, but it's so much more than that now. There's so much more to him, and I don't even really understand my feelings for him. All I know is that I don't *need* to understand how I feel about him because it doesn't matter. We need to stay friends, no matter how I feel. And to maintain that boundary, I can't be blurring lines in my head and think that Friday is anything more than an evening shared between two friends.

Jude snickers before standing up with Ava. "Whatever you say," he practically sings. Why does he look so amused by this? We started this interaction with him seeming reserved and not warm to the idea of leaving the house or seeing anyone, but now it's ending with the return of his casual smirk and effortless flirting. His demeanor has changed, and I don't know why. Is he excited about getting out of the house? Maybe the knowledge that he's finally going to stop hiding here with Ava and shielding her from the world feels like a weight off his shoulders.

Or maybe he's excited about the date.

The thought pops into my mind without warning, and it's completely unwelcome because I know it isn't the truth. Or if it is, his mood change isn't because the date is with *me*. It's probably that he's just finally excited to see his other friends.

That's got to be it.

"How about I take Ava for a bit so you can finish those emails?" I offer, needing a change of subject. Now that he's standing up, he seems way too close.

Or maybe I'm just all too aware of his presence after he called me *his* and then called our plans together a *date*, all within a few minutes.

"You worked all day. You aren't taking her."

I ignore him and reach for Ava. Her entire face lights up, and I can't help but return her smile because she's too damn cute. I wrap my hands underneath her armpits and go to grab her, but he keeps a soft hold on her.

I meet his gaze, and I don't know what he sees in my stare, but he relents. His hold loosens, and I'm able to pull her to me.

I line our faces up, reveling in the wide, gummy smile she gives me. "Hi, sweet girl," I coo. "I missed you today. You ready to have some real fun while your dad works?"

"Hey, you didn't tell me you missed *me*."

I shoot Jude a look. "Maybe that's because I didn't miss you."

He swallows, and I swear for a moment there might actually be hurt in his eyes. It's only a flash of it, but it seems like he might actually be disappointed by what I said. "Well, I missed you," he gets out hoarsely. "*We* missed you."

I have to look away from his warm, brown eyes. I don't

know if he even realizes how much weight the words he keeps saying have. I know he doesn't mean them the way that I hope him to, but I can't pretend that hearing him say he missed me—especially in that raw and real tone he used—doesn't do things to me.

I'm desperately trying to be his friend. To be there for him and Ava and make sure he has someone to lean on. I want to be that person for him more than I've ever wanted anything else. But my stupid heart has a mind of its own, and it doesn't care about all the reasons I shouldn't fall for him. It hears things like "my girls" and "it's a date" and "I missed you" and thinks that maybe Jude is feeling every single thing I am.

And that's dangerous.

Because as much as I try to tell my heart not to feel that way, it doesn't matter.

I'm developing real feelings for Jude Kensington—my best friend—and I don't think there's anything I can do to stop it. All I can do is hide it and try my best to pretend it isn't the truth.

"I'm going to go feed Ava, and you work on your emails." I don't even wait to hear a response from him. I make sure my grip on Ava is tight before I rush out of his office.

"Still waiting for you to tell me you missed me!" he calls after me. There's humor to his voice, but there's something else. Something more vulnerable. Something that makes my stomach do a flip.

I don't answer him. I make my way to the kitchen and begin to prepare a bottle. When I look down at Ava, I find her watching me with a smile.

"Is this funny to you?" I ask, whispering even though I know it isn't necessary. If Jude followed us, I would've heard his footsteps. He's all the way on the opposite side of the house, thankfully.

As if she can understand me, Ava lets out the smallest little laugh.

I groan. "Oh, so it *is* funny to you. I'm glad you think me catching feelings for your dad when I absolutely shouldn't is hilarious. Well, it isn't funny to me, baby girl. What am I going to do?"

Ava's no help because all she does is laugh, having no idea how serious it is that somehow in the span of a few weeks, I've gone from caring about Jude as a friend and knowing we're better off that way, to getting to know him on a deeper level and starting to fall for him anyway.

35
Jude

I swore I was only going to answer a couple of emails before taking Ava from Charlotte and allowing her to actually have a break after getting off work, but when I stepped out of my office and made my way down the hallway to the living room, Charlotte had Ava laughing so hard that I didn't want to disturb them.

For a few minutes, I stood there and watched them. My heart ached, seeing them together. It's clear how much she loves Ava, and seeing her interact with my daughter makes me feel things I shouldn't. A few weeks ago, I felt so much guilt that Ava wouldn't have a mother in her life.

Now, that feeling is forgotten. For Ava's sake, I wish her mother had wanted to be involved, but I know it's for the best that she'll have no memory of the mother who didn't want to be in her life. Ava is still a very lucky little girl because she has Charlotte. I can't even be jealous that Char is getting belly laughs out of Ava—far louder than I've been able to—because it's just so sweet to watch the two of them together.

Instead of interrupting their time together, I backed away

and dove into more work. I hadn't even realized a couple of hours had gone by until I looked out my office window and saw the sun setting.

I pull my glasses from my face and sit back in my office chair. I let out a loud sigh as I think about the plan Charlotte came up with earlier. Tomorrow, I'll be leaving Ava alone with her while I leave the house, and I know I should feel nervous about it—and I do—but not because I don't trust Charlotte. I just haven't really left Ava alone fully yet. Charlotte's watched her for me, but I've always been around. Tomorrow will be different, and while there are nerves that come with that, I am excited to get back to Pembroke.

I'm ready to tell more people about Ava. Because of Charlotte—and finally telling people, like my parents and Cal—I'm realizing it's okay if I don't give every detail of how Ava came to be mine to others. All they need to know is that she's my daughter and that I'm excited for the rest of the world to meet her. Eventually, I'll have to explain it to the bigger social scene of Manhattan, but for now, I can dip my toes in by just telling those at Pembroke.

And then there's the party on Friday with Charlotte.

I called it a date as a test, to see if maybe things are changing for her the way they are for me. Her reaction made it feel like maybe it is, but I'm still too nervous to ask that outright.

The reality is that I want Charlotte. I want her in any way she'll give me, and it's getting harder to accept her as just a friend. There are so many reasons why she and I should never cross the boundary we set between us, but the more time that passes, the more it feels like maybe I've had it wrong since Ava came into my life. I drew a line between us because I thought it was the right thing to do. Now, lying to her—and myself—about how my feelings for her have grown deeper doesn't feel right at all. It feels wrong.

I pinch the bridge of my nose as I try to think through the last few weeks. It's felt like a whirlwind, and I haven't even had time to process it all. I've been so busy—and rarely alone—that I've been able to push a lot of things to the back of my mind.

Now, they won't stay silent any longer.

Sitting alone in my office, I can't help but wonder what would happen if I were honest with Charlotte. I have no idea what my life will look like with Ava, and I'm terrified about what Charlotte sees as her future, but I'm also trying to live in the present. I want to live in the *right now*.

And right now, I want to tell Charlotte the last thing I want to be is her friend. I want to see if we could be more, and I don't want to keep trying to prevent that from happening. I just don't know if that's what she wants, and I don't know if I have the nerve to ask.

It's unknown territory for me.

Women typically come to me. Their feelings for *more* are obvious. They chase me, and that's all I've ever known. It works. I smile at them, and they eat out of the palm of my hand.

Until Charlotte.

She brushed me off from the moment we met. It didn't used to bother me. It was still fun.

Now, if she told me that she isn't feeling the same way I am, it'd crush me. I wouldn't be able to brush it off and pretend that it's fine. She's the first woman to ever have the power to hurt me, and I don't know how to handle that.

"I didn't know if you wanted to do her bedtime routine or if you wanted me to." Charlotte's soft voice pulls me from my thoughts.

I try not to jump. I was so locked into thinking of her that I didn't even realize she walked in holding Ava.

I immediately stand up and take my daughter from her. Ava melts against me instantly, and the tightness in my chest I felt while thinking about Charlotte disappears. "I can put her to bed. Go take a break. I'm sorry I got lost in work. I didn't mean to make you watch her that long."

Charlotte smiles. She stands close to me, close enough that she can reach out and run a hand over Ava's hair. "It's fine. You needed to work, and us girls had a good time together. I am going to finally get out of my work clothes, and I told my sister Carly I'd call her tonight while she's at home visiting Mom and Dad, so I'll probably go do all that if you're fine with Ava."

"Of course. I'm sorry again that I took so long."

Charlotte looks up at me through her long eyelashes and gives me that soft smile that I dream about at night. "Don't be sorry." She leans in and presses a kiss against Ava's head, and I can't help but wish that she were kissing me instead. "Good night, Ava girl. Let's try and get some good sleep tonight...what do you think?"

I laugh. "We'll see. If her refusal to nap anywhere but on me earlier is any indication, we might be taking a drive tonight. What secrets do you have for me?"

It's Charlotte's turn to laugh. "I don't have any good secrets tonight, so let's hope Ava sleeps."

Before I can respond, she leaves my office, which is probably a good thing because I was about to tell her that I have a big enough secret for the both of us. I want her, and if I knew she wanted me too, I'd say fuck the rules and boundaries we've put between us.

I watch the doorway for a few moments, wondering if

for some reason Charlotte will appear in it again. When she doesn't, I look down at my daughter. Her eyebrows are red, and instead of her eyes being wide open, her lids are heavy.

"You tired, baby girl?" I lean in to kiss her, and I catch a whiff of the familiar scent of her baby soap mixed with the specific smell of Charlotte. I inhale again, my eyes closing for a moment. It isn't lost on me how much comfort I find in not only the smell of my daughter but of Charlotte as well. She always smells like vanilla mixed with something else…maybe cherry. Whatever it is, the scent is intoxicating. It's been weeks of being taunted by so many things when it comes to her, her smell being one of them. I have to push the feeling away of how much I love the vanilla and cherry scent that I now associate with her. Not only that, but the smell now brings me comfort, something I'm trying to ignore.

I shake my head, ridding my mind of thoughts of her as I make the mental note to thank her for already giving Ava a bath. All there's left to do is give Ava a bottle and rock her to sleep—two of my favorite things to do with my daughter.

I use my free hand to close my laptop lid and leave my office. I actually feel really good about how much work I was able to get done today. For the first time in a long time, I think I'll be able to go to bed without feeling guilty about all the things I left for my assistant to do. I know eventually I'll have to find a better childcare situation than asking Charlotte to step in, but for now, I think it'll work.

I walk to my room and fight the urge to stop at Charlotte's door on the way. She's done enough for me today, I need to leave her alone, but even though I just saw her, I still miss her. We live in the same house, and I still find myself missing her when she's not around. It's a foreign feeling, but one I'm tired of fighting.

Ava lets out a little coo, as if she's excited about being near Charlotte too. I can't help but smile. It seems like I'm not the only one who Charlotte has wrapped around her finger; she's got my daughter obsessed with her too.

"I know," I tell my daughter. "I want to see her too, baby girl. But you've got to go to bed, and I've got to leave her alone." I walk by Charlotte's door without stopping. Once Ava's milk is made, I go right to my room without even glimpsing in the direction of Charlotte's room.

The entire time I feed my daughter and rock her to sleep, I can't help but let my mind replay every moment between Charlotte and me over the last few weeks. I think about every interaction, trying to figure out if all of this is one-sided or in my head, or if there's a chance she's feeling the same way I am.

I let my head fall against the rocking chair in the corner of my room as I rock back and forth. "What do you think? Do I tell her how I feel, or do I keep pretending not to like her?" I ask Ava as if she can actually respond. It's quiet, so quiet that I look down and find that she's popped off the bottle and has fallen fast asleep.

"So you're leaving me to decide that by myself?" I mutter. "You're supposed to tell me what to do here because this is new territory for me, and I don't know what to do."

Ava stays fast asleep, and I stay in the chair, thinking about all the things that could go wrong if I confess my feelings to Charlotte.

36

Charlotte

The hot water of the shower feels amazing against my tense muscles. I've probably been in the shower longer than I need to be, but it feels good to let the water run over me.

My entire body is on edge, and it's because of Jude.

Weeks of pent-up tension catch up to me as I stand underneath the stream of water.

I can't get the way Jude called me *his girl* out of my head.

I can't get anything he's done in the last few weeks out of my head.

I've been pushing every interaction between us to the back of my mind in an attempt to keep things platonic, but left with nothing but my own thoughts in this shower, everything catches up to me.

The lingering looks Jude gives me.

The way he finds ways to touch me, even when it's not necessary.

Memories of him without a shirt.

The sight of him in those gray sweatpants, which leave little to the imagination.

His glasses—*the slutty glasses*, as I've nicknamed them.

The way he placed his hand over mine.

The feeling of his skin against mine.

Him calling our time together this Friday a date.

It's all become too much.

I've never wanted anyone as badly as I want Jude. I need him, even though I know I shouldn't. I've tried to fight it, but it's no use.

He used to flirt with me, and it was harmless.

Now when he flirts…it feels more intentional. It feels like there's more behind it. And I can't pretend not to notice anymore. I notice it all, and now I'm left with the constant feeling of needing him. There's a constant ache between my thighs that I owe to him and him alone.

I close my eyes as the water sprays down my body.

I know I shouldn't, but I let my hand drift down until my fingers brush over my clit.

I'd be lying if I said this was the first time I've closed my eyes and imagined Jude touching me since I moved in with him. I feel like every night over the last week or two, I'm having to touch myself to thoughts of him just to be able to get to sleep.

My need for him is desperate. And since I can't have him, pretending it's him touching me is the next best thing.

I circle my clit once, tingles spreading throughout my entire body at the touch.

I do it again, imagining it is Jude instead of me.

I've stared at his hands often, wondering what it'd be like to feel his thick fingers inside me.

I let out a moan as I continue to circle my clit, imagining it's his hand. I bet he'd tease me just like this. He'd press lightly, going around the most sensitive part of my body before actually giving me what I want and fully pressing his fingers inside.

Heat spreads throughout me, and even with the water running over me, I know I'm soaking wet thinking of him. I continue to circle my clit, letting my pace pick up as I wish more than anything that it was Jude doing it instead.

I imagine him kissing me as his fingers explore. Our kiss was brief, just the whisper of our lips against one another, but I am still confident he's an excellent kisser. I wish I knew more about how he kissed. Would he kiss me nice and slow and draw it out as he continued to touch me? Or would he kiss me with a fiery intensity as his fingers worked slowly against my swollen clit?

God, I wish I knew.

"Jude," I moan, unable to stop myself.

He's on the other side of the house and still managing to drive me absolutely wild.

I slowly inch my finger inside myself as I think of him. I think of him in his fitted gray sweatpants. I'd give anything to have him touch me the way I'm touching myself right now. While he played with me, I'd let my fingers drift down his stomach, tracing every single one of his abs that he constantly has on display.

I know I'd tease him. Even if he gave me what I wanted and slowly pushed his fingers inside me, I'd draw it out for him. I imagine letting my fingers trace his waistband as I paid close attention to his every reaction.

Another moan leaves my lips as I slide a second finger in. A delicious tension builds throughout my entire body. I pulse my fingers in and out, but I need more.

I quickly turn off the shower and grab my towel from the hook. There's a throbbing between my legs from being teased without a release. I slide the towel over my body to dry myself off just enough to leave the bathroom.

My heart races from the rush of pleasure as I make my way to my bed. It's dark in my room, thanks to the late hour of the evening and because I pulled my curtains shut. There's enough light filtering in from the bathroom that I'm able to open up the bottom drawer of my dresser and grab my bag of toys. I settle on my vibrator and hastily shove the bag in my drawer and slam it shut.

My entire body feels like it's on fire. I've worked myself up with thoughts of Jude, and I'm now desperate for a release.

I throw my towel to the ground and climb into bed. I haphazardly pull the comforter over me before lying back. My legs shake in anticipation as I let out a heady breath. I adjust my body until I'm comfortable, lining up the head of the vibrator against my clit.

I don't turn it on at first. Instead, I close my eyes and circle my clit with the tip, going back to imagining it's Jude doing it instead of a toy. I continue to move in circles around the swollen bud until I need more. Clicking the top of the vibrator, I turn it on and stifle a moan at the pleasure it immediately brings.

It feels so fucking good.

I move my hips as I let the vibrator press against my clit. In a moment, I'll begin to inch it inside myself, little by little, but for right now, I revel in the feeling of it just pressed against me.

God, I wish it were Jude's fingers instead. Or even better, the tip of his dick.

Another moan leaves my lips as I imagine him on top of me. I imagine the feeling of his body pressed to mine, of the dirty things he'd say to me as he played with my clit with the tip of his dick.

I want it so bad.

I use my free hand to pull the comforter up my body, hoping the thickness of the material covers the sound of the vibrator. It's my quietest one, and with Jude's room across the house, I shouldn't have to worry about him hearing anything anyway.

But I bite my lip and do my best to stay quiet as I think about what it'd be like if he *weren't* across the house from me.

I imagine him in my bed. My eyes flutter open and shut in pleasure as I think about how good it'd feel to have the weight of him on top of me. I want to feel the scrape of his five o'clock shadow on my skin. I want to feel his thick fingers inside me as he gets me ready to take his dick.

I want to know the dirty things he'd say to me if he were in bed with me right now. I blush at the memory of him telling me how dirty he could talk. Is he demanding in bed? Or would he prefer me to take the lead? I'd do anything to find out.

"Jude." His name comes out as a moan again. I can't help it. I'm so turned on by thoughts of him that I'm desperate to come as I imagine it's him making me orgasm instead of the vibrator.

I circle my clit one more time with the toy before slowly inching it inside myself.

"Oh my God," I pant, my toes curling underneath the comforter. With every inch I push in, I imagine it's Jude's dick instead.

My entire body feels hot as fire builds low in my abdomen. I know I'm close to coming. I rock my hips up and down, pushing the vibrator deeper. I let out another moan at the feeling of it pulsing inside me.

This isn't the first time I've imagined what it'd feel like to have sex with Jude. In the last couple of weeks, I've touched myself thinking of him more times than I'd like to admit. But there's something about tonight that feels more intense. I think it was the way he let his thumb dance across the top of my hand when we were in his office. Or the intensity in his eyes that felt like he wanted to say more when he called the Pembroke event this Friday a date.

It's like the floodgates of my desire for him have been fully opened, and instead of feeling guilty for wanting him so badly, I'm giving in to it, just for tonight. I could've waited for him to put Ava to bed tonight and cornered him in the kitchen and kissed him the way I've dreamed about, but instead, I hid in my room alone.

Imagining him fucking me isn't crossing a line…right? If I don't act on my desperate need for him, I'm technically still keeping him in the friend zone.

At least that's what I'm telling myself as I pick up the speed at which I push the vibrator in and out of me as I imagine it being his length instead.

Goosebumps pop up on my skin as I imagine him kissing along my neck as he thrusts.

I need more. My fingers trail along my ribs as I guide them to my nipple, squeezing the sensitive bud to feel more. The comforter slides off the top half of my body slightly, but I don't care enough to fix it.

I'm too close.

My hips circle as pressure begins to build.

I'm going to come.

Heat pools low in my core, and I know I'm seconds away from a release.

I squeeze my eyes shut and arch my back, reveling in the way my entire body feels lit with desire because of the building orgasm.

"Jude," I moan, this time a little louder.

I pull the vibrator all the way out, and I'm about to push it as deep as I can to hit the spot I need it to hit most…when a sound has my eyes popping open.

My entire body stills as my gaze immediately connects with Jude's. He leans against the doorframe, wearing nothing but his glasses and a pair of gray sweatpants. One hand grabs onto the doorframe like it's the only thing keeping him in place, while the other strokes up and down his bulging length.

I'm too stunned to say anything. I've been caught. Before my brain can even process what's happening, he's clearing his throat. "If you're going to come thinking of me, the least you could do is let me be the one to do it."

37

Jude

Ava's been asleep for over two hours, which has me hopeful that tonight might not have to be a night we go for a drive to keep her that way.

I'm so excited about the fact that Ava's actually sleeping in her crib without needing to be driven around that I feel like I should tell Charlotte the sleep training might be working.

I make my way to her room, trying not to read into why she hasn't left her room since we spoke in my office. She said good night to Ava, but I figured that after she spoke with her family and changed from work, she'd come back out. She never did, not even to eat. I know because I sat in the kitchen waiting for her. The more time that passed by, the more I worried that maybe she was avoiding me.

Maybe calling it a date was too much.

I couldn't help it. The words slipped out, and even after I said them, I didn't regret it. But even so, the fact that she hasn't come out tonight after I held her hand in the office and called our plans *a date* has me worried.

I quietly walk to her room. Maybe she fell asleep early. Or

maybe she's avoiding me. Either way, I'm using the guise of telling her about Ava's great job sleeping as an excuse to check in on her.

Before I get to her door, I double-check that Ava is still down before sliding the monitor back into my pocket and lifting my hand to knock. My knuckles are about to hit the wooden door when a noise makes me pause.

My entire body freezes.

Was that a moan?

My heart rate accelerates at the idea, and I think I must have imagined it when I hear another one, this one louder and longer.

Blood immediately goes to my cock. Hearing her moan like that has my entire body heated.

Is she touching herself? Fuck, I'd give anything to see that.

I stifle a groan at the mental picture. I couldn't pinpoint what the soft humming noise was, but now, paired with her moans, I guarantee that's the sound of a vibrator.

I've never been so turned on in my life. I run my palm over my cock to get some sort of relief as I imagine what she must look like on the other side of the door.

I want to go in there. I *need* to, and I know I have no right feeling that way.

I'm crossing so many fucking lines just by standing here and eavesdropping on what is clearly a moment she's taking for herself, but I can't move. It's like she's a magnet, and instead of pulling away like I should, I'm being drawn to her. I'm sure she'd be furious to find me standing here, but even knowing that, I can't move.

I flex my jaw, the movement so intense that I can hear my teeth grinding. It's taking every ounce of my restraint to not push the door open.

I need to go.

I need to back away and go back to my side of the house and stay there.

If I open the door, there's no going back. I won't be able to stop myself from going after what I want—*her.* I won't be able to tell myself that it's better if we never cross the line. I still have no idea what she wants or how she feels about me, and the best choice for everyone would be for me to leave.

I'll leave.

I'm about to back away and leave her alone, because I'm trying really hard not to break the rules we put in place, and I'm clearly not thinking straight…when I hear another moan.

"Jude." My name comes out like a damn plea. And every bit of self-control I had is gone. She said my fucking name while touching herself, and the knowledge has my entire body ablaze.

I know I shouldn't, but I can't help it. I grab the handle of her door and push it open slowly, making sure I stay quiet while doing so.

The scene in front of me makes me lightheaded.

Charlotte is lying on her bed, her head resting against the pillow as the comforter moves up and down where she plays with her pussy. She's never looked as beautiful as she does right now. Wet hair sticks to her face, making me wonder if maybe she was in the shower before deciding to get herself off. Even in the darkness of the room, I can tell that her cheeks are flushed.

"Oh my God," she mutters, and it's so fucking sexy that I can't help but run my hand over my length again.

I wish I knew what she was picturing right now.

Is she thinking about me fingering her? Fucking her? Worshipping her pussy with my tongue the way I've dreamed of doing too many times to count? Whatever it is, I know I could make it better than whatever she's imagining. If she just gave me the chance, I know I could give her one orgasm after the next—each one better than the last.

I watch her closely, committing to memory every single thing she does so I know how to do it better. Now that I've seen her like this—heard my name fall from her lips—there's no going back. I don't care that I told her we'd just be friends. I don't care about how complicated things will be.

All I care about is her letting me give her the real thing and making her feel good.

Nothing else matters.

Her movements under the comforter pick up. She gets faster, and I'd give anything to rip the comforter away so I could see the way she fucks herself with the toy.

She lets out small moans and whimpers that have my cock aching for some sort of relief. I feel dizzy from being so turned on. My head spins because I'm so desperate for her.

Char's hand dances along her skin until she pinches her nipple between two fingers.

I imagine taking that nipple into my mouth. I want to bite and suck and bite and suck some more until she's begging me for more. How much could I turn her on just by playing with her nipples?

I'm hard as a fucking rock imagining it.

The comforter slips down her body, and now I have a view of her perfect, round tits. She continues to play with her nipple as her hand underneath the comforter moves faster and faster.

I'm stuck in a trance.

Watching her like this is both the sexiest thing I've ever seen and the most tortured I've ever felt. I want to watch her come undone, but at the same time, I want to be the one to make her fall over the edge.

"Jude." This time, my name is said so loudly that I can't not react. She's fucking herself with a vibrator, thinking of me, and that seems permission enough to let my presence be known.

I push the door open, and for a few seconds, the only thing I can hear is the sound of my own beating pulse. I grip the doorframe so tightly that my nails might bite into the wood. I couldn't care less. All I can do is stare at her, anxious to find out what happens next. Letting her know I'm here instead of backing away and pretending this never happened is something we can't come back from. This isn't us just kissing briefly or stolen touches—this is full-blown lust and pure, hot need that will be hard to move on from.

Charlotte's eyes pop open, and her entire body stills as her eyes meet mine.

I fight the urge to tell her she's the most beautiful woman I've ever seen. My every thought seems to be consumed by her, and I've never wanted something more than I want her.

Her only movement is the quick rise and fall of her chest as she stares at me. She blinks, as if she's trying to figure out if she's imagining me or not. I run my hand up and down my length through the fabric of my pants, needing some sort of relief from how much she's turned me on without even realizing it.

I swallow, knowing my next words could change everything between us. I don't care if things change. I want them to. I can't go on wanting her like this and pretending I don't. I need her more than I've ever needed anything in my life, and I'm over pretending otherwise. Something's snapped inside me, and all I can do is hope that with my next words, she doesn't push me away.

"If you're going to come thinking of me, the least you could do is let me be the one to do it." My words come out thick and raspy. I let the weight of them linger between us, my gaze focused on her as I wait for her response.

I continue to brush up and down my cock. Everything hurts from how turned on I am. Even stroking myself through the fabric of my pants isn't enough to dull the ache.

"Jude," she whispers, blinking again as if she's still trying to figure out if I'm here or not. She's completely still as she stares back at me in shock. "What are you doing here?"

My hand drops from the doorframe as I take a step inside her room. I pull the door closed behind me as I pay close attention to her reaction. If it feels like she wants me to leave, I'll go, but I hope that isn't the case.

I hope she lets me finish her off. I know by the pants and moans she was letting out that she was close to coming. I only hope that she doesn't stop whatever's happening between us, and she'll let me finish the job for her.

I take another step toward her. "Were you touching yourself while thinking of me?"

Her eyes go wide. "Jude." My name comes out like a pant. It's so sexy that my cock jerks just at the sound of my name coming from her mouth.

"I'm right here, sweetheart," I respond, continuing to close the distance between us until I'm standing at the foot of her bed. "Now, tell me if you were thinking about me."

I don't know how long it stays silent between us. The only sound is the buzzing of her vibrator that I can't see. There's still a bulge in the comforter from where she holds her hand, and it's still right above her pussy, meaning she hasn't moved the vibrator from where she was fucking herself.

The realization sends a shiver down my spine. Everything about this moment is so fucking hot that I can barely take it. I might combust at any minute.

Charlotte closes her eyes for a minute. I use it as an opportunity to trail my gaze along the bare skin not hidden by the comforter.

Up close, I find that her nipples are hard and pink, the peaks begging for my touch—or maybe even my mouth. Even her chest has a perfect pink flush to it, the color something I can only see because of the light that filters out from the bathroom.

I trace over her ribs and her stomach, wishing that the comforter weren't resting right underneath her belly button so I could see even more of her. I take my time letting my eyes return to her face. When our gazes finally meet, I find her staring back at me expectantly.

"Tell me to leave," I rasp. It takes every fiber in my being to get the words out. I don't want to leave. I want to stay right here and finish what she started, but I know I've walked in on her, and I need to give her the chance to stop this if she doesn't want anything to happen.

"Why?"

"Because if you don't tell me to leave, then I'm going to crawl into this bed with you and show you how much better I am at making you come."

38

Charlotte

I don't know what's happening. Did I somehow fall asleep and this is all a dream? It wouldn't surprise me. I've had dirty dreams of him recently.

Jude stares at me, his hand running over the thick outline of his dick over and over again, as he waits for me to answer.

Did I slip in the shower and hit my head? Did I get too distracted touching myself with the hot water running over me that I somehow fell and I'm concussed?

This can't be happening. Jude can't be standing at the foot of my bed, wanting to make me come.

But I swear he's real.

I should feel embarrassed at the fact that he caught me masturbating and that he might've even heard me moaning his name, but I'm not. I can't possibly be when he looks at me like a man starved. He licks his lips as he waits for me to tell him to leave, and I don't know how to tell him that now that he's here, I don't think I have the strength to stop whatever's about to happen.

"We shouldn't," I manage to get out. The vibrator barely

pushes against my clit from where I was seconds away from pushing it inside when he caught me. It's so soft that it's like a tease, but with enough of that, paired with the hot desire in his eyes, I still feel incredibly close to coming.

"I don't care if we shouldn't." The bed dips underneath his weight. I squeeze my thighs together at the hungry way he looks at me. Squeezing them together does nothing. In fact, it traps the vibrator between my thighs, making my entire body hum with arousal.

"We're supposed to be friends."

"Friends help friends, don't they?"

I shake my head. "Not like this." Why does he have to be so sexy? How can he possibly expect me to do the right thing here when he looks at me like nothing else matters in the world other than making me come?

He grabs onto the comforter, his eyebrows lifting in a silent question. He wants to know if he can pull it off me, and I don't know what to say. Never in my life have I ever been caught like this. If it were any other person, I might feel embarrassed, but it's impossible to feel that way when it's so obvious how turned on he is right now. I glance down at his groin, finding his gray sweatpants tented with his very obvious erection.

I did that.

Me.

Warmth spreads through my entire body, knowing that just the thought of me made him hard like that.

"We said we'd keep each other in the friend zone." My voice comes out weak and breathy. I'm throwing out excuses about why we shouldn't do this, and it's glaringly obvious that I don't even believe the words I'm saying.

"If I were in the friend zone, would you be fucking yourself with a toy while imagining it was me?"

I moan. I can't help it. His words are so sexy, and paired with the raspy, desperate tone of his voice, it's one of the hottest things I've ever heard.

"I just..." I pause when he just barely pulls on the comforter. It only exposes the tops of my hip bones, but it's still more skin than a few moments ago, and he watches me carefully to see if I'll stop him or not. "We said we'd be friends and not make things complicated."

"You need to come...I've never wanted anything more than to make you come. Nothing about that seems complicated."

He pulls the comforter down enough that all he'd need to do is tug it another two inches, and he'd see all of me.

He licks his lips again. They're wet and shiny, and I have to close my eyes when I can't help but wonder what his smirk would look like covered in my arousal. I squeeze my thighs together again, trying not to moan when the vibrator pulses against my clit with the movement.

"*Char.*" My name comes out so tightly, I wonder if he's saying my name through gritted teeth.

I open my eyes, finding the muscle of his jaw ticking away as he stares at me so intensely that it takes my breath away.

My heart jolts at the way he looks at me, and my pulse pounds in anticipation. "What?"

His eyes flick down to the comforter before meeting my gaze. "This is your last chance to stop this. I'm trying to give you an out, but I'm at the end of my restraint. I don't care what we've said in the past. I don't care about what happens next. All I fucking care about is making you come so hard that touching yourself will never compare again."

I moan and arch my back, the movement causing the

comforter to slip completely.

Jude lets out a loud groan at the same moment air hits my lower half.

I don't know what he can see with my thighs still squeezed together, but he stares at me in a way no man has ever looked at me before. He looks starved and desperate. I wonder if he even realizes that his tongue has peeked out to wet his lips again.

It's clear the moment his resolve fully snaps. He lets out a low noise at the back of his throat that sounds a lot like a growl as he rips the comforter from my body completely and tosses it to the foot of the bed.

He slides off the bed, and before I can ask him what he's doing, his fingers wrap around my ankle, and he yanks my body down the bed. I yelp, the vibrator falling to the side as I stare at him wide-eyed, wondering what's going to happen next.

"You're beautiful," he marvels, his eyes raking over my naked body.

I squirm at his words—or maybe it's the primal way he looks at me. Either way, he's barely even touched me yet, and my entire body feels on edge with desire for him.

"Jude." I know I should say something else, *anything* else, but I can't. I can barely form a coherent thought—let alone words—right now. I've never been so turned on in my life. It feels like my entire body is a live wire, and at any moment, I could catch fire.

He groans, his eyes closing for a minute. His fingers tighten against my ankle, and while I appreciate him touching me in some capacity, I need more. I want him to touch me in other places. I want him to touch me everywhere.

He opens his eyes, and the normal blue irises I love to stare into are all but gone. His pupils are large as he watches me closely. "You're so fucking sexy when you moan my name like that, sweetheart."

Sweetheart.

I'm a puddle at the nickname, and wetness pools between my thighs at his use of it.

He swipes his thumb along the inside of my ankle, the movement making me jerk. I'm so sensitive right now that even the smallest touch has me aching for more.

Jude runs a hand over his dick, his eyes focused on me. I don't think he's looked away once. I love the power I feel underneath his stare. He watches me like I'm the only thing to exist, and I can't deny how good it feels to be looked at like that.

I'm about to beg him to touch me anywhere but just my ankle when he quickly moves, taking me by surprise. One minute, he's staring at me with a look of pure need; the next, his hand wraps behind my neck, and he's pulling my body off the mattress.

I blink, coming face-to-face with Jude. His breath hits my cheek as he places his thigh between my legs.

He moves to grab my face with both of his hands. It's possessive and sexy, and my chest heaves with my labored breaths because of how turned on I am. His eyes rake over my face before he opens his mouth to speak. "Before we do anything else, there's something I've been needing to do."

"What?"

His only answer is to crush his mouth against mine.

Our first kiss—if you could really even call it that—was featherlight. It was calm and sweet and quick. Just as soon as it began, it ended.

This kiss is the opposite.

It's desperate and hungry. Fervent. Heated. It's so electrifying that I feel the kiss throughout my entire body.

Jude's hands grip my face like I'm his lifeline. His fingertips dig into my scalp as his tongue pushes into my mouth with skilled determination.

I can't believe I've gone this long without kissing him. His kiss is like a brand. It's as if he knows this might be the one time we both let down the walls and give in to our attraction, and he's going to make damn sure it's a kiss I could never forget.

He tastes like wine, making me wonder if he had a glass after getting Ava to bed.

My hands find his chest as I try to steady myself. Our heads move back and forth as we kiss each other like two people desperate for air, and the only way to get it is from each other. My hands trail across his abs, and I try to commit the feeling of them to memory. They jump underneath my touch, his skin warm and his toned muscles hard.

His tongue circles mine as his fingers tangle in my wet hair, and I can't help but moan. I move my hips, the movement causing my clit to press against his knee. I moan again at the sensation, grinding against his thigh to get some sort of friction.

I was so close to an orgasm before he even walked in that my entire body still feels pulled taut. I'm like a rubber band, threatening to snap at any second because of the desire coursing through my veins.

One of Jude's hands slides down until he grips my neck possessively. He forces my head up, deepening the kiss, something I didn't even know was possible.

This is bad.

Not the kiss.

The kiss is *everything.*

But the way in which he kisses me is something I'll never be able to wipe from my memory. I don't think I'll ever be able to look at him and pretend he's just my friend when he's kissed me like this.

Maybe that's what he wants.

Or maybe this is just how he kisses.

Either way, I soak in the moment because if I'm going to give in, I'm going to revel in this with him.

I grind against his leg, letting out another moan.

He groans at the sound. He rips his mouth away just far enough to be able to talk. "No coming yet." His fingertips tighten slightly around my throat, and why do I find the possessive hold so hot?

A small whine escapes me at his words. I need a release. He steals any argument I might have by leaning in and kissing me again.

This time, it's a bit slower, but the possessiveness is still there. His tongue dips into my mouth slightly, and I eagerly meet his tongue with mine.

I'm so lost in the kiss that I don't even notice that he's somehow reached and grabbed for the vibrator until I feel him press it into my inner thigh.

The feeling is too much. I pull away and bury my face in the crook of his neck. "Oh God," I pant, my hips bucking as he guides the vibrator up.

I feel Jude's deep, throaty laugh in the hand against the back of my neck. He uses the hand not holding the vibrator to force me to look at him once again.

"No, sweetheart. God's not here. I want you to say *my* name."

I have to close my eyes because everything is too much.

The vibrator reaching the apex of my thighs.

The tight grip he has on my face.

His words.

The way he looks at me.

We've barely even started doing anything, and it still feels like everything has changed. I'll never forget him just like this. He isn't Jude, my charming best friend. He's someone entirely different. Someone possessive and in control, and someone really good at making me feel like the only woman in the world.

I know I should stop this before letting anything else happen. I'm scared he's already ruined any shot I had at pretending to just be his friend, but I could at least try to stop it.

I can't.

He glides the vibrator over my clit at the same time he leans in to kiss me, and I know that, at least for tonight, I don't have the power to stop anything with him.

I want it all, consequences be damned.

39

Jude

I'm fucking ruined.

I never should've opened the door to Charlotte's room. The moment I heard her moan, I should've turned around and run back to my room and locked myself inside.

But I didn't.

And now, I don't think I'll ever forget the sounds of her moans. I'll never forget the fervent way in which she kisses me back. Any hope to ever look at her and not remember how fucking perfect she is all but vanishes.

I'm battling with myself to savor every single moment of this with her, not knowing if this is something that'll happen again or not, and wanting nothing more but to push her back into the mattress and slide my cock into her the way I've imagined doing so many times before.

I could get lost in kissing her. She grabs my hair as I lightly circle her clit with the vibrator.

I love tasting her moans. I press the vibrator against her clit harder this time, holding it there for a few seconds just so I can taste her moan again.

I moan right along with her. I don't even know what sounds leave my body as I get lost in everything that is her.

Charlotte's fingertips tighten in my hair, and I know if I keep the vibrator there for even a moment longer, she'd come. But I don't want her to come. Not yet. I'm having too much fun.

Instead of giving her what she wants, I move the vibrator. The moment I pull it away, she lets out a whimper that I swear makes my heart stop. Why does she have to be so fucking sexy? She's so perfect, and it's killing me. I wonder if she knows how gone I am for her.

"No," she pleads, her back arching and her head falling backward as she tries to find any kind of relief. "Jude, I'm so close."

I run the fingers of my free hand along my forehead, committing to memory the way she looks right now. Her hair's wet from a shower; it sticks to her flushed cheeks as her hooded eyes watch me carefully. There's not a single wall between us right now, and I want to remember it forever. At least for this very moment, she's mine and I'm hers, and nothing else can stop that. It's fucking perfect.

"I know, sweetheart." The raspiness of my voice takes me by surprise. It's thick with lust and desire. "You need to come, don't you?"

She nods, letting out another whimper.

I lift the vibrator and stare at it for a moment, marveling at the wetness that coats the tip of it. It makes me glance between her thighs, and I can't help but smirk at the sight. She's soaking wet. Not only does her pussy gleam with her arousal, but her thighs are slick too.

I lick my lips, wondering if I should stop teasing her and press my mouth to her perfect pussy instead.

When I look at her again, I find her gaze still focused on me. Her ragged breaths mirror my own, and I try to decide what I want to do next. I have her just the way I want her right now. She's practically begging me to come, and it's the sexiest thing in the world. If I knew that tomorrow I'd be able to do this very thing with her without her having any reservations, I might speed things up between us.

But I have no idea what tomorrow will bring. Tonight might be my only chance with her. I've got to make it count.

I press my free hand to her chest and gently coax her back down on the mattress. I stand above her, taking in the sight for a moment as the vibrator continues to pulse in my hands.

Charlotte laid out completely naked on the edge of the bed is a sight to see. She keeps a close eye on me as she waits for what I'm going to do next.

My cock aches, and my balls tighten. I don't think I've ever been so worked up in my life. If she keeps moaning the way she is—paired with the way she pants my name—I don't know if she'll even have to touch me to make me come. That's how bad I want her. How desperately I need her.

She opens her mouth—to argue, I'm sure—but before she can get any words out, I guide the vibrator to her nipple.

She bucks at the feeling, her eyes snapping shut as she lets out a cry of pleasure. I circle her nipple with the vibrator, loving how I can see the goosebumps popping up on her skin.

"Tell me that you need me to make you come." I don't realize how desperately I need to hear her say the words until I give the command.

"I need you to make me come," she hurriedly gets out, not giving my demand a second thought before she's begging for more.

I smirk. I love her like this. Needy and desperate for me. "I don't know if you've convinced me you mean it. You were in here touching yourself thinking of me instead of just asking me to do it. Make me believe that you need me to make you come. Make believe that you need *me*."

I don't know why I tease her. I want this just as badly as she does—probably more. I've just been so in my head trying to figure out if she's as attracted to me as I am to her that I need any proof that I'm not alone in this pure, desperate need.

She lets out a cry of displeasure. I can't wait until she actually comes. She'll realize all of the waiting and edging was worth it. But until then, it's so fucking sexy to see how needy she is for me.

"I need you. I need to come." Her eyes find mine, and I can't help but shiver at the intensity with which she looks at me. I have to palm my cock just to find even a second of relief.

"Say *please*. Beg for me, sweetheart."

She jumps when I move the vibrator to her other nipple. I circle it before pressing it hard against the tender skin. "I'm going to get you back for this."

It feels like all the blood in my body is already in my cock, but somehow, more rushes to it at her words. I smile. "Is that a promise?"

She smiles, her hips arching as she places her hand between her legs. Before she can touch herself, I swat her hand away.

"I'm all yours, Char. I'm ready to make you come so hard you won't even remember your name, but first, you need to beg for it, baby. I've been thinking about you every damn night, wishing you were in my bed, wishing I was inside you, wishing I could taste you. I can't even put into words how badly I want you, and before I make you come, I need to know you feel the same."

She tries to clench her thighs together, but my knee prevents her from doing it. I'm so happy she isn't able to obstruct my view of her. I love looking at how wet she is. I love knowing that I made her this way. That even when I wasn't in the room with her, she was still thinking of me to get herself off.

"I need you, Jude. *Please.*"

"'Atta girl." I don't need anything else. I click the vibrator off and toss it to the side. The first time I make her come, I want to be the one doing it. I want to feel her against my tongue and taste her. The toy can be fun for later, but for right now, she's going to come because of me and me alone.

I crouch to my knees before wrapping my arms around her thighs and pulling them open wide for me.

"Funny you made me beg for you, but you're the one on your knees right now."

I smile up from between her thighs at the comment. Her breathing is ragged as she watches me closely with a slight tilt to her lips. I love that even in the heat of a moment like this, her sass is still there.

"Anytime you want me on my knees for you like this, you just have to ask." Before she can say anything else—something that'll crush me, like telling me this will be the only time she lets me have her—I lightly circle her clit with my tongue.

She hisses, her hips bucking just from the small lick. I smile, even though I don't think she can see it.

Fuck, she tastes incredible. I lick her again, this time pressing my tongue flat against her swollen clit. I can't help but groan. She tastes so fucking good I might get addicted. How do I convince her that this one time won't be enough? I've only had the smallest taste of her, and I'm already sure that I don't think I'll ever get enough of her.

I let my tongue circle her clit one more time before I can't hold back anymore. I bury my face in her pussy and seal my mouth to her.

40

Charlotte

I'm going to come.

Jude's just started eating me out, and I already feel lightheaded from the building orgasm.

There's so much tension in my body that it feels almost unbearable. My fingers grasp at anything I can find as Jude brings me incredibly close to coming. I twist and yank at locks of Jude's hair as he licks and laps like a man who's been starved.

I'm already so close to toppling over the edge before he slides two fingers inside me. He doesn't even start with just one. His two thick fingers stretch me in a way that has my back arching and my toes curling.

"Jude," I say desperately before I let out a moan.

It's all too much.

I've imagined what it'd feel like to have his face between my thighs before, but nothing compares to the real thing. Nothing's ever felt so good. I'm almost scared of the intensity of the orgasm that I know is close.

Jude hooks his fingers inside me at the same time he sucks my clit. That's all it takes to finally push me over the edge.

"I'm coming," I cry, shocked I can even get the two words out.

An explosion of pleasure takes over my entire body as the orgasm crashes through me. I moan, I pant, I'm pretty sure I repeat Jude's name over and over as I ride out every wave. I've never had one this intense. My eyes squeeze shut, and my fingers desperately hold on to Jude's hair as he doesn't take his mouth from me.

Because I'd been worked up for so long, it feels like the orgasm lasts forever. It's so strong that it almost hurts as it takes over my entire body.

For however long it takes, it feels like I can't think straight. The only thing I can think about is the immense pleasure from between my thighs, the feeling only heightened by the fact that Jude doesn't take his mouth from me the entire time.

I try to catch my breath as I come down from the orgasm. Jude's tongue circles my clit as he lets out a loud moan of his own, making me squirm. I tighten my hold on his hair and try to lift his head.

"Jude," I pant, his name coming out strangled. "I…I need a minute."

I open my eyes to find his gaze already on me.

He lifts his head, and if I hadn't just come, the smirk he gives me would've sent me over the edge.

His lips are wet—from me—and his hair sticks up in different directions, also my doing. His eyes stay focused on me as he slowly removes his fingers.

"That was…everything," he mutters.

His own chest heaves as he stares at me with such an intensity that despite the exhaustion I feel from my orgasm, my skin still tingles underneath his stare. He stands up, and before I can say anything, he's climbing onto the mattress and bringing his face close to mine. He leans in to kiss me, and I let him, unable to deny that it's hot to taste myself on his lips.

He kisses me slowly for a minute, giving me time to regroup after he just gave me what I can only describe as a mind-blowing orgasm.

Finally, he pulls away, a smirk immediately finding his lips. "Did you know the sight of you coming was the sexiest thing I've ever seen?"

Blood rushes to my cheeks. "I don't even remember half the things I said."

His smile gets wider as his fingers softly move a piece of wet hair from my face. "Oh, I remember every single thing you said. Every sound you made. I'll never be able to forget any of it."

I squirm at his words, unable to fight my own smile. I know I shouldn't, but I melt at his admission. I want him to remember because I know there's no way I'll ever forget the way he made me come. I couldn't even if I wanted to. That was the best orgasm I've ever had, and it wasn't even because of Jude's obvious skill. It's the fact that it was…Jude.

I bite my lip as an idea pops into my head. Jude presses a soft kiss to my neck as I let my hand drift down his body. The moment my fingertips press against his lower abs, he jumps. His muscles tighten underneath my skin as he brings his head to mine.

"Char…" he rasps, air hissing through his teeth when I let my hand drift even lower.

He looks at me through his glasses as I continue to move my hand lower until I find the waistband of his sweatpants.

"Your turn," I whisper, wanting to make him feel as good

as he made me feel. I don't want this to stop between us, at least not yet; not until I can make him come too.

Before I can get my hand under his waistband, Jude's fingers are wrapping around my wrist, preventing me from going any further. "Wait," he mutters, his features unrecognizable as he looks into my eyes.

Embarrassment courses through my veins at the way he stops me from doing anything. Does he not want me to?

"It isn't that I don't want you to," he hurriedly gets out, his words hoarse. It's as if he can read my mind. I swear there's a blush creeping on his cheeks as he looks down for a moment before meeting my eyes again.

"Then let me make you come," I plead, not caring that there's a neediness to my tone. Maybe tomorrow, I'll be embarrassed about the way he caught me touching myself, followed by begging him to let me make him come moments after he gave me the best orgasm of my life, but tonight, I don't let the embarrassment in. I can't, not when I want him as much as I do right now.

Jude smiles, and something about it soothes the part of me that was still a little nervous that now that he made me come, he was done with whatever's happening between us tonight.

His cheeks get even more red. I have no idea why he's blushing, but I love it. I don't know if I've ever seen him this affected, and there's a certain power I feel knowing I have the ability to make him react that way. He rubs his lips together for a moment before he traces my cheekbone with the hand not holding my wrist. "You know how I said watching you come was the sexiest thing I'd ever seen?"

I nod, even though I can't help but be confused by the question.

He sighs. "Well, I meant that. It was so sexy watching you—tasting you—come…that I couldn't help it." He pauses for a moment, looking down at where my hand rests against his waistband before looking at me again.

"You couldn't help what?"

He closes his eyes. "I came."

My eyes go wide as I process his words. "But I didn't…"

He lets out a nervous laugh before opening his eyes to look at me, and something about the sound of his laugh makes my heart squeeze in my chest. I've always seen the confident, charming side of him, but I can't help but love seeing this side of him too. The one that blushes and chuckles nervously.

"I didn't touch you yet," I finish, my voice quiet.

He groans, and it's just another thing I love hearing the sound of. "You didn't have to. I don't think you understand how much I've wanted you, how much I've thought about finally touching you and tasting you. The moment that finally happened, I was done for. You were moaning my name, and your pussy was greedily hugging my fingers as you came on my tongue, and it was so sexy that it made me come undone."

My heart pounds at his admission. I look between us, noticing for the first time the wet stain on the front of his sweatpants.

I did that.

I wet my lips as I stare at it. I didn't even have to touch him, and I did that.

My entire body heats again at the realization.

"Are you thinking that I'm pathetic for coming in my pants before you ever got the chance to touch me?" I love the vulnerability in his voice. I'm realizing that even after a year of friendship, I really haven't seen Jude become fully vulnerable until recent weeks. Now that he's not afraid to show me this side of him, it's hard not to continue to fall for him.

I bite my lip and shake my head before I let my fingers dance over the thick outline tenting his sweatpants. Even though he already came, he's still hard. "No, I'm not thinking you're pathetic at all. I'm thinking that I love that I had the power to make you come without even touching you, but I'm still really looking forward to touching you, and I'm hoping you'll let me."

He clenches his jaw as I stroke up and down him again. "You have so much power over me, and you don't even realize it. I'm yours to touch and do whatever you want with, Char. But first, let's both clean up a little bit, then I need you to eat something because you never came out to eat, and *then* you're mine for the night."

I groan because I don't want to wait. "What if I want you right now?"

He presses his forehead to mine; his glasses press into me, but I don't even care. I love him in glasses too much to say anything. "You're killing me, you know that?"

I smile. I don't know if I should do it or not, but I press my lips to his because I want to feel his lips against mine again. If he doesn't want me to kiss him, he doesn't act like it. He immediately meets my tongue with his, the two of us taking a moment for a lazy kiss before I pull away enough to talk. "If I'm killing you, does that mean you'll let me make you come right now?" As if to prove a point, I run my hands along his length, hoping he'll give in and let us continue instead of waiting.

"You already made me come, sweetheart. And you will again. But you need to eat before I spend all night fucking you the way I've been imagining for weeks."

My cheeks flush at the way he says *fucking*. It's raspy and makes my clit throb all over again.

He smiles before pressing a kiss to the tip of my nose. "I love making you blush. I can't wait to see what other dirty things I can say to you later to make those cheeks even redder than they are now."

I know it's ridiculous, but I jut my bottom lip out because as much as I love the thought of having him later, I want him right now too. Now that we've started, I don't want to stop. What happens if we go out into the kitchen and eat, and he realizes that none of this is a good idea and that we shouldn't continue? I wouldn't blame him for it. I know that starting whatever's going on right now probably won't end well, but I'm too caught up in the desperate need for him to care. I'd hate that he never got the opportunity to come from my touch or if I never got to feel him move inside me. Now that I've had a teaser of Jude in bed, I want it all.

Jude slides off the bed, and I hate the feeling of his body not being pressed to mine. I want to touch him again, to feel his skin against mine. He pulls the baby monitor from his pocket, reminding me of Ava in the first place.

He turns it around and shows a sleeping Ava. "Look who's still asleep."

I smile. "Maybe we should take this opportunity to finish what we started right now while we can. She might wake up later, and then we'd miss our chance."

Jude shakes his head. "If you think Ava waking up would stop me, then you really don't understand how fucking desperate I am to feel your pussy around my cock, sweetheart. If she wakes up, I'll deal with it, and the moment she's back asleep, we're finishing what we started. But you'll need your energy for that, so stop arguing with me, and let's get in the shower to get both of us cleaned up, eat some food, and spend the rest of the night doing everything I've been imagining for so long."

He holds out his hand for me to take, and I let out a small whine before I put my hand in his. Between my thighs, I'm sticky from my own arousal, and he did run the vibrator all over my body before finally giving me what I wanted. A shower probably wouldn't hurt—especially since he came on himself too—but there's still a small part of me that's worried that once we leave this room, things will change. There's a reason we've fought the attraction between us. What if leaving pops the bubble that we're in, and reality sneaks back in?

But Jude still stares at me with a heated gaze as he pulls me off the bed. He doesn't look at me any differently. In fact, instead of going straight to the bathroom to shower, he pulls my body flush to his and grabs both sides of my face. "I meant it when I said you don't even realize how much power you have over me." Instead of letting me respond, he leans in and kisses me slowly. It isn't rushed like when he first kissed me tonight. It's as if now he realizes that he'll have another chance to kiss me later, like he knows it's not the last.

I kiss him back, wishing I had the nerve to tell him that I don't think he realizes it isn't me that holds all the power; it's him. If he just said the word, I'd be his. The truth is, he doesn't even have to say anything.

I'm already his, whether he truly wants that or not. I know giving in to the attraction between us might hurt me in the end. He's got so much going on in his life that he might not be ready for the things that I want, but knowing that about him doesn't matter. It doesn't stop my heart from wanting him, from wishing we could figure it out.

Plenty of relationships stem from friendships. Is it naive of me to believe maybe ours can too?

I kiss him back, knowing that tonight might be the only night that I can have him this way. Tomorrow, we'll probably both go back to realizing the reasons we fought our attraction, and we'll go back to pretending it isn't there, but tonight, I'll be his. And that'll have to be enough.

41

Jude

I've never been nervous around a woman, ever, yet here I am, my heart racing and my mouth dry as Charlotte and I stand in front of the shower. Steam begins to fill her bathroom as she keeps her eyes aimed at me.

She smiles before looking at her feet. "Hopefully, there's still warm water. My thoughts of you started in the shower, and it was a fairly long one before I got out."

I stifle a groan at the mental picture she gives me. I love the fact that she was thinking of me in the shower. I love that she was thinking of me at all. There are so many questions I want to ask her, but I keep them to myself. I want to know how often she thinks of me. I want to know what she wants when it comes to me. I want to know if this thing between us is just physical for her or if she wants me on a deeper level, the way that I want her. I don't ask any of them, though, because right now, just knowing that she's thinking about me at all is all I need to know. It's answer enough, and I don't want to scare her away.

But I'm desperate for answers. I want to know every thought and feeling she has because she makes me feel things I've never felt before. She makes me want things I've never wanted with anyone else. Her ability to make me nervous is proof enough that Charlotte has a hold on me that no one's had before. It's scary, not knowing if she wants that or not, but it's also freeing, finally accepting that I can't change it. All I can do is savor the moments I do have with her and hope that whatever we started doesn't have to end.

I open the glass door and stick my hand underneath the water. "It's warm, but maybe we should get in before that changes."

Charlotte glances down at her naked body before her eyes move across my body. "Just waiting on you." She smiles as she lifts an eyebrow, pointing out that I still need to take my sweatpants off.

I sigh. I don't know why I feel so nervous to get undressed, but it's just another thing that's new when it comes to Charlotte. I turn the volume up on the monitor and set it on the bathroom counter. I make sure my gaze stays locked on her as I grab onto the fabric at my sides. I slide the pants down my legs before kicking them to the side. My hand finds my cock immediately as I wrap my fingers around myself and pump up and down once, just to give myself some kind of relief from the need I still feel for her.

Charlotte stares at me for a few seconds longer before she lets her gaze travel down. My cock jerks in my hand the moment her eyes go wide, and she licks her lips.

"That's not going to fit," she whispers.

I stifle yet another groan because I swear she's trying to kill me. I want to bury myself inside her and not leave all night, and I know I need to feed her before doing that, but she's making it incredibly hard to do the right thing and wait. Even though

I came only minutes ago, I know it'd be easy to get worked up all over again. In fact, I'm already incredibly hard and ready for her despite just having come. It's the effect she has on me.

She stares at my cock greedily, and it takes everything in me to not say fuck eating and slide inside her while we take a shower, just like I'm sure she was imagining before I caught her.

I hold the door open for her and nod in the direction of the shower so she gets in. "The sooner we shower, the sooner we eat, and then the sooner I can show you just how perfectly my cock fits inside you."

She bites her lip before turning around and following directions. As she steps in, I can't help but playfully swat her ass.

Charlotte yelps and looks over her shoulder as she steps underneath the water. "Hey! What was that for?"

I let out a low chuckle as I step in behind her. I pull the shower door closed, trapping the heat in the shower with us as steam billows around our bodies. "For being you," I answer, immediately grabbing her by the hips and guiding her under the spray so the water from the showerhead cascades over her shoulders.

"What's that supposed to mean?"

"It means you're perfect."

She smiles as she looks up at me with wet eyelashes, and it occurs to me that I don't know if I'll ever feel about someone the way that I feel about her. No one's ever had a hold of my heart just by smiling at me, yet here she is, giving me a beautiful upturn of her lips that feels as if she's got her fingers wrapped around my most vital organ.

"Does that line work with everyone else?" she asks, a teasing tone to her voice.

I smirk as I lift my shoulders in a casual shrug. "Couldn't tell you. I've never used it before."

Her smile falters for a moment as she stares at me, complete surprise written all over her face. I truly don't think she realizes that I forget other women even exist when I'm in her presence. No one else matters when she's around.

"Now you're the one killing *me*," she points out, her gaze darting to my erection for a moment before looking back at me again.

"Good." I grab one of her soap bottles and squeeze the liquid into my hand. Once I have enough, I set the bottle down before rubbing my hands together to get them nice and sudsy. Notes of cherries and vanilla fill the shower as I begin to work the soap against her skin.

"I can wash myself." Charlotte looks down at where my hands travel over her stomach, making sure I begin to cover every inch of her skin in the soap.

"I know." I don't stop. I don't want to stop. I want the excuse to keep my skin pressed to hers as I make sure her entire body is lathered. She doesn't stop me either; instead, she keeps her eyes glued to every movement as I continue to cover her soft, tan skin in bubbles.

Every inch of her is perfect. I've seen her in bikinis too many times to count. It's taunted me, imagining what she looks like underneath the scrappy pieces of fabric she's paraded around me in. Seeing every inch of her is something I'll never forget. I couldn't if I tried.

I bring my hand over her full breasts, loving the way she gasps when my fingers travel over her hardened nipple.

"Jude," she warns, her tone thick with lust.

"What?" I ask innocently, my thumb traveling over her

nipple again. I can't help it. She's so damn reactive to every touch that I can't resist teasing her a little. She's tempted me for weeks, and she doesn't even know it. It doesn't hurt to get her back just a little.

"You said we're taking a shower to get clean."

I move my hand to her other breast, this time letting myself feel the full weight of it in my hand. She moans, and the sound makes my cock throb. She watches me carefully as I pinch her nipple between my thumb and pointer finger. It isn't technically necessary to help get her clean, but that doesn't matter. I do it anyway because I love to see her reaction to my touch. "We are taking a shower to get clean," I finally respond, my voice thick with lust. "I'm just making sure every inch of you is clean."

Charlotte playfully rolls her eyes before they flutter shut when I pinch her nipple again, this time harder. I want to test what she likes and doesn't like, committing her reactions to memory so I know for later.

I continue to wash the top of her body, too distracted by watching my hands move against her skin to realize she got her own squirt of soap until her hand wraps around the base of my cock.

Air hisses through my teeth, and my vision gets blurry for a moment as I look down at her fingers wrapped around me. She squeezes a little tighter, attempting to get her fingertips to touch at the base but failing to make it work. I meet her gaze and find her wearing a satisfied smile.

"I'm just making sure every inch of you is clean," she says innocently, throwing my own words back at me.

I can't respond at first.

This is the first time she's ever really touched me there, and it feels so fucking good that I can't form words. The only thing

I can focus on is the way it feels to finally have her hands on me.

She uses my silence to her advantage. Her hand pumps up and down my shaft, and if she hadn't already ruined me, she'd be doing it right now. If I keep letting her move up and down the way she is right now, she'd be able to make me come again in no time. And if her hand feels this fucking good, I can't imagine what her mouth or her pussy will do to me.

I'm a fucking goner for Charlotte. I knew it before she ever touched me, but now that she has, it just solidifies the truth.

I let her continue to stroke me up and down for a few more minutes before the pleasure is too much. I knock her hand away and quickly grab her waist and spin her around, pressing her back to my front so she can't keep stroking me.

She lets out a yelp of surprise as I keep my arms locked around her, preventing her from teasing me the way that she was. I thought stopping her would help, but I don't know if I fully thought through what I was doing. The new position has my cock pressed into her back in a way that forces me to close my eyes for a moment because of just how close I am to her ass cheeks. If I adjusted myself, I could trace the seam of her ass with the tip of my cock, something that's incredibly tempting, given our current position.

"I wasn't done cleaning you," she says with easy defiance.

I can't help but smirk, loving the sass in her tone. My answer is to splay my hand out over her stomach, using it to keep her pressed to me as I let my other hand wander over her hips. "I'm clean," I say, leaning in before pressing a kiss to her neck. Her long hair falls in careless, wet waves down her back. It being pushed from her shoulders gives me free rein to kiss along the tender skin of her back. My fingertips brush over her inner thigh. "You, on the other hand, are still a very dirty girl.

Let me help you with that."

I press the back of my hand against her inner thigh, forcing her legs a little wider so I have better access to her. I run my fingertips over her clit, loving the way she arches against me at the small touch.

The movement makes her grind against my cock, and even though it's such a fucking tease, I love it. Feeling her pressed against me like this encourages me to keep going. I massage over her pussy again, my fingers circling her clit as I use the pretense of cleaning her to tease her.

"Still getting you clean," I rasp, circling again.

She moans, and it's the first time I realize just how hard it's going to be to make it out of this shower without fucking her. I thought I had more self-control, but it turns out that with her, it's almost all but gone. It'll take every ounce of willpower to get out of this shower without burying my cock inside her.

"Jude, it feels too good," she manages to get out, her words broken because of the way I continue to play with her pussy. Hot water cascades over us, bubbles from the soap dripping down our skin as I continue to hold her close to me.

"No such thing," I tell her, wondering if I should give her one more orgasm before we get out of the shower. The next time I come, I want to be buried inside her pussy as she greedily clenches my cock, but that doesn't mean I can't give her one more orgasm before feeding her. She's so reactive to every single thing I do that there's not a doubt in my mind that even if I get her to come again in this shower, I'll be able to have her coming multiple times after we eat as well.

I smile, even though she can't see it. I press my mouth against her throat, loving how I can feel her racing pulse against my lips. I trail kisses along her neck as my fingers circle her clit.

I let the water wash over them, watching the soap run off them until they're free of bubbles before I move them down.

She gasps at the same moment my fingers slide inside her.

"I thought you said we were done until I ate," she pants, her body relaxing against mine as I work my fingers in and out of her.

"I changed my mind."

She attempts to reach around her back to touch me, but it doesn't work. "That isn't fair. If you get to touch me, I get to touch you."

I bite her neck, quickly letting my tongue run over the spot my teeth just were. "It isn't fair how much you've teased me recently just by existing. I promise you'll get to touch me later. But right now, I need you to be a good girl and come on my fingers. Let me give you another."

She moans. "I don't want to come again unless you're inside me."

I slowly coax a third finger inside her, giving her time to adjust around them. "I am inside you." I move them in and out, loving how tight she clenches around me. I can't fucking wait until I feel this same thing around my cock.

"Not what I meant."

"I'm going to try my best to take it slow with you, but you have to understand just how badly I want you. You drive me fucking crazy, and I don't know how long I'll be able to be gentle. Stretching you like this is me getting you ready to take my cock later."

"I don't want you to be gentle."

"Good. Now, I need to feel you come again."

She doesn't answer me. All she does is moan, her body relaxing even more. I hold her up by keeping my other hand pinned against her abdomen, relishing in the fact that she's not stopping this.

Now that I've made her come once, I think I might be addicted. I had the purest intentions to not start anything when I first recommended the shower, but things changed. I can't let either of us leave until she's come around my fingers again, her body relaxed and her pussy prepped to take my cock instead of my fingers next time.

I press the heel of my hand against her clit as I work my fingers in and out of her, desperate to feel her come again. I trail kisses along her neck, biting and sucking a trail along the skin as I continue to bring her close to another orgasm.

The closer she gets, the more her body relaxes, and I end up supporting her weight. I don't mind. In fact, I love it.

Her moans get louder and freer, telling me she's got to be close. She arches her back, her breathing turning ragged and quick as I move in and out of her faster and faster, making sure the heel of my hand stays pressed against her clit the entire time.

"Jude," she pants.

I kiss her neck, wanting her to feel me everywhere when she comes. "I know," I say against her skin. "Come for me, baby."

It's like my permission was the final thing she needed. She lets out a strangled cry as her pussy tightens around my fingers. Her moans are depraved and sexy as hell as the orgasm takes over her body.

"Jude, Jude, Jude." She moans my name over and over so many times I lose count. It drives me to continue to kiss her neck, probably leaving a trail of hickeys, as she rides out the waves of her orgasm.

Feeling her come against my tongue with my fingers inside

her was sexy as hell, but there's something about only using my fingers and still making her come so hard that drives me fucking wild.

I make sure not to stop until she feels every last second of the release, the entire time wondering how the hell I can convince her that whatever we started can never end. She's my best friend, but it's so much more than that. I'll never have enough of her, and it was crazy for me to think I ever could.

Now, I'll do whatever it takes to convince her of the same thing.

42

Charlotte

"What do you want for dinner?" Jude asks me from across the kitchen.

I sit on one of the barstools, staring at him and wondering if I'm somehow dreaming all of this or if he really did have me coming over his fingers ten minutes ago, and now he's standing in front of his fridge, shirtless, offering to make me food.

"What's the fastest thing you can make?"

He wears nothing but a towel tied around his waist, and it's teasing me like crazy. Now that I've seen him—*all* of him—I don't want to eat. I want to get back to my room and finally make him come the way he's done for me—twice.

He lets out a long, throaty laugh as he shakes his head. "Eager to get dinner over with?"

I nod immediately. "Yes. I'm not hungry. I'm horny."

Jude smiles, and somehow, even from across the room, he makes my entire body feel warm just from his heated gaze alone. "I've given you two orgasms, and you're still greedy for more."

I press my thighs together underneath the counter. I've

never come twice in a row, and here I am, begging for a third because of how much I want him. He has this ability to turn me on moments after I've already had a release. What we've done so far has already been incredible, but I want more. I want to go all the way with him, and feeling his tongue or his fingers isn't enough. It won't be enough until I feel him inside me.

"You started it," I tell him, leaning back in my chair as I watch him begin to collect things from the fridge and set them on the counter. "I was minding my own business"—a flush creeps across my cheeks at the memory of him catching me in my room—"taking care of myself, before you interrupted."

"And I've made you come—*twice*—far harder than you would've with the toy you were trying to pretend was me." He shuts the fridge before meeting my gaze. "Don't worry, sweetheart, you'll feel my cock inside you soon enough." He winks, and it's both incredibly hot and extremely frustrating at the same time. He's having fun dragging this out, and there's nothing I can do but eat the damn food he's insistent I have before finally getting what I want.

"I want a peanut butter and jelly," I announce.

He pauses, looking down at the array of ingredients he's laid out on the counter before looking back at me. "I was going to make you a chicken pasta."

I shake my head. "I want a peanut butter and jelly."

His lips twitch with the threat of a smile. "I'm offering to make you any meal you want, and what you want is a peanut butter and jelly?"

I give him a confident nod before crossing my arms over my chest. The movement makes the plush robe I'd haphazardly thrown on after the shower fall open. I let it, hoping that putting the red marks he's left all over me—which will be incredibly hard to hide tomorrow, by the way—on display will make him remember what we could be doing right now instead of eating. "Or maybe just some crackers and cheese. Something fast."

"Or you could let me cook for you and make you a nice meal before I fuck you so hard that you won't be able to walk straight tomorrow."

My mouth snaps shut as my heart hammers inside my chest. He stares at me with raised eyebrows, just waiting for me to respond to the filthy words he just said. Wetness pools between my thighs at the mental picture of him fucking me. I can't help it. He's promised it so many times that I'm wet at the thought of it.

A pit forms in my stomach as I fight the urge to tell him he could make a nice meal for me tomorrow. Saying that would imply how badly I want this to be something that isn't just for tonight, but I don't know how much of what he's saying is because he just wants to give in to the sexual attraction between us or if there are feelings involved too.

For me, the feelings run deep. It isn't just my body that wants him; it's my heart too. But this is Jude we're talking about. No matter how vulnerable he's gotten, I don't know if he's in the right spot to allow himself to feel anything more for me. I'm too nervous to ask, preferring to take what he'll give me, even if that means that this is something more along the lines of friends with benefits.

"Does your silence mean you're going to let me make you a nice meal?" Jude asks, interrupting my thoughts.

I shake my head and smile. "No. I want a peanut butter and jelly. Should I make it, or are you going to make it for me?"

• • •

"I'm done," I announce, pushing my plate away from me.

"You didn't even finish your sandwich," Jude argues, pushing my plate in front of me once again.

"I'm done," I repeat, sliding out of my chair and looking at him with a smile. I did what he wanted. I ate some of the damn PB&J that seemed like it took forever for him to make, and now I'm ready for what comes next.

I'm ready for him to fuck me.

And instead of begging him to do it, I'm taking matters into my own hands.

"It's going to be a long night. Eat the rest of your sandwich, Char. You'll need the energy."

Goosebumps break out all over my skin at what he's insinuating with his words. I hope I need the energy. I hope he can't get enough and that he's inside me all night. There's really only one way to find out.

I slowly back away toward my room. My teeth rake against my bottom lip as I keep my gaze locked on his.

"Char," Jude warns, his voice deep as he drags my name out slowly.

Instead of answering him, I grab the robe tied around my waist. Jude watches me carefully as I pull at one end, loosening the knot until it's undone completely.

His broad shoulders heave up and down with each breath as he focuses on me. I use his focus to my advantage. I let the tie of the robe drop from my hand, forcing both sides open.

He sucks in a deep breath, his eyes immediately following the curves of my naked body.

I love the way he looks at me. He's had me twice now, and you wouldn't know by the way his gaze travels over every inch of my exposed skin. He looks at me as if he'll never have enough, and all I can do is hope that's really the truth.

My pulse spikes with excitement over what's to hopefully come.

I continue to back up in the direction of my bedroom, letting one side of the robe fall down my shoulder in the process.

"Get back here and eat," Jude demands, but there isn't the same control in his tone that there was earlier. He doesn't say the words with conviction. The realization makes me smile.

"No," I answer simply, letting the other side of the robe fall off my shoulder until the only thing keeping it on my body at all is my arms being in the sleeves. "I did what you told me to. I ate. Now I'm ready for you to fuck me."

Jude closes his eyes for a moment, his fingers reaching up to pinch the bridge of his nose. I'll hand it to him—he really is trying to stick to his guns on making me finish my food, but it isn't going to work. I'm done, and I'm ready for what comes next between us.

While his eyes are closed, I let the robe drop to the floor. I don't know if he opens his eyes yet or not, because I quickly spin and make a run for my room, hoping that if he finds me naked in bed again, he'll finally let me be the one to help him find some relief.

My heart hammers in my chest at the sound of the barstool scraping against the hardwood. He's noticed I'm gone, and adrenaline courses through my veins at the idea of him catching up to me.

I run through the hallway naked, wanting to make it to my bed before he catches up to me.

There's some sort of thrill about running from him. I don't know what he'll do when he catches up, but I'm excited to find out.

It doesn't take him long. One moment, I'm running down the hallway, my bedroom door in sight, and the next, his large arm is snaking around my waist and pulling my body against his.

Our chests both heave in unison as we stand in the dark hallway. "What do you think you're doing?" he all but growls, his lips moving close to my ear.

His breathing is uneven as he keeps me pinned against his body. "I thought you were going to be a good girl and follow my directions, but it turns out you're just a dirty slut eager for my cock instead."

I press my thighs together as my entire body goes tight at his words. No one's ever talked to me like that, but it sends waves of heat throughout my body. It's hot hearing those words from his lips, making my clit ache for him.

Somehow, the towel has stayed wrapped around his waist, even with him chasing me. I almost wish it weren't there. I wish I could feel his dick pressed against my back again without a layer of fabric between us.

Even with the towel between us, I do what I can to drive him crazy. I grind my ass against him, tingles running down my spine at the idea of how close I am to finally feeling him inside me.

"I need you."

Jude lets me grind against him a few more times before he sighs. "If my girl is being so needy, then who am I to say no?"

43

Jude

Charlotte's entire body stills against mine.

I can't help but smile, loving the way she clenches her thighs together the moment the words leave my mouth. I think my girl is more than ready for me, and that makes my cock get even harder at imagining how wet she is right now because of my words.

Before she can respond, I quickly spin her around and lift her from the ground. She lets out a loud yelp as I throw her over my shoulder. I tried to do the right thing and make sure she had a good meal before getting fucked all night, but in true Charlotte fashion, she's stubborn and won't even let me try to be a gentleman before I'm inside her all night long.

"I can walk," she tells me, her body squirming as I carry her to her room.

"I'm having fun just like this."

"Jude, I can walk."

It's soft, but I let my hand slap against her ass once.

"Ow! What was that for?"

"For always being stubborn and arguing."

I use my shoulder to push her bedroom door open before immediately letting it shut behind us.

"I'm never stubborn," she argues.

I smile as I toss her onto the bed, remembering just earlier tonight when I found her fucking herself thinking of me. Fuck, I'll never be able to wipe that from my memory. Just like I won't be able to forget the way she looks right now either.

There's a defiant glint to her eyes as she stares up at me.

She's so fucking perfect it makes my chest hurt.

All of a sudden, a realization crashes into me. I want to fuck her—desperately—but I'm also terrified of it. She already owns me in a way that nobody has before, and I just know the moment I feel myself inside her, the moment we become one, it'll truly be over for me. I'll never recover from her. There will never be anyone else for me; it'll just be her. It's like the wool has been pulled from my eyes, and I'm realizing that for a year, I thought I was doing a great job at not falling for Charlotte, but that was all a lie. I pretended I didn't have real feelings for her because she shut me down from the beginning.

But the truth is, I think Charlotte owned my heart even before Ava came into the picture. And once we go all the way, there's no coming back. I'll be hers whether she wants me to be or not.

"What are you waiting for?" Charlotte's words break me from my thoughts. I blink, my gaze focusing on her as I realize she's moved in the time I've been lost in my thoughts of her.

"What?" I ask, taking a step closer to the bed. She kneels, her knees almost coming off the bed as she stares at me with wide eyes.

"I said, *what are you waiting for*?" I love the confident tone of her voice. It's sexy and sure, and it beckons me to take another step closer to her.

Before I can answer her, I close the distance between us and grab her by the back of the neck. My lips immediately find hers, claiming them as mine once again. Our mouths fuse together as I trace her tongue with mine.

The kiss is slow and passionate. I'm so lost in the taste of her that I don't even realize her hands are at my waist until I feel the towel fall from my hips.

I pull away, looking down and finding Charlotte wearing a smug smile. "My turn," she mutters, her gaze moving from my face and down my body.

Her hand wraps around my cock again. It feels so good that my head falls back as I let out a groan of pleasure.

Fuck. It's already too damn much, and she's barely touched me.

She pumps up and down a few times, and I look down again so I can commit the sight of her on her knees to memory. I look at her just in time to see her push her damp hair off her shoulders before leaning forward. Her breath hits my cock, and it jerks in her grasp in anticipation.

This makes Charlotte smile. She looks up at me, and having her on her knees, her mouth inches from my cock, is something I'll never forget.

"Fuck," I rasp, my hand reaching out to trace her cheekbone before I lift her chin to me for a moment. "I've imagined you like this so many times."

She bites her lip, her hand still stroking my cock in a perfect rhythm. "Like this?" There's a sultry tone to her voice I'd never heard before tonight. It sends shivers down my spine. Before I can respond, she leans forward and takes me into her mouth.

Air hisses through my teeth, and I grab onto her hair just to steady myself. I knew it'd feel good, but from the moment her warm tongue circles my tip, I'm fucking gone.

My fingers tangle in her hair, my fingertips pressing into her scalp as she hollows out her cheeks. I try to keep my eyes open to watch her, but it feels so fucking good that all I can do is watch her through hooded eyelids.

She keeps her hand wrapped around the base of my cock, still stroking up and down, while she focuses on the tip for a moment. I feel dizzy because of the white-hot pleasure taking over my entire body.

Her hand continues to work up and down when she pulls away and looks up at me. "Is this what you imagined?" She does a slow, wet drag of her tongue along my entire length, and it makes my entire body rigid with how turned on I am because of her.

I nod, my grip on her hair tightening because I need something to hold on to. "Yes," I manage to get out, my voice thick with lust.

"What else did you imagine?"

My eyes close for a moment because her asking me what I've imagined when it comes to her is so personal but so fucking sexy. When I open them, I find her watching me with wide, expectant eyes.

"You taking me all the way," I answer honestly. I've thought about so many things when it comes to her. One of them being how good it would feel for her to take all of me in her mouth, how it'd feel to have her moan around my cock as I hit the back of her throat.

"You're too big."

"I've always imagined you taking me anyway."

She must take my words as a challenge because instead of

responding, she opens her mouth wide and pulls me in once again. This time, she hollows her cheeks out even more, sucking me so tight that my balls tighten.

My other hand tangles in her hair as well. I want to give her the power to do whatever she wants, but I can't help it. I push her head forward, coaxing her mouth along my shaft so she takes me even deeper.

She moans, and the vibration around my cock has me echoing the sound.

"Good girl," I praise. I look down at her, finding her eyes watching me carefully. "Fuck, you're so goddamn sexy with your mouth full of me."

Her eyelids flutter shut, and I don't miss how the hand not wrapped around my cock moves along her inner thigh until she plays with herself.

"More," I demand. If the tight grip I have on her hair hurts her, she doesn't say anything. I move my hips, forcing more of myself into her mouth.

"Just like that," I grit out. It feels too fucking good. I'm not even fully inside her, and the head of my cock already hits the back of her throat. She gags but doesn't stop. She presses her tongue flat against my shaft and uses her hand to stroke the part of me not in her mouth.

I can't help it.

My hips begin to move faster and faster until I'm fully fucking her mouth.

She lets me do it, her eyes staying focused on me the entire time. Tears prick her eyelids from how deeply she takes me, but she doesn't stop. The way she hurriedly circles her clit with her own fingers encourages me to keep going.

"Fuck, baby, you like your mouth being fucked like this?"

She nods with her mouth still full of me. Tears run down her cheeks, but she keeps going.

It's so fucking sexy, but I know I need to stop. As good as this feels, I don't want to come before I've buried myself in her pussy. With how good she's sucking me right now, if I let her go much longer, I'll be coming down her throat instead of inside her.

"This is exactly what I imagined," I confess, my hips still moving at a fast pace as I fuck her mouth. "You on your knees for me, taking my cock like the good little slut that you are."

She lets out a loud moan, one that I feel not only around my cock but throughout my entire body.

"Actually, this is better than anything I've ever imagined. Have you imagined this too, sweetheart?"

Charlotte nods with her eyes still glued to me. And as much as I fucking love the feeling of my cock in her mouth, I need more. I pull myself from her before she can stop me. I use her shock to my advantage.

One moment, she's still on her knees with my cock all the way down her throat, and the next, I have her pressed into the mattress as I get myself seated between her thighs.

"I wasn't done," Charlotte says, her chest heaving up and down as she props herself up on her elbows to look at me.

I smirk. "Say the word and you can have me just like that any other time. But right now, I need to feel your perfect cunt squeeze around my cock."

Charlotte moans, her eyelids fluttering shut. With me between her legs, her thighs are spread open, showing her pussy already glistening with need for me.

Her lips are red and swollen, beckoning me to kiss them before doing anything else. I bring my face closer to hers, trying to ignore the way my cock brushes over her pussy with the new position.

I love how natural it feels to kiss her. It's a euphoric mixture of the familiarity of feeling like I've spent my entire life kissing her, mixed with the thrill of it feeling like a first kiss every time our lips brush.

I'm so fucking gone for this woman. I've dragged out joining our bodies completely, knowing it'll be the end for me, but it's already too late. I'm hers, and denying both of us the pleasure of finally having sex won't change any of that.

Our tongues tangle with heat and passion. My hand snakes between her thighs, loving how wet and ready she already is for me.

"You ready to be fucked, sweetheart?"

44

Charlotte

"Please fuck me already," I beg, my back arching as Jude slides two fingers inside me.

I wanted to have my fun and give him a blow job to make him feel as good as he's made me feel, but if he won't let me make him come with my mouth, I'm more than ready to feel him inside me.

"Fuck, I love how eager you are for my cock," Jude growls, his teeth scraping against my throat.

He keeps making all of these promises of fucking me and still hasn't yet. Of course I'm eager for it. The orgasms he's given me with his fingers and tongue have already made me see stars. I can't imagine what it'll feel like when he's fully inside me, coming at the same time I am.

My skin prickles at the thought.

As if he can read my mind, Jude pauses the trail of kisses and bites along my neck to look me in the eyes. "I don't have a condom."

I groan because even though I'm on the pill, I know after Ava being a surprise, he's going to want to use one. "Maybe in your room? Your wallet?"

An unreadable look washes over Jude's face for a moment. I so badly want to know what it means, but I'm too distracted by the way his fingers still move in and out of me to ask about it. He shakes his head. "I don't think so. I've never brought a woman here for that, and to be honest, I don't know the last time I needed one."

I blink as I try to process what he's saying. It doesn't make sense, but I'm too lost in my desperation for him to put any more thought into it.

"I don't want to stop," I whine. "I want you to fuck me."

Jude lets out a groan of his own. His forehead falls to mine as he continues to let his fingers slowly move in and out of me. "Are you on the pill?"

I nod excitedly. "Yes. And my recent checkup was clear."

"Mine too. We don't have to if you don't want to. I've always used a condom, but there's nothing I'd love more than to fuck you without anything between us. Char, I want to feel all of you."

I knew I was already falling fast and hard for him, but there's something about the desperation and vulnerability in his voice that splits me wide open.

He must take my silence as hesitation because he pulls his head away to meet my eyes. "We don't have to. I can stop now or try to get condoms delivered or—"

I can't help but laugh at the thought of someone delivering condoms. I shake my head. "I don't want anything between us either."

He lets out a breath of relief. "Fuck, I've dreamed of this so many times, I can't believe it's going to happen."

My eyes close at his words. Jude's always been upfront

about his attraction to me, but flirting is a personality trait for him. I don't know how deep his attraction goes, but it means everything to know that he's imagined us just like this. That maybe even in his sleep, he's wanted me the way I find myself wanting him.

I arch my hips, a silent plea for him to replace his fingers with his dick. They feel incredible inside me, but I still need more. "I need you," I pant, goosebumps popping up on my skin when he pulls my nipple into his mouth.

"Not as much as I need you, sweetheart," he responds before gently biting my peaked nipple.

"Jude." I moan, my entire body once again feeling like I could combust at any moment when he pulls his fingers from inside me and circles my clit with the tip of his dick.

His eyes rake over my face as he pushes hair from my forehead and smooths it out. "Yes, baby?"

I tremble under his touch. He's teasing me, pressing just the tip of his length against me without pushing in. "Please," I manage to get out. My entire body feels like it's on fire. Sweat sticks to my skin as I wait for him to give me what I want.

"Please what?"

"Please, fuck me."

He lets out a deep, throaty chuckle that makes my toes curl. "I've got to give my girl what she wants."

He lines himself up perfectly and pushes in. The moment the tip of him is inside, he lets out a whimper that sends tingles down my spine. It's the hottest sound I've ever heard. It's vulnerable and erotic, and I want to hear him do it again, knowing he made that sound because of the way it felt for him to be inside me.

I run my hands down his back, needing to feel him

everywhere I can as he continues to slowly seat himself.

His head falls to the crook of my neck as his broad shoulders heave up and down from his heavy breathing. "You feel so fucking good, Char."

I arch my hips at his words, the movement allowing him a little deeper. I don't know how much of him is even inside me, but it feels like too much and perfect at the same time.

"I don't know if I can take any more," I confess. I don't want him to stop, but the way he stretches me is already painful.

He presses a soft kiss to my collarbone. His body sticks to mine from the sweat beginning to coat both of us. "Yes, you can," he encourages. His voice is soft, but firm. As if to prove a point, he slides even further into me, something I didn't realize was possible.

I gasp at how good it feels despite the ache that follows from being so full of him.

"You're too big." I moan, my head falling to the side as his tongue trails under my earlobe.

His lips tickle my ear as he lets out a deep growl. "You can take it, sweetheart."

I shake my head. I don't know if I can. It feels like he's in as far as physically possible. My nails rake against his spine as he gives me time to adjust to the fullness of him.

I can't see the familiar shade of blue in his eyes because of the darkness of the room paired with the fact that they're dilated, but he brings his gaze to mine so I can't see anything but him. "I was made for you, just like you were made for me. You're going to take every fucking inch of me because we're perfect for each other."

His body shakes as if he's desperate for more but holding back. I don't want that. I want all of him, to feel him so deep that I'll never be able to forget what it was like to feel him move inside me.

"Keep going," I demand, both needing more from him and not knowing how much more I can actually take.

He smirks, and there's something about seeing that upturn of his lips while he's pushing himself inside me that makes my thighs tremble with desire. He pushes in another inch, and I let out a moan at the feeling. I'm slowly adjusting to the thickness of him, immense pleasure replacing the pain at the sheer size of him.

Jude's hands find both sides of my face. He grips me possessively, his gaze flicking to where our bodies are joined.

"Look at us," he demands. I don't follow his directions at first. I can't. I'm too lost in staring at the way his hair sticks to his forehead and his glasses sit crooked on his face. He's never looked hotter, and the sight of him like this steals my breath for a moment as it hits me that this is really happening.

"Char." His voice somehow gets even raspier—and sexier. I like this controlling side of him. I meet his gaze.

"Yes?"

He looks down again, pulling himself all the way out of me before slowly pushing himself back inside. "Look at how perfectly you take me. You're doing so fucking good, sweetheart."

I do as he says, but the moment is too much. The nickname. The huskiness to his voice. The possessive way he holds on to my face, his fingertips digging into my skin as he holds my head in place. Seeing him inside me. Feeling him inside me. I've never been so turned on in my life, and I'm overwhelmed with the pleasure overtaking my senses.

"Does it feel good?" I ask, my words coming out rushed. I hope it feels as good for him as it does for me. He's barely started moving, but this is already the best sex of my life because it's with him.

"Good isn't even the right way to explain it," he begins, his voice tight as he rocks slowly in and out of me. "The only way to describe it is *perfect*. You're perfect, Char."

He doesn't wait for me to respond, something I'm thankful for because I don't even know what to say back. He's claiming my body as his, but my heart as well. I don't know how he can say things like he is and not expect me to fall for him.

"I'm trying to be slow, baby. I know you need time to adjust, but..."

I shake my head. "I don't want slow. I need more. Faster. Give me more."

His thumb tenderly brushes over my cheekbone. "You sure? You said it's too much, and I'm barely halfway. I don't want to hurt you."

"Give me more," I beg, regretting ever telling him I didn't think I could take it all. I want to, no matter if it hurts or not. Now that he's given me time to adjust, I'm desperate for more. I welcome the ache of him stretching me. Now I want faster and harder. I want to feel it all.

He laughs before pressing a soft kiss to my cheek. It's tender and intimate and makes my heart leap inside my chest. "Tell me if it becomes too much. I'll stop. Just remember how fucking gone I am for you and that you own me, even if I'm fucking you fast and hard like you're my greedy little slut."

I moan at his words. "Yes. Please."

"Since you said *please*." He takes my breath away when he slams his hips into me, fully pushing himself inside the rest of the way.

45

Jude

The moment I push all the way inside Charlotte, I know that she's officially ruined me for anyone else. There will never be another woman in my life. There's just Charlotte.

She lets out a loud moan as I pause, letting her feel all of me for a moment and get adjusted. She asked for more, and I'm going to give it to her. It took everything in me to take it slow and give her time to acclimate. But now, with this little taste of her taking every inch of my cock, I know slow isn't a possibility anymore.

I need fast. Hard. I want her to still feel me tomorrow and the day after that. I want to ruin her for anyone else the way she's ruined me. It's only fair. I want to fuck her so good that she'll realize just how perfect we are together.

"Jude." She moans my name loudly, her pussy hugging me tight.

I trap her mouth with mine, wanting to taste the next time she moans. I intended the kiss to be gentle as I pick up pace with my hips, but she's the one to deepen it. She tilts her head to the side and meets my tongue with hers. I kiss her back, putting the same intensity into the kiss that she is. My glasses bump against her cheek and get in the way of me kissing her the way that I want to. In one quick motion, I'm pulling them from my face and tossing them to the side.

Charlotte pulls away, her lips red and swollen as they turn into a smile. "What if I liked the glasses on? I think you've given me a glasses kink."

I laugh, leaning in to kiss her again as I roughly rock my hips into her. We get lost in the kiss and the feeling of our bodies moving together before I pull away just enough to get words out. "I'm never wearing my contacts again, then."

She wraps her legs around my back, her heels pushing into my ass as she gives me a satisfied smile. "Good." Her new position allows me even deeper inside her the next time I rock my hips back and forth.

It feels too good. She fits too perfectly around me, and I know that I'm not going to last as long as I'd like to. Everything with her is too fucking perfect. The way she hungrily kisses me back, always eager for me. The way her nails bite into my back as I push myself in and out of her. The moans she lets out. The way she reaches inside my chest and grabs me by the heart without even realizing it.

This woman owns me in a way no one has—or ever will again. It's on the tip of my tongue to tell her how I feel, but I can't. I'm too nervous. I don't know if this is just physical for her or if she sees any kind of future with me, and I don't have the nerve to find out. I don't want to ruin things with her. I'll hide my feelings and pretend they aren't there if it means I have any part of her at all—even if it's just the physical side.

"Jude." She moans my name, and I kiss her before she's able to do it again. As much as I love hearing her say my name desperately, if she says it again, I really will be coming before I've had the chance to make her finish before me.

The kiss is messy. We're teeth and tongues and moans as I pick up the pace. I know my hips slam against her in a punishing rhythm, but she doesn't seem to care. Instead, her moans get louder and more depraved. My girl likes to be fucked deep and hard, and it drives me fucking wild.

"God, you feel too fucking good," I say, ripping my mouth from hers. I kiss along her neck, creating a trail of red marks that joins the ones I left earlier. I've never cared about leaving a hickey, but with her, I want them on every inch of her body. I want to claim her in a way that is so raw and primal, and I can't even pretend to feel any different.

Everything with Charlotte is different. I've never wanted—needed—someone the way that I do her. It's both exhilarating and terrifying.

Charlotte moves one of her hands from my back to cup the back of my neck instead. Her fingers latch onto the hair at the base of my head as her nails bite into my skin. She holds me there, keeping our faces close as I continue to slam into her.

Her gaze locks with mine, and there's something so intimate about the moment that I feel the base of my spine tingle with the threat of an orgasm. I've never been inside someone without a barrier or craved the eye contact, but with her, I don't want anything between us, and I don't want to look away.

I want to see her reaction when she comes. I want her to watch *me* when I come. If I'm too nervous to use words to convey how gone I am for her, maybe my reaction will be enough.

"I'm close," she pants, her heels digging more into my ass as she keeps me deep inside her.

"I can tell," I grit out, letting out a shaky breath as I push myself as deep as I can. My hips hit the back of her thighs, making a slapping sound because of the sweat coating both our bodies.

"Come for me, baby," I demand, needing to feel it. "Come around my cock."

Her eyes shut as she shakes her head. "Not until you come. I want to come with you."

Pleasure courses through my veins at her words. "I'm going to," I say through gritted teeth as I continue to fuck her rough and hard. "I want you to come around my cock as I fill you with my cum."

Charlotte squeezes her eyes shut even tighter at my words. Her cunt squeezes me, telling me she loves the idea of me feeling her with my cum.

"Is that what you want?" I grit, reaching between us and taking her nipple between my fingers to turn her on even more.

"Yes," she pants, her back arching. I know she's close with how tight she's getting around me, which is good because I'm seconds away from my own orgasm.

"Good girl. Do it now for me, baby. Let me feel it."

I pinch her nipple and dive in for a kiss, wanting our bodies to touch in every place physically possible. I swallow her loud cry of pleasure as she's finally sent over the edge.

Her nails dig into the back of my neck as I taste her moans, my hips slamming against her a few more times before my own orgasm rips through me. For a moment, my vision fades to black as I ride out the waves of pleasure. Nothing's ever compared to the overwhelming amount of pleasure taking over my entire body.

We're a mix of moans and groans and curse words as we both get lost in the feeling of each other. Both orgasms seem to last forever as our tongues clash in the same passionate manner as our bodies.

Everything about it is fucking perfect. I can't think straight. I can't focus on anything other than the way it feels to finally experience this with her.

We both ride out the orgasm, my hips slowing with each moment that passes by until I go completely still with my cock still buried inside her.

I fall into her, pressing her body into the mattress as we both try to catch our breath. My face finds the crook of her neck as I try to come back to Earth after the mind-blowing orgasm I just had.

I love that she doesn't move. In fact, her legs stay wrapped around me, and her fingers absentmindedly play with the hair at the back of my neck as we both regain our footing.

"That was..." she pants, her chest heaving underneath mine. Her room smells like sweat and sex, and it turns me on again, even though I just came.

"Everything," I finish for her, lifting my head just enough to be able to look her in the eye.

She pulls her bottom lip between her teeth before giving me a smile. "Yes. Everything." Her gaze softens as she continues to play with my hair, and it's at the tip of my tongue to tell her that I've fallen for her. I'll be anything she wants me to be, but I don't want to just be her friend. I want to be more; I'm just too fucking scared of being rejected by her to tell her that.

What if I confess how I feel and I lose her completely? I can't do that. I need her. Ava needs her. So I force myself to keep the words to myself, no matter how much I want to say them out loud.

I never knew if I'd be able to have her like this. I buried the feelings and pretended it was fun to flirt with her, but that it was nothing more. I thought that'd work, but I could only pretend for so long.

From the moment I first saw Charlotte, she captured my attention and has kept it ever since. Little by little, I was giving her my heart without even realizing I was doing so. Nothing in my life used to make sense. It was like a puzzle where I had all the pieces but had no idea how to put them together. But now, the pieces fit together perfectly. I know exactly how I feel—how I've always kind of felt about her deep down —and it all makes sense.

I've fallen for my best friend. Having her like this was the final piece to finally admit to myself that she owns my heart.

I'm hers.

Now, all I have to do is muster up the courage to ask her if that's something she'd ever even want.

"Tell me a secret." Charlotte's words break me from my thoughts of her.

Her words catch me off guard. I open my mouth, not knowing how to even respond. If I were brave, I'd tell her exactly what I was thinking, but for the first time in my life, I'm not confident. I'm not able to say exactly what's on my mind. I care about something enough that I can get hurt, and instead of allowing myself to be vulnerable, I rack my mind for something else I can say instead.

Something safer.

I force a smile, wishing I could tell her what I really want to say. Maybe another time, I'll be brave enough. I just need more time to figure out where her head's at before I put my own heart on the line. I push the wet pieces of hair from her face, my chest aching at just how beautiful she is.

"You want a secret?" I ask, my voice hoarse.

She nods, her fingers still absentmindedly playing with my hair.

I lean in to softly kiss her for a moment to buy myself time. So many different things run through my mind regarding what I could tell her, but I still settle on something that seems safe. I pull away as I let my mouth turn into a smirk. "My secret is that I'm considering hiding your toy from you so next time you get dirty thoughts about me, you just come to me instead."

It isn't the most vulnerable thing I could say to her, but it's a way for me to test the waters. I want to know if she thinks this is a one-time thing or if she wants this to happen again as badly as I do.

"Is that an invitation?"

My chest loosens ever so slightly at her question. "Yes. An invitation. A demand. However you want to look at it, I want you to come straight to me next time."

"What if I tell you that I think about you like that far more often than you think? You might get sick of me wanting you."

My jaw clenches for a moment. I fight the urge to throw a question right back at her: *What if I tell you that I've fallen in love with you and it pretty much feels like, besides my daughter, you're the only thing I think about?*

I keep that question to myself. For right now, it's enough to know that at least she's open to this happening again between us. Now that I've had her, it'll never be enough.

"Oh, Char," I begin, peppering kisses against her forehead. "Listen to me when I say this, sweetheart. I'll never get sick of you wanting me. You got that?" I bring my gaze to hers, loving that despite already having a flush to her cheeks because of the way we fucked each other, she still blushes at my words.

"Got it," she whispers. And before I can do something crazy like tell her I'm in love with her, I kiss her, hoping that maybe another night, I'll have the nerve to tell her my biggest secret… the one about being head over heels in love with my best friend.

46

Charlotte

I wake up to Jude's warm body pressed against mine. His arm is draped across my middle, and his large hand is splayed out across my stomach.

I don't think I've ever slept so well.

When we were sleeping, at least.

He kept his promise by fucking me so hard and long that today my muscles are already sore from the night we shared.

But it was perfect.

Part of me was nervous that I'd wake up and he'd be gone, that he'd regret what we shared last night, but instead of finding my bed empty, he holds me against him like he never wants to let go.

I can't help but smile. Last time I woke up in his arms, I wanted to do everything possible to make sure I got away from him before he woke up and realized the position we were in.

Now, I want to soak in having him like this. I have no idea what things are going to look like for us going forward, so I want to savor every second of the walls being down between us.

Before I can turn my head to see if he's awake or not, he

presses his lips to my bare shoulder.

"Good morning." I try not to shiver at the raspiness of his voice. He sounds sexy in the morning.

I turn a little so I can meet his gaze, and my entire body feels warm at just the way our stares connect.

"Morning," I whisper.

"How'd you sleep?" he asks, the hint of a smirk on his lips.

I blush at the memories of last night. The dirty words he said. The possessive way in which he fucked me. The soft caress of his lips against mine and the way he kissed me as if he planned on doing it forever.

"Good. How about you?"

His smile gets wider, and it's just another moment that grabs hold of my heart. "Never better."

My cheeks feel even hotter at his words. Why does he have to be so perfect? He makes it almost impossible not to fall for him.

He glances over to where the baby monitor rests. At some point, he must've gotten up to get the charger because I know it wasn't in here last night.

"Ava's still asleep. I woke up in the middle of the night to check on her and make sure everything was okay, and she was passed out the entire time."

This makes me smile as I turn my body so I fully face him. I love how his arms tighten around me and pull my body completely flush against his. We're so close our noses almost touch.

"Maybe the sleep schedule is working," I note. Since Ava was dropped off almost a month ago, she's never slept through the entire night. This would be a first, and I can't help but feel a rush of pride that maybe my idea for the sleep schedule is working.

Jude smiles before reaching out and cupping my cheek. I can't help but immediately nestle into his touch. He moved in and out of me for a good chunk of last night, but something about this moment feels even more intimate. "I definitely think it's working. I think I'm going to have to wake her up so she stays on it for the rest of the day."

"Speaking of today, are you excited to go to Pembroke?"

Jude's gaze rakes over my face as he pushes a piece of hair from my cheek. I don't even want to know what my hair looks like. Between the two showers and getting fucked all night, I'm sure it's a tangled mess. Luckily, it's my day off, and my only plans are to hang out with Ava, so it doesn't matter what it looks like. "I was thinking I could tell Tyson I'll join him another day. We were up so much of last night; I don't want to leave you with Ava while I go have fun."

I shake my head before placing my palm against his chest and pushing myself up so I hover slightly over him. "No, not happening. You're not getting out of this, Jude Kensington. You're going to Pembroke today."

His eyes go wide for a moment before a huge grin takes over his face. "I really love it when you're bossy."

My cheeks heat, but I don't let the flirting deter me from making sure he doesn't use us having sex all night to get out of going to the club. "Then you're really going to love it because I'm putting my foot down. You're going to see your friends today and tell them about Ava and stop hiding out here."

"But what if I like it here with just you and Ava? It's like we're a little family that never has to leave."

My mouth snaps shut for a moment because the tenderness in his voice about does me in. I can't help but remember the way Lucy pointed out that we were playing house and how dangerous that might be. Now, with him saying those words, I realize just how much I *like* playing house with him and just how much it doesn't feel like playing at all. It feels real. I want it to be real. Why does everything have to be so complicated?

"You can like it here all you want," I manage to get out despite the thickness that has suddenly clogged my throat due to emotion. "But you're still going to Pembroke today."

Jude moves his hand to behind my neck. Instead of saying anything, he pulls my head down and brings our faces close to each other once again before pressing his lips to mine.

We kiss for a moment. This one is tender and sweet and makes butterflies take flight in my stomach. It seems to last forever, but not long enough either.

Eventually, I pull away just enough to get words out. "Are you kissing me to distract me from forcing you to finally get out of this house?"

He shows off his perfect dimples with a cocky smirk. "Is it working?"

I shake my head and playfully swat at his chest. "No. You're going out, Jude. I promise I slept great and am looking forward to some alone time with Ava."

His face softens as he reaches up to move hair from my forehead once again. "I just feel bad leaving you alone with her while I go out and have fun with the guys."

I frown. "Why? I told you to do it."

He's quiet for a moment, and I wish that I could get into his head to read his thoughts. It feels like there's something he's keeping to himself as his gaze travels over me, and I'd give anything to know what it is. "I don't know," he finally gets out. "I just don't want you to feel like I'm taking advantage of you or anything."

My heart melts at his words. I put my hand over his, keeping his palm placed firmly against my cheek. "I don't think that. I'm the one who made the plans for you."

His fingertips twitch against my skin, and he's quiet for longer than I like all over again. My heart hammers in my chest because no matter how perfect the morning has been so far, it's obvious there's something he wants to say and isn't, and that makes me nervous.

I try to keep quiet for as long as possible in hopes that he'll say whatever's on his mind, but he doesn't. And as much as I wish I had the courage to just ask him what he's thinking, I don't know if I want to know. I don't want to ruin whatever bubble we're in, the one where I got to have him all night and still wake up next to him in the morning.

I can't take the silence any longer, so I plaster on a smile. "So it's settled. You're going to Pembroke. You're going to have fun. And you're going to tell whoever you're comfortable with that you're an amazing dad to an incredible daughter."

He smiles, and the sight of it calms my nerves slightly. His eyelids crinkle at the corner, and his dimples make an appearance, and seeing that makes me believe that maybe I'm overthinking what's going on in his head. "Is that so?"

I nod. "It is."

"Fine. But for the record, I'm kind of sad at the thought of getting out of the house. I like spending my time with my girls."

My girls.

This isn't the first time he's called me his girl, but something about now hits harder than it did before. I want to be his more than ever.

I don't know if he can see the flush to my cheeks with the early morning sunlight filtering in through the window or not.

Whether he can see it or not doesn't matter. It's there because I enjoy Jude calling me his girl far more than I want to admit to myself.

"We'll be here when you get back," I assure him.

"Good. I can't wait."

He leans in for another kiss, and I close my eyes and get lost in it, trying not to let my heart get too excited about being called his. No matter how much I want that to be true, and despite the two of us finally giving in to the physical attraction between us last night, there's still so much we need to work out. I don't know what's going to happen, and there's still a chance I can get hurt at the end of all of this. I try to remind my heart of that as it hammers against my chest at the way he possessively kisses me.

I want to be Jude's as much as I want him and Ava to be mine. With each passing moment with them, that becomes more and more obvious. I just don't know what the future holds, and having so many unknowns is terrifying.

So for now, I push all thoughts of what's to come from my mind and focus on the present. I get lost in kissing Jude, trying my best not to worry about the future.

47

Jude

"Are you sure you're okay with me leaving?" I ask Charlotte for what might actually be the hundredth time.

She rolls her eyes before yanking open the front door. "Jude, I'm positive. Give me Ava, and go have fun."

I look down to where I hold my daughter in my arms. She gives me a gummy smile when our eyes connect, and it does nothing to encourage me to leave. As much as I'd enjoy catching up with friends at Pembroke, I meant it when I told Charlotte I prefer to be home with her and Ava. "How am I supposed to leave her when she's smiling at me like this?"

Charlotte smiles before taking a step closer to us. "Just think of the smile she'll give you when you get home."

I sigh before pulling my gaze from Charlotte. If I look at her too long, I'm afraid I won't leave. I've seen her in the morning numerous times since she first moved in here weeks ago. But this morning is different. Her hair is untamed, memories of tangling my fingers in it all night flooding my mind at the sight. Her lips are red and swollen from where I kissed them all night, and there are even small red marks along her neck that I left there.

Seeing her this morning is different from all the other mornings, because this morning, it felt like she was actually mine. I didn't wake up to find my arms empty. She woke up in my arms the way I'd dreamed about many times before but never got to actually experience until today. She was there, in bed with me, and I can't deny how perfect and normal sharing the morning with her has been.

We kissed in bed before both getting dressed and waking up Ava together. It was perfect, and it's hard not to insist on spending the rest of the day together.

"Now tell me, am I golfing eighteen holes today or just nine?" I ask, leaning in to press a kiss to my daughter's head. After sleeping all night, she's happy as can be. Seeing her in such a good mood doesn't do anything to help me leave the house alone for the first time since she came into my life.

This makes Charlotte laugh. "I've already answered this. You're golfing eighteen, and you're going to enjoy every second."

I let out a groan as I pull Ava tightly to my chest. I've already loaded my SUV with my clubs, and I really should leave so I make it to Pembroke in time to make my tee time. It's just so hard to leave both Ava and Charlotte.

"I miss you already," I mutter against the top of Ava's head. My lips move against a giant bow Charlotte insisted on putting in her hair.

"She misses you too," Charlotte confirms. She takes a step closer until her body presses slightly against mine as she puts her hand against Ava's back.

I meet her blue gaze and can't help but let my lips turn up

in a smile. "I meant I'll miss both of you."

I love how she blushes immediately. She's so reactive, even to just my words, and it drives me crazy. Her mouth opens and shuts as she tries to get words out. The sight makes my smile get even wider. It isn't often that Charlotte is rendered speechless, but it seems that admitting I'll also miss her, in addition to my daughter, has done the trick.

"You will?" she finally asks, her voice quiet and unsure.

I nod before wrapping my arm around her and pulling her body against mine. I love how right it feels to hold both Ava and Charlotte in my arms. We stay locked in the embrace for a few moments as I try to come up with an excuse to ditch the guys and stay home instead. It's not even that I don't want to tell them about Ava. I'm actually really excited to let my friends know about how great she is. It's just that I don't want to be apart from Charlotte and Ava that has me hesitant to leave.

"Of course I'll miss you. With you two is where I always want to be."

She doesn't pull away or do anything to make me think my words scare her. The realization makes me smile. We probably need to talk about what happened last night and what happens next, but I push it away for now. There isn't time to get into it this morning, and I don't even know if I want to have that conversation yet. I'm good with how things are right now, and maybe talking about it will make it too complicated. I can't tell her that I've fallen for her...that'll probably scare her away.

And it probably isn't even fair for me to confess my feelings to her yet. There's still a lot I'm figuring out with my life now that Ava is in the picture, and when I tell Charlotte how I feel about her, I don't want her to question it at all. I need more time to prove to her just how deep my feelings have become and show her that I'd do anything to make it work between us.

"As much as I'm loving this hug, I think it's time for you to go," Charlotte speaks up, pulling me from my thoughts of her.

I let out another sigh because I know it's true. I give her one last squeeze before letting my arm drop.

I pull Ava away from me just enough to see her face. "You be good for Char, okay, baby girl?"

"She'll be perfect," Charlotte assures me. She holds her hands out to take Ava. I press one more kiss to my daughter's head before handing her over.

"You promise you'll call if you need anything?"

Charlotte nods. "Of course. But everything will be fine, and we'll be here when you're done."

I stand there, wondering if it's too much to kiss her. I've stolen kisses from her all morning, but there's something about leaning in for a goodbye kiss that feels like…more.

She stares at me, her grip on Ava tight as Ava starts to babble to herself and wiggle.

My heart begins to double in speed because I want to lean in and kiss her, but I'm just scared she might push me away.

Char watches me closely. I lean in, watching her every move to gauge if I'm making a mistake or not. I can't help but smile when she rises to her tiptoes to meet me halfway.

We both move slowly as we bring our heads close together. Our gazes stay locked as I bring my lips to hers.

We've kissed plenty of times at this point, but I think this one might be my favorite.

It might be because it's sweet and tender, done with both our mouths slightly upturned as we both can't help but smile. Or maybe it's the fact that my hand rests on my daughter's back, and a kiss goodbye seems like the most normal thing in the world to do. I'm saying goodbye to the two people who matter most to me in the world, and I can't help but hope I'm lucky enough to have goodbye kisses with the two of them just like this for the rest of my life.

Charlotte's the first one to pull away. There's still the whisper of a smile on her lips as she takes a step back and points to the open door. "It's really time for you to go, or you're going to be late."

I sigh but nod. "Okay, I'm leaving. Goodbye, girls."

"Say goodbye to Daddy," Charlotte says. She lifts Ava's hand to her little mouth and makes her blow a kiss. It's so precious that I commit the sight of the two of them to my memory.

Fuck, I don't want to go. I want to stay home with the two of them and pretend the rest of the world doesn't exist, but I can't. I need to get out and find a way to merge my old life with my new one.

I press a kiss to both of their foreheads and rush out the door before I talk myself out of leaving. Once I get to Pembroke, I'll have fun and will thank Charlotte for giving me the time out with my friends. It's just hard. I'm not used to having people waiting at home for me, and now that I do, I'm realizing how lucky I am. I used to do everything in my power to avoid being home because I hated being alone.

Now, home is the place I want to be the most, because home is not only my daughter, but it's Charlotte too.

48

Charlotte

Jude

How's everything going?

I smile as I look down at my phone. I lie next to Ava on her playmat in the living room, shaking my head at her dad already checking in when it feels like he just left.

I pull up the camera app on my phone and switch it to selfie mode. I make sure both Ava and I are in frame before snapping a photo and sending it to Jude.

Charlotte

We're doing just fine without you ;)

Charlotte

Have fun!!

Jude

This photo is a tease. Now I want to leave Pembroke and race home to my girls.

I close my eyes and clutch my phone to my chest. He's really got to stop doing that. My heart can't handle it. I don't think he realizes what he does to me every time he calls me *his*.

I groan and open my eyes. The sound catches the attention of Ava. She rolls to her belly and looks at me with a gummy smile.

"Don't laugh at me, Ava girl," I whine. "Your dad is just too cute, and it's killing me."

She excitedly kicks her legs and lets out a tiny little giggle that has me smiling despite my current predicament of catching feelings for her dad, even though I know I shouldn't. I'm about to tickle her for laughing at me when my phone vibrates again.

Jude

Keep sending photos of the two of you.

Charlotte

Deal. But also put your phone away and enjoy your time with the guys. I'll get ahold of you if anything happens, but I promise we'll be fine.

Jude

If I put my phone away do you promise to keep sending photos that I can look through later?

Charlotte

Yes. Now go have fun.

Jude

I love it when you're bossy.

I roll my eyes and toss my phone to the side. I already can't wait to hear all about his day golfing and how it went to tell more people about Ava, but I also want him to enjoy his time with the guys. Ava and I will have fun in his absence, while also being excited for him to get home.

• • •

My day with Ava has been amazing so far. We played, read some books, and she drank some milk before doing a great job at sleeping in her crib for an almost two-hour nap. We're back on the floor, playing on her playmat and listening to the same song she's obsessed with from one of her toys, when the doorbell rings.

I pause, wondering who it could even be. The doorknob moves as if someone's trying to get in. I immediately grab Ava and pull her to my chest.

There's beeping and then the sound of the door unlocking. My heart thuds because I have no idea who is coming into Jude's house right now, but it's obvious that whoever it is knows the passcode to his locks.

My heart hammers as I stumble to stand up with Ava in my arms.

"Jude," a woman's voice calls out.

I frown because I have no idea whose voice that is.

The door swings open, and I come face-to-face with a woman I recognize, but only because of photos on the internet and the photos Jude showed me before. A man steps through the door behind her, the two of them immediately looking at me.

"Hi," I mutter, my heart racing as I try to think of what to say to Jude's parents.

"Charlotte," Jude's mom says sweetly, her features softening as she looks from me to the baby in my arms. "And is this Ava?"

I nod because I don't know how to respond. I guess it makes sense that they would know who I am because of Jude. I've been excited to possibly meet them one day. Jude's talked so much about them, and they obviously raised an incredible son. I just wasn't expecting to be meeting them today, and I definitely wasn't expecting to meet them without Jude here too.

"We thought we'd surprise Jude and meet our granddaughter," Jude's mom explains as she walks to the kitchen counter. She sets down her large designer bag and gives me a warm smile. "We told him our trip didn't end for a few more days, but we finished business early and couldn't wait to get home to meet Ava. I guess I should've thought about calling him first."

I swallow as his dad shuts the door and also gives me a smile. I'm wondering if I should call Jude and tell him that his parents are here or ask him what I'm even supposed to do in this situation. "He went to golf at Pembroke. I'm sure he'll be done soon. Maybe we should call him?"

Jude's mom waves her hand dismissively through the air. "Not necessary. Let him enjoy his time. Last time we spoke, he told me he hadn't gone to the club or told anyone there about his daughter yet."

She walks up to me, and I keep Ava clutched to my chest, not knowing what to do. I know these are her grandparents—they share blood with her when I don't—but I still feel weird just handing her over to them without Jude here.

"This is his first time going," I confirm.

Jude's mom holds her hand out. "I'm Florence, by the way. And this is my husband, Nathaniel."

I smile because I appreciate that she's introducing herself and not immediately taking Ava from my arms. My heart still beats erratically, but something about her warm smile helps ease my nerves.

I shift Ava so I hold her with one arm and hold out my other hand. "I'm Charlotte."

Florence's smile grows. "I know who you are. Jude's talked a lot about you over the past year."

I can't help but smile while my heart leaps in my chest. I've certainly mentioned Jude to my mom—my entire family, really—but there's something about knowing he's talked about me as well that makes my heart melt.

"Oh, really?"

Florence's gaze rakes over me as she drops my hand. I try not to squirm underneath her stare. She's got the same big, almond eyes that Jude has, but instead of being brown like his, they're more hazel. "He talks about you often. There was a time when I thought you might be his girlfriend and he was too nervous to admit that to his nosy mother."

I choke on my own spit at her comment. It was the last thing I was expecting her to say, and she said it so casually. "Not his girlfriend," I rush to get out in between coughing fits.

Ava grabs at my cheek and smiles, clearly finding me choking on my own saliva hilarious.

Florence just watches me with a lifted brow and an unreadable stare.

"We're just friends," I finally get out.

Florence's gaze drops.

My jaw clenches, and my cheeks feel like they're on fire when I realize what she's looking at.

I hadn't expected visitors this morning when I got dressed. I thought it was just going to be me and Ava hanging out. If we were to leave for a walk or something, I would've changed. But because we were having fun inside, I didn't think twice about throwing on a tank top and leggings. The leggings are fine, although I do feel underdressed compared to Florence in her linen dress, but it's the tank top that's the problem. It does nothing to hide the hickeys left all over my neck.

I keep a tight hold on Ava as my cheeks continue to flush. I don't even know what to say to Florence. I don't know if I lie and say that the hickeys are not from Jude—that doesn't seem right—or if I just tell her that they are from her son, but we're still just friends.

My mouth stays shut because neither option seems like a great idea.

"As a *friend*," Florence begins, putting emphasis on *friend* and letting me know she doesn't believe me whatsoever, "are you also Ava's nanny now? I thought Jude told me you worked at Pembroke."

I nod. "I do. I'm a cart girl there, but I only work the weekend shift. Since I have most weekdays off, we're trying this thing where I watch Ava a couple of days during the week so Jude can get out and also work when he needs to."

Nathaniel speaks up from where he stands by the couch a few feet away from us. "That's kind of you to step in. I was wondering why he was falling behind at work; that wasn't like Jude. Since he told us about Ava, I've been trying to delegate his workload to others, but there's stuff that needs to be overseen by him. Good to know he has a plan moving forward."

"He's been doing his best," I say, meeting Nathaniel's gaze. The first thing I think when our eyes meet is that Jude has the same warm, brown eyes as his father. "It's been hard for him to not take on the full load of caring for Ava, but hopefully soon, we'll find a rhythm," I continue, wondering why it's so important to me that his parents know how hard he's been trying to juggle it all. They haven't seen him every day, navigating all of this, the way I have. He's doing the best he can, and they should know that.

"She really looks just like him," Florence notes, completely changing the subject.

My gaze moves from Nathaniel back to Ava. I focus on her the same way Florence does, remembering how I thought the same thing the first time I saw her. Ava looks almost identical to her dad. I have no idea who her mother is, but I really can't see anyone else in Ava's features besides Jude.

"She's perfect," I whisper, leaning in and pressing a soft kiss to the top of her head.

"Do you know who her mother is?" Florence asks, taking me by surprise that she would ask the question so quickly.

I immediately shake my head. "I don't know her name. Jude didn't tell me, and I didn't ask."

Florence frowns for a moment as if she doesn't believe me. I can't help but feel a tinge of pain in my chest because…is that something he should've told me? His mom clearly expects me to know, but it isn't something I ever wanted to push Jude on. I didn't really care to know. If Ava's mother didn't want to be in her life, then it isn't necessary for me to know her identity.

She looks a little disappointed that I don't have the answer. "He told us it was someone in his past, but that's as far as he'd go. He hired his own lawyers and didn't involve us in any of the legal dealings, so I can't even find out from the lawyers who her mother is. From the sound of it though, it seems like he's getting closer every day to having full parental rights to Ava," Florence continues. "I don't want to ask him if he doesn't want to share. I just feel like I could be doing more to help him, but it doesn't seem like he wants the help."

I don't say anything in response. Jude's kept me updated about the legal proceedings. It's a long process, but so far, it seems like everything is going according to plan for him to have full rights to Ava.

"Can I hold her?" Florence asks, pulling me from my thoughts.

I blink, trying to regain focus as I think about the right thing to do in this situation. Jude adores his parents. I know there isn't any reason he wouldn't want his mom holding his daughter…it just feels weird that he isn't here for the moment.

I nod. "Do you mind if I take some photos of it though?" I point to where my camera sits on the end table by the couch. Since it was just me and Ava, I spent some of our playtime getting photos of her. My memory cards are filled with photos of her over the last month. I want to start putting together a gift for Jude to give him on Ava's first birthday, something filled with photos of her from every month she's been with us. "I just feel bad Jude isn't here for the moment, and he'll want to be able to see the two of you holding her for the first time."

Florence looks over to where Nathaniel closes the distance to her and places a hand on her shoulder.

Nathaniel stares at me with the same brown-eyed gaze as Jude, his lips pressed into a thin line before he gives one curt nod. "That's very thoughtful of you."

Florence nods along with her husband. "We'd love that."

I smile and squeeze Ava once before handing her over to Florence. Jude's mom's eyes immediately glass over when Ava goes to her without any protests. I take in the moment for a second before hurrying over to grab the camera.

I take as many photos as I can, wishing Jude were here to see this moment with his parents but doing everything I can to make it feel like he didn't miss a thing when he returns home from his day at Pembroke.

49

Jude

"There he is," Tyson teases as I step into the pro shop at Pembroke. "I was worried that you completely disappeared. Charlotte's been telling me you're fine and just busy, but if you didn't show up today, I was going to call *Dateline*."

I roll my eyes as I come to a stop next to him. "No need. I'm here. It's just been a crazy few weeks."

Tyson stares at me for a moment. I shift under his stare, wondering if he somehow knows about Ava already or if he's thinking something else as he watches me closely. I didn't know anyone could hide their emotions better than Cal, but it turns out Tyson has a better poker face. He nods. "Glad you could make it, then."

I give him a smile as a little bit of guilt hits me. I still don't know Tyson as well as I know other members at the club, but I'm enjoying getting to know him, and I feel bad that the craziness with Ava paused that for a moment. Tyson hasn't been as active a member in the past as his sister, Winnie, or her husband, Archer, but it seems like he's making an effort to be here more. Now that I'm figuring out my footing with Ava, I make the mental note to put more effort into getting to know Tyson more. I really like him, and I hope the month of ignoring him reaching out hasn't upset him.

"Is it just us today, or is anyone else joining?" I ask. I know Charlotte had mentioned that some others might come out, but I was so wrapped up in what happened between us last night and not wanting to leave her and Ava today that I forgot to ask.

"Archer, Cal, and Beck are coming. Ryker, Camille, Preston, and Emma all come in later this week, so they want to join in another day."

I nod. Part of me was hoping all the guys would be here so I could tell them about Ava all at once instead of having to do it multiple times, but telling Tyson, Archer, and Beck about my daughter will still be a way to get the word out. My chest feels tight with nerves, but I know I'll feel better once I'm finally able to tell them.

Everyone else will find out when I show up at the party on Friday with Ava in tow. The small group today will allow me to dip my toes into sharing the news before the big reveal later this week.

"It'll be nice to catch up with everyone," I note. When Tyson doesn't answer me, I follow his gaze to see what's caught his attention. He's always quiet, but there's something about the way he stares out the pro shop window that catches my attention.

I follow his gaze until I see a woman with shoulder-length blonde hair standing on the sidewalk, speaking with a Pembroke employee. I don't know if Tyson is staring at the blonde or the employee, but whichever one it is, when I look back at him, I find that his gaze still hasn't wavered.

"How are you feeling about today? You ready to actually win against me this time?" I ask. All of them are probably going to beat me because I haven't swung a club in weeks. I'm used to golfing a few times a week, so it'll probably take some time for me to get back in the groove.

I stare at Tyson, a grin tugging at my lips as he still doesn't respond to me. His blue eyes stay pinned on the two people having a conversation out the window. His face is stone-cold as he pays close attention to them. I wish I knew which one he was staring at, but they're too far away to be able to tell. But whatever it is, I can't help but be curious why Tyson is so focused.

"You know all the Pembroke members, don't you?" Tyson asks, completely ignoring my question.

My eyebrows pull in on my forehead in confusion. "I'd like to think I do. Why?"

He finally looks away long enough to meet my gaze for one moment before his attention goes back to the two people on the sidewalk. "Then do you know the name of that blonde woman?"

I strain my neck to see if I can catch her at a different angle. I don't know how he expects me to fully recognize someone just by the back of her head, but I try anyway. She finally turns just enough for me to see her profile, but she's still too far away for me to know who it is.

"I don't think I can tell from here. Why?"

Tyson shakes his head. He keeps his attention on the blonde I don't recognize. I can't tell what he's thinking by the look on his face, but something about her definitely steals his attention. Eventually, he shakes himself out of whatever trance he's locked in and returns to look at me. "No reason. Ready to get checked in? We'll share a cart and wait for the others. Someone's going to have to ride solo and tag along. Charlotte sweet-talked Teddy into letting us have a fifth person out with us today." Typically, there are only four people for each group, but since it's a private club where everyone knows everyone, sometimes the rules can be bent.

I can't help but frown at his mention of Teddy. My mind immediately remembers the way that it felt to read his name across her chest the day she was wearing his jacket. That same familiar twinge of jealousy hits me at just the mere mention of him.

"Is that so?" I grit out, my teeth grinding against each other as I look across the shop at Teddy. I hadn't even noticed he was working today until Tyson mentioned it.

"Why do you look like you want to kill the poor pro shop employee?" Tyson asks, humor in his tone. He seems to have all but forgotten about the woman he was staring at moments ago. I don't look at him as an idea pops into my head.

"Let's get checked in. I need to talk to Teddy anyway."

Tyson hums a response, but I feel him follow close behind me as I walk up to the desk.

Teddy immediately smiles at me, but it falters when I don't return the smile. "Hi, Mr. Kensington. We've been wondering where you've been."

"Mm-hmm." I stare at him, jealousy blooming in my chest again at the memory of Charlotte wearing his jacket. It's ridiculous. The guy has always been nothing but nice to me. "I'd like to purchase a Pembroke jacket," I tell him.

Teddy looks at me, confused for a moment, but regains his composure. "Okay. What size?"

"Small."

"Small?" Tyson asks from right behind me.

Teddy looks just as confused as Tyson sounds.

I nod. "Yes. A small. And then can you make sure you hang it up in Charlotte's employee locker or wherever she keeps her things?"

Teddy's eyes go wide as it seems he finally comprehends the reason behind my purchasing a jacket. I meant to buy Charlotte one the moment I saw her wearing Teddy's, but then Ava was brought into my life, and I got distracted. She's been coming to work since, and I can't help but wonder if there were any other days she wore his jacket that I don't know about.

"Sure thing," Teddy gets out nervously. His eyes look to Tyson for some sort of help. "Are you ready to be checked in?"

I step aside, not wanting to have any more of a conversation with Teddy. If I do, I might be a dick, and I'm not used to being that. I'm also not used to being jealous, so allowing Tyson to finish getting us checked in while we wait for the others is probably best.

• • •

"So," I begin, meeting the gazes of my friends as we all stand in a circle deciding the order for golfing today. "There's something I just want to tell everyone before we get the day started."

Cal gives me a smile as his eyebrows lift on his forehead. I can't help but wonder if he thought I might back out of telling the others about Ava today. I can't wait to prove him wrong and finally tell the guys about Ava so they will better understand my absence recently.

I scan the rest of the guys in the group, my heart suddenly

thundering in my chest. I took a few sips of beer in an attempt to get some liquid courage for the news, but the alcohol hasn't kicked in at all. They all just stare at me expectantly, waiting for me to continue.

I swallow. "I'm a dad." The words come out hurried, and they're muttered to my feet instead of to the guys, but still they're out.

I don't look up, not wanting to see their faces at first.

"A dad?" Beck asks.

"Who's pregnant?" Archer questions moments later.

I press the toe of my shoe into the golf green for a moment before working up the courage to look at them. I focus on Cal since he already knows the news.

"No one is pregnant. The baby is here. She's almost five months old, and her name is Ava."

It's silent for a few beats before Beck is the one to speak up. "Being a girl dad is the best."

I meet his stare, relief flooding through me that he didn't ask another question. I smile. "Yeah, she's got me wrapped around her finger, that's for sure. Since I found out about her, it's been kind of crazy. Her mother doesn't want to be involved, and I'm working on getting full parental rights to her. It came as a surprise that she even existed…so that's where I've been recently." By the end of me talking, my words come out hurried and almost blur together. I was just so ready to get the news of Ava out on the table that I couldn't even slow down when talking.

It's quiet for a few beats as all of them soak in what I said. I know me being a dad was probably the last thing they were expecting to hear today, but I'm glad I've now told them.

Tyson clears his throat. "That's amazing, and it explains a

lot. Happy for you, Kensington."

I give him a relieved smile. "Yeah, sorry I ignored your invites to hang out. You can now understand that I've been preoccupied."

He nods. "All good. I'm excited to meet her."

Archer chimes in. "Winnie will be thrilled to find out there's another baby in the crew. She's always talking about how much she adores Celeste."

"Margo will also be so excited that we aren't the only ones with a baby. Although it makes me sad… I don't know if I can even call Celeste a baby anymore because she's getting so big," Beck notes.

I can't help but let out a sigh of relief at how easy they react to the news. I've spent the last month worrying that anytime I told anyone about Ava, they'd grill me with questions, but I'm learning that maybe all of those fears were just in my head. So far, no one's pressured me to speak about Karina, for which I'm incredibly grateful. They've been nothing but encouraging after learning about Ava, and it makes me feel bad for taking weeks to tell everyone about her in the first place.

All the tension in my body dissipates as they ask me questions about Ava without ever being intrusive. They listen intently as I give them the details I'm willing to share before we start our round of golf.

Time flies by, and all I can think about is how excited I am to get home once the eighteen holes are over and tell Charlotte how appreciative I am of her getting this all set up. No matter how much I miss my girls, the time with my friends today is just what I needed to finally feel comfortable finding a new normal that involves Ava in my life at Pembroke.

50

Charlotte

It's been almost two hours since Jude's parents showed up, and I don't want to admit the number of times I've checked my phone since they've been here. I keep expecting to see a notification from Jude, but I haven't gotten anything. He's got to be done with the eighteen holes by now, but my guess is he's probably still hanging out with the rest of the guys or doing something at the club. I was the one who told him to have fun and stop checking in, but now that his parents are here, it feels weird to still not have told him that they arrived unexpectedly. I can't help but wonder if I should text him and tell him anyway even though Florence didn't want me to.

I quietly shut the door to Jude's room, making sure I don't wake up a sleeping Ava. She had a great time playing with Florence and Nathaniel for the last hour, but it was obvious she was getting tired. Florence was thrilled to give her a bottle before I grabbed Ava and put her down for a nap. Once I leave Jude's room, I sneak down the hallway and into my room to grab some clothes to cover the hickeys Jude left before returning to the main living space.

I walk into the living room at the same time I watch Nathaniel step out to the back porch. My stomach drops at the idea of being alone with Jude's mom. She's been nothing but nice to me since they showed up, but I'm nervous that being alone with her will lead to her asking questions I don't have the answers to.

"I probably should've asked this earlier, but do you need anything to drink? Some food?" I ask, trying to make idle conversation with her.

Florence shakes her head. She sits on the couch with her ankles crossed, her hazel gaze locked on me. There's a hint of a smile on her lips, but something about the way she looks at me makes me nervous. "No, thank you. Want to come sit next to me?"

My feet pause as I stare at the empty spot on the couch next to her. If I were honest, I'd tell her "not really," but instead, I find myself closing the distance and taking the seat next to her.

I give her a tight-lipped smile, my heart beginning to race at the way she looks at me. It almost looks like she pities me, and I don't like the sight of it. I don't know why she'd look at me like that, but something about her demeanor tells me I'm about to find out.

"It's very kind of you to step in and help Jude like this," she begins.

I try to take a deep breath because maybe I'm overreacting and that's all she wants to talk about. It'd make sense that she just wants to extend her gratitude for stepping in and helping Jude when he needed it. "Oh, thank you, but I'm happy to help out," I respond, my voice a little unsteady. I don't know why I'm suddenly so nervous, but my intuition tells me this conversation is going to go in a direction I might not like.

She solidifies my gut feeling by clearing her throat and giving me a pensive stare. "Tell me, Charlotte...do you care about my son?"

My mouth opens and closes as I think of how to respond to her question. "Of course I do. We've grown close over the last year. He's my friend."

Her gaze slips to the marks that are now hidden underneath the fabric of my sweater. "And the way you care about him...it's *just* as a friend?"

I twist my hands in my lap. I'm tired of having to lie to everyone when they ask me how I feel about Jude, but I'm also not ready to say out loud just how deep my feelings have gotten for him. When I finally make sense of them and am finally ready to talk about them, I want Jude to be the first to hear it, not anyone else.

"Yes," I lie. Truthfully, when I look at Jude, he feels like so much more than a friend, but I can't say that to his mom. Not when I'm still figuring out what exactly it means to be falling for my best friend and especially not when I haven't been honest with him about them either.

She stares at me for I don't even know how long. Her posture is rigid, and her face is unreadable as she scans my face. Eventually, she sighs. "For your sake, I hope that's the truth."

My head rears back at her comment. "What's that supposed to mean?"

"It means I hope that you mean it when you say Jude is just your friend."

All I can do is stare at her. If I ask her for more details, will it make it obvious to her that I definitely view him as more than just a friend?

Her shoulders fall as she lets out a long sigh. She takes me by surprise by reaching out and clutching my hand in hers. Despite the gesture, it still feels like you can cut the tension in the room with a knife. "I love my son," she begins, her tone cautious. "He's my only child. I'm lucky enough that even after he became an adult, we remained close. I have friends whose sons never call them or make an effort to see their parents. That isn't Jude. He's always called home and made a point to visit us, even when he's busy with work and life."

I nod because I don't know what else to do. It seems like there's a *but* coming, and I'm nervous for what that'll be.

"We made sure we gave him the world. He's our only son and the heir to a company the family's worked incredibly hard to build. He's worked hard his entire life, but he's also had it easier than some. Things have always come easily to him, and I'm worried that this next season of his life will really test him."

"He's doing great," I whisper, wishing I could put more strength into my words, but I'm too nervous for wherever this conversation seems to be leading to lace too much conviction into my words.

Florence nods. "I'm really proud of him for the way he's handling things, but I just don't want you to get hurt in the process of him figuring out his life."

Even though I knew the *but* was coming, it doesn't make what she says hurt any less. Especially when she's bringing up one of my biggest fears when it comes to falling for him.

"Why would I get hurt?" I manage to get out, wanting to know her take on the situation.

She frowns for a moment as her gaze sweeps over me. It feels like she was hoping I wouldn't ask, but I can't help it. I've just met the woman, and she already feels the need to give me a warning when it comes to her son. I want to use the opportunity to figure out why she feels the need to do that in the first place.

"Because...Jude's always had this mental picture in his head that he would take over the family business, eventually settle down, get married, and have kids. I know he didn't put a time frame on it for himself, but he's always mentioned the desire for a family. I know he loves Ava, and she's now his entire world, but the way things have panned out isn't what he imagined for himself. I'm worried with you being here, and the two of you spending so much time together, that he—and maybe even you—will get swept up in playing the part, and in the end, someone will get hurt. I don't want it to be my son, but I don't want it to be you either."

I swallow as I try to fight the stinging in my eyes. She's basically echoing the same thing that Lucy said. I've tried to push Lucy's fear of me playing house to the back of my mind because it was only one opinion, but now with Florence saying the same thing, I can't help but think a little deeper into both of their points.

Are we just playing house? Are the feelings between us only because of the situation we're in? I've been so worried about messing up the friendship Jude and I have worked hard to build that I've tried not to even think too hard about Lucy's words.

"Nothing's happened," I lie. My words come out weak, and the way she closes her eyes in disappointment for a moment before opening them to look at me again tells me she doesn't believe me in the slightest.

"I think you're a fantastic woman," Florence begins. "It takes someone special to jump in and help raise someone else's baby. I'm not taking that away from you. I truly don't know what my son would do without you, but I think that might also be a problem. I don't want him to depend on you, let you in, and you decide that it's all too much."

I shake my head, hating the fact that she thinks I'd ever be able to just walk away. "I wouldn't be here if it was too much."

Florence lets out a deep sigh. "You're young, Charlotte. You still have so much life to live and to figure out. What happens when you realize that at twenty-four, you don't want to settle down and raise someone else's baby?"

I keep my mouth shut, even though I want to point out that I love Ava because she's Jude's. I know she isn't my blood, but that doesn't make me care about her any less. It doesn't matter that she isn't my blood. I don't love her any less. "I care about Jude, and I care about Ava. I don't have plans to go anywhere."

Florence lets out a defeated sigh while she looks me in the eyes. "You say that now. But things change. And I'd give the same advice to my son too. I don't want him to get lost in the idea of creating a family with you and having you step in for Ava and then one day wake up and realize he moved too quickly and you get hurt in return."

My eyes burn because she's pointing out my biggest fear with all of this. It's something I haven't even wanted to think about because it hurts too much. But now that she's said it out loud, I can't think of anything else.

It's only been a month since Ava came into our lives, and things have changed so quickly. Before Ava, Jude and I were just fine being friends. Is it because of Ava that we started feeling more for each other? Are we both so swept up in this idea of a family together that we've convinced ourselves that we feel things for each other that wouldn't be there if Ava weren't in the picture?

Florence squeezes my hand, reminding me that she'd even

reached out to hold it in the first place. "Just be careful with my son's heart and with yours, okay? Really think about things."

I nod. I can't say anything because my throat is clogged with emotion. Even if I could manage to get words out, I don't even know what I'd say in the first place. I'm too lost in analyzing her words and the last month of my life to even respond.

"And as much as I like you—and appreciate you stepping in and doing something not many women would—I want you to know my son and my granddaughter come first. If you hurt either of them..." She shakes her head and lets her words hang in the air for a moment.

She never gets to finish them before Jude walks in the door. "I'm home!" he exclaims, looking at the ground. "Now, where are my gir—" He looks up and pauses, his head cocking to the side.

"*Mom*?"

51

Jude

The day at the club was just what I needed. I was having so much fun that I even lost track of time talking with my friends after we finished the eighteen holes. As soon as I realized the time, I raced home without even letting Charlotte know I was coming. I was so excited to thank her for forcing me out of the house and for watching Ava that all I could think about was getting back to my girls.

Maybe that's why I walked in the front door without even looking up first.

Or maybe why I didn't even notice the fact that there was a car parked on the street that isn't typically there.

Either way, finding my mom sitting in the living room next to Charlotte was the last thing I was expecting.

"What are you doing here?" I ask, setting my golf bag down in the entryway and closing the door. "Is Dad here? I thought you both were still out of the country."

Mom immediately pushes herself off the couch and closes the distance to me. "My boy," she mutters, grabbing my face in her hands before lifting to her tiptoes to place a kiss to my cheek. "We finished up our business early and couldn't wait any longer to come meet our granddaughter. We took the first flight home. We didn't even go to our house here first; we came straight to your house from the airport."

I wrap my arms around my mom and pull her in for a hug. I'm a little in shock to find her here. It was the last thing I expected, but I'm so happy to see her. I hadn't realized how much I needed the embrace from her until right now. She immediately hugs me back, bringing me the relief only a hug from a mother can give.

I don't know how long we stay that way. Eventually, I pull away and shake my head. "I can't believe you were here and didn't tell me. I would've left golf early or picked you up from the airport."

Mom waves at the air dismissively. She takes a step back, but her gaze stays on me. "I wanted you to have the time out with your friends. If you're going to be staying in the Hamptons for the summer with our granddaughter, then we plan on being here a lot. We'll have lots of time together."

"Does that mean you already met Ava?" I ask. Sadness tugs at my heart at the thought of missing that special moment. Guilt immediately follows when I realize I might've missed it because I was out golfing instead.

"We did—very briefly before she made it clear she needed a nap—but your friend Charlotte made sure to take photos of all of it. She said you wouldn't want to miss it."

Relief and another feeling I can't put my finger on run through me at her words. I look over my mom's shoulder to Charlotte, who still sits on the couch with an unreadable look on her face. Her hands are in her lap, and there doesn't seem to be any color in her face as she looks between my mom and me.

"Thank you," I get out, my voice suddenly hoarse. I'm sure it was a lot for my parents to show up unannounced, and I appreciate that even in the chaos, she thought of me enough to capture the moment so I can look back on it.

Charlotte gives me a forced smile, and I fight the urge to ask why she seems uncomfortable. She lets out a long sigh before standing up and walking closer to us. She stops a few feet away, clearly unsure of where she's supposed to stand in all of this. I want to wrap my arm around her and pull her into my side, but I don't know if that's something she'd want me doing with my mom here.

"It was no problem," she mutters. "I really wanted you to feel like you didn't miss anything."

"Thanks, Char. I really appreciate that." I stare at her, trying to figure out if she's acting weird. Maybe she just doesn't know how to act with my parents showing up unexpectedly. I feel bad she was here alone and that she didn't have any kind of warning. My parents love to get involved in my life, and they do meddle, but I thought they'd give me a warning before showing up.

Charlotte looks at my mom for a moment before her gaze returns to me. "Well, I've got to get out and run some errands, so I'm going to let you guys catch up while I'm gone."

She grabs her keys and bag from the entryway table before slipping on her shoes and leaving without saying anything else.

I watch the door for a moment, wondering why I have a gut feeling that something is wrong.

I know my mom just got here, and I might be overthinking it, but I follow Charlotte out the front door anyway, leaving my mom standing inside alone.

"Hey," I call after Charlotte, shocked by how far she's made it in the little time it took for me to follow her out.

She doesn't look back. "I'm just going to run some errands. The baby monitor is in the living room. Enjoy the time with your parents."

A knot forms in my stomach because she hasn't even looked at me, but I can tell by her voice that something is wrong. I grab her by the arm, needing her to look at me. "Char," I all but plead. "Don't go. You can stay."

She turns to look at me, and it feels like a punch to the gut the moment her eyes meet mine. Something's definitely wrong, and I don't know what. When I left this morning, everything seemed perfect. Now, I can almost see her physically building back up the walls between us.

"You should get back inside," she tells me, her voice composed but void of any emotion.

I shake my head. "Not when I feel like there's something you're not telling me. What's wrong? Did something happen?"

She shakes her head, but it's hard to miss the way her lip slightly trembles. "Nothing's wrong. Nothing's happened. I just feel like you should have some time with Ava and your parents that doesn't involve me." The smile she gives me is completely fake, and I don't want it. I want the one she gave me this morning. The one that reached her eyes. The one where she looked at me like I was something special. Now, she looks at me like all she wants to do is get away.

"You're lying," I say, hating the hurt that's clear in my voice. "Is it my parents? I'm sorry. I'm sure it was a shock for them to just show up, and I'm sorry you were alone when they arrived. I shouldn't have left; I should've been home."

Charlotte's eyes soften slightly as she shakes her head again. "No. They were insistent they were happy you got out.

Everything's fine. I just need out of the house to run some errands."

My jaw clenches as I fight the urge to press her for more. I know her well enough to know that something had to have happened and that something's bothering her. There's nothing I want more for her than to just tell me so we can figure it out together, but if she doesn't trust me enough to confide in me, then there's nothing I can do. I hate the feeling of her keeping something from me. I thought we were working past that, but it's clear she doesn't want to tell me what's upset her, and I can't force her to want to talk to me.

I reach out and cup her cheek. She flinches at first, and it breaks something inside me. Still, she leans into my touch and doesn't pull away. I soak in the feeling of my skin against hers, trying to tell myself that everything will be fine.

"Whatever it is, just talk to me. We'll figure it out."

Her eyes scan my face, and for a brief moment, it feels like she just might tell me. Hope blooms in my chest as her shoulders relax and her eyes soften. I stay quiet, hoping that if I don't break the silence, she'll tell me whatever it is so we can handle it together.

"Can I ask you somethin—"

"Everything okay out here?" my mom calls out.

Charlotte's posture immediately goes rigid all over again. She swats my hand away and backs up until her body is pressed against her car.

My hand drops as I look over my shoulder at my mom. She's walked out far enough that she stands on the sidewalk, her arms folded across her chest as she watches Charlotte and me closely.

"I'll be back in a minute," I assure my mom, unsure why she even felt the need to come out here in the first place. I know she means well to check in, but I was so close to getting Charlotte to just tell me what's wrong, but the moment my mom showed up, Charlotte went back to shutting me out.

When I look back at Charlotte, dread seeps into my bones because it's obvious the walls are back up. She stares at my mom, an unreadable look in her eye before she looks back at me. I get another fake smile from her, and I hate it.

"Go back inside," she tells me, her voice shaking slightly. "I'll see you later."

I sigh, but with my mom still standing out here, I don't want to make a scene. "But I'll see you later?" I confirm, needing to know eventually she'll open up to me about what's wrong. "We'll talk more about this then?" I ask, not missing how pitiful my voice sounds.

Charlotte pulls her bottom lip between her teeth but nods. "Ava went down not too long ago, so she should sleep for a while. Enjoy the time with your parents."

Before I can even respond, she's yanking open the door to her car and immediately shutting it. I hate that she doesn't even spare me a second glance as she backs out of the driveway and leaves.

When I left this morning, everything seemed great. I had my girls, and I was able to get out and see my friends and finally accept there's a way for me to balance my old life with my new one. Somehow, in the span of a few hours, everything seems to have gone wrong, and I don't even know why.

"She's a nice girl," my mom notes, interrupting me from my thoughts.

I turn around and face her. I scan her face, wondering if she has any idea why Charlotte is acting weird. If my mom knows, she doesn't give any indication. She stares back at me with a soft smile, acting as if nothing has happened at all.

"Yes, she is. She's the best," I say, watching my mom closely.

I want to add that no one compares to her. That she's mine, but judging by the way she just ran out, I don't even know if that's the case. I *want* her to be mine. But the way she just looked at me makes it feel like she wants nothing to do with me.

"Let's get inside and say hi to your father."

I stare at my mom for a little longer. I search her face, trying to figure out if something happened with her and Charlotte. I don't think so. They're both so easy to love, I can't imagine them not getting along. But I can't help but shake the uneasy feeling that something clearly did happen. I don't think Charlotte would've run out the way she did if it didn't.

I nod, knowing there's nothing else I can do until Charlotte comes back home. When she does, I'll ask her what's wrong and what happened. Until then, I'll try to enjoy having my parents here to meet my daughter and spend time with us.

For the next few hours, I can't shake that even though it's great to spend time with Ava and my parents, it still doesn't feel like my entire family is together. It feels like there's a missing piece, and that piece is Charlotte.

52

Charlotte

Jude

How are your errands going?

Jude

Had to wake Ava up from her nap. This sleep schedule is really working, all thanks to you.

Jude

Just checking in…

Jude

Ordering dinner for all of us. What do you want for dinner?

Charlotte

I'm actually busy helping Lucy with cookbook stuff. I might just crash here tonight.

Jude

Are you sure?

Charlotte

Yes, I'm sure. It'll be nice to spend some time with Lucy anyway.

Jude

But you're coming back tomorrow? I want to know what's bothering you.

Charlotte

Yes I'll be back.

• • •

Jude

Ava slept through the night last night. I thought you'd want to know.

Charlotte

Yay! Look at her go. Hope you managed to get some sleep as well.

Jude

I would've slept better if it was next to you.

Charlotte

Are you planning on working at all today?

Jude

No

Jude

Why?

Charlotte

Lucy's still needing help so I was going to stay and help her if you didn't need someone to watch Ava.

Charlotte

If you need me to watch Ava I can just come home, but if you don't, I might stay here.

Jude

I don't want you home because I need you to watch Ava. I want you home because I miss you and think we need to talk.

Jude

Is everything okay?

Charlotte

Everything's fine. Just letting you enjoy your family time without me tagging along, and using the time to help Lucy with everything she needs.

Jude

Okay. I still really want to talk about things.

Charlotte

We will, I promise. Just going to keep helping Lucy while you spend time with your parents.

Jude

Will you be coming home tonight? I'm bringing Ava to the club to meet everyone and having dinner at Pembroke Grill with my parents. We'd love to have you join if you want.

Charlotte

Good for you for taking her to the club! I'll let that be a family moment for all of you, but let me know how it goes. Since you'll be out, I might just sleep here again tonight.

Jude

Okay.

Charlotte

All the girls are going to melt at seeing you with a baby.

Jude

I don't care about other girls. I care about you.

Charlotte

I'm so proud of you for taking Ava to Pembroke. I can't wait to hear how it goes.

• • •

Charlotte

I fell asleep early last night. Lucy's been putting me to work testing out different recipes. How did it go?

Charlotte

I bet everyone at the club loved her.

Charlotte

Was looking through my photos and found this one of Ava. It was too cute not to share.

Charlotte

sends attachment

Jude

Love it

Jude

I'm going to lock up the house before getting to bed. Are you coming back tonight or staying at Lucy and Cal's?

Charlotte

I can stay here so I don't wake you up coming home.

Jude

I wish you'd just come home. I want to talk.

Charlotte

I know, I will I promise. I think I just realized some time away from each other might be good for us both. I'll be back and we'll talk.

• • •

I stare at my phone, wondering if I should send the text I've typed out to Jude. I left his house on Monday, and now that it's Thursday and days later, I'm ready to get back home. When I first left, I really intended on only being gone a few hours, but the longer I was gone, the more I realized how much the conversation with Florence had gotten to me. I needed time to work out my thoughts and I didn't want to mess up Jude's time with his parents. I look back down at my phone, getting the courage to send the text.

Charlotte

Is it okay if I come back today?

I toss my phone onto the counter, nervous about what Jude's response will be. I know he's got to have questions about why I stayed away in the first place and I need to be honest with him about the reason, I'm just nervous about approaching the conversation with him. After some time away, I've realized that I can't avoid having more serious conversations with him any longer.

I jump when my phone vibrates.

Jude

Of course. This is your home, Char. I didn't want you to stay anywhere else in the first place.

I stare at the text on my phone, rereading it for what feels like the hundredth time. When I left his house on Monday, I didn't have the intention of staying away for days. But one day led to the next, and the more time that passed, the more I replayed Jude's mom's words over and over in my head. I've wanted to go home, but I also wanted to make sure I took the time away from Jude to really sort out how I was feeling before returning home to talk with him. I've taken the time needed, and now I'm just ready to see him again.

"Okay, I tried giving you a pass, but we have to talk about it," Lucy declares, breaking me from my thoughts.

I jolt in my barstool at her kitchen counter, my eyes immediately finding hers. She stands on the opposite side of the island from me, her gaze pinned squarely on me.

"What?" I ask, placing my phone down on the counter.

Lucy shakes her head. "Don't play coy with me. You've been here since Monday, and while I love all the catching up we've been able to do, I know there's a reason you aren't going back to Jude's, and I want you to tell me why."

I try to make sure my face doesn't give any hint of what's been going on. "His parents are in town, so I wanted to give them space to spend time together...and you've needed the help."

"You're not using me as an excuse for avoiding Jude."

I groan before scrubbing my hands over my face. "I'm not avoiding Jude."

"Yes you are. Tell me why."

"You don't know that," I toss out, fully recognizing how weak my voice is. I don't even believe myself; I don't know how I expect her to believe me either.

Lucy rolls her eyes—something I've rarely seen her do. "Yes I do. Now, stop moping and holding it in and talk to me."

"I'm not moping."

She snorts and aims a spoon in my direction before she stirs the food in front of her. "You're absolutely moping. Spill."

I sigh. Maybe it'll be good to tell her about my conversation with Florence. I thought about talking to one of my sisters about it all, but it seemed like too much to relay to them. Plus, I don't want them to get the wrong impression of Florence. I don't think she meant any of her words to be cruel—she just cares for her son—but I can't help but worry that she has a point about everything. Although Lucy has kind of echoed the same things as Florence, maybe it'll still help bring some clarity to the entire thing to have an outside source give their opinion.

"You know when I told you that Jude and I were just friends?"

"You mean, do I remember when you lied to my face? I sure do."

I narrow my eyes at her for a moment before continuing. "Well, things happened. When you and I first spoke about it, the only thing Jude and I had done was kiss. And it was barely a kiss. The night before Ava showed up, we both drank a lot and shared a moment. After Ava, I thought it was only ever going to be that…a moment."

Lucy tosses the spoon in the bowl, rounds the counter, and takes the seat next to me. "But…"

"But it wasn't just a moment. It was just the moment that was a catalyst for a bunch of other moments."

"Tell me everything."

I close my eyes for a second, trying to ignore the stabbing pain in my chest that I feel when talking about Jude. I know to the outside world it may seem too fast, how quickly things changed between us, but we were spending every second of every day together. I couldn't help but develop feelings for him.

I don't know how long it takes to tell Lucy everything that happened between Jude and me. I try to give her every detail, hoping that maybe she can give insight that I haven't thought of. As nervous as I am to tell her everything, I want her honest opinion on the situation.

When I woke up on Monday, I felt good about the direction Jude and I were heading in. I know we still needed to have some serious conversations, but I felt hope. But after his mom questioned if Jude and I were only feeling things because of the situation we're in, I don't know what to believe anymore. I know I want to be honest with Jude about how I feel and about my talk with his mother and the fears it brought to light, but it's still complicated. I know how I feel about Jude, but I can't help but wonder if Florence was right about her son. What if he's just lost in playing house with me? What if he doesn't feel the same way about me that I feel about him? Maybe Lucy can give more insight into the situation and help me with what I should say when I do go back home and talk to Jude.

I finish relaying the entire conversation with Florence to Lucy. She listens the entire time, letting me explain everything before she offers any insight.

I lean back in my chair. "And just the way he looked at me, Lucy, I can't get it out of my head. It looked like I was breaking his heart. If the feelings weren't real, would he really look so crushed when I left?"

Lucy puffs out her cheeks and nods. I appreciate that she doesn't feel the need to fill the silence at first. She gathers herself before speaking. My heart races as I wait for her to answer, but I don't say anything. I've told her everything, now I just want to know what she thinks.

"Do you want me to be honest with you?" Lucy asks. She sits up and places her elbows on the counter, her gaze solely focused on me.

"Of course."

"My first thought when I saw you and Jude with Ava was how terribly this was going to end. I must admit, I wondered if the two of you basically raising a child together would blur lines, but I think I was wrong, and I think Florence is wrong too."

"Why do you think that?"

"Because I know you and I know Jude. I think the attraction has always been there for both of you. It's not like it suddenly came on the moment Ava arrived. You guys kissed after drinking for a reason. The tension finally snapped, and that didn't have anything to do with Ava coming into the picture."

I nod as I mull over her words. She isn't wrong. The kiss

happened before Jude found out he was a dad. If I had stayed that morning instead of rushing to get to work, what would've happened? Would he have asked me out on a date? He mentioned he wanted to before Ava showed up, and we decided to remain friends instead. Did he mean that? I can't help but wonder if things would be any different if I'd just stayed the next morning and talked about the night before with him instead of leaving.

"Yeah, but Jude's had a year to act interested. I just can't help but read into how quickly things changed for him once Ava was involved. What if his mom is right? What if he wants that conventional family picture so badly that it's making him believe he feels things for me that he doesn't?"

"Okay, don't hate me, but can I chime in here?" a voice interjects.

My eyes go wide, and Lucy lets out a gasp when we find Cal standing in the entryway to the hallway. He holds up his hands like he's taming a bear, which he very well might be with the shriek that leaves Lucy.

"Callahan Hastings!" she scolds, pointing a finger at her fiancé. "How dare you eavesdrop on this conversation."

He takes a hesitant step forward, his hands still out in front of him as he walks into the kitchen. "I didn't mean to. I walked out of my office, and the two of you were so locked in conversation you didn't even notice me standing there."

He aims an apologetic look in my direction, but I'm too busy trying to process the embarrassment of him hearing everything I just said to respond.

"I'm mad at you," Lucy admonishes. She tosses her long hair over her shoulder and rips her gaze from Cal and looks at me. "I'm so sorry, Charlotte. He said he was in meetings for the rest of the day. I didn't even think about him hearing us."

"It's fine," I whisper, even though it definitely doesn't feel fine. Is he going to tell everything I said to Jude? My cheeks heat at the thought. I don't want anything I've said relayed back to Jude unless it comes from me. I'm still trying to wrap my head around everything so I feel comfortable enough to see him again and explain why I ran off in the first place.

"If it's fine, can I give my opinion, then?" Cal asks. His gaze nervously bounces between Charlotte and me. "Jude's my best friend, and I think you might want to hear what I have to say."

I sigh but nod. Lucy reaches across the counter and puts her hand over mine. I squeeze hers, loving the connection with my friend as I wait for whatever Cal's about to say.

Cal closes the distance before he leans against the counter, his gaze focused on me. "I think Jude's had feelings for you from the moment you guys met."

I shake my head. "That's not possible. It's *Jude*."

Cal lifts an eyebrow. "I used to hear all about the women he took on dates and his adventures. It's all he ever wanted to talk about. But after he met you, it stopped. In fact, it felt like if he wasn't giving me shit about how obsessed I was with Lucy, he was talking about you. *Charlotte this, Charlotte that.* He talked about you like you hung the damn moon."

My mouth hangs open as I stare at him in disbelief. "There were tons of women after he met me. I saw him flirt with them with my own eyes."

Cal lifts a shoulder in a casual shrug. "Sure, he flirted, but I think it was all for show. I love Jude, but I don't think even Jude realized how he felt about you until Ava came into his life. He's grown up a lot in the last month, and if you ask me what I think, I'd tell you that I believe he has feelings for you that have been there all along and have nothing to do with Ava or wanting a family."

I blink a few times as I try to process what Cal's saying.

Could it be true? I want to believe it's true because, in my gut, I know that what I feel for Jude is real. The only reason I was ever able to push him away was because I didn't want to be someone he slept with and left. I didn't want things to be awkward, and I didn't want to lose him as a friend. But now, I can't hide from what I feel for him. I'm falling for him.

"What if you're wrong?" I whisper. "What if he breaks my heart and I lose not only him but Ava too? What if it doesn't work out?" I ask. I shake my head back and forth, trying to process how I could ever cope with losing either of them.

Lucy squeezes my hand. "What if it *does* work out? What if letting go of the fear of losing them and allowing yourself to love them is the best thing that happens to all of you?"

53

Jude

My house has never felt so empty.

I sit in my room, staring at Ava's empty bed, wondering if I should've thought twice before letting my parents take her for the evening.

My mother was thrilled about the idea of Ava staying with them overnight. I didn't know this, but after I first told them about Ava, they had workers come to their house to make a nursery for my daughter. She even made sure to purchase all the necessities for Ava to have at her house as well.

When she offered to take Ava for the night, I thought it'd be nice to have a night alone with Charlotte since she said she'd be coming home. I thought it would give us the chance to talk about whatever is clearly bothering her and what made her stay away for days. But she still hasn't returned home. And no matter how many photos my mom sends of Ava looking happy as can be at their house, I can't help but miss my daughter.

I also can't help but miss Charlotte.

I thought with each day she didn't come back that maybe her absence would make me understand why she felt the need to leave in the first place, but it hasn't. All I've done is miss her and solidify that I'm in love with her.

I've fallen for my best friend.

How could I not?

It feels like I've fallen for her twice. Once, the very moment I met her. It was the sudden kind of love that I didn't have the capacity to understand at the time. She was so magnetic that I found myself thinking about her all the time. All I wanted to do was find ways to spend time with her. I'd never felt such an intense pull to another person before until Charlotte. I pushed it away until I couldn't anymore. I tried to pretend it wasn't there until I fell for her a second time. The second time was after Ava. She stepped in so effortlessly that I couldn't pretend any longer. She was there for me in a time when she didn't have to be, and it was the first time I had real hope that maybe she could feel the same way I felt about her.

I've been terrified of telling her how I feel because I hate the thought of her not feeling the same way, but at this point, I hate the thought of keeping it to myself even more. She has to know how I feel, and I have to deal with whatever happens after I'm honest with her. I'll tell her the moment she finally decides to come home, risking whatever happens next.

I don't know how long I sit in my room, staring at Ava's empty bed. It could be minutes; it could be over an hour. I get so lost in thinking about how I'm going to tell Charlotte I'm in love with her that I don't even notice when she gets home.

There's a soft knock on the door. "Jude? Are you in here?"

A knot loosens in my chest at the sound of Charlotte's voice. I turn around, coming face-to-face with the woman who owns my heart. "Char," I breathe, blinking a few times to make sure she's here.

She gives me a tentative smile. "Hi."

I stand up and take a step closer to her before stopping. I want to pull her in for a hug and press my lips to hers, but I don't know if that's something she wants me to do. It takes everything in me to keep my feet planted. "I missed you," I blurt out, my eyes immediately closing because I couldn't sound any more pathetic.

She doesn't say anything at first. She's quiet long enough for me to work up the nerve to open my eyes and look at her once again.

"I missed you too," she responds the moment our gazes meet.

My shoulders sag with a sigh of relief. I clear my throat. "Really?"

She nods. "Where's Ava?" Her focus travels over my shoulder to the empty bed behind me.

"She's with my parents for the night. Her first official sleepover."

She raises her eyebrows. "How do you feel about that?"

My lip twitches with the hint of a smile. "They're probably incredibly annoyed with the number of times I've checked in on her."

My words earn me another one of her beautiful smiles. "I'm shocked you even agreed to it in the first place."

I scratch at my neck. "I wanted the night to talk to you."

Her eyes go wide, and I don't know if it's a good reaction or a bad one, but either way, I tell myself that I still need to be honest about what I want to talk to her about.

"Oh," she whispers, giving no indication of what's going through her head.

"Do you want to sit?" I ask, pointing to my bed. I pause,

wondering if I should offer for us to go out into the living room instead.

Why do I suddenly feel so awkward? This is Charlotte. I don't need to feel anxious around her, but nerves are the only thing I'm feeling right now.

Charlotte doesn't answer, but she does step into my room before walking past me and taking a seat on the bed. "Sure," she finally gets out once she's sitting down.

I nod before I follow her lead and sit down on the edge of my bed. I want to sit so close to her that our bodies touch, but I make sure to leave room between us just in case that's what she wants.

My heart pounds. I'm not used to ever feeling uneasy. I'm never nervous. But now that she's here and willing to talk, I'm so anxious I can barely form a coherent thought. Every speech I made up in my head disappears with her so close to me.

I swallow and turn my body to face hers. "Can we talk about why you left Monday? I want to know what happened."

Charlotte winces before nodding. "I spoke with your mom."

I already suspected it had to have been something with my mom, but no matter how many times I asked my mom about it while Charlotte was gone, she found ways to avoid the question. Because of my mom acting like she didn't know what I was talking about, I couldn't help but wonder if maybe there was another reason Charlotte left and stayed away that didn't have anything to do with my mom. "And?" I ask, my voice quiet. There's a tightness in my chest at learning that the reason Charlotte left was because of a conversation with my mom, but I wait to hear more about it before getting worked up about it.

"And she brought up some things that scared me. I'm sorry for leaving the way that I did, but I didn't know how to process what she was saying, and I needed to get away to work through it."

It feels like my heart might pound right out of my chest. I could throw up from nerves alone. "What did she say?" I ask hoarsely. I want to know, but I'm also not sure if I want the answer.

Charlotte's eyes rake over my face. She rubs her lips together as she thinks about my question. "She was worried we were going to hurt each other."

"How so?"

"She was worried that maybe one—or both—of us will get so lost in the living together and taking care of Ava that we'll think we're feeling things we're not. It was clear she thought we were better off as friends and nothing more."

I don't know what to say back to her. All I do is stare, wondering how I can even begin to form the right words to convey to her that everything I'm feeling is real. I've come up with a million different speeches in my head to tell her how I feel, but now that she sits next to me, staring back at me with her beautiful blue eyes, nothing feels like enough. I don't know if I can put into words how much she means to me…how much I love her.

"Why are you looking at me like that?" she whispers.

I can't help but smile, remembering another time she asked me that same question. The night I kissed her for the first time.

"Because, Char, you're not just my friend. You're my every thought. My every feeling. My *everything*."

Her lips part with her sharp intake of breath. "But…" She shakes her head. "We were friends for so long. What changed? What about our friendship?"

I scoot closer to her, close enough that I cup her cheek in my palm. She leans into my touch, and I savor the connection of our skin. “I mean this in the nicest way possible, but fuck the friendship. I love being your friend, but I want to be more too. So much more.”

“But…I don’t want to ruin our friendship.”

“The friendship isn’t ruined. It’s just…more. It isn’t ruining the friendship exactly, but opening it up to be something better. And I’ve caught feelings for you, sweetheart. It’s more than that.” I grab the other side of her face until I cup both her cheeks in my hands. I press my forehead to hers for a moment, breathing in at the same time she breathes out. We sit like that for a moment as I work up the courage to say more.

I slide my fingers under her chin and tip her head so our gazes connect again. “I love you.” I make sure the words come out confident and with conviction. “And I don’t need you to say it back right now. I know it might take time for you, but I don’t want to keep it to myself anymore. I think I’ve loved you since the moment we met; it just took me a while to put a name to the feeling. But I love you. Not because we live together. And not because of things with Ava. I love you because you’re the easiest person in the world to love.”

Tears run down her cheeks as she lets out a sound that’s a mix between a hiccup and a laugh. “Jude.” She shakes her head in disbelief. I’d be worried about the tears, but she wears a smile that’s so radiant it steals my breath.

“I love you,” I repeat. “And I know there are a lot of things we still need to figure out, but I don’t want to keep how I feel about you to myself anymore.”

“What if you only think that because we’ve spent all this time together? What if I give you my heart and you change your mind down the road? What if you realize you mixed up being grateful that I’ve helped with Ava with being in love?”

I shake my head, wishing there was a way she could read my mind so she could see just how much I love her. "I'm not changing my mind. And the only thing I'm going to realize is that just when I feel like I couldn't love you more, I'll find a way to fall in love with you even more anyway."

Charlotte's gaze flicks down to my lips for a moment before she meets my stare again. "I don't even know what to say. I want to believe everything you're saying, but you've known me for a year. What makes you sure now when you weren't sure before?"

It's a valid question, and I love that she's asking me questions instead of shutting down. It gives me hope that with time, she'll feel the same way about me that I feel about her. Obviously, it's important for her to be sure of how I feel about her, and if she didn't think she felt the same, or eventually could, I don't think she'd even be asking.

"I think I was scared. I didn't even realize what I was feeling. I've never been in love before, and since we were so close, I pretended how I felt about you was the way a friend should feel about another friend. I'm not used to being rejected so it was easier to pretend to just be your friend than to open myself up to the hurt I'd feel if I told you how I felt and you still weren't interested. I was terrified of you seeing the real me and the man I want to be and you still not wanting me or you still not feeling the same. So, I just pretended I was fine just being friends. But the last few weeks… I can't pretend. I don't want to pretend. You're my best friend, but also the woman I'm in love with."

"Jude, I—" I kiss her before she can get any more words out. I want to know that she loves me too, but I want to give her time to really think about it before saying the words out loud. Once she says them, there's no taking them back, and I just want to make sure she means them first.

54

Charlotte

I hadn't realized how tense I'd been the entire week until Jude's lips meet mine. With his mouth against mine, life finally feels like it makes sense again.

I missed him so much. My fingers tangle in his hair as I pull his face closer to mine. His tongue coaxes my mouth open, and I welcome him in.

"I missed you," I tell him, pulling away. "And I just need you to know that I—"

He presses his fingertips against my lips. "I want to hear you tell me you love me back so badly, but I just don't want to hear you say it unless you're sure. I don't want you to feel like you have to say it just because I did."

I smile despite his fingers still pressed to my mouth. "Jude, I love you." The words roll off my tongue easily. After my talk with Lucy and Cal, I realized that I wasn't just falling for Jude. I've *fallen*. Hearing him tell me the same, without asking for me to say it in return, only solidified how I feel about him.

"What?" he rasps, staring at me in disbelief.

"I love you."

He smiles so wide that both his dimples make an appearance. "Say it again."

I run my thumb over his bottom lip, trying to comprehend how lucky I am to be loved by this man. "I love you," I repeat, making sure my words are strong and clear.

He closes his eyes for a moment. His next words are said with his eyes still shut, as if he's too afraid to look me in the eye and see my reaction. "And you mean it? I want to let you fully in, but it isn't just my life. It's Ava's too. I want to make sure that you won't be changing your mind."

My heart breaks at the vulnerability in his voice. If only he knew how much I cared about him and Ava. "Open your eyes," I whisper, wanting to be able to look him in the eye when I say what I'm about to say.

He does as he's told, his chestnut gaze focused solely on me. "I love you, Jude. I can't pinpoint the moment I fell. I think it's similar to your experience…that for so long, I assured myself that you were just a friend that I even had myself believing it too. I don't know the moment I fell. But I've been falling for you longer than Ava's been around. I don't just want to play family with you. I want to *be* your family. I want you and Ava to be mine. I want to figure out life together, and I can't imagine ever going back to pretending we're just friends. I want to be more than friends forever with you."

He lets out a sigh of relief before his mouth crashes against mine.

We make up for lost time with the kiss. His tongue against mine. Teeth hitting teeth. Hands in hair and tugging at clothes. One moment, I'm still in clothes Lucy loaned me; the next moment, they're on the ground.

"I love you," Jude declares as he kisses a trail along my

collarbone. "I'm sorry I didn't show it enough and I'm sorry I made you question if this was all just pretend." He continues to pepper more kisses along my skin.

"I love you too," I respond breathlessly, my hips arching when he playfully bites at my neck. "And don't be sorry. I think it was good someone brought it up, and I think it was good we had some time apart. I don't know if I would've faced my fears about us without your mom bringing them to light."

Jude brings his head in front of mine. "None of this is pretend. You're it for me, sweetheart. I love you. I'm in love with you."

I smile because I didn't know I could ever feel so happy. When I left on Monday, I was so devastated by what Florence had said. It was an echo of what Lucy had mentioned and I let the words get to me, but I also appreciate both of them for saying them. I think maybe Jude and I were both too nervous to ask the other about what was real and what wasn't, and the time apart and the reality check with Lucy and Cal only proved to me what I already knew deep down.

I was in love with Jude Kensington. He owned my heart. I can't pinpoint the moment I gave it to him, but it's his to keep. And I'm so incredibly grateful that he's trusting me with not only his heart, but Ava's as well.

"I'm so in love with you, Jude Kensington," I say, my fingers gripping at his hair as he kisses along my hip bone.

"Feel free to tell me that as often as you want," he responds, his breath hitting my inner thigh.

"Same to you. I want to hear it all the time. Tell me how much you love me all day, every day, and I wouldn't complain about you even adding in the reasons you love me," I tease.

He places his hands between my thighs and pushes them

open. Goosebumps develop on my skin in anticipation.

He runs his fingers through my wetness, letting out a growl of approval at how wet I already am for him.

"I love you because you're you," he declares before leaning in and pressing his mouth to me.

My eyelids flutter shut, and I let out a loud moan at the feeling of having his mouth there. I let my hands grab onto his hair as he continues to make me see stars just with his tongue.

Eventually, I get too close, and as much as I love the feeling of his mouth against my clit, I want to come with him inside me.

"Jude," I pant, pulling on his hair to lift his head.

His eyes meet mine, and it's like he reads my mind. He presses a soft kiss against my inner thigh before he trails kisses all the way up my body until his head is above mine. "Need me to fuck you, sweetheart?"

I nod, letting out an eager cry at the idea. "Yes."

He strokes himself up and down a few times before he lines himself up with my entrance. My toes curl in anticipation. It's only been a few days since he was last inside me, and yet it feels like a lifetime ago.

I let out a loud moan as he pushes inside me at the same moment I get the words out.

His arms reach behind my back, and he coaxes my body off the mattress and onto his lap instead. Now I'm on top, my thighs on either side of his as I ride him and take him even deeper.

"I love you because it feels like you see the real me and the man I want to be," he mutters against my skin, thrusting his hips slowly.

My head falls back. There's something about the slow, deep way he pushes in and out of me, mixed with his words, that doesn't feel like he's fucking me.

It feels like he's making *love* to me.

"I love you because you're the most selfless person I know."

Another rock in and out, and I find myself getting even closer to an orgasm.

"I love that you leave a little trail around the house of where you've been. It's a reminder that you're here, with me, and I love the proof of you sharing the same space as me."

I begin to trail kisses along his neck as he continues to rock in and out of me at a pace that has me edging closer to the brink of an orgasm.

"And I fucking love the way you smell. While you were gone, I kept going into your shower and smelling your fucking shampoo because I missed you so much."

I let out a laugh that quickly turns into a moan when his fingertips find my clit.

"I missed you too," I hurriedly get out as his fingers begin to work even faster against me.

Jude lets out a low growl. "Good. Now, prove it."

He slams into me, and it's the final thing to send me over the edge. I come at the same time as he does, both of us chanting *I love you* over and over as we ride out the highs of our orgasms.

55

Jude

"I still can't believe this is happening," Charlotte whispers with her cheek pressed to my chest.

My fingers run through the long, blonde strands of her hair as we lie in bed together. "What can't you believe?"

"That you love me. That I got the nerve to tell you I love *you*." She turns so her chin rests against my chest, and her big eyes focus on me. "Just…all of it. It feels too perfect to be real."

I smile because she's saying exactly what I've been thinking. It's been an hour since we got cleaned up after having sex. It's been nice to not be in a hurry after; to just lie in bed, saying everything out loud that we've been too afraid to say until now. "It is perfect, but it's also real."

Charlotte gives me a wide smile as she shakes her head in disbelief. "My family is going to lose it when I tell them about us. My sister Hailey has been telling me to hook up with you for months."

I can't help but laugh at her comment. For some reason, it feels good that she's been talking to her family about me. Pride blooms in my chest that I was important enough to Charlotte for her to tell them about me. "Has she? I can't wait to meet her, then. I can't wait to meet all of them."

"You'd want that?" she asks, her eyes lighting up. She watches me closely, almost as if she can't believe I'd want to meet her family.

I continue to run my fingers through her hair as I look into her eyes. "Of course. I'd love to see where you come from. I can't wait to tell them about how amazing a daughter and a sister they have, and to let them know how wildly in love with you I am."

She playfully rolls her eyes. "My mom's going to be obsessed with you." Her nose scrunches as her lips turn into a smile. "Actually, she might already be."

I can't help but return her smile. "Moms always love me."

Charlotte lets out a dramatic groan. "Well, I can't say the same about your mom. I'm scared she might hate me. What's she going to think when we tell her we're together?"

I shrug. "I love my mom, but she doesn't get a say in my life." I make sure to keep my voice calm and composed, wanting her to know that I mean every word that leaves my mouth.

Charlotte watches me closely. Her blue gaze rakes over my face as if she's trying to find any indication that I'm just telling her what she wants to hear. "But she's your mom; I know you care about what she thinks. What if she thinks we're rushing into things or that this isn't real?"

I shake my head and use the hand not in her hair to hold the side of her face. "Do you feel like this isn't real or that we're rushing into things?"

She doesn't answer at first, but eventually, she shakes her head. "No."

"Good. I don't think so either. I think the timing for

everything has worked out just the way it was supposed to."

Her bottom lip juts out slightly, and a tiny crease appears between her eyebrows. "But I still want your mom to like me." Her words come out a little shaky, and it feels like a punch to the gut.

"She will. I think she already does," I assure her. "From what you've told me, she didn't care about just *my* heart, but yours too. I think she thought she was doing what was best for everyone. I'll have to talk with her about staying out of it next time, but it worked out in the end. We were both finally able to say how we feel without the fear of being hurt, and that's all that matters in the end."

I wish my mom had talked things over with me before going straight to Charlotte, but I know she thought she was doing the right thing by intervening. If she hadn't brought up her concerns to Charlotte, I'm not sure we'd be in this place now. As much as I hated Charlotte leaving the way that she did, now in hindsight, I think it was good for both of us to have a few days apart. After not seeing each other for a few days, we were able to see each other again and both be open and honest about how we were feeling.

Charlotte stares at me, the hint of a smile on her lips.

My heart squeezes because she's just so damn beautiful.

"What?" I ask.

Her smile grows, and she attempts to hide it by pulling her bottom lip between her teeth. "Nothing."

"Tell me."

"I just hope you're right. I love you. I know you're close with your parents, and I just can't help but be worried that it'll take some time for your mom to warm up to the idea of me… to the idea of *us*."

"I promise I'll talk to her, but I also don't want you worrying about her. We both know how we feel. No one else has to understand it but us."

Charlotte gives me a smile before laying her head back down on my chest. She doesn't argue, which I hope means she's satisfied with my answer for the time being. Warmth spreads throughout my entire body to have her body pressed against mine. I can't wait for countless more nights spent just like this. The two of us in bed, talking about anything and everything.

"I miss Ava," Charlotte announces, pulling me from my thoughts.

I can't help but smile because I love how much Charlotte cares for Ava. It means the world to me how much she loves my daughter. "I miss her too. Think we should go pick her up in the middle of the night?"

This makes Charlotte laugh against my chest. "I'm trying to get on your mom's good side."

I play with her hair before pressing a kiss to her forehead. "You already are, trust me. Even when you were gone, she spoke highly of you. She wouldn't tell me anything happened between the two of you. She played coy about that. But she did compliment you countless times. I promise everything will be fine."

"If you say so," Charlotte responds before letting out a long sigh.

We lie in silence for I don't know how long. I run my fingers through her hair while she absentmindedly traces circles on my bare chest. I didn't know happiness like this even existed, but something as simple as lying in bed with her has made me feel a bliss I can't even put into words.

Part of me is nervous I might wake up and find out all of

this is just a dream. I have to remind myself it's real. She's here. She loves me. She's in my arms, and we're going to figure things out together.

I don't want to rush things, but there is one more thing I want to talk about with Charlotte. The only thing that'd make this better is having the chance to put a label on the woman that I love.

I clear my throat, nervous to say my next words but choosing to say them anyway. "Tomorrow at the Pembroke party, I'm excited you'll be my date, but I'd also love to tell everyone in attendance that you're my girlfriend."

Charlotte spins to her stomach and looks at me with an excited spark in her eyes. Her mouth hangs open for a moment as she stares at me in disbelief. "Jude, is this you officially asking me to be your girlfriend?"

The excitement in her voice makes my heart soar. "Only if you say yes."

"Have you ever even had a girlfriend?"

I give her a smirk. "Not really. I haven't cared about someone enough before to make them mine. You're my first… and my last."

Her lips dance with the hint of a smile. The moonlight filtering through my bedroom windows illuminates the blues of her eyes, creating an almost twinkle in them as she stares at me. "God, why do you have to be so good with your words?"

"I'm just telling the truth. You're it for me, Char. And if you want to wait to put a label on this, then that's fine…I'll wait. But I love you, and there's nothing I'd love more than to show up at Pembroke tomorrow telling everyone you're my girlfriend."

The sides of her eyes crinkle as her smile grows. "I'd be honored to be your girlfriend, Jude Kensington."

I pull her face to mine, my lips hovering over hers. "No, sweetheart, the honor is all mine."

She closes the small distance between our mouths. Our lips connect in a kiss that is tender and tugs at my heartstrings.

Eventually, we pull away, but I keep my fingers tangled in her hair as our gazes meet once again. "So is that a yes?" I ask, my heart hammering in my chest at the question. I know she's pretty much already said yes, but I need to hear the words to make sure I got it right the first time.

Charlotte nods. "Of course it's a yes."

My mouth slams against hers as happiness takes over my entire body. I woke up this morning worried about what the future held for Charlotte and me, and now I'm ending the night with her as my girlfriend.

I don't know how long we stay that way, but I love that nothing is rushed, and we kiss as if we have all the time in the world. In a way, we do. There's no fear of what happens in the morning, and there are no barriers between us. It's perfect.

56

Charlotte

"Ready?" Jude asks me, holding his hand out as he holds open the passenger door to his SUV. I place my hand in his and nod, carefully stepping out of the car, making sure I don't step on the skirt of my dress.

"Why am I so nervous?" I whisper, giving him a hesitant smile as he shuts my passenger door.

We stand in the busy Pembroke parking lot. People walk by us, all of them dressed up for the welcome party tonight. All day, I was excited to finally experience a Pembroke party from the vantage point of a member—at least the guest of one—but now that we're here, I'm so nervous I feel like I might actually throw up.

"Don't be nervous, sweetheart. Tonight will be fun." Jude gives me an encouraging smile before leaning in and pressing a kiss to my forehead. He's careful not to kiss me on the lips, per my own request. He complained about not being able to kiss me for five minutes before he finally accepted that I wanted to at least make it to the party before he messed up my makeup.

I watch Jude as he opens the back door of the SUV and pulls

Ava out of her car seat. She wears a baby pink dress and a giant bow on top of her head. My heart melts at the sight. It's absolutely adorable. I ordered the outfit the moment Jude agreed to come to the event, and I'm happy it made it here in time for Ava to wear it.

"Hi, sweet girl," I get out, loving that she immediately smiles when her eyes meet mine.

"There you are!" Florence calls from a few cars down. She and Nathaniel close the distance to us, the two of them dressed up for the party tonight.

Florence gives me a warm smile, and it helps loosen the knot I felt in my stomach at seeing her for the first time since I ran out of Jude's house on Monday. "You look radiant this evening," Florence tells me. She surprises me by pulling me in for a hug and giving me a squeeze. "I'm sorry," she whispers, keeping her voice low enough that only I hear it.

I hadn't realized how badly I needed the hug and apology from her until now. When Jude went to pick up Ava from his parents' house this morning, he had a talk with his mom about everything. Eventually, I think it'll be a good idea for me and Florence to speak again and finish the conversation we started earlier in the week, but I'm not rushing it. The apology, paired with the warm smile and Jude's adamance that their talk went great, gives me the reassurance I need for now.

I give her a tight squeeze back before we both pull away. I make sure my smile matches hers. While I was nervous to see her again, I understand why she said the things she said to me. She cares about her son and granddaughter, and I appreciate the way she was looking out for all of us.

"You look absolutely beautiful," I tell her, my eyes traveling over the gown she wears.

"She does, doesn't she?" Nathaniel chimes in, putting his

arm around his wife's waist.

"Charlotte," a familiar voice calls. I turn around and find Lucy and Cal making their way in our direction.

"Oh my God, you look hot," I tell Lucy, taking in her outfit. She wears a long black dress and a pair of black gloves that help show off her diamond engagement ring.

She smiles and looks down at the ground for a moment before returning my stare. "Right back at you. I love the pink."

I smile and do a quick spin for her. "Thank you. I somehow was able to find a dress last minute that matched Ava's almost perfectly."

Lucy's eyes soften as she looks behind me, where Jude holds Ava. "Stop it," she mutters, closing the distance so she can walk up to Ava. "Look how cute you are."

Jude smiles before pressing a kiss to his daughter's cheek. "I have a feeling she's going to be stealing everyone's heart tonight."

I can't help but smile and nod my head. "As she should."

Mini conversations break out between the small group before Jude finally clears his throat and talks over everyone. "Should we get inside?" Jude asks, his eyes find mine, and he holds out his free hand for me to take.

I gladly close the distance between us and put my hand in his. Butterflies take flight in my stomach at the thought of arriving hand in hand with him. He's asked me countless times today if I was sure that I was okay with us telling everyone about our relationship, but I've never been more sure about something in my life. I want everyone to know that he's mine, but it's still a little nerve-racking.

"Let's get in there," I answer, both nerves and excitement making my voice shake ever so slightly.

There are echoes of agreement before we walk toward the

club. There's a long line of cars waiting in the valet line that we walk past to get inside.

The moment we step through the doors, I can't help but gasp. I worked this morning, but when my shift ended in the afternoon, Pembroke still looked the same as it always did. Now, it's been completely transformed. There are green and cream elements everywhere, making the club feel even more elegant and classy than it already is.

"This is stunning," I marvel. I'm so swept up in looking around the club that I don't even notice the curious stares from both Pembroke members and employees.

"*You're* stunning," Jude whispers, leading us down the hallway to the ballroom of the club. The lights are dimmed, but I can't help but wonder if the flush that blooms on my cheeks is noticeable.

We pass by many people, some who wave and try to stop us, but Jude keeps walking. I got a text from Margo as soon as we pulled into the parking lot that they were already here, so my guess is that Jude is on a mission to find our friends before engaging in small talk with anyone.

I clutch Jude's hand as we continue to make our way to the main event space. At first, I try to focus on the decorations and soak in how beautiful the transformation of the club is, but eventually, I can't help but notice the people watching us as we walk by. "I think people are staring at us," I declare before letting out a nervous laugh.

"Let them stare," Florence notes from closely behind us. I love how casually she offers the advice. It's a gentle reminder that it doesn't matter if people look or not.

I look over my shoulder and give her an appreciative smile. "You're right. We all look too good. Of course they're staring."

She winks at me at the same moment Jude squeezes my hand.

"They could also be staring at the absolutely adorable baby on Jude's hip," Lucy pipes up from my other side.

Her words earn a chuckle from both Jude and Cal.

"That's definitely it," Jude responds.

We step into the room, and the sight in front of me steals my breath. It's like a picture out of a magazine, and I can't help but wish I had thought to bring my camera. We walk next to a champagne tower, and I gape at it. I've worked around the wealthy for the last year, but there's something about seeing a champagne tower with two waitstaff dressed in black tie to serve you that makes you realize just how rich the party is.

"I can't believe this," I marvel as I look around wide-eyed.

"There's Camille!" Lucy says excitedly, pulling me from the trance of looking around at the party setup.

I follow Lucy's gaze to find Camille waving us down from across the room.

"We're going to go find our friends," Florence announces to Jude.

We stop as Jude turns to his mom for a moment. "Tell Grandma you'll see her later," Jude says in the adorably sweet voice he saves for talking to his daughter.

Florence smiles before she and Nathaniel both lean in to press a kiss to Ava's round little cheeks. "We'll see her later. Let us know when you want us to take her home."

I know Jude kept telling his mom it wasn't necessary, but his parents offered to take Ava back home once she got tired so Jude and I could still enjoy the event. She tried convincing him to let Ava stay the night at their house for a second night in a row, but he wasn't having it. Them taking Ava home early and waiting at the house for us to return was the compromise.

"Love you," Jude tells his mom before they walk away.

"Oh, this is going to be good." Lucy laughs as she looks across the room. "By the look on her face, Camille's definitely going to have some questions for you."

I blush as I follow Lucy's line of sight to find Camille, Jude's publicist and Ryker's fiancée and someone I've grown closer to over the last year, gawking. It looks like she mouths something like *What the fuck*, but I can't be exactly sure.

"Oh boy," I mutter. My words make both Lucy and Jude laugh at the same time.

"Wait until I introduce you as my girlfriend," Jude snickers.

Lucy gasps. Her hand finds my stomach as she forces me to come to a stop.

"Excuse me? Girlfriend?"

"Girlfriend?" Cal echoes as he wraps his arm around Lucy's and pulls her into his body.

Jude and I look at each other. His lips twitch with a growing smirk. "I finally got Charlotte to say yes to being my girlfriend."

I roll my eyes at his comment. "I said yes the first time you asked."

Jude leans in and presses a kiss to my lips, making my cheeks heat because he does it without a care in the world about how many people are watching.

Ava lets out an excited squeal before her little hand finds my cheek. Jude laughs against my lips before pulling away.

"What is happening?" Camille asks, breathing heavily as if she just ran across the room to us.

"What do you mean?" Jude coyly asks. He begins to walk in the direction Camille just came from.

Camille's eyes bounce between me and Jude as we walk toward the table filled with our friends. "Oh, I don't know…the fact that you and Charlotte just kissed and you're holding an adorable baby that looks identical to you."

No one answers as we close the distance to the table filled with people I've been fortunate to grow close with ever since working at Pembroke Hills. Directly in front of me is Tyson, whose face lights up the moment he sees Ava. I don't know if I've seen him smile much, but he melts at the sight of Ava.

Next to him is his sister, Winnie, and her husband, Archer. Next to Archer is Preston Rhodes—someone my dad often asks about—and Emma stands next to him, her face entirely lit up when she spots Ava. On Emma's hip is Celeste, Beck and Margo's daughter. Both Margo and Beck stand next to Emma, their attention focused on us, watching closely as we stop in front of everyone.

"Good evening," Jude croons. He squeezes my hand and pulls me closer to him until I'm flush against his side. I reach out and playfully tap Ava's nose, unable to resist making her laugh in this moment.

"Some of you already met or heard about her, but if you haven't, this is my daughter, Ava." He props her up on his hip slightly to show her off. The movement makes her let out an adorable little giggle that can be heard even over the live band playing in the far corner of the ballroom.

"Daughter?" Camille asks, her voice calm and composed but her face showing shock.

Jude grins as if he couldn't be more proud to be introducing his daughter to everyone. It makes my heart completely melt. "Yes. My daughter."

"It's my job to know everything about everyone. How did I not know you had a daughter?" Camille asks, her voice full of disbelief.

She looks to her fiancé, Ryker, but he's too busy looking at Jude to give her a response. "That's amazing," he marvels, giving Jude a smile. "Jude…a *dad*." He shakes his head as if he can't believe it.

"Yep. I'm a dad. Don't seem too shocked." His attention focuses on Camille as he gives her an apologetic smile. "And don't feel bad about not knowing. I've only begun to tell people recently."

"But I'm your publicist," she tosses out. "You're supposed to tell me everything."

Jude laughs. "I know. We'll talk more about things regarding Ava later. I'm still gaining my footing with it."

Camille gives a nod before her eyes slice to me. "And can we talk about the fact that you guys are clearly together? About damn time."

Ryker echoes her sentiment by whistling and clapping his hands. The noise catches the attention of the people around us, but I don't pay them any mind.

I can't.

The way Jude turns to look at me takes my breath away. It's one of those moments where everyone else fades away and all I see is him. He looks at me with so much love that I wonder if he's always looked at me like this and I just somehow missed it, or if this is something new.

"I'm obsessively in love with Charlotte, and she's made me the luckiest guy in the world by saying yes to being my girlfriend." His words come out a little raspy as he stares at me adoringly. He blinks a few times before his dimples make an appearance with the deep curve of his lips. "And yeah. There's my life update. Should we have some champagne?"

Our friends stare at us with wide smiles. It's a moment I'll never forget, a time I want to remember forever.

One by one, they come up to us and give us hugs and congratulations. We get settled at our table, and the entire night, I find myself wondering how I got to be so lucky.

Tears sting my eyes as I look around at the small group of people who have become my family here in the Hamptons. When I first moved out here, I didn't know a single soul. All I knew was that it felt like I belonged in the Hamptons. I couldn't have known that a job offer at an elite country club would lead me to finding so many incredible people…and falling in love.

Jude watches as Margo holds Ava and Beck holds Celeste and the two girls interact with each other. He wears a wide grin. It's almost as if he can sense me watching him because he looks over at me and immediately pulls my body against his.

"I love you," he tells me, his lips moving against my forehead before he presses a soft kiss there.

"I love you too." I snuggle into him, soaking in the moment. It's just the start of the summer season here in the Hamptons, but I'm so excited to spend it surrounded by the people here tonight.

Most of all, I'm excited to see what the summer—and the future—has in store for the two people I love most—Jude and Ava.

I can't help but smile as I imagine all the memories we're going to create.

If someone had told me I'd be starting the summer with Jude Kensington as my boyfriend, I would've never believed them. I would've told them that Jude and I were just friends.

But the universe has a funny way of working things out, and I can't help but wonder if, all along, Jude and I were always meant to be more than friends.

EPILOGUE

Jude

SIX MONTHS LATER

"This shouldn't be allowed," I mutter, staring at my daughter in her bright pink birthday hat.

"Right?" Charlotte echoes with her camera in front of her face. "I cried the entire time I was getting this set up."

We stand in the brand-new studio Charlotte just began renting. It's on one of the busiest streets here in the Hamptons, and she's going to be turning the former boutique into the photography studio of her dreams. I'm so proud of her for finally making this dream a reality. I know she first moved to the Hamptons with the dream of eventually opening up a photography business here, and she's done it. She saved all the money from working at Pembroke and finally took the leap of faith and signed a one-year lease for the space we stand in. It needs some work to convert it from its previous function as a retail store, but I'm excited to see what she does with the place, and I'm ready to help her however I'm needed. I'm so damn proud of her for all of the hard work she's put into this and I can't wait to see her new business flourish.

Ava sits in a white high chair with a pink birthday banner strung behind her. It felt right that the very first session at Charlotte's new studio would be Ava's first birthday pictures. Her birthday isn't technically for a month, but we're getting the photos done now so we can send them out as invitations.

"How is our baby girl going to be one?" I mutter, staring at our daughter. She sits in her high chair, cautiously looking at the pink cake in front of her that she refuses to touch.

Charlotte puts the camera down for a moment and looks at me, her eyes glassing over slightly. "I don't want to talk about it," she tells me before shaking her head. "It seems like just yesterday when she came into our lives. Where did the time go?"

I shrug because I don't know where the time went either. It feels like Karina was just dropping Ava off with me yesterday, but in reality, that was over six months ago.

The last six months have been the best of my life, and they've passed all too quickly.

Memories of the last six months race through my mind in a blur.

We spent the summer in the Hamptons with our closest friends and family. After Charlotte's family visited from Arizona, my parents and Charlotte's parents quickly became best friends. They even went on vacation together in Colorado in the fall. Last summer was a perfect bubble where I got to spend all my time with my girls and the people I love most.

Charlotte never moved out, even when her previous landlord begged her to take over the rental again in the off-season. We split our time between the Hamptons and Manhattan. My work schedule has been busier than ever. Kensington Corporation has been expanding into many new markets and my dad's allowed me to take the helm on all of it. It's kept me busy, but I've made sure to never let work get in the way of spending time with my girls. We spent weekends in the Hamptons when Charlotte had to work and moved our schedules around to be in Manhattan if I had to report to Kensington Corporation's headquarters. We've made it work without jeopardizing any family time and I'm proud of us.

At the end of the summer, Ava officially became mine. Karina stuck to her word and signed all of the parental rights to me. We got to celebrate the victory by going to Italy for Lucy and Cal's wedding. It was Charlotte's first time in Italy and Ava's first real trip ever, and we had the trip of a lifetime together.

Over the last six months, I've fallen even more in love with Charlotte each day. She has both me—and my daughter—wrapped around her finger. It was in the little moments where we had spa nights and she convinced me to do a face mask with her or asked me to paint her toes. Or in the times when I woke up in the middle of the night to an empty bed, only to find that she was fast asleep after she'd crawled into Ava's crib with her. Or when Charlotte threw a half-birthday party for Ava because she felt that every milestone should be celebrated together as a family. There were tons of little moments—and big ones—that made me fall even more in love with Charlotte.

I'm so in love with her that I'm planning to propose to her sometime this summer. I'm working with Lucy to figure out the perfect time and somehow trying to make it a surprise for Charlotte, even though she's impossible to surprise. I would've proposed to her sooner, but Charlotte's insisted that we should at least be in a relationship for a year before getting engaged.

As soon as we hit that year mark this summer, I'll be popping the question. I don't want to wait any longer to put a ring on her finger.

"C'mon, just put your finger in it. I promise it's yummy," Charlotte coaxes, stepping forward and attempting to push Ava's hand into the frosting.

Ava immediately lets out a cry of protest.

Charlotte and I both laugh. Ava never likes to be messy, and we knew she might not be into the smash cake for her first birthday, but Charlotte was insistent we needed the photos anyway.

Charlotte dips her finger into the pink frosting and holds it up to Ava's mouth. Ava stares at Charlotte curiously.

"Taste it," Char tells her, pushing her finger a little closer. Ava stares a little bit longer before she finally opens her mouth.

The moment the icing hits her tongue, her entire face lights up.

"Oh my God," Charlotte mutters, a radiant smile on her face.

Deciding she actually does like frosting, Ava takes us both by surprise—instead of putting her hands in the cake and eating, she just leans down and takes a bite out of it.

"Ava!" we both say in unison, followed by laughter.

Charlotte immediately grabs her camera, and the familiar sound of clicking fills the space as Ava sticks her entire face in the smash cake.

"This is so good." Charlotte laughs, continuing to take photo after photo of our daughter.

I watch, unable to wipe the smile from my face. It's really sad to think about how little Ava was when she first came into my life and how big she is now. She says words—my favorite being *Dada*, of course—and crawls everywhere and will be walking any day now. Her cheeks aren't as round as they used to be, and the giant bows that used to be as big as her face don't look so big on her. She has little opinions and loves to snuggle and suddenly hates the car, and it's bittersweet to think of how quickly time has passed and how big she's gotten.

"Nice job, baby girl," I marvel. Ava still completely buries her face in the cake. You'd never know that moments ago, she didn't even want to touch it.

Charlotte continues to get all the pictures she needs as Ava chows down on the cake. Eventually, she decides she's all done, and she pushes the cake off the high chair and lifts her arms up.

"Mama," she declares, making it known she wants Charlotte to pick her up.

Charlotte gasps and it feels like my heart takes flight from inside my chest.

Char looks at me with tears in her eyes. "Did I just hear that right?"

All I can do is nod as I swallow past the lump of emotion in my throat.

"Did you just call me mama?" Charlotte asks, her voice full of disbelief.

Ava smiles at Charlotte. "Mama," she repeats, reaching for Charlotte.

Charlotte puts her camera down and pulls Ava from her high chair. I can't help but fall in love with Char all over again when Ava immediately melts against her.

"Yeah, baby girl, that's your Mama," I rasp.

Charlotte cries as she clutches Ava to her chest. It's another one of the beautiful moments that I'll remember for the rest of my life.

I smile, wondering how I got to be the luckiest man in the world to not only fall in love with Charlotte, but to call her my best friend too. She's my partner in life for all things, and as incredible as the last six months have been together, I'm excited about what the next six will look like. And then the next six... until the rest of forever.

I fell in love with Charlotte without ever really knowing what love was. I don't know if there was ever really one thing that made me fall in love with her. It was just *her.* She's my everything. She and Ava are my world. Sometimes I lie in bed next to the love of my life and wonder what I ever did to deserve her. She didn't have to selflessly step up the way she did for Ava and me. She didn't have to stick around as I learned what it was like to love someone. She's been there for me every step of the way, and I look forward to a lifetime of happiness with her.

I can't wait to have it all with her.

Charlotte looks up at me as she balances Ava on her hip. There's still tears in her eyes as she smiles at me. "What?" she asks.

I shake my head. "I just really love you, Charlotte Mitchell."

Her entire face lights up, and I feel like I fall in love with her all over again. "I love you too, Jude Kensington."

"But not as much as I love you," I immediately respond.

She rolls her eyes before pressing a kiss to Ava's head. "Daddy is just really always trying to win on that one, isn't he?"

All I do is smile and shrug before tucking my hands into my pockets. I keep my mouth shut, even though I know I do win. I win because I get to love her and be loved by her.

She's my best friend. My love. My world.

ACKNOWLEDGMENTS

There are so many people who supported me while writing this book. Writing it wasn't easy, and I'm so happy for the team of people I had surrounding me that pushed me to finish *More than Friends*. Without them, this book wouldn't be what it is now, and I'm eternally grateful for their support.

To my husband, thank you for being there for me throughout the entire process. You do so much behind the scenes to allow me to live out my dreams. I'm so grateful for all that you do. I love you.

To Meg, Lauren, and Chasity, thank you for pushing me to finish this book when all I wanted to do was quit. Thank you for helping me perfect Jude and Charlotte's love story and for never getting sick of my endless voice memos plotting everything out. I couldn't have finished this book without you three and I hope you know you're stuck with me forever. I love you girls so much and am so grateful for you.

Kelsey, thank you for holding my hand throughout the many breakdowns I had while writing this book. I'm so fortunate to be able to work with my best friend and I appreciate everything you do to keep all things Kat Singleton running. I wouldn't be able to function without you. I love you.

To Rae, thank you for not laughing at me when I asked you to help me with this release. I wouldn't have been able to organize anything without and I'm so grateful to call you a friend. Thank you for being my organization and AirTable queen.

Summer, my cover queen, thank you for bringing Jude and Charlotte to life perfectly. You took my vision for what I wanted for the cover and absolutely PERFECTED it. I couldn't be more obsessed and am so grateful to be working on this series with you.

Jade, thank you so much for creating the custom title PNG for me! You made it exactly what I wanted and I love how it turned out so much.

To Maren, who cheered me on and forced me to write this book when I wanted to give up. Thank you for pushing me to meet the deadline and for cheering me on. I love you forever. Let's try not to get behind on deadlines again!

To Holly, Salma, and Sandra. Thank you for all your help in making this book perfect for release. You worked tirelessly to help me meet my deadline and never once complained about me being a hot mess. You're my editing dream team. I appreciate your help so much!

To Nina, thank you for being my agent. Working with you is a dream and I'm so lucky to have you. You're always championing my books and I appreciate it so much. I can't wait for all the amazing things we'll do together!

To Jess, Sarah, and everyone at Entangled, thank you for believing in me and my books. It's such a dream to see my book on shelves and I appreciate all your hard work in my making my dreams come true. I'm so happy I found a home with Entangled and can't wait for everything that's to come! I know I didn't make this deadline easy on anyone and I appreciate your patience and for always being in my corner. I'm so thankful for Entangled!

To Valentine and everyone with VPR. Thank you for everything you do to keep me in check. It's not a secret that I'm a constant hot mess, and all of you are the reason I'm able to function. Thank you for making all things Kat Singleton run smoothly and amazing. I'm so thankful to call VPR home and for your help in getting *More than Friends* out to the world.

To the content creators and people in this community that share my books, I'm so eternally grateful for you. I've connected with so many amazing people since I started this author adventure and it means the world to me to have all of you to connect with. I'm appreciative of the fact that you take the time to talk about my stories on your platform. I notice every single one of your posts, videos, pictures, etc. It means the world to me that you share about my characters and stories. You make this community such a special place. Thank you for everything you do.

To the amazing humans on my own personal content team, thank you for making every release amazing. You babes are forever blowing my mind with the unique content you create based on my words and I'm so grateful to have all of you on this journey with me. I love and appreciate you so much.

I have the privilege of having a growing group of people I can run to on Facebook for anything–Kat Singleton's Sweethearts. The members there are always there for me, and I'm so fortunate to have them in my corner. I owe all of them so much gratitude for being there on the hard days and on the good days. Sweethearts, y'all are my people.

And last but certainly not least, thank you to you, the

reader. Whether this is the first book you've read of mine, or you've been around for many releases, your endless support means the world to me. It is you who is the lifeblood of this community. It is you that keeps me going even on the hard days. You're the reason I get to wake up every single day and work my dream job, and for that, I'm so freaking grateful. Thank you for choosing my words to read. Thank you for supporting me. You've given me the greatest gift by choosing *my* book to read. I love you so much. I hope I made you proud with this book.